W9-BGO-406

Praise for Glen Cook

"Cook's talent for combining gritty realism and high fantasy provides a singular edge."

— *Library Journal*

"Cook provides a rich world of assorted races, cultures, and religions; his characters combine the mythic or exotic with the realistic, engaging in absorbing alliances, enmities, and double-crosses."

— *Publishers Weekly*

"Over the past twenty-five years, Cook has carved out a place for himself among the preeminent fantasy writers of his generation.... His work is unrelentingly real, complex, and honest. The sense of place that permeates his narrative and characters gives his 'fantasies' more gravitas and grit than most fictions set in the here-and-now."

— Jeff VanderMeer, author of *Finch* and
City of Saints and Madmen

"The thing about Glen Cook is that... he single-handedly changed the field of fantasy—something a lot of people didn't notice, and maybe still don't. He brought the story down to a human level... Reading his stuff was like reading Vietnam War fiction on Peyote."

— Steven Erikson, author of *Gardens of the Moon*
and *Dust of Dreams*

"Most of these stories are told at ground level... Confusion reigns. Motivations are obscure, intentions often irrelevant. Magic is to be feared, not only by those who face it, but by those who wield it, and every sword seems as apt to turn against its holder or against a friend as to strike down an enemy."

— *Locus*

"The man is a master stylist—he doesn't let you go. He's become my literary equivalent to Beethoven: I can read him anytime."

— *Green Man Review*

Aп Empire
Uпacquaiптed with Defeat

Other books by Glen Cook

The Heirs of Babylon
The Swordbearer
A Matter of Time
Passage at Arms
The Dragon Never Sleeps
The Tower of Fear
Sung in Blood

Dread Empire
A Cruel Wind
    (Containing *A Shadow of All
    Night Falling, October's Baby*
    and *All Darkness Met*)
A Fortress in Shadow
    (Containing *The Fire in His
    Hands* and *With Mercy
    Toward None*)

Starfishers
Shadowline
Starfishers
Stars' End

Darkwar
Doomstalker
Warlock
Ceremony

The Black Company
The Black Company
Shadows Linger
The White Rose
The Silver Spike
Shadow Games
Dreams of Steel
Bleak Seasons
She Is the Darkness
Water Sleeps
Soldiers Live

The Garrett Files
Sweet Silver Blues
Bitter Gold Hearts
Cold Copper Tears
Old Tin Sorrows
Dread Brass Shadows
Red Iron Nights
Deadly Quicksilver Lies
Petty Pewter Gods
Faded Steel Heat
Angry Lead Skies
Whispering Nickel Idols
Cruel Zinc Melodies

**Instrumentalities of
the Night**
The Tyranny of the Night
Lord of the Silent Kingdom

AN EMPIRE
UNACQUAINTED WITH DEFEAT
STORIES OF THE DREAD EMPIRE

GLEN COOK

NIGHT SHADE BOOKS
SAN FRANCISCO

An Empire Unacquainted with Defeat © 2009 by Glen Cook
This edition of *An Empire Unacquainted with Defeat*
© 2010 by Night Shade Books

Jacket art © 2008 by Raymond Swanland
Jacket design by Claudia Noble
Interior layout and design by Jeremy Lassen

All rights reserved

"Soldier of an Empire Unacquainted with Defeat" first appeared in *The Berkley Showcase*, Volume 2, Berkley Books, August 1980, Victoria Schochet & John Silbersack, editors. ©1980 by Glen Cook.

"The Nights of Dreadful Silence" first appeared in *Fantastic Stories*, September, 1973. ©1973 by Ultimate Publishing Co., Inc.

"Finding Svale's Daughter" appears here for the first time.

"Ghost Stalk" first appeared in *The Magazine of Fantasy & Science Fiction*, May 1978. ©1978 by Mercury Press, Inc.

"Filed Teeth" first appeared in *Dragons of Darkness*, Ace Books, November 1981, Orson Scott Card, editor. ©1981 by Glen Cook.

"Castle of Tears" first appeared in *Whispers*, October 1979. ©1979 by Stuart David Schiff.

"Call for the Dead" first appeared in *The Magazine of Fantasy & Science Fiction*, July 1980. ©1980 by Mercury Press, Inc.

"Severed Heads" first appeared in *Sword & Sorceress I*, DAW Books, 1984, Marion Zimmer Bradley, editor. ©1984 by Glen Cook.

"Silverheels" first appeared in slightly different form in *Witchcraft & Sorcery*, May 1971. ©1971 by Fantasy Publishing Co., Inc.

"Hell's Forge" appears here for the first time.

Certified Chain of Custody
Promoting Sustainable
Forest Management
www.sfiprogram.org
PwC-SFICOC-272

Printed in Canada

First Printing

978-1-59780-188-1

Night Shade Books
Please visit us on the web at
http://www.nightshadebooks.com

Contents

INTRODUCTION

The world of the Dread Empire, from the beginning, was conceived as the stage for numerous, often unrelated stories. The earliest were intended to center on the characters Bragi Ragnarson, Mocker, and Haroun bin Yousif. Most of those stories have never been published. Some were quite amusing. Like the novelette about the sorcerers' convention inspired by the insanity witnessed at my first science fiction convention, the St. Louis Con Worldcon of 1969. There were a whole string of stories, back to back, that, in time, would have filled several volumes set before the events chronicled in *The Fire in His Hands* and, mainly, between *With Mercy Toward None* and *A Shadow of All Night Falling.* Only a minority of those got written and fewer saw publication. Of those actually written only a handful can be located anymore. See below.

The Dread Empire world grew fast, over a decade, going through several reincarnations, before *A Shadow of All Night Falling* actually found a publisher capable of surviving long enough to get it into the bookstores. It was accepted twice in the earlier 1970s. The first publisher went bankrupt. The second suffered a devastating fire in its production and storage facilities. Its business response was to turn back all non-bestseller titles scheduled for the next two years.

In 1980, when the first books appeared, the Dread Empire series was expected to consist of fourteen volumes, the central feature of which would be one vast mega-novel, in multiple volumes, spanning the lives of Bragi Ragnarson and Haroun bin Yousif. Seven of those titles did see print. Two more, *Wake the Cruel Storm* and *The Wrath of Kings,* were started but never finished. The former, following on from *An Ill Fate Marshalling*, was 85% complete. The manuscript and all associated developmental materials have disappeared, presumably appropriated by a visitor to my home who just had to know what would happen next. There are no viable suspects in this or several other disappearances of rare artifacts from my earliest writing career.

About 15% of *The Wrath of Kings* survives, fragments of draft material that happened to be outside my filing cabinets, lost in the mess of the house, whenever the rest of the material disappeared. A few of the short pieces, some of which appear here for the first time, survived by hiding in my agent's files and came home to Papa when the passing of the head of the agency caused it to shut down. Among these was a novelette entitled "The Funeral," which would be the capstone—or headstone—for the entire series. I'd completely forgotten having written it till I came on it while putting this collection together.

The published stories are presented here as they appeared in print, less typographical errors, however tempted I was to make improvements. Bad grammar, run-on sentences, squirrelly punctuation and all. Much of the latter not having been my fault but that of a couple of editors whose relationship with proper punctuation was somewhere beyond the second cousin twice removed state. Only "Silverheels" received even cosmetic revisions. I felt it important to show any evolution that might have occurred.

SOLDIER OF AN EMPIRE UNACQUAINTED WITH DEFEAT

The following novella was the longest of the published short fiction pieces in the Dread Empire world setting. It is a sidelight involving none of the characters from the several novels.

Possibly the best received of all my short fiction, this garnered numerous excellent reviews, was on the Locus *recommended reading list, and was chosen one of the five best novellas of 1980 in the Locus Readers' Poll.*

The world of the Dread Empire is, of course, the most important character of the series. It is always there, always on stage, always a stage, but never to be taken for granted.

I

His name was Tain and he was a man to beware. The lacquered armor of the Dread Empire rode in the packs on his mule.

The pass was narrow, treacherous, and, therefore, little used. The crumbled slate lay loose and deep, clacking underfoot with the ivory-on-ivory sound of punji counters in the senyo game. More threatened momentary avalanche off the precarious slopes. A cautious man, Tain walked. He led the roan gelding. His mule's tether he had knotted to the roan's saddle.

An end to the shale walk came. Tain breathed deeply, relieved. His muscles ached with the strain of maintaining his footing.

A flint-tipped arrow shaved the gray over his right ear.

The black longsword leapt into his right hand, the equally dark short-sword into his left. He vanished among the rocks before the bowstring's echoes died.

Silence.

Not a bird chirped. Not one chipmunk scurried across the slope, pursuing the arcane business of that gentle breed. High above, one lone eagle floated majestically against an intense blue backdrop of cloudless sky. Its shadow skittered down the ragged mountainside like some frenetic daytime ghost. The only scent on the breeze was that of old and brittle stone.

A man's scream butchered the stillness.

Tain wiped his shortsword on his victim's greasy furs. The dark blade's polish appeared oily. It glinted sullen indigoes and purples when the sun hit right.

Similar blades had taught half a world the meaning of fear.

A voice called a name. Another responded with an apparent, "Shut up!" Tain couldn't be sure. The languages of the mountain tribes were mysteries to him.

He remained kneeling, allowing trained senses to roam. A fly landed on the dead man's face. It made nervous patrols in ever-smaller circles till it started exploring the corpse's mouth.

Tain moved.

The next one died without a sound. The third celebrated his passing by plunging downhill in a clatter of pebbles.

Tain knelt again, waiting. There were two more. One wore an aura of Power. A shaman. He might prove difficult.

Another shadow fluttered across the mountainside, Tain smiled thinly. Death's daughters were clinging to her skirts today.

The vulture circled warily, not dropping lower till a dozen sisters had joined its grim pavane.

Tain took a jar from his travel pouch, spooned part of its contents with two fingers. A cinnamon-like smell sweetened the air briefly, to be pursued by an odor as foul as death. He rubbed his hands till they were thoroughly greased. Then he exchanged the jar for a small silver box containing what appeared to be dried peas. He rolled one pea round his palm, stared at it intently. Then he boxed his hands, concentrated on the shaman, and sighed.

The vultures swooped lower. A dog crept onto the trail below, slunk to the corpse there. It sniffed, barked tentatively, then whined. It was a mangy auburn bitch with teats stretched by the suckling of pups.

Tain breathed gently between his thumbs.

A pale cerulean light leaked between his fingers. Its blue quickly grew as intense as that of the topless sky. The glow penetrated his flesh, limning his finger bones.

Tain gasped, opened his hands. A blinding blue ball drifted away.

He wiped his palms on straggles of mountain grass, followed up with a dirt wash. He would need firm grips on his swords.

His gaze never left the bobbing blue ball, nor did his thoughts abandon the shaman.

The ball drifted into a stand of odd, conical rocks. They had a crude, monumental look.

A man started screaming. Tain took up his blades.

The screams were those of a beast in torment. They went on and on and on.

Tain stepped up onto a boulder, looked down. The shaman writhed below him. The blue ball finished consuming his right forearm. It started on the flesh above his elbow. A scabby, wild-haired youth beat the flame with a tattered blanket.

Tain's shadow fell across the shaman. The boy looked up into brown eyes that had never learned pity. Terror drained his face.

A black viper's tongue flicked once, surely.

Tain hesitated before he finished the shaman. The wild wizard wouldn't have shown him the same mercy.

He broke each of the shaman's fetishes. A skull on a lance he saved and planted like a grave marker. The witch-doctor's people couldn't misapprehend that message.

Time had silvered Tain's temples, but he remained a man to beware.

Once he had been an Aspirant. For a decade he had been dedicated to the study of the Power. The Tervola, the sorcerer-lords of his homeland, to whose peerage he had aspired, had proclaimed him a Candidate at three. But he had never shown the cold will necessary, nor had he developed the inalterable discipline needed, to attain Select status. He had recognized, faced, and accepted his shortcomings. Unlike so many others, he had learned to live with the knowledge that he couldn't become one of his motherland's masters.

He had become one of her soldiers instead, and his Aspirant training had served him well.

Thirty years with the legions. And all he had brought away was a superbly trained gelding, a cranky mule, knowledge, and his arms and armor. And his memories. The golden markings on the breastplate in his mule packs declared him a leading centurion of the Demon Guard, and proclaimed the many honors he had won.

But a wild western sorcerer had murdered the Demon Prince. The Guard had no body to protect. Tain had no one to command.... And now the Tervola warred among themselves, with the throne of the Dread Empire as prize.

Never before had legion fought legion.

Tain had departed. He was weary of the soldier's life. He had seen too many wars, too many battles, too many pairs of lifeless eyes staring up with "Why?" reflected in their dead pupils. He had done too many evils without questioning, without receiving justification. His limit had come when Shinsan had turned upon herself like a rabid bitch able to find no other victim.

He couldn't be party to the motherland's self-immolation. He couldn't bear consecrated blades against men with whom he had shared honorable fields.

He had deserted rather than do so.

There were many honors upon his breastplate. In thirty years he had done many dread and dire deeds

The soldiers of Shinsan were unacquainted with defeat. They were the world's best, invincible, pitiless, and continuously employed. They were feared far beyond the lands where their boots had trod and their drums had beaten their battle signals.

Tain hoped to begin his new life in a land unfamiliar with that fear.

He continued into the mountains.

One by one, Death's daughters descended to the feast.

II

The ivory candle illuminated a featureless cell. A man in black faced it. He sat in the lotus position on a barren granite floor. Behind a panther mask of hammered gold his eyes remained closed.

He wasn't sleeping. He was listening with a hearing familiar only to masters of the Power.

He had been doing this for months, alternating with a fellow Aspirant. He had begun to grow bored.

He was Tervola Candidate Kai Ling. He was pursuing an assignment which could hasten his elevation to Select. He had been fighting for the promotion for decades, never swerving in his determination to seize what seemed forever beyond his grasp.

His body jerked, then settled into a tense lean. Little temblors stirred his extremities.

"West," he murmured. "Far, far to the west." The part of him that listened extended itself, analyzed, fixed a location.

An hour passed.

Finally, Kai Ling rose. He donned a black cape which hung beside the nearly invisible door. He smiled thinly behind his mask. Poor Chong. Chong wouldn't know which of them had won till he arrived for his turn on watch.

III

Tain rested, observing.

It seemed a calm and peaceful hamlet in a calm and peaceful land. A dozen rude houses crowded an earthen track which meandered on across green swales toward a distant watchtower. The squat stronghold could be discerned only from the highest hilltops. Solitary shepherds' steads lay sprinkled across the countryside, their numbers proclaiming the base for the regional economy.

The mountains Tain had crossed sheltered the land from the east. The ivory teeth of another gigantic range glimmered above the haze to the north. Tain grazed his animals and wondered if this might be the land he sought.

He sat on a hillside studying it. He was in no hurry to penetrate it. Masterless now, with no fixed destination, he felt no need to rush. Too, he was reluctant. Human contact meant finalization of the decision he had reached months ago, in Shinsan.

Intellectually he knew it was too late, but his heart kept saying that he could still change his mind. It would take the imminent encounter to sever his heartlines home.

It was… *scary*… this being on his own.

As a soldier he had often operated alone. But then he had been ordered to go, to do, and always he had had his legion or the Guard waiting. His legion had been home and family. Though the centurion was the keystone of the army, his father-Tervola chose his companions, and made most of his decisions and did most of his thinking for him.

Tain had wrestled with himself for a year before abandoning the Demon Guard.

A tiny smile tugged his lips. All those thousands who wept on hearing the distant mutter of drums—what would they think, learning that a soldier of the Dread Empire suffered fears and uncertainties too?

"You may as well come out," he called gently. A boy was watching him from the brushy brookside down to his right. "I'm not going anywhere for hours."

Tain hoped he had chosen the right language. He wasn't sure where he had exited the Dragon's Teeth. The peaks to the north, he reasoned, should be the Kratchnodians. That meant he would be in the part of Shara butting against East Heatherland. The nomadic Sharans didn't build homes and herd sheep, so these people would be immigrants from the west. They would speak Iwa Skolovdan.

It was one of four western tongues he had mastered when the Demon Prince had looked westward, anticipating Shinsan's expansion thither.

"I haven't eaten a shepherd in years." An unattended flock had betrayed the boy.

The lad left cover fearfully, warily, but with a show of bravado. He carried a ready sling in his right hand. He had well-kempt blond hair, pageboy trimmed, and huge blue eyes. He looked about eight.

Tain cautioned himself: the child was no legion entry embarking upon the years of education, training, and discipline which gradually molded a soldier of Shinsan. He was a westerner, a genuine child, as free as a wild dog and probably as unpredictable.

"Hello, shepherd. My name is Tain. What town would that be?"

"Hello." The boy moved several steps closer. He eyed the gelding uncertainly.

"Watch the mule. She's the mean one."

"You talk funny. Where did you come from? Your skin is funny, too."

Tain grinned. He saw things in reverse. But this was a land of round-eyes. He would be the stranger, the guest. He would have to remember, or suffer a cruel passage.

Arrogant basic assumptions were drilled into the soldiers of Shinsan. Remaining humble under stress might be difficult.

"I came from the east."

"But the hill people…. They rob and kill everybody. Papa said." He edged closer, fascinated by Tain's swords.

"Sometimes their luck isn't good. Don't you have a name?"

The boy relented reluctantly. "Steban Kleckla. Are those swords? Real swords?"

"Longsword and shortsword. I used to be a soldier." He winced. It hurt to let go of his past.

"My Uncle Mikla has a sword. He was a soldier. He went all the way to Hellin Daimiel. That was in the El Murid Wars. He was a hero."

"Really? I'll have to meet your uncle."

"Were you a hero when you were a soldier? Did you see any wars?"

"A few. They weren't much fun, Steban." How could he explain to a boy from this remote land, when all his knowledge was second-hand, through an uncle whose tales had grown with the years?

"But you get to go places and see things."

"Places you don't want to go, to see things you don't want to see."

The boy backed a step away. "I'm going to be a soldier," he declared. His lower lip protruded in a stubborn pout.

Wrong tack, Tain thought. Too intense. Too bitter. "Where's your dog? I thought shepherds always had dogs."

"She died."

"I see. I'm sorry. Can you tell me the name of the village? I don't know where I am."

"Wtoctalisz."

"Wtoctalisz." Tain's tongue stumbled over the unfamiliar syllables. He grinned. Steban grinned back. He edged closer, eying Tain's swords.

"Can I see?"

"I'm sorry. No. It's an oath. I can't draw them unless I mean to kill." Would the boy understand if he tried to explain consecrated blades?

"Oh."

"Are there fish in the creek?"

"What? Sure. Trout."

Tain rose. "Let's see if we can catch lunch."

Steban's eyes grew larger. "Gosh! You're as big as Grimnir."

Tain chuckled. He had been the runt of the Demon Guard. "Who's Grimnir?"

The boy's face darkened. "A man. From the Tower. What about your horse?"

"He'll stay."

The roan would do what was expected of him amidst sorcerers' conflicts that made spring storms seem as inconsequential as a child's temper tantrum. And the mule wouldn't stray from the gelding.

Steban was speechless after Tain took the three-pounder with a casual hand-flick, bear fashion. The old soldier was *fast*.

"You make a fire. I'll clean him." Tain glowed at Steban's response. It took mighty deeds to win notice in the Dread Empire. He fought a temptation to show off.

In that there were perils. He might build a falsely founded, over-optimistic self-appraisal. And a potential enemy might get the measure of his abilities.

So he cooked trout, seasoning it with a pinch of spice from the trade goods in his mule packs.

"Gosh, this's good." As Steban relaxed he became ever more the chatterbox. He had asked a hundred questions already and seldom had he given Tain a chance to answer. "Better than Ma or Shirl ever made."

Tain glowed again. His field cooking was a point of pride. "Who's Shirl?"

"She was my sister."

"Was?"

"She's gone now." There was a hard finality to Steban's response. It implied death, not absence.

IV

Steban herded the sheep homeward. Tain followed, stepping carefully. The roan paced him, occasionally cropping grass, keeping an eye on the mule. For the first time Tain felt at ease with his decision to leave home.

It was unlikely that this country would become his new home, but he liked its people already, as he saw them reflected in Steban Kleckla. He and the boy were friends already.

Steban jerked to a stop. His staff fell as he flung a hand to his mouth. The color drained from his face.

That Aspirant's sense-feel for danger tingled Tain's scalp. In thirty years it had never been wrong. With the care of a man avoiding a cobra, he turned to follow Steban's gaze.

A horse and rider stood silhouetted atop a nearby hill, looking like a black paper cutout. Tain could discern little in the dying light. The rider seemed to have horns.

Tain hissed. The roan trotted to his side. He leaned against his saddle, where his weapons hung.

The rider moved out, descending the hill's far side. Steban started the sheep moving at a faster pace. He remained silent till the Kleckla stead came into view.

"Who was that?" Tain hazarded, when he reckoned the proximity of lights and parents would rejuvenate the boy's nerve.

"Who?"

"That rider. On the hill. You seemed frightened."

"Ain't scared of nothing. I killed a wolf last week."

He was evading. This was a tale twice told already, and growing fast. First time Steban had bragged about having driven the predator away. Then he had claimed to have broken the beast's shoulder with a stone from his sling.

"I misunderstood. I'm sorry. Still, there was a rider. And you seemed to know him."

The lights of Steban's home drew nearer. Boy and sheep increased their pace again. They were late. Steban had been too busy wheedling stories from his new friend to watch the time closely.

"Steban? That you, boy?" A lantern bobbed toward them. The man carrying it obviously was Steban's father. Same eyes. Same hair. But worry had etched his forehead with deep lines. In his left hand he bore a wicked oaken quarterstaff.

An equally concerned woman walked beside him.

Once, Tain suspected, she had been beautiful. In a round-eye sort of way. Doubtlessly, life here quickly made crones of girls.

"Ma. Papa. This's my new friend. His name is Tain. He used to be a soldier. Like Uncle Mikla. He came across the mountains. He caught a fish with his hands and his horse can do tricks, but his mule will bite you if you get too close to her. I told him he should come for supper."

Tain inclined his head. "Freeman Kleckla. Freelady. The grace of heaven descend." He didn't know an appropriately formal Iwa Skolovdan greeting. His effort sounded decidedly odd in translation.

Man and wife considered him without warmth.

"A Caydarman watched us," Steban added. He started coaxing the sheep into pens.

The elder Kleckla scanned the surrounding darkness. "An evil day when we catch their eye. Welcome, then, Stranger. We can't offer much but refuge from the night."

"Thank you, Freeman. I'll pay, that your resources be not depleted without chance of replacement." There was a stiffness about Kleckla which made Tain feel the need to distance with formality.

"This is the Zemstvi, Stranger. Titles, even Freeman and Freelady, are meaningless here. They belong to tamed and ordered lands, to Iwa Skolovda and the Home Counties. Call me Toma. My wife is Rula. Come. I'll show you where to bed your animals."

"As you will… Toma." He bowed slightly to the woman. "Rula." She frowned slightly, as if unsure how to respond.

This would be harder than he had anticipated. At home everyone had positions and titles and there were complicated, almost ritualized protocols and honorifics to be exchanged on every occasion of personal contact. "They'll need no fodder. They grazed all afternoon."

One bony milk cow occupied Kleckla's rude barn. She wasn't pleased by Tain's mule. The mule didn't deign to acknowledge her existence.

Toma had no other stock save his sheep. But he wasn't poor. Possessing cow and flock, he was richer than most men. Richer, in some ways, than Tain, whose fortune was in metal of changeable value and a few pounds of rare spice. Which would bring more in the marketplace of the heart?

"You'll have to sleep out here," Toma informed him. "There's no room…."

Tain recognized the fear-lie. "I understand." He had been puzzling the word *zemstvi,* which seemed to share roots with *frontier* and *wilderness.* Now he thought he understood.

"Are you a new Caydarman?" Toma blurted. He became contrite immediately. "Forget that. Tell me about the man you saw."

Because Toma was so intent, Tain cut off all exterior distractions and carefully reconstructed the moment in the manner he had been taught. A good scout remembered every detail. "Big man. On a big horse, painted, shaggy. Man bearded. With horns."

"Damned Torfin." Toma sublimated anger by scattering hay. "He didn't have horns. That was his helmet."

There was a lot to learn, Tain thought. This was an odd land, not like the quiet, mercantile Iwa Skolovda he had studied at home.

He considered the little barn. Its builders had possessed no great skill. He doubted that it was two years old, yet it was coming apart.

"Might as well go eat. It isn't much. Boiled mutton with cabbage and leeks."

"Ah. Mutton. I was hoping." Responding to Toma's surprise, "Mutton is rare at home. Only the rich eat it. Us common soldiers made do with grain and pork. Mostly with grain."

"Home? Where would that be?"

"East. Beyond the Dragon's Teeth."

Toma considered the evasion. "We'd better get inside. Rula gets impatient."

"Go ahead. I have a couple of things to do. Don't wait on me. I'll make do with scraps or leftovers."

Toma eyed him, started to speak, changed his mind. "As you will."

Once Toma departed, Tain pursued the Soldier's Evening Ritual, clearing his heart of the day's burdens. He observed the abbreviated Battlefield Ritual rather than the hour of meditation and exercise he pursued under peaceful circumstances. Later he would do it right.

He started for the door.

His neck tingled. He stopped, turned slowly, reached out with an Aspirant's senses.

A man wearing a horned helmet was watching the stead from the grove surrounding the Klecklas' spring. He didn't see Tain.

Tain considered, shrugged. It wasn't his problem. He would tell Toma when they were alone. Let the Freeman decide what ought to be done.

V

The sun was a diameter above the horizon.

Tain released the mule and roan to pasture. He glanced round at the verdant hills. "Beautiful country," he murmured, and wondered what the rest of his journey would bring. He ambled a ways toward the house. Rula was starting breakfast.

These people rose late and started slowly. Already he had performed his Morning Ritual, seen to his travel gear and personal ablutions, and had examined the tracks round the spring. Then he had joined Toma when his host had come to check the sheep.

Toma had first shown relief, then increased concern. He remained steadfastly close-mouthed.

Tain restrained his curiosity. Soldiers learned not to ask questions. "Good morning, Steban."

The boy stood in the door of the sod house, rubbing sleep from his eyes. "Morning, Tain. Ma's cooking oats."

"Oh?"

"A treat," Toma explained. "We get a little honeycomb with it."

"Ah. You keep bees?" He hadn't seen any hives. "I had a friend who kept bees...." He dropped it, preferring not to remember. Kai Ling had been like a brother. They had been Aspirants together. But Ling hadn't been able to believe he hadn't the talent to become Tervola. He was still trying to scale an unscalable height.

"Wild honey," Toma said. "The hill people gather it and trade it to us for workable iron."

"I see." Tain regarded the Kleckla home for the second time that morning. He wasn't impressed. It was a sod structure with an interior just four paces by six. Its construction matched the barn's. Tain had gotten better workmanship out of legion probationers during their first field exercises.

A second, permanent home was under construction nearby. A more ambitious project, every timber proclaimed it a dream house. Last night, after supper, Toma had grown starry-eyed and loquacious while discussing it. It was symbolic of the Grail he had pursued into the Zemstvi.

Its construction was as unskilled as that of the barn.

Rula's eyes had tightened with silent pain while her husband penetrated ever more deeply the shifting paths of his dreams.

Toma had been an accountant for the Perchev syndicate in Iwa Skolovda, a tormented, dreamless man using numbers to describe the movements of furs, wool, wheat, and metal billets. His days had been long and tedious. During summer, when the barges and caravans moved, he had been permitted no holidays.

That had been before he had been stricken by the cunning infection, the wild hope, the pale dream of the Zemstvi, here expressed rudely, yet in a way that said that a man had tried.

Rula's face said that the old life had been emotional hell, but their apartment had remained warm and the roof hadn't leaked. Life had been predictable and secure.

There were philosophies at war in the Kleckla home, though hers lay mute before the other's traditional right. Accusing in silence.

Toma was Rula's husband. She had had to come to the Zemstvi as the bondservant of his dreams. Or nightmares.

The magic of numbers had shattered the locks on the doors of Toma's soul. It had let the dream light come creeping in. *Freedom*, the intellectual chimera pursued by more of his neighbors, meant nothing to Kleckla. His neighbors had chosen the hazards of colonizing Shara because of the certainties of Crown protection.

Toma, though, burned with the absolute conviction of a balanced equation. Numbers proved it impossible for a sheep-herding, wool-producing community not to prosper in those benign hills.

What Tain saw, and that Toma couldn't recognize, was that numbers wore no faces. Or were too simplistic. They couldn't account the human factors.

The failure had begun with Toma. He had ignored his own ignorance of the skills needed to survive on a frontier. Shara was no-man's-land. Iwa Skolovda had claimed it for centuries, but never had imposed its suzerainty.

Shara abounded with perils unknown to a city-born clerk.

The Tomas, sadly, often ended up as sacrifices to the Zemstvi.

The egg of disaster shared the nest of his dream, and who could say which had been insinuated by the cowbird of Fate?

There were no numbers by which to calculate ignorance, raiders, wolves, or heart-changes aborting vows politicians had sworn in perpetuity. The ciphers for disease and foul weather hadn't yet been enumerated.

Toma's ignorance of essential craft blazed out all over his homestead. And the handful of immigrants who had teamed their dreams with his, and had helped, had had no more knowledge or skill. They, too, had been hungry scriveners and number-mongers, swayed by a wild-eyed false prophet innocent of the realities of opening a new land. All but black sheep Mikla, who had come east to keep Toma from being devoured by his own fuzzy-headedness.

Rula-thinking had prevailed amongst most of Toma's disciples. They had admitted defeat and ventured west again, along paths littered with the parched bones of fleeting hope.

Toma was stubborn. Toma persisted. Toma's bones would lie beside those of his dreams.

All this Tain knew when he said, "If you won't let me pay, then at least let me help with the new house."

Toma regarded him with eyes of iron.

"I learned construction in the army."

Toma's eyes tightened. He was a proud man.

Tain had dealt with stiff-necked superiors for ages. He pursued his offer without showing a hint of criticism. And soon Toma relaxed, responded. "Take a look after breakfast," he suggested. "See what you think. I've been having trouble since Mikla left."

"I'd wondered about that," Tain admitted. "Steban gave the impression that your brother was living here. I didn't want to pry."

"He walked out." Toma stamped toward the house angrily. He calmed himself before they entered. "My fault, I guess. It was a petty argument. The sheep business hasn't been as good as we expected. He wanted to pick up a little extra trading knives and arrowheads to the tribes. They pay in furs. But the Baron banned that when he came here."

Tain didn't respond. Toma shrugged irritably, started back outside. He stopped suddenly, turned. "He's Rula's brother." Softly, "And that wasn't true. I made him leave because I caught him with some arrowheads. I was afraid." He turned again.

"Toma. Wait." Tain spoke softly. "I won't mention it."

Relief flashed across Kleckla's face.

"And you should know. The man with the horns. The… Caydarman? He spent part of the night watching the house from the grove."

Toma didn't respond. He seemed distraught. He remained silent throughout breakfast. The visual cues indicated a state of extreme anxiety. He regained his good humor only after he and Tain had worked on the new house for hours, and then his chatter was inconsequential. He wouldn't open up.

Tain asked no questions.

Neither Toma nor Rula mentioned his departure. Toma soured with each building suggestion, then brightened once it had been implemented. Day's end found less of the structure standing, yet the improvement in what remained had Toma bubbling.

VI

Tain accidentally jostled Rula at the hearth. "Excuse me." Then, "Can I help? Cooking is my hobby."

The woman regarded him oddly. She saw a big man, muscled and corded, who moved like a tiger, who gave an impression of massive strength kept under constant constraint. His skin was tracked by a hundred scars. There wasn't an ounce of softness in or on him. Yet his fingers were deft, his touch delicate as he took her knife and pan. "You don't mind?"

"Mind? You're joking. Two years I haven't had a minute's rest, and you want to know if I mind?"

"Ah. There's a secret to that, having too much work and not enough time. It's in the organization, and in putting yourself into the right state of mind before you start. Most people scatter themselves. They try everything at once."

"I'll be damned." Toma, who had been carrying water to the sheep pens, paused to watch over Tain's shoulder.

Turning the browned mutton, Tain said, "I love to cook. This is a chance for me to show off." He tapped a ghost of spice from an envelope. "Rula, if we brown the vegetables instead of stewing them…."

"I'll be damned," Toma said again. He settled to the floor to watch. He pulled a jar of beer to his side.

"One should strive to achieve the widest possible competence," Tain remarked. "One may never *need* a skill, but, again, one can't know the future. Tomorrow holds ambushes for the mightiest necromancers. A new skill is another hedge against Fate's whimsy. What happens when a soldier loses a limb here?"

"They become beggars," Rula replied. "Toma, remember how it was right after the war? You couldn't walk a block…."

"My point made for me. I could become a cook. Or an interpreter. Or a smith, or an armorer, according to my handicap. In that way I was well-served. Where's Steban? I asked him to pick some mushrooms. They'll add the final touch. But don't expect miracles. I've never tried this with mutton…. Rula? What is it?"

Toma had bounced up and run outside. She was following him.

"It's Steban. He's worried about Steban."

"Can you tell me?"

"The Caydarmen…." She went blank, losing the animation she had begun showing.

"Who are they?"

"Baron Caydar's men." She would say no more. She just leaned against the door frame and stared into the dusk.

Toma returned a moment later. "It's all right. He's coming. Must have spent the day with the Kosku boy. I see his flock too."

"Toma…." Fear tinged Rula's voice.

"The boy can choose his friends, woman. I'm not so weak that I'll make my children avoid their friends because of my fears."

Tain stirred vegetables and listened, trying to fathom the situation. Toma *was* scared. The timbre of fear inundated his voice.

He and Rula dropped the subject as if pursuing it might bring some dread upon them.

Steban had collected the right mushrooms. That had worried Tain. He never quite trusted anyone who wasn't legion-trained. "Good, Steban. I think we'll all like this."

"You're cooking?"

"I won't poison you. The fish was good, wasn't it?"

Steban seemed unsure. He turned to his father. "Wes said they were fined five sheep, five goats, and ten geese. He said his dad said he's not going to pay."

Dread and worry overcame his parents' faces.

"Toma, there'll be trouble." Rula's hands fluttered like nervous doves.

"They can't afford that," Toma replied. "They wouldn't make it through winter."

"Go talk to him. Ask the neighbors to chip in."

"It's got to end, Rula." He turned to Tain. "The Crown sent Baron Caydar to protect us from the tribes. We had less trouble when we weren't protected."

"Toma!"

"The tribes don't bother anyone, Rula. They never did. Hywel goes out of his way to avoid trouble. Just because those royal busybodies got themselves massacred…. They asked for it, trying to make Hywel and Stojan bend the knee."

"Toma, they'll fine us too."

"They have to hear me first."

"They know everything. People tell on each other. You know…."

"Because they're scared. Rula, if the bandits keep pushing, we won't care if we're afraid."

Tain delivered the meal to table. He asked, "Who are the Caydarmen? The one I saw was no Iwa Skolovdan."

"Mercenaries." Toma spat. "Crown wouldn't let Caydar bring regulars. He recruited Trolledyngjans who escaped when the Pretender overthrew the Old House up there. They're a gang of bandits."

"I see." The problem was taking shape. Baron Caydar would be, no doubt, a political exile thrust into an impossible position by his enemies. His assignment here would be calculated to destroy him. And what matter that a few inconsequential colonists suffered?

Tain's motherland was called Dread Empire by its foes. With cause. The Tervola did as they pleased, where and when they pleased, by virtue of sorcery and legions unacquainted with defeat. Shinsan did have its politics and politicians. But never did they treat civilians with contempt.

Tain had studied the strange ways of the west, but he would need time to really grasp their actuality.

After supper he helped Toma haul more water. Toma remarked, "That's the finest eating I've had in years."

"Thank you. I enjoyed preparing it."

"What I wanted to say. I'd appreciate it if you didn't anymore."

Tain considered. Toma sounded as though he expected to share his company for a while.

"Rula. She shouldn't have too much time to worry."

"I see."

"I appreciate the help you're giving me...."

"You could save a lot of water-hauling with a windmill."

"I know. But nobody around here can build one. Anyway. I couldn't pay much. Maybe a share of the sheep. If you'd stay...."

Tain faced the east. The sunset had painted the mountains the color of blood. He hoped that was no omen. But he feared that legionnaires were dying at the hands of legionnaires even now. "All right. For a while. But I'll have to move on soon."

He wondered if he could outrun his past. A friend had told him that a man carried his pain like a tortoise carried his shell. Tain suspected the analogy might be more apt than intended. Men not only carried their pain-shells, they retreated into them if emotionally threatened.

"We need you. You can see that. I've been too stubborn to admit it till now...."

"Stubbornness is a virtue, properly harnessed. Just don't be stubborn against learning."

Steban carried water with them, and seemed impressed. Later, he said, "Tell us about the wars you were in, Tain."

Rula scowled.

"They weren't much. Bloody, sordid little things, Steban. Less fun than sheep-shearing time."

"Oh, come on, Tain. You're always saying things like that."

"Mikla made a glory tale of it," Rula said. "You'd think…. Well…. That there wasn't any better life."

"Maybe that was true for Mikla. But the El Murid Wars were long ago and far away, and, I expect, he was very young. He remembers the good times, and sees only the dullness of today."

"Maybe. He shouldn't fill Steban's head with his nonsense."

So Tain merely wove a tale of cities he had seen, describing strange dress and customs. Rula, he noted, enjoyed it as much as her son.

Later still, after his evening ritual, he spent several hours familiarizing himself with the countryside. A soldier's habits died hard.

Twice he spied roving Caydarmen. Neither noticed him.

Next morning he rose early and took the gelding for a run over the same ground.

VII

Rula visited Tain's makeshift forge the third afternoon. Bringing a jar of chill spring water was her excuse. "You've been hammering for hours, Tain. You'd better drink something."

He smiled as he laid his hammer aside. "Thank you." He accepted the jar, though he wasn't yet thirsty. He was accustomed to enduring long, baking hours in his armor. He sipped while he waited. She had something on her mind.

"I want to thank you."

"Oh?"

"For what you're doing. For what you've done for Toma. And me."

"I haven't done much."

"You've shown Toma that a man can be proud without being pig-headed. When he's wrong. But maybe you don't see it. Tain, I've lived with that man for eighteen years. I know him too well."

"I see." He touched her hand lightly, recognizing a long and emotionally difficult speech from a woman accustomed to keeping her own counsel.

He didn't know how to help her, though. An unmarried soldier's life hadn't prepared him. Not for a woman who moved him more than should be, for reasons he couldn't comprehend. A part of him said that women were people too, and should respond the same as men, but another part saw them as aliens, mysterious, perhaps even creatures of dread. "If I have done good, I have brought honor to the house."

He chuckled at his own ineptitude. Iwa Skolovdan just didn't have the necessary range of tonal nuance.

"You've given me hope for the first time since Shirl…." she blurted. "I

mean, I can see where we're getting somewhere now. I can see Toma seeing it.

"Tain, I never wanted to come to the Zemstvi. I hate it. I hated it before
I left home. Maybe I hated it so much I made it impossible for Toma to
succeed. I drove Shirl away…."

"Yes. I could see it. But don't hate yourself for being what you are."

"His dreams were dying, Tain. And I wouldn't give him anything to replace them. And I have to hate myself for that. But now he's coming alive.
He doesn't have to go on being stubborn, just to show me."

"Don't hate anybody, Rula. It's contagious. You end up hating everything,
and everybody hates you."

"I can't ever like the Zemstvi. But I love Toma. And with you here, like
a rock, he's becoming more like the boy I married. He's started to find his
courage again. And his hope. That gives me hope. And that's why I wanted
to thank you."

"A rock?"

"Yes. You're there. You don't criticize, you don't argue, you don't judge,
you don't fear. You know. You make things possible…. Oh, I don't know
how to say what I want. I think the fear is the biggest thing. It doesn't
control us anymore."

"I don't think it's all my fault, Rula. You've done your part." He was growing unsettled. Even embarrassed.

She touched his arm. "You're strong, Tain. So strong and sure. My brother
Mikla…. He was sure, but not always strong. He fought with Toma all the
time."

Tain glanced south across the green hills. Toma had gone to the village
in hopes of obtaining metal that could be used in the windmill Tain was
going to build. He had been gone for hours.

A tiny silhouette topped a distant rise. Tain sighed in a mixture of disappointment and relief. He was saved having to face the feelings Rula was
stirring.

Toma loved the windmill. He wanted to let the house ride till it was
finished. Tain had suggested that they might, with a little ingenuity, provide running water. Rula would like that. It was a luxury only lords and
merchant princes enjoyed.

Rula followed his gaze. Embarrassment overtook her. Tain yielded the
jar and watched her flee.

Soon Toma called, "I got it, Tain! Bryon had an old wagon. He sold me
enough to do the whole thing." He rushed to the forge, unburdened himself
of a pack filled with rusty iron.

Tain examined the haul. "Good. More than enough for the bushings. You
keep them greased, the windmill will last a lifetime."

Toma's boyish grin faded.

"What happened? You were gone a long time."

"Come on in the house. Share a jar of beer with me."

Tain put his tools away and followed Toma. Glancing eastward, he saw the white stain of Steban's flock dribbling down a distant slope, heading home. Beyond Steban, a little south, stood the grotesque rock formation the locals called the Toad. The Sharans believed it was the home of a malignant god.

Toma passed the beer. "The Caydarmen visited Kosku again. He wouldn't give them the animals."

Tain still didn't understand. He said nothing.

"They won't stand for it," Rula said. "There'll be trouble."

Toma shrugged. "There'll always be trouble. Comes of being alive." He pretended a philosophical nonchalance. Tain read the fear he was hiding. "They'll probably come tonight...."

"You've been drinking," Rula snapped. "You're not going to...."

"Rula, it's got to stop. Somebody has to show them the limits. We've reached ours. Kosku has taken up the mantle. The rest of us can't...."

"Tain, talk to him."

Tain studied them, sensed them. Their fear made the house stink. He said nothing. After meeting her eyes briefly, he handed Toma the beer and ignored her appeal. He returned to his forge, dissipated his energies pumping the bellows and hammering cherry iron. He didn't dare insinuate himself into their argument. It had to remain theirs alone.

Yet he couldn't stop thinking, couldn't stop feeling. He hammered harder, driven by a taint of anger.

His very presence had altered Toma. Rula had said as much. The man wouldn't have considered supporting this Kosku otherwise. Simply by having entered the man's life he was forcing Toma to prove something. To himself? Or to Rula?

Tain hammered till the hills rang. Neutral as he had tried to remain, he had become heir to a responsibility. Toma had to be shielded from the consequences of artificial bravado.

"Tain?"

The hammer's thunder stammered. "Steban? Home so early?"

"It's almost dark."

"Oh. I lost track of time." He glanced at his handiwork. He had come near finishing while roaming his own mind. "What is it?"

"Will you teach me to be a soldier?"

Tain drove the tongs into the coals as if their mound contained the heart of an enemy. "I don't think so. Your mother...."

"She won't care. She's always telling me to learn something."

"Soldiering isn't what she has in mind. She means your father's lessons."

"Tain, writing and ciphers are boring. And what good did they do my dad? Anyway, he's only teaching me because Mother makes him."

What kind of world did Rula live in, there behind the mask of her face? Tain wondered.

It couldn't be a happy world. It had suffered the deaths of too many hopes. Time had beaten her down. She had become an automaton getting through each day with the least fuss possible.

"Boring, but important. What good is a soldier who can't read or write? All he can do is carry a spear."

"Can you read?"

"Six languages. Every soldier in my army learns at least two. To become a soldier in my country is like becoming a priest in yours, Steban."

Rula, he thought. Why do I find you unique when you're just one of a million identical sisters scattered throughout the feudal west? The entire subcontinent lay prostrate beneath the heel of a grinding despair, a ponderous changelessness. It was a tinder-dry philosophical forest. The weakest spark flung off by a hope-bearing messiah would send it up.

"A soldier's training isn't just learning to use a sword, Steban. It's learning a way of life. I could teach you to fence, but you'd never become a master. Not till you learned the discipline, the way of thinking and living you need to...."

"Boy, you going to jabber all night? Get those sheep in the pens."

Toma leaned against the doorframe of the house. A jar of beer hung from his hand. Tain sensed the random anger rushing around inside him. It would be as unpredictable as summer lightning.

"Take care of the sheep, Steban. I'll help water them later."

He cleaned up his forge, then himself, then carried water till Rula called them to supper.

Anger hung over the meal like a cloying fog rolling in off a noisome marsh. Tain was its focus. Rula wanted him to control Toma. Toma wanted his support. And Steban wanted a magical access to the heroic world his uncle had created from the bloodiest, most ineptly fought, and most pointless war of recent memory. Tain ate in silence.

Afterward, he said, "I've nearly finished the bushing and shaft bearings. We can start the tower tomorrow."

Toma grunted.

Tain shrugged. The man's mood would have to take care of itself.

He glanced at Rula. The appeal remained in her eyes. He rose, obtained a jar of beer, broke the seal, sipped. "A toast to the windmill." He passed it to Toma.

"Steban, let's get the rest of that water."

A breeze had come up during supper. Good and moist, it promised rain. Swift clouds were racing toward the mountains, obscuring the stars. Maybe, Tain thought, the weather would give Rula what he could not.

"Mom and Dad are mad at each other, aren't they?"

"I think so."

"Because of the Koskus?"

"Yes." The walk from the spring seemed to grow longer.

"Dad's afraid. Of the Caydarmen." Steban sounded disappointed.

"With good reason, I imagine." Tain hadn't met any of the Baron's merce-naries. He hadn't met any of the neighbors, either. None had come calling. He hadn't done any visiting during his reconnaissances.

"Soldiers aren't ever afraid."

Tain chuckled. "Wrong, Steban. Soldiers are always afraid. We just learn to handle fear. Your Dad didn't have to learn when you lived in the city. He's trying to catch up now."

"I'd show those Caydarmen. Like I showed that wolf."

"There was only one wolf, Steban. There're a lot of Caydarmen."

"Only seven. And the Witch."

"Seven? And a witch?"

"Sure. Torfin. Bodel. Grimnir. Olag. I don't remember the others."

"What about this witch? Who's she?"

Steban wouldn't answer for a while. Then, "She tells them what to do. Dad says the Baron was all right till she went to the Tower."

"Ah." So. Another fragment of puzzle. Who would have thought this quiet green land, so sparsely settled, could be so taut and mysterious?

Tain tried pumping Steban, but the boy clammed up about the Baron.

"Do you think Pa's a coward, Tain?"

"No. He came to the Zemstvi. It takes courage for a man to leave every-thing just on the chance he might make a better life someplace else."

Steban stopped and stared at him. There had been a lot of emotion in his voice. "Like you did?"

"Yes. Like I did. I thought about it a long time."

"Oh."

"This ought to be enough water. Let's go back to the house." He glanced at the sky.

"Going to rain," he said as they went inside.

"Uhm," Toma grunted. He finished one jar and started another. Tain smiled thinly. Kleckla wouldn't be going out tonight. He turned his smile on Rula.

She smiled back. "Maybe you'd better sleep here. The barn leaks."

"I'll be all right. I patched it some yesterday morning."

"Don't you ever sleep?"

"Old habits die hard. Well, the sheep are watered, I'm going to turn in."

"Tain?"

He paused at the door.

"Thanks."

He ducked into the night. Misty raindrops kissed his cheeks. A rising wind quarreled with itself in the grove.

He performed the Soldier's Ritual, then lay back on the straw pallet he had fashioned. But sleep wouldn't come.

VIII

The roan quivered between his knees as they descended the hill. It wasn't because of the wind and cold rain. The animal sensed the excitement and uncertainty of its rider.

Tain guided the animal into a brushy gully, dismounted, told the horse to wait. He moved fifty yards downslope, sat down against a boulder. So still did he remain that he seemed to become one with the stone.

The Kosku stead looked peaceful to an untrained eye. Just a quiet rural place passing a sleepy night.

But Tain felt the wakefulness there. Someone was watching the night. He could taste their fear and determination.

The Caydarmen came an hour later. There were three of them, bearing torches. They didn't care who saw them. They came down the hill from behind Tain and passed within fifty yards of him. None noticed him.

They were big men. The one with the horn helm, on the paint, Tain recognized as the Torfin he had seen before. The second was much larger than the first. The third, riding between them, was a slight, small figure in black.

The Witch. Tain knew that before she entered his vision. He had sensed her raw, untrained strength minutes earlier. Now he could feel the dread of her companions.

The wild adept needed to be feared. She was like as untrained elephant, ignorant of her own strength. And in her potential for misuse of the Power she was more dangerous to herself than to anyone she threatened.

Tain didn't doubt that fear was her primary control over the Baron and his men. She would cajole, pout, and hurt, like a spoiled child....

She *was* very young. Tain could sense no maturity in her at all.

The man with the horns dismounted and pounded on the Kosku door with the butt of a dagger. "Kosku. Open in the name of Baron Caydar."

"Go to Hell."

Tain almost laughed.

The reply, spoken almost gently, came from the mouth of a man beyond fear. The Caydarmen sensed it, too, and seemed bewildered. That was what amused Tain so.

"Kosku, you've been fined three sheep, three goats, and five geese for talking sedition. We've come to collect."

"The thieves bargain now? You were demanding five, five, and ten the other day."

"Five sheep, five goats, and ten geese, then," Torfin replied, chagrined.

"Get the hell off my land."

"Kosku...."

Assessing the voice. Tain identified Torfin as a decent man trapped by circumstance. Torfin didn't want trouble.

"Produce the animals, Kosku," said the second man. "Or I'll come after them."

This one wasn't a decent sort. His tone shrieked bully and sadist. This one *wanted* Kosku to resist.

"Come ahead, Grimnir. Come ahead." The cabin door flung open. An older man appeared. He leaned on a long, heavy quarterstaff. "Come to me, you Trolledyngjan dog puke. You sniffer at the skirts of whores."

Kosku, Tain decided, was no ex-clerk. He was old, but the hardness of a man of action glimmered through the gray. His muscles were taut and strong. He would know how to handle his staff.

Grimnir wasn't inclined to test him immediately.

The Witch urged her mount forward.

"You don't frighten me, little slut. I know you. I won't appease your greed."

Her hands rose before her, black-gloved fingers writhing like snakes. Sudden emerald sparks leapt from tip to tip.

Kosku laughed.

His staff darted too swiftly for the eye to follow. Its iron-shod tip struck the Witch's horse between the nostrils.

It shrieked, reared. The woman tumbled into the mud. Green sparks zig-zagged over her dark clothing. She spewed curses like a broken oath-sack.

Torfin swung his torch at the old man.

The staff's tip caught him squarely in the forehead. He sagged.

"Kosku, you shouldn't have done that," Grimnir snarled. He dismounted, drew his sword. The old man fled, slammed his door.

Grimnir recovered Torfin's torch, tossed it onto the thatch of Kosku's home. He helped the Witch and Torfin mount, then tossed his own torch.

Tain was inclined to aid the old man, but didn't move. He had left his weapons behind in case he encountered this urge.

He didn't need weapons to fight and kill, but he suspected, considering Kosku's reaction, that Grimnir was good with a sword. It didn't seem likely that an unarmed man could take him.

And there was the Witch, whose self-taught skill he couldn't estimate.

She had had enough. Despite Grimnir's protests, she started back the way they had come.

Tain watched them pass. The Witch's eyes jerked his way, as if she were startled, but she saw nothing. She relaxed. Tain listened to them over the ridge before moving.

The wet thatch didn't burn well, but it burned. Tain strode down, filled a bucket from a sheep trough, tossed water onto the blaze. A half-dozen throws finished it.

The rainfall was picking up. Tain returned to the roan conscious that eyes were watching him go.

He swung onto the gelding, whispered. The horse began stalking the Caydarmen.

They weren't hurrying. It was two hours before Tain discerned the deeper darkness of the Tower through the rain. His quarry passed inside without his having learned anything. He circled the structure once.

The squat, square tower was only slightly taller than it was wide. It was very old, antedating Iwa Skolovda. Tain assumed that it had been erected by Imperial engineers when Ilkazar had ruled Shara. A watchtower to support patrols in the borderlands.

Shara had always been a frontier.

Similar structures dotted the west. Ilkazar's advance could be chronicled by their architectural styles.

IX

Toma was in a foul mood next morning. Toma was suffering from more than a hangover. Come mid-morning he abandoned his tools, donned a jacket and collected his staff. He strode off toward the village.

He had hardly vanished when Rula joined Tain. "Thanks for last night," she said.

Tain spread his hands in an "it was nothing" gesture. "I don't think you had to worry."

"What?"

"Nothing." He averted his gaze shyly.

"He's gone to find out what happened."

"I know. He feels responsible."

"He's not responsible for Kosku's sins."

"We're all responsible to one another, Rula. His feelings are genuine. My opinion is, he wants to do the right thing for the wrong reasons."

"What reasons?"

"I think he wants to prove something. I'm not sure why. Or to whom. Maybe to himself."

"Just because they blame him…." Her gaze snapped up and away, toward the spring. Tain turned slowly.

A Caydarman on a painted horse was descending the slope. "Torfin?" Today he wore no helmet.

"Oh!" Rula gasped. "Toma must have said something yesterday."

Tain could sense the unreasoning fear in her. It refused to let the Caydarman be anything but evil. "You go inside. I'll handle him."

She ran.

Tain set his tools aside, wiped his hands, ambled toward the spring. The Caydarman had entered the grove. He was watering his mount.

"Good morning."

The Caydarman looked up. "Good morning."

He's young, Tain thought. Nineteen or twenty. But he had scars.

The youth took in Tain's size and catlike movements.

Tain noted the Caydarman's pale blue eyes and long blond hair, and the strength pent in his rather average-appearing body. He was tall, but not massive like Grimnir.

"Torfin Hakesson," the youth offered. "The Baron's man."

"Tain. My father's name I don't know."

A slight smile crossed Torfin's lips. "You're new here."

"Just passing through. Kleckla needed help with his house. I have the skills. He asked me to stay on for a while."

Torfin nodded. "You're the man with the big roan? I saw you the other day."

Tain smiled. "And I you. Several times. Why're you so far from home?"

"My father chose a losing cause. I drifted. The Baron offered me work. I came to the Zemstvi."

"I've heard that Trolledyngjans are terse. Never have I heard a life so simply sketched."

"And you?"

"Much the same. Leaving unhappiness behind, pursuing something that probably doesn't exist."

"The Baron might take you on."

"No. Our thinking diverges on too many things."

"I thought so myself, once. I still do, in a way. But you don't have many choices when your only talent is sword work."

"A sad truth. Did you want something in particular?"

"No. Just patrolling. Watering the horse. Them." He jerked his head toward the house. "They're well?"

"Yes."

"Good." The youth eyed the stead. "Looks like you've gotten things moving."

"Some. Toma needed help."

"Yes. He hasn't made much headway since Mikla left. Well, good-day, Tain. Till we meet again."

"Good-day, Torfin. And may the grace of heaven guide you."

Torfin regarded him with one raised eyebrow as he mounted. "You have an odd way of putting things," he replied. He wheeled and angled off across the hillside. Tain watched till the youth crossed the low ridge.

He found Rula hunkered by the cookfire, losing herself in making their noonday meal.

"What did he want?" she demanded.

"To water his horse."

"That's all?"

"That and to look at me, I suppose. Why?"

"He's the dangerous one. Grimnir is big and loud and mean. The others are bullies too. But Torfin…. He's quiet and quick. He once killed three of Stojan's warriors when they tried to steal horses from the Tower corrals."

"Has he given you any trouble?"

She hesitated. Tain knew she would hide something.

"No. To hardly anybody. But he's always around. Around and watching. Listening. Then the others come with their fines that aren't anything but excuses to rob people."

So much fear in her. He wanted to hold her, to tell her everything would be all right. "I have to get to work. I should finish the framework today. If Toma remembers to look for lumber, we might start the tank tomorrow." He ducked out before he did anything foolish.

He didn't understand. He was Tain, a leading centurion of the Demon Guard. He was a thirty-year veteran. He should be past juvenile temptation. Especially involving a woman of Rula's age and wear….

He worked hard, but it did no good. The feelings, the urges, remained. He kept his eyes averted during lunch.

"Tain…." she started once

"Yes?"

"Nothing."

He glanced up. She had turned toward the Tower, her gaze far away.

Afterward, he saddled the roan and led out the mule and took them on a short patrol. Once he spied Torfin in the distance, on a hilltop, watching something beyond. Tain turned and rode a few miles westward, till the Tower loomed ahead. He turned again, for home, following a looping course past the Kosku stead. Someone was repairing the thatch.

Rula was waiting, and highly nervous. "Where have you been?" she demanded.

"Exercising the animals. What happened?"

"Nothing. Oh, nothing. I just hate it when I have to be alone."

"I'm sorry. That was thoughtless."

"No. Not really. What claim do I have on your time?" She settled down. "I'm just a worrier."

"I'll wait till Toma's home next time." He unsaddled the roan and began rubbing him down. The mule wandered away, grazing. Rula watched without speaking.

He was acutely conscious of her gaze. After ten minutes, she asked, "Where did you come from, Tain? Who are you?"

"I came from nowhere and I'm going nowhere, Rula. I'm just an ex-soldier wandering because I don't know anything else."

"Nothing else? You seem to know something about everything."

"I've had a lot of years to learn."

"Tell me about the places you've been. I've never been anywhere but home and the Zemstvi."

Tain smiled a thin, sad smile. There was that same awe and hunger that he heard from Steban.

"I saw Escalon once, before it was destroyed. It was a beautiful country." He described that beauty without revealing his part in its destruction. He worked on the windmill while he reminisced.

"Ah. I'd better start supper," Rula said later. "Toma's coming. He's got somebody with him."

Tain watched her walk away and again chastised himself for unworthy thoughts.

She had been beautiful once, and would be still but for the meanness of her life.

Toma arrived wearing an odd look. Tain feared the man had divined his thoughts. But, "The Caydarmen went after Kosku last night. The old coot actually chased them off."

"Heh?" Tain snorted. "Good for him. You going to be busy?" He glanced at the second man. "Or can you help me mount these bearings?"

"Sure. In a couple minutes. Tain, this is my brother-in-law."

"Mikla?" Tain extended his hand. "Good to meet you. I've heard a lot about you."

"None of it good, I'm sure." Laughter wrinkled the corners of Mikla's eyes. He was a lean, leathery man, accustomed to facing hard weather.

"More good than bad. Steban will be glad to see you."

Rula stuck her head out the door. Then she came flying, skirts a-swirl. "Mikla!" She threw her arms around her brother. "Where *have* you been? I've been worried sick."

"Consorting with the enemy. Staying with Stojan and trying to convince him that we're not all Caydarmen."

"Even Caydarmen don't all seem to be Caydarmen," Tain remarked as he hoisted a timber into position.

Mikla watched the ease with which he lifted. "Maybe not. But when the arrows are flying, who wonders about the spirit in which they're sped?"

"Ah. That's right. Steban said you were a veteran."

A whisper of defensiveness passed through Mikla's stance. "Steban exaggerates what I've already exaggerated silly."

"An honest man. Rare these days. Toma. You said Kosku chased the Caydarmen away? Will that make more trouble?"

"Damned right it will," Mikla growled. "That's why I came back. When the word gets around, everybody in the Zemstvi will have his back up. And those folks at the Tower are going to do their damnedest to stop it."

"Kind of leaves me with mixed feelings. I've been saying we ought to do something ever since the Witch turned the Baron's head. But now I wonder if it'll be worth the trouble. It'll cause more than beatings and judicial robberies. Somebody'll get killed. Probably Kosku."

"I really didn't think it would go this far," Toma murmured. Tain couldn't fathom the pain in Kleckla. "I thought she'd see where she was heading...."

"Enough of this raven-cawing," Mikla shouted. He swept Rula into a savage embrace. "What's for supper, little sister?"

"Same as every night. Mutton stew. What did you expect?"

"That's a good-looking mule over there. She wouldn't miss a flank steak or two."

Rula startled them with a pert, "You'll get your head kicked in for just thinking about it. That's the orneriest animal I ever saw. She could give mean lessons to Grimnir. But maybe you could talk Tain into fixing supper. He did the other day. It was great."

Tain thought he saw a glimmer of the girl who had married Toma, of the potential hiding behind the weary mask.

"He cooks, too? Mercy. Toma, maybe you should marry him."

Tain watched for visual cues. How much of Mikla's banter had an ulterior motive? But the man was hard to read.

Rula bounced off to the house with a parting shot about having to poison the stew.

"That story of Kosku's is spreading like the pox," Toma observed. He reassumed the odd look he had worn on arriving.

So, Tain thought. Kosku is talking about the mystery man who doused the fire in his thatch. Was that what had brought Torfin?

"A Caydarman stopped by," he told Kleckla. "Torfin. He watered his horse. We talked."

"What'd he want?"

"Nothing, far as I could tell. Unless he was checking on me. Seemed a pleasant lad."

"He's the one to watch," Mikla declared. "Quiet and deadly. Like a viper."

"Rula told me about Stojan's men."

"Them? They got what they asked for. Stojan didn't like it, but what could he do? Torfin cut them down inside the Baron's corral. He let a couple get away just so they could carry the warning."

"With only seven men in his way I wouldn't think Stojan would care how things looked."

"Neither Stojan's nor Hywel's clans amount to much. They had small-pox bad the year before we came out. Stojan can't get twenty warriors together."

"Steban must have heard the news," Tain observed. "He's coming home early."

The boy outdistanced his flock. Toma hurried to meet him.

Tain and Mikla strolled along behind. "What army were you in?" the latter asked.

Tain had faced the question since arriving. But no one had phrased it quite this directly. He had to tell the truth, or lie. A vague reply would be suspicious. "Necremnen." He hoped Mikla was unfamiliar with the nations of the Roë basin.

"Ah." Mikla kept asking pointed questions. Several tight minutes passed before Tain realized that he wasn't fishing for something. The man just had the curiosities.

"Your sister. She's not happy here."

"I know." Mikla shrugged. "I do what I can for her. But she's Toma's wife."

And that, thought Tain, told a whole tale about the west. Not that the women of his own nation had life much easier. But their subjugation was cosmeticized and sweetened.

Toma reached Steban. He flung his arms around wildly. Mikla started trotting.

Tain kept walking. He wanted to study Mikla when the man wasn't conscious of being observed.

He was a masculine edition of Rula. Same lean bone structure, same dark brown hair, same angular head. Mikla would be several years older. Say thirty-six. Rula wouldn't be more than thirty-three, despite having been married so long.

The world takes us hard and fast, Tain thought. Suddenly he felt old.

Toma and Mikla came running. "Steban saw smoke," Toma gasped. "Toward Kosku's place. We're going over there." They ran on to the house.

Tain walked after them.

He arrived to find Toma brandishing his quarterstaff. Mikla was scraping clots of earth off a sword he had dug out of the floor.

X

Sorrow invaded Tain's soul. He couldn't repulse it. It persisted while he helped Steban water the sheep, and worsened while he sat with Rula, waiting for the men to return. Hours passed before he identified its root cause. Homesickness.

"I'm exhausted," he muttered. "Better turn in."

Rula sped him a look of mute appeal. He ignored it. He didn't dare wait with her. Not anymore. Not with these unsoldierly feelings threatening to betray all honor.

The Soldier's Rituals did no good. They only reminded him of the life he had abandoned. He was a soldier no more. He had chosen a different path, a different life.

A part of life lay inside the sod house, perhaps his for the asking.

"I'm a man of honor," he mumbled. Desperation choked his voice.

And again his heart leaned to his motherland.

Sighing, he broke into his mule packs. He found his armorer's kit, began oiling his weapons.

But his mind kept flitting, taunting him like a black butterfly. Home. Rula. Home. Rula again.

Piece by piece, with exaggerated care, he oiled his armor. It was overdue. Lacquerwork needed constant, loving care. He had let it slide so he wouldn't risk giving himself away.

He worked with the unhappy devotion of a recruit forewarned of a surprise inspection. It required concentration. The distractions slid into the recesses of his mind.

He was cleaning the eyepieces of his mask when he heard the startled gasp.

He looked up. Rula had come to the barn.

He hadn't heard her light tread.

She stared at the mask. Fascination and horror alternated on her face. Her lips worked. No sound came forth.

Tain didn't move.

This is the end, he thought. She knows what the mask means....

"I.... Steban fell asleep.... I thought...." She couldn't tear her gaze away from that hideous metal visage.

She yielded to the impulse to flee, took several steps. Then something drew her back.

Fatalistically, Tain polished the thin traceries of inlaid gold.

"Are you?... Is that real?"

"Yes, Rula." He reattached the mask to his helmet. "I was a leading centurion of the Demon Guard. The Demon Prince's personal bodyguard." He returned mask and helmet to his mule packs, started collecting the rest of his armor.

He had to go.

"How?... How can that be? You're not...."

"We're just men, Rula. Not devils." He guided the mule to the packs, threw a pad across her back. "We have our weaknesses and fears too." He threw the first pack on and adjusted it.

"What are you doing?"

"I can't stay now. You know what I was. That changes everything."

"Oh."

She watched till he finished. But when he called the roan, and began saddling him, she whispered, "Tain?"

He turned.

She wasn't two feet away.

"Tain. It doesn't matter. I won't tell anyone. Stay."

One of his former master's familiar spirits reached into his guts and, with bloody talons, slowly twisted his intestines. It took no experience to read the offer in her eyes.

"Please stay. I…. We need you here."

One treacherous hand overcame his will. He caressed her cheek. She shivered under his touch, hugging herself as if it were cold. She pressed her cheek against his fingers.

He tried to harden his eyes. "Oh, no. Not now. More than ever."

"Tain. Don't. You can't." Her gaze fell to the straw. Savage quaking conquered her.

She moved toward him. Her arms enveloped his neck. She buried her face in his chest. He felt the warm moistness of tears through his clothing.

He couldn't push her away. "No," he said, and she understood that he meant he wouldn't go.

He separated himself gently and began unloading the mule. He avoided Rula's eyes, and she his whenever he succumbed.

He turned to the roan. Then Mikla's voice, cursing, came from toward Kosku's.

"Better go inside. I'll be there in a minute."

Disappointment, pain, anger, fear, played tag across Rula's face. "Yes. All right."

Slowly, going to the Rituals briefly, Tain finished. Maybe later. During the night, when she wouldn't be here to block his path….

Liar, he thought. It's too late now.

He went to the house.

Toma and Mikla had arrived. They were opening jars of beer.

"It was Kosku's place," Toma said. Hate and anger had him shaking. He was ready to do something foolish.

"He got away," Mikla added. "They're hunting him now. Like an animal. They'll murder him."

"He'll go to Palikov's," Toma said; Mikla nodded. "They're old friends. Palikov is as stubborn as he is."

"They can figure the same as us. The Witch…." Mikla glanced at Tain. "She'll tell them." He finished his beer, seized another jar. Toma matched his consumption.

"We could get there first," Toma guessed.

"It's a long way. Six miles." Mikla downed his jar, grabbed another. Tain glanced into the wall pantry. The beer supply was dwindling fast. And it was a strong drink, brewed by the nomads from grain and honey. They traded it for sheepskins and mutton.

"Palikov," said Tain. "He's the one that lives out by the Toad?"

"That's him." Mikla didn't pay Tain much heed. Toma gave him a look that asked why he wanted to know.

"We can't let them get away with it," Kleckla growled. "Not with murder. Enough is enough. This morning they beat the Arimkov girl half to death."

"Oh!" Rula gasped. "She always was jealous of Lari. Over that boy Lief."

"Rula."

"I'm sorry, Toma."

Tain considered the man. They were angry and scared. They had decided to do a deed, didn't know if they could, and felt they had talked too much to back down.

A lot more beer would go down before they marched.

Tain stepped backward into the night, leaving.

XI

He spent fifteen minutes probing the smoldering remnants of Kosku's home and barn. He found something Toma and Mikla had overlooked.

The child's body was so badly burned he couldn't tell its sex.

He had seen worse. He had been a soldier of the Dread Empire. The gruesome corpse moved him less than did the horror of the sheep pens.

The animals had been used for target practice. The raiders hadn't bothered finishing the injured.

Tain did what had to be done. He understood Toma and Mikla better after cutting the throats of lambs and kids.

There was no excuse for wanton destruction. Though the accusation sometimes flew, the legions never killed or destroyed for pleasure.

A beast had left its mark here.

He swung onto the roan and headed toward the Toad.

A wall collapsed behind him. The fire returned to life, splashing the slope with dull red light. Tain's shadow reached ahead, flickering like an uncertain black ghost.

Distance fled. About a mile east of the Kleckla house he detected other night travelers.

Toma and Mikla were walking slowly, steering a wobbly course, pausing frequently to relieve their bladders. They had brought beer with them.

Tain gave them a wide berth. They weren't aware of his passing.

They had guessed wrong in predicting that they would beat the Caydarmen to Palikov's.

Grimnir and four others had accompanied the Witch. Tain didn't see Torfin among them.

The raiders had their heads together. They had tried a torching and had failed. A horse lay between house and nightriders, moaning, with an arrow in its side. A muted Kosku kept cursing the Witch and Caydarmen.

Tain left the roan. He moved downhill to a shadow near the raiders. He squatted, waited.

This time he bore his weapons.

The Toad loomed behind the Palikov home. Its evil god aspect felt believable. It seemed to chuckle over this petty human drama.

Tain touched the hilt of his longsword. He was tempted. Yet…. He wanted no deaths. Not now. Not here. This confrontation had to be neutralized, if only to keep Toma and Mikla from stumbling into a situation they couldn't handle.

Maybe he could stop it without bloodshed.

He took flint and steel from his travel pouch. He sealed his eyes, let his chin fall to his chest. He whispered.

He didn't understand the words. They weren't in his childhood tongue. They had been taught him when he was young, during his Aspirant training.

His world shrank till he was alone in it. He no longer felt the breeze, nor the earth beneath his toes. He heard nothing, nor did the light of torches seep through the flesh of his eyelids. The smell of fetid torch smoke faded from his consciousness.

He floated.

He reached out, locating his enemies, visualizing them from a slight elevation. His lips continued to work.

He struck flint against steel, caught the spark with his mind.

Six pairs of eyes jerked his way.

A luminous something grew round the spark, which seemed frozen in time, neither waxing nor dying. The luminosity spread diaphanous wings, floated upward. Soon it looked like a gigantic, glowing moth.

The Witch shrieked. Fear and rage drenched her voice.

Tain willed the moth.

Its wings fluttered like silk falling. The Witch flailed with her hands, could touch nothing. The moth's clawed feet pierced her hood, seized her hair.

Flames sprang up.

The woman screamed.

The moth ascended lightly, fluttered toward Grimnir.

The Caydarman remained immobile, stunned, till his hair caught fire. Then he squealed and ran for his horse.

The others broke a moment later. Tain burned one more, then recalled the elemental.

It was a minor magick, hardly more than a trick, but effective enough as a surprise. And no one died.

One Caydarman came close.

They were a horse short, and too interested in running to share with the man who came up short.

Whooping, old man Kosku stormed from the house. He let an arrow fly. It struck the Caydarman in the shoulder. Kosku would have killed him had Tain not threatened him with the moth.

Tain recalled the spark again. This time it settled to the point it had occupied when the moth had come to life. The elemental faded. The spark fell, dying before it hit ground.

Tain withdrew from his trance. He returned flint and steel to his pouch, rose. "Good," he whispered. "It's done."

He was tired. He hadn't the mental or emotional muscle to sustain extended use of the Power. He wasn't sure he could make it home.

But he had been a soldier of the Dread Empire. He did not yield to weariness.

XII

The fire's smoke hung motionless in the heavy air. Little more than embers remained. The ashes beneath were deep. The little light remaining stirred spooky shadows against the odd, conical rocks.

Kai Ling slept soundly. He had made his bed there for so long that his body knew every sharp edge beneath it.

The hillmen sentinels watched without relaxing. They knew this bane too well. They bothered him no more. All they wanted of him was warning time, so their women and children could flee.

Kai Ling sat bolt upright. He listened. His gaze turned west. His head thrust forward. His nose twitched like that of a hound on point. A smile toyed with his lips. He donned his golden panther mask.

The sentinels ran to tell their people that the man-of-death was moving.

XIII

Toma and Mikla slept half the day. Tain labored on the windmill, then the house. He joined Rula for lunch. She followed him when he returned to work.

"What happened to them?" he asked.

"It was almost sunup when they came home. They didn't say anything."

"They weren't hurt?"

"It was over before they got there." The fear edged her voice again, but now she had it under control.

I'm building a mountain of responsibility, Tain thought.

She watched him work a while, admiring the deft way he pegged timbers into place.

He clambered up to check the work Toma had done on the headers. Out of habit he scanned the horizon.

A hill away, a horseman watched the stead. Tain balanced on the header. The rider waved. Tain responded.

Someone began cursing inside the sod house. Rula hurried that way. Tain sighed. He wouldn't have to explain a greeting to the enemy.

Minutes later Mikla came outside. He had a hangover. A jar of beer hung from his left hand.

"Good afternoon," Tain called.

"The hell it is." Mikla came over, leaned against a stud. "Where were you last night?"

"What? Asleep in the barn. Why?"

"Not sure. Toma!"

Toma came outside. He looked worse than his brother-in-law. "What?"

"What'd old man Kosku say?"

"I don't know. Old coot talked all night. I quit listening to him last year."

"About the prowler who ran the Caydarmen off."

"Ah. I don't remember. A black giant sorcerer? He's been seeing things for years. I don't think he's ever sober."

"He was sober last night. And he told the same story the first time they tried burning him out."

Toma shrugged. "Believe what you want. He's just crazy." But Toma considered Tain speculatively.

"Someone coming," Tain said. The runner was coming from the direction of the Kosku stead. Soon Toma and Mikla could see him too.

"That's Wes. Kosku's youngest," Toma said. "What's happened now?"

When the boy reached the men, he gasped, "It's Dad. He's gone after Olag."

"Calm down," Mikla told him. "Catch your breath first."

The boy didn't wait long. "We went back to the house. To see if we could save anything. We found Mari. We thought she ran to Jeski's…. She was all burned. Then Ivon Pilsuski came by. He said Olag was in town. He was bragging about teaching Dad a lesson. So Dad went to town. To kill him."

Tain sighed. It seemed unstoppable now. There was blood in it.

Toma looked at Mikla. Mikla stared back. "Well?" said Toma.

"It's probably too late."

"Are you going?"

Mikla rubbed his forehead, pushed his hair out of his eyes. "Yes. All right." He went to the house. Toma followed.

The two came back. Mikla had his sword. Toma had his staff. They walked round the corner of the house, toward the village, without speaking.

Rula flew outside. "Tain! Stop them! They'll get killed."

He seized her shoulders, held her at arm's length. "I can't."

"Yes, you can. You're…. You mean you won't." Something had broken within her. Her fear had returned. The raid had affected her the way the Caydarmen wanted it to affect the entire Zemstvi.

"I mean I can't. I've done what I could. There's blood in it now. It'll take blood to finish it."

"Then go with them. Don't let anything happen to them."

Tain shook his head sadly. He had gotten himself cornered here.

He had to go. To protect a man who claimed the woman he wanted. If he didn't, and Toma were killed, he would forever be asking himself if he had willed it to happen.

He sealed his eyes briefly, then avoided Rula's by glancing at the sky. Cloudless and blue, it recalled the day when last he had killed a man. There, away toward Kosku's, Death's daughters planed the air, omening more dying.

"All right." He went to the Kosku boy, who sat by the new house, head between his knees.

"Wes. We're going to town. Will you stay with Mrs. Kleckla?"

"Okay." The boy didn't raise his head.

Tain walked toward the barn. "Take care of him, Rula. He needs mothering now."

Toma and Mikla traveled fast. Tain didn't overtake them till they were near the village. He stayed out of sight, riding into town after them. He left the roan near the first house.

There were two horses in the village. Both belonged to Caydarmen. He ignored them.

Kosku and a Caydarman stood in the road, arguing viciously. The whole village watched. Kosku waved a skinning knife.

Tain spotted the other Caydarman. Grimnir leaned against a wall between two houses, grinning. The big man wore a hat to conceal his hairless pate.

Tain strolled his way as Mikla and Toma bore down on Olag.

Olag said something. Kosku hurled himself at the Caydarman. Blades flashed. Kosku fell. Olag kicked him, laughed. The old man moaned.

Mikla and Toma charged.

The Caydarman drew his sword.

Grimnir, still grinning, started to join him.

Tain seized his left bicep. "No."

Grimnir tried to yank away. He failed. He tried punching himself loose. Tain blocked the blow, backhanded Grimnir across the face. "I said no."

Grimnir paused. His eyes grew huge.

"Don't move. Or I'll kill you."

Grimnir tried for his sword.

Tain tightened his grip.

Grimnir almost whimpered.

And in the road Tain's oracle became fact.

Mikla had been a soldier once, but now he was as rusty as his blade. Olag battered his sword aside, nicked him. Toma thrust his staff at the Caydarman's head. Olag brushed it away.

Tain sighed sadly. "Grimnir, walk down the road. Get on your horse. Go back to the Tower. Do it now, or don't expect to see the sun set." He released the man's arm. His hand settled to the pommel of his longsword.

Grimnir believed him. He hurried to his horse, one hand holding his hat.

Olag glanced his way, grinned, shouted, "Hey, join the game, big man." He seemed puzzled when Grimnir galloped away.

Tain started toward Olag. Toma went down with a shoulder wound. Mikla had suffered a dozen cuts. Olag was playing with him. The fear was in him now. His pride had neared its snapping point. In a moment he would run.

"Stop it," Tain ordered.

Olag stepped back, considered him from a red tangle of hair and beard. He licked his lips and smiled. "Another one?"

He buried his blade in Mikla's guts.

Tain's swords sang as they cleared their scabbards. The evening sun played purple and indigo upon their blades.

Olag stopped grinning.

He was good. But the Caydarman had never faced a man doubly armed.

He fell within twenty seconds.

The villagers stared, awed. The whispers started, speculating about Kosku's mystery giant. Tain ignored them.

He dropped to one knee.

It was too late for Mikla. Toma, though, would mend. But his shoulder would bother him for the rest of his life.

Tain tended Kleckla's wound, then whistled for the roan. He set Toma in the saddle and laid Mikla behind him. He cleaned his blades on the dead Caydarman.

He started home.

Toma, in shock, stared at the horizon and spoke not a word.

XIV

Rula ran to meet them. How she knew, Tain couldn't fathom.

Darkness had fallen.

Steban was a step behind her, face taut and pallid. He looked at his father and uncle and retreated into an inner realm nothing could assail.

"I'm sorry, Rula. I wasn't quick enough. The man who did it is dead, if that helps." Honest grief moved him. He slid his arm around her waist.

Steban slipped under his other arm. They walked down to the sod house. The roan followed, his nose an inch behind Tain's right shoulder. The old soldier took comfort from the animal's concern.

They placed Mikla on a pallet, and Toma in his own bed. "How bad is he?" Rula asked, moving and talking like one of the living dead.

Tain knew the reaction. The barriers would relax sometime. Grief would demolish her. He touched her hand lightly. "He'll make it. It's a clean wound. Shock is the problem now. Probably more emotional than physical."

Steban watched with wide, sad eyes.

Tain squatted beside Toma, cleansing his wound again. "Needle and thread, Rula. He'll heal quicker."

"You're a surgeon too?"

"I commanded a hundred men. They were my responsibility."

The fire danced suddenly. The blanket closing the doorway whipped. Cold air chased itself round the inside walls. "Rain again," Rula said.

Tain nodded. "A storm, I think. The needle?"

"Oh. Yes."

He accepted needle and thread. "Steban. Come here."

The boy drifted over as if gripped by a narcotic dream.

"Sit. I need your help."

Steban shook his head.

"You wanted to be a soldier. I'll start teaching you now."

Steban lowered himself to the floor.

"The sad lessons are the hardest. And the most important. A soldier has to watch friends die. Put your fingers here, like this. Push. No. Gently. Just enough to keep the wound shut." Tain threaded the needle.

"Uncle Mikla…. How did it happen?" Disbelief animated the boy. His uncle could do anything.

"He forgot one of a soldier's commandments. He went after an enemy he didn't know. And he forgot that it's been a long time since he used a sword."

"Oh."

"Hold still, Steban. I'm going to start."

Toma surged up when the needle entered his flesh. A moan ripped from his throat. "Mikla! No!" His reason returned with his memory.

"Toma!" Tain snapped. "Lie down. Rula, help us. He's got to lie still."

Toma struggled. He started bleeding.

Steban gagged.

"Hold on, Steban. Rula, get down here with your knees beside his head. Toma, can you hear me?"

Kleckla stopped struggling. He met Tain's eyes.

"I'm trying to sew you up. You have to hold still."

Rula ran her fingers over Toma's features.

"Good. Try to relax. This won't take a minute. Yes. Good thinking, Steban."

The boy had hurled himself away, heaved, then had taken control. He returned with fists full of wool. Tain used it to sponge blood.

"Hold the wound together, Steban."

The boy's fingers quivered when the blood touched them, but he persevered.

"Good. A soldier's got to do what's got to be done, like it or not. Toma? I'm starting."

"Uhm."

The suturing didn't take a minute. The bandaging took no longer.

"Rula. Make some broth. He'll need lots of it. I'm going to the barn. I'll get something for the pain. Steban. Wash your hands."

The boy was staring at his father's blood on his fingers.

A gust of wind stirred fire and door covering. The wind was cold. Then an avalanche of rain fell. A more solid sound counterpointed the patter of raindrops.

"Hailstones," Rula said.

"I have to get my horse inside. What about the sheep?"

"Steban will take care of them. Steban?"

Thunder rolled across the Zemstvi. Lightning scarred the night. The sheep bleated.

"Steban! Please! Before they panic."

"Another lesson, Steban." Tain guided the boy out the door. "You've got to go on, no matter what."

The rain was cold and hard. It fell in huge drops. The hailstones stung. The thunder and lightning picked up. The wind had claws of ice. It tore at gaps in Tain's clothing. He guided the roan into the rude barn. The gelding's presence calmed the mule and cow. Tain rifled his packs by lightning flashes.

Steban drove the sheep into the barn too. They would be crowded, but sheltered.

Tain went to help.

He saw the rider in the flashes, coming closer in sudden jerks. The man lay against his mount's neck, hiding from the wind. His destination could be nowhere but the stead.

Tain told Steban, "Take this package to your mother. Tell her to wait till I come in."

Steban scampered off.

Tain backed into the lee of the barn. He waited.

The rider passed the spring. "Torfin. Here."

The paint changed direction. The youth swung down beside Tain. "Oh, what a night. What're you doing out in it, friend?"

"Getting the sheep inside."

"All right for a Caydarman to come in out of it?"

"You picked the wrong time, Torfin. But come on. Crowd the horse inside."

Lightning flashed. Thunder rolled. The youth eyed Tain. The ex-soldier still wore his shortsword.

"What happened?"

"You haven't been to the Tower?"

"Not for a couple days."

"Torfin, tell me. Why do you hang around here? How come you're always watching Steban graze sheep?"

"Uh…. The Klecklas deserve better."

Tain helped with the saddle. "Better than what?"

"I see. They haven't told you. But they'd hide their shame, wouldn't they?"

"I don't understand."

"The one they call the Witch. She's their daughter Shirl."

"Lords of Darkness!"

"That's why they have no friends."

"But you don't blame them?"

"When the Children of Hell curse someone with the Power, is that a parent's fault? No. I don't blame them. Not for that. For letting her become a petulant, spoiled little thief, yes. I do. The Power-cursed choose the right- or left-hand path according to personality. Not so?"

"It's debatable. They let me think she was dead."

"They pretend that. It's been a little over a year since she cast her spell on the Baron. She thought he'd take her to Iwa Skolovda and make her a great lady. But she doesn't understand politics. The Baron can't go back. And now she can't come home. Now she's trying to buy a future by stealing."

"How old are you, Torfin?"

"Nineteen, I think. Too old."

"You sound older. I think I like you."

"I'm a Caydarman by chance, not inclination."

"I think you've had pain from this too."

A wan smile crossed Torfin's lips. "You make me wonder. Do you read minds? What are you, carrying such a sword?" When Tain didn't respond, he continued bitterly, "Yes, there's pain in it for Torfin Hakesson. I was in love with Shirl. She used me. To get into the Tower."

"That's sad. We'd better go in. Be careful. They're not going to be glad to see you. Caydarmen burned the Kosku place. One of his girls was killed."

"Damn! But it was bound to happen, wasn't it?"

"Yes. And that was just the beginning. Kosku went after Olag and Grimnir. He was killed too."

"Which one did it?"

"Too late. Olag, but he's dead too. He killed Mikla and wounded Toma first, though."

"Help me with the saddle. I can't stay."

"Stay. Maybe together we can stop the bloodshed here."

"I can't face them. They already hate me. Because of Shirl."

"Stay. Tomorrow we'll go to the Tower. We'll see the Baron himself. He can stop it."

"Mikla lived with Stojan's daughter. The old man will want to avenge him."

"All the more reason to stop it here."

Torfin thought again. "All right. You didn't cut me down. Maybe you have a man's heart."

Tain smiled. "I'll guard your back, Trolledyngjan."

XV

Rula and Toma were talking in low, sad tones. Tain pushed through the doorway. Silence descended.

Such hatred! "Torfin will stay the night. We're going to the Tower in the morning. To talk to the Baron." Tain glared, daring opposition.

Toma struggled up. "Not in my house."

"Lie down, damn it. Your pride and fear have caused enough trouble."

Toma said nothing. Rula tensed as if to spring.

"Tain!" Steban whined.

"Torfin has said some hard things about himself. He's almost too eager to take his share of responsibility. He's willing to try to straighten things out.

"In no land I know does a father let his daughter run away and just cry woe. A man is responsible for his children, Toma. You could have gone after her. But it's easier to play like she's dead, and the Witch of the Tower has nothing to do with you. You sit here hating the Baron and refuse to admit your own part in creating the situation...."

He stopped. He had slipped into his drillmaster's voice. Pointless. Recruits had to listen, to respond, to correct. These westerners had no tradition of personal responsibility. They were round-eyes. They blamed their misfortunes on external forces....

Hadn't Toma blamed Mikla? Didn't Rula accuse Toma?

"That's all. I can't do any good shouting. Torfin is spending the night. Rula. Steban gave you a package."

She nodded. She refused to speak.

"Thank you."

For an instant he feared she hadn't understood. But the packet came with a murmured, "It's all right. I'll control my feelings."

"Is the broth ready?" He felt compelled to convince Rula.

She ladled a wooden bowl full. "Tain."

"Uhm."

"Don't expect me to stop feeling."

"I don't. I feel. Too much. I killed a man today. A man I didn't know, for no better reason than because I responded to feelings. I don't like that, Rula."

She looked down, understanding.

Steban chimed, "But you were a soldier...."

"Steban, a soldier is supposed to keep the peace, not start wars." The almost-lie tasted bitter. The Dread Empire interpreted that credo rather obliquely. Yet Tain had believed he was living it while marching to conquest after conquest. Only when Shinsan turned upon itself did he question his commanders.

"Tain...." There was a life's worth of pain in Steban's voice.

"People are going to get killed if we don't stop it, Steban." Tain tapped herbs into Toma's broth. "Your friends. Maybe there are only six Caydarmen. Maybe they could be beaten by shepherds. But what happens when the Baron has to run?" He hoped Toma was paying attention. Steban didn't care about the long run.

Toma's eyes remained hard. But he listened. Tain had won that much respect.

"Governments just won't tolerate rebellion. It doesn't matter if it's justified. Overthrow the Baron and you'll have an army in the Zemstvi."

Toma grunted.

Rula shrieked, "Tain!"

He whirled, disarmed Steban in an eye's blink. Torfin nodded in respect. "Thank you."

"Steban," Toma gasped. "Come here."

"Dad, he's a Caydarman!"

Tain pushed the boy. A soul-searing hatred burned in his young eyes. He glared at Mikla, Torfin, and Tain.

Tain suddenly felt tired and old. What was he doing? Why did he care? It wasn't his battle.

His eyes met Rula's. Through the battle of her soul flickered the feelings she had revealed the day before. He sighed. It *was* his battle.

He had killed a man. There was blood in it. He couldn't run away.

XVI

"I want to see Shirl," Rula declared next morning. "I'm going too."

"Mom!" Steban still didn't understand. He wouldn't talk to Tain, and Torfin he eyed like a butcher considering a carcass.

Tain responded, "First we take care of Mikla. Steban. The sheep. Better pasture them." To Toma, "Going to need sheds. That barn's too crowded."

Toma didn't reply. He did take his breakfast broth without difficulty.

He finally spoke when Steban refused to graze the sheep. "Boy, come here."

Steban went, head bowed.

"Knock it off. You're acting like Shirl. Pasture the sheep. Or I'll paddle your tail all the way out there."

Steban ground his teeth, glared at Tain, and went.

Rula insisted that Mikla lie beside the new home's door. Tain and Torfin took turns digging.

Tain went inside. "We're ready, Toma. You want to go out?"

"I've got to. It's my fault.... I have to watch him go down. So I'll remember."

Tain raised an eyebrow questioningly.

"I thought about what you said. I don't like it, but you're right. Four dead are enough."

"Good. Torfin! Help me carry Toma."

It was a quiet burial. Rula wept softly. Toma silently stared his brother-in-law into the ground. Neither Torfin nor Tain spoke. There were no appropriate words.

Tain saddled the roan and threw a pad on the mule. He spoke to her soothingly, reassuringly.

He knelt beside Toma while Torfin readied the paint. "You'll be all right?"

"Just leave me some beer. And some soup and bread."

"All right."

"Tain?"

"Yes?"

"Good luck."

"Thanks, Toma."

The mule accepted Rula's weight, though ungraciously. Tain donned his weapons. Little was said. Tain silently pursued his Morning Ritual. He hadn't had time earlier. Torfin watched. He and Rula couldn't talk. There were too many barriers between them.

The Tower was a growing, squat, dark block filled with frightening promise. A single vermilion banner waved over its ramparts. A feather of smoke curled from an unseen chimney.

"Something's wrong," Torfin remarked. They were a quarter mile away. "I don't see anybody."

Tain studied their surroundings.

Sheep and goats crowded the pens clinging to the Tower's skirts. Chickens and geese ran free. Several scrawny cattle, a mule, and some horses grazed nearby.

No human was visible.

"There should be a few women and children," Torfin said. "Watching the stock."

"Let's stop here."

"Why?" Rula asked.

"Beyond bowshot. Torfin, you go ahead."

The youth nodded. He advanced cautiously. The closer he drew, the lower he hunched in his saddle.

"Rula, stay here." Tain kicked the roan, began trotting round the Tower. Torfin glanced back. He paused at the Tower gate, peered through, dismounted, drew his sword, went it.

"Whoa." The roan stopped. Tain swung down, examined the tracks.

"Six horses," he murmured. "One small." He leapt onto the roan, galloped toward the Tower gate. "Torfin!" He beckoned Rula.

Torfin didn't hear him. Tain dismounted, peered through the gate into a small interior court. Quarters for the garrison had been built against the bailey walls.

"What is it?" Rula asked.

"Six riders left this morning. The Witch and the other five Caydarmen, probably."

Rula's cheek twitched. She wove her fingers together. "What about the people here?"

"Let's find Torfin."

The youth appeared above. "They're up here." He sounded miserable.

Tain guided Rula up the perilous stair. Torfin met them outside a doorway.

"In here. They saw us coming."

Tain heard muted weeping.

"Trouble," Torfin explained. "Bad trouble."

"I saw the tracks."

"Worse than that. She'll be able to cut loose for real…." The youth pushed the door. Frightened faces peered out at Tain.

The three women weren't Trolledyngjan. And their children were too old to have been fathered by the mercenaries.

Tain had seen those faces countless times, in countless camps. Women with children, without husbands, who attached themselves to an occupying soldiery. They were always tired, beaten, frightened creatures.

Mothers and children retreated to one corner of the Spartan room. One woman brandished a carving knife. Tain showed his palms. "Don't be afraid. We came to see Baron Caydar."

Rula tried a smile. Torfin nodded agreement. "It's all right. They mean no harm."

The knife-woman opened a path.

Tain got his first glimpse of Caydar.

The Baron lay on a pallet in the corner. He was a spare, short man, bald, with a scraggly beard. He was old, and he was dying.

This was what Torfin had meant by saying the trouble was big. There would be no brake on the Witch with the Baron gone. "Torfin. Move them. I'll see if I can do anything."

The Baron coughed. It was the first of a wracking series. Blood froth dribbled down his chin.

Torfin gestured. The Tower people sidled like whipped dogs. Tain knelt by the old man. "How long has he been sick?"

"Always. He seldom left this room. How bad is it?"

"Rula. In my left saddle bag. The same leather packet I had when I treated Toma." She left. "He'll probably go before sundown. But I'll do what I can."

"Tain, if he dies.... Grimnir and the others.... They'd rather take the Witch's orders. Her style suits them better."

Tain checked the Baron's eyes and mouth, dabbed blood, felt his chest. There was little left of Caydar. "Torfin. Anyone else shown these symptoms?"

"I don't think so."

"They will. Probably the girl, if she's been intimate with him."

Rula reappeared. She heard. "What is it?"

"Tuberculosis."

"No. Tain, she's only a child."

"Disease doesn't care. And you could say she's earned it."

"No. That isn't fair."

"Nothing's fair, Rula. Nothing. Torfin. Find out where she went." Tain took the packet from Rula, concentrated on Caydar.

He left the room half an hour later, climbed the ladder to the ramparts. Hands clasped behind him, he stared at the green of the Zemstvi.

A beautiful land, he thought. About to be sullied with blood.

Fate, with a malicious snicker, had squandered the land's last hope.

Torfin followed him. "They're not sure. She just led them out."

"Probably doesn't matter. It's too late. Unless...."

"What?"

"We smash the snake's head."

"What? He's going to die? You can't stop it?"

"No. And that leaves Shirl."

"You saying what I think?"

"She has to die."

Torfin smiled thinly. "Friend, she wouldn't let you do it. And if she couldn't stop you with the Power, I'd have to with the sword."

Tain locked eyes with the youth. Torfin wouldn't look away. "She means a lot to you, eh?"

"I still love her."

"So," Tain murmured. "So. Can you stand up to her? Can you bully the others into behaving themselves."

"I can try."

"Do. I'm into this too deep, lad. If you don't control her, I'll try to stop her the only way I know." He turned to stare across the Zemstvi again.

Though the Tower wasn't tall, it gave a view of the countryside matched only from the Toad. That grim formation was clearly visible. The rain had cleared the air.

Someone was running toward the Tower. Beyond, a fountain of smoke rose against the backdrop formed by the Dragon's Teeth.

A distance-muted thunderclap smote the air.

"That's your place," Torfin said softly.

XVII

A man in black, wearing a golden mask, rounded a knoll. He paused above the Palikov stead. Bloody dawn light leaked round the Toad. It splashed him as he knelt, feeling the earth. It made his mask more hideous. The faceted ruby eyepieces seemed to catch fire.

Thin fingers floated on the air, reaching, till they pointed westward. The man in black rose and started walking. His fingers led him on.

He went slowly, sensing his quarry's trail. It was cold. Occasionally he lost it and had to circle till he caught it again.

The sun scaled the sky. Kai Ling kept walking. A gentle, anticipatory smile played behind his mask.

The feel of the man was getting stronger. He was getting close. It was almost done. In a few hours he would be home. The Tervola would be determining the extent of his reward.

He crossed a low hilltop and paused.

A shepherd's stead lay below. He reached out....

One man, injured, lay within the crude sod house. A second life-spark lurked in the grove surrounding the nearby spring.

And there were six riders coming in from the southwest.

One seized his attention. She coruscated with a stench of wild, untrained Power.

"Lords of Darkness," Kai Ling whispered. "She's almost as strong as the

Demon Princess." He crouched, becoming virtually invisible in a patch of gorse.

Five of the riders dismounted. They heaped kindling round the timbers of a partially finished house.

A man staggered from the sod structure. "Shirl!" he screamed. "For god's sake...."

A raider tripped him, slipped a knife into his back as he wriggled on the earth.

Kai Ling stirred slightly as two blasts of emotion exploded below.

A child burst from the grove, shrieking, running toward the killer. And the wild witch lashed the man with a whip. He screamed louder than the boy.

Kai Ling reeled back from the raw surge. She *was* as strong as the Prince's daughter. But extremely young and undisciplined.

He stood.

The tableau froze.

The boy thought quickest. He paused only a second, then whirled and raced away.

The others regarded Kai Ling for half a minute. Then the witch turned her mount toward him. He felt the uncertainty growing within her.

Kai Ling let his Aspirant's senses roam the stead. The barn stood out. That was his man's living place. But he was gone.

Faceted rubies tracked the fleeing boy. Lips smiled behind gold. "Bring him to me, child," he whispered.

The raiders formed a line shielding the woman. Swords appeared. Kai Ling glanced at the boy. He waited.

She felt him now, he knew. She knew there had been sorcery in the Zemstvi. She would be wondering....

A raider wheeled suddenly. Kai Ling could imagine his words.

He had been recognized.

He folded his arms.

What would she try?

The fire gnawed at the new house. Smoke billowed up. Kai Ling glanced westward. The child had disappeared.

The witch's right arm thrust his way. Pale fire sparkled amongst her fingertips.

He murmured into his mask, readying his defenses.

She was a wild witch. Untrained. She had only intuitive control of the Power. Her emotions would affect what little control she had. He remained unworried despite her strength.

Kai Ling underestimated the size of the channel fear could open in her. She hit him with a blast that nearly melted his protection.

He fell to his knees.

He forced his hands together.

Thunder rolled across the Zemstvi. The timbers of the burning house leapt into the air, tumbled down like a lazy rain of torches. The sod house twisted, collapsed. The barn canted dangerously. The cow inside bawled.

The witch toppled from her horse, screaming, clawing her ears. She thrashed and wailed till a raider smacked her unconscious.

The Caydarmen looked uphill. Kai Ling, though unconscious, remained upon his knees. Golden fire burned where his face belonged. They tossed the witch aboard her horse, fled.

Kai Ling eventually fell forward into the gorse, vanishing.

Then only the flames moved on the Kleckla stead, casting dancing color onto the man whose dreams were dying with him.

XVIII

Tain pushed the roan. He met Steban more than a mile from the Tower. The boy was exhausted, but his arms and legs kept pumping.

"Tain!" he called. "Tain, they killed Pa." He spoke in little bursts, between lung-searing gasps.

"You go on to your mother. She's at the Tower. Come on. Go." He kicked the roan to a gallop.

Steban didn't reach the Tower. Rula, having conquered Tain's mule, met him. She pulled him up behind her and continued toward her home.

Tain saw the Caydarmen to the south, but didn't alter course. He would find them when their time came.

It was too late now. Absolutely too late. He had switched allegiance from peace to blood. He would kill them. The Witch would go last. After she saw her protectors stripped away. After she learned the meaning of terror.

He was an angry, unreasoning man. Only craft and cunning remained.

He knew he couldn't face her wild magic armed only with long and shortsword. To do so he had to resume his abandoned identity. He had to become a soldier of the Dread Empire once more. A centurion's armor bore strong protective magicks.

What amazing fear would course through the Zemstvi!

He pulled up when he topped the last hill.

The after-smell of sorcery tainted the air round the stead. The familiar stench of the Dread Empire overrode that of the Witch....

He hurled himself from the horse into the shelter of small bushes. His swords materialized in his hands. His emotions perished like small flames in a sudden deluge. He probed with Aspirant senses.

They had come. Because of the civil war he hadn't believed they would bother. He had fooled himself. They couldn't just let him go, could they? Not a centurion with his background. He could be too great a boon to potential enemies.

The heirs of the Dread Empire, both the Demon Princess and the Dragon Princes, aspired to western conquests.

Tain frowned. Sorceries had met here. The eastern had been victorious. So what had become of the victor?

He waited nearly fifteen minutes, till certain the obvious trap wasn't there. Only then did he enter the yard.

He couldn't get near Toma. The flames were too hot.

Kleckla was beyond worry anyway.

Tain was calm. His reason was at work. He had surprised himself in the jaws of a merciless vice.

One was his determination to rid the Zemstvi of the Witch and her thieves. The other was the hunter from home, who would be a man stronger than he, a highly ranked Candidate or Select.

Where was he? Why didn't he make his move?

Right now, just possibly, he could get away. If he obscured his trail meticulously and avoided using the Power again, he might give his past the slip forever. But if he hazarded the Tower, there would be no chance whatsoever. He would have to use the Power. The hunter would pin him down, and come when he was exhausted....

Life had been easier when he hadn't made his own decisions. Back then it hadn't mattered if a task were perilous or impossible. All he had had to do was follow orders.

He released the old cow, recovered his mule packs. He stared at them a long time, as if he might be able to exhume a decision from their contents.

He heard a noise. His hands flew to his swords.

Rula, Steban, and the mule descended the hill.

Tain relaxed, waited.

Rula surveyed the remains. "This's the cost of conciliation." There was no venom in her voice.

"Yes." He searched her empty face for a clue. He found no help there.

"Rula, they've sent somebody after me. From the east. He's in the Zemstvi now. I don't know where. He was here. He chased the Caydarmen off. I don't know why. I don't know who he is. I don't know how he thinks. But I know what his mission is. To take me home."

Steban said, "I saw him."

"What?"

"A stranger. I saw him. Over there. He was all black. He had this ugly mask on...."

A brief hope flickered in Tain's breast.

"The mask. What did it look like? What were his clothes like?"

Steban pouted. "I only saw him for a second. He scared me. I ran."

"Try to think. It's important. A soldier has to remember things, Steban.

Everything."

"I don't think I want to be a soldier anymore."

"Come on. Come on." Tain coaxed him gently, and in a few minutes had drawn out everything Steban knew.

"Kai Ling. Can't be anybody else." His voice was sad.

"You know him?" Rula asked.

"I knew him. He was my best friend. A long, long time ago. When we were Steban's age."

"Then...."

"Nothing. He's still a Tervola Aspirant. He's been given a mission. Nothing will deflect him. He might shed a tear for our childhood afterward. He was always too emotional for his chosen path."

She surveyed his gear while he helped Steban off the mule. "You mean you have to run to have a chance?"

"Yes."

"Then run. Anything you did now would be pointless, anyway."

"No. A soldier's honor is involved. To abandon a task in the face of a secondary danger would be to betray a code which has been my life. I'm a soldier. I can't stop being one. And soldiers of the Dread Empire don't retreat. We don't flee because we face defeat. There may be a purpose in sacrifice. We withdraw only if ordered."

"There's nobody to order you. You could go. You're your own commander now."

"I know. That's why it's so difficult."

"I can't help you, Tain." The weight of Toma's demise had begun to crack her barriers against grief.

"You can. Tell me what you'll do."

"About what?"

He indicated the stead. "You can't stay. Can you?"

She shrugged.

"Will you go with me if I go?"

She shrugged again. The grief was upon her now. She wasn't listening.

Tain massaged his aching temples, then started unpacking his armor.

Piece by piece, he became a leading centurion of the Demon Guard. Steban watched with wide eyes. He recognized the armor. The legions were known far beyond lands that had endured their unstoppable passing.

Tain donned his helmet, his swords and witch kit. He paused with his mask in hand. Rula said nothing. She stared at Toma, remembering.

Tain shook his head, donned the mask, walked to the roan. He started toward the Tower

He didn't look back.

The armor began to feel comfortable. The roan pranced along, glad to be a soldier's steed once more. He felt halfway home....

What he had said penetrated Rula's brain soon after he passed out of view. She glanced around in panic.

The mule remained. As did all Tain's possessions except his weapons and armor. "He left his things!"

Quiet tears dribbled from Steban's eyes. "Ma. I don't think he expects to come back. He thinks he's going to die."

"Steban, we've got to stop him."

XIX

Tain came to the dark tower in the day's last hour. Caydarmen manned its ramparts. An arrow dropped from the sky. It whistled off his armor.

Torfin stood beside the Witch. Tain heard her say, "He's not the same one. He wore robes. And walked."

And Torfin responded, awed, "It's Tain. The man who stayed with your father."

There was no thought in the old soldier. He was a machine come to destroy the Tower. He let decades of combat schooling guide him.

He began with the gate.

From his witch pouch he drew a short, slim rod and a tiny glass vial. He thrust the rod into the vial, making sure the entire shaft was moist. He spoke words he had learned long ago.

Fire exploded in his hand. He hurled a flaming javelin.

It flew perfectly flat, immune to gravity. It struck the gate, made a sound like the beating of a brass gong.

Timbers flew as the gate shattered.

Caydarmen scrambled down from the ramparts.

Tain returned to his pouch. He removed the jar and silver box he had used in the pass. He greased his hands, obtained one of the deadly peas. He concentrated, breathed. The cerulean glow came into being. He hurled a fiery blue ball upward.

It rose slowly, drifted like gossamer toward the ramparts.

The Witch didn't recognize her peril until too late. The ball jumped at her, enveloping her left hand.

She screamed.

Torfin bellowed, followed his confederates downstairs.

Tain dismounted and strode through the gate.

Grimnir met him first. Fear filled the big man's eyes. He fought with desperate genius.

And he died.

As did his comrades, though they tried to team against the man in black.

Trolledyngjans were feared throughout the west. They were deadly fighters. These were amazed by their own ineffectuality. But they had never faced a soldier of the Dread Empire, let alone a leading centurion of the Demon Guard.

The last fell. Tain faced Torfin. "Yield, boy," he said, breaking battle discipline. "You're the one good man in this viper's nest. Go."

"Release her." The youth indicated the ramparts. The girl's screams had declined to moans. She had begun fighting the ball. Tain knew she had the strength to beat it, if she could find and harness it.

He smiled. If she failed, she would die. Even if she succeeded, she would never be the same. No matter what happened to him, he had won something. At her age pain could be a powerful purgative for evil.

Still, he had to try to make the situation absolute. "Stand aside, Torfin. You can't beat me."

"I have to try. I love her, Tain."

"You're no good to her dead."

At the bottom of it, Torfin was Trolledyngjan. Like Tain, he could do nothing but be what he was. Trolledyngjans were stubborn, inflexible, and saw all settlements, finally, in terms of the stronger sword.

Torfin fell into a slight crouch, presenting his blade in a tentative figure eight.

Tain nodded, began murmuring the Battle Ritual. He had to relax, to give his reflexes complete control. Torfin was more skilled than his confederates. He was young and quick.

He shrieked and lunged.

Tain turned his rush in silence. The soldiers of Shinsan fought, and died, without a word or cry. Their silence had unnerved men more experienced than Torfin.

Tain's cool, wordless competence told. Torfin retreated a step, then another and another. Sweat ran down his forehead.

Tain's shortsword flicked across and pinked Torfin's left hand. The dagger flew away. The youth had used the weapon cunningly, wickedly. Its neutralization had been Tain's immediate goal.

Torfin danced away, sucked his wound. He looked into faceted crystal and knew the old soldier had spoken the truth when claiming he couldn't be beaten.

Both glanced upward. Shirl's moans were fading.

Tain advanced, engaging with his longsword while forcing Torfin to give ground to the short. Torfin reached the ladder to the ramparts. He scrambled up.

Tain pursued him mercilessly, despite the disadvantage. The youth was a natural swordsman. Even against two blades he kept his guard almost impenetrable.

Tain pushed. Torfin was relying on youth's stamina, hoping he would tire. Tain wouldn't. He could still spend a day in his hot armor, matching blows with the enemy. He hadn't survived his legion years by yielding to fatigue.

Tain stepped onto the battlements. Torfin had lost his last advantage. Tain paused to glance at the Witch.

The blue ball had eaten half her arm. But she was getting the best of it. Only a few sparks still gnawed at her mutilated flesh.

She looked extremely young and vulnerable.

Torfin looked, too.

Tain feinted with the longsword, struck with the short.

It was his best move.

Torfin's blade tumbled away into the courtyard. Blood stained both of his hands now.

He backed away quickly, seized a dagger his love carried at her waist.

Tain sighed, broke battle discipline. "Boy, you're just too stubborn." He sheathed his swords, discarded their harness. He removed his helmet, placed it between his blades.

He went to Torfin.

The youth scoured Tain's armor twice before the soldier took the dagger and arced it out into the grass of the Zemstvi.

Torfin still would not yield.

Tain kicked his feet from beneath him, laid the edge of one hand across the side of his neck.

Tain backed away, glanced down. Torfin's dagger had found a chink. Red oozed down the shiny ebony of his breastplate. A brutalized rib began aching.

He recovered his shortsword, went toward the Witch.

In seconds she would complete her conquest of his magick. In seconds she would be able to destroy him.

Yet he hesitated.

He considered her youth, her vulnerability, her beauty, and understood how she had captivated Torfin and the Baron.

She bleated plaintively, "Mother!"

Tain whirled.

Rula stepped onto the ramparts. "Tain. Don't. Please?"

Seconds fled.

Tain sheathed his blade.

Shirl sighed and gave up consciousness.

"Tain, I brought your things. And your mule." Rula pushed past him to her daughter.

"The wound is cauterized. I'll take care of the bone."

"You're wounded. Take care of yourself."

"It can wait."

He finished Shirl's arm ten minutes later. Then he removed his breastplate and let Rula tend to his injury. It was minor. The scar would become lost among its predecessors.

Rula finished. "You'd better go. The hunter...."

"You're staying?" An infinite sadness filled him as he drew his eyes from hers to scan the Zemstvi. Kai Ling was out there somewhere. He could sense nothing, but that had no meaning. His hunter would be more cunning than he. The trap might have closed already.

"She's my daughter. She needs me."

Sadly, Tain collected his possessions and started for the ladder.

Torfin groaned.

Tain laid his things aside, knelt beside the youth. "Ah. She does have this stubborn ass, you know." He gathered his possessions again. This time he descended without pausing.

Soldiers of the Dread Empire seldom surrendered to their emotions.

He had a hand on Steban's shoulder, trying to think of some final word, when Rula came to him. "Tain. I'll go."

He looked into her eyes. Yes, he thought. She would. Dared he?...

Sometimes a soldier did surrender. "Steban. Go find you and your mother some horses. Rula, get some things from the Tower. Food. Utensils. Clothes. Whatever you'll need. And hurry." He scanned the horizon.

Where was Kai Ling?

"Old friend, are you coming?" he whispered.

Not even the breeze responded. It giggled round the Tower as if the gathering of Death's daughters were a cosmic joke.

Their shadows scurried impatiently round the old stronghold.

They were a hundred yards along the road to nowhere.

"Tain!"

He whirled the gelding.

Torfin leaned on the battlements, right hand grasping his neck. Then he raised the other. "Good luck, centurion."

Tain waved. He didn't reply. His ribs ached too much for shouting.

The day was dead. He set a night course for the last bit of sunlight. Rula rode to his left, Steban to his right. The mule plodded along behind, snapping at the tails of the newcomers.

He glanced back just once, to eye the destruction he had wrought. Death's daughters had descended to the feast. The corner of his mouth quirked downward.

His name was Tain, and he was still a man to beware.

XX

The wind of dark wings wakened Kai Ling. The daughters of Death circled close. One bold vulture had landed a few feet from his outstretched hand.

He moved.

The vulture took wing.

He rose slowly. Pain gnawed his nerve ends. He surveyed the stead, the smoking ruins, and understood. He had survived his mistake. He was a lucky man.

Slowly, slowly, he turned, feeling the twilight.

There. To the west. The centurion had called on the Power yet again.

THE NIGHTS
OF DREADFUL SILENCE

This was the first Dread Empire world story published, appearing in the September 1973 issue of Fantastic Science Fiction & Fantasy Stories. *At the time the story was written its world existed principally to support short fiction involving Leiberesque characters Bragi Ragnarson, Mocker, and Haroun bin Yousif. That world had evolved into something much larger, more complex, and deadlier even before this story appeared.*

An ominous thing was happening at Itaskia's Royal Palace. Aristithorn of Necremnos, the infamous sorcerer, was being cheated by King Norton.

The wizard repeated, "Your Highness, your servant is certain he heard the promise of the Princess Yselda's hand to the man who could slay that up-country ogre."

Norton asked, "Vizier, did we make that ridiculous promise?"

"No, Majesty."

"You see, wizard?" The King glared. Of course he had made the proclamation—he made it every time a dragon, troll, or other disaster arose—but he had no intention of following through. Never had.

Aristithorn sighed. "Ah, so that's the way of it. Hast heard of Ainjar, King of Alfar, Majesty? He cheated Silmagester the Dark—sad, his reward. Three plagues: first, dragons; then locusts in swarms; later, thirty-three daughters so ugly they were unmarriageable, and each of whom eats with the appetite of ten lusty men…."

"You threaten?" the King roared.

"Nay, Illustrious. I merely make a moral: dishonesty seldom pays."

"Seize him!" Norton bellowed. Softer, "Good an excuse as I'll find, I guess."

Aristithorn shook his head sadly as pikemen closed in. "Hate to do it, but:

"Past six night and come seventh sun.
Itaskia's lying shall be done;
This treacher Norton's wicked realm
Black vengeance mine shall overwhelm;
Then ever after shall be heard
No slightest sound of singing bird.
No low of cow, nor spoken word."

There was more, equally bad poetry, which does not bear repeating. He finished with a muttered, "Not bad for spur-of-the-moment." He threw his staff to the marble floor, watched it become a huge serpent, mounted it and rode from the palace, past horrified guards.

That was the same day Bragi Ragnarson suffered a fit of nostalgia and, to the hoots and jeers of his friends, galloped off north toward Trolle-dyngja, a place someone once described as, "the arse of the world on ice." Bragi only remembered the good things, though, until, two days north of Itaskia, a sudden rain squall came rumbling along and pounced. He had equally sudden visions of himself forced to face the weather as it would be a few hundred miles farther along—snow and sleet and ice and all that. Quickly, he turned back for the warm taproom at Itaskia's Red Hart Inn, all pride fled.

Shortly, he fell asleep. And shortly, his scatter-brained mare had them hopelessly lost. Bragi woke to find himself being carried through unfamiliar forest typical of the kingdom anywhere north of the Silverbind.

Three days later he was still searching for the road home, completely miserable. The cold drizzle would not stop. Then he heard someone sing-ing. Also hearing his indignant stomach rumbling, Bragi thought he might cadge something to eat. He studied the camp of the singer from hiding, saw a bedraggled old donkey and a ragged old man huddling around a small fire where a cauldron exuded aromatics. The clearing around the old man was dry, but, being so hungry, Bragi did not notice. He stepped out of the underbrush.

"Hello, grandfather," he said, "could you spare a starving man a smallish bite?" He waved a hand in the direction of the pot.

The old man, bent over something he was trying to sew, started. He looked at Bragi uncertainly. "You're a long way from Trolledyngja," he observed. "You're welcome, sure. I've no extra gear, not being accustomed to guests."

"Thanks. Say, how'd you know where I'm from?" While talking, he dug battered utensils from his saddlebag.

The old man rummaged through his own gear, found a spoon and bowl, joined the other man over the pot. "Where else do men grow big as bears, and twice as ugly?" he asked. "Who else butchers the King's Tongue such a way? You're one of those wandering heroes, eh? Dragon-slaying and maiden-rescuing. Ah, what a life. Wish I were young again…. What would you be doing out here?"

"Times are tough," Bragi grumbled. "Too much competition. In the old days, before King Norton, it was 'a dragon in every cave and a troll under every mountain.' But since Norton killed King Willem, things have gotten worse. Trolls and dragons're almost gone…. Willem was a conservationist." Then he remembered the question. "I fell asleep in the saddle coming down the North Road. Stupid horse decided to go exploring. Been lost three days." He finished filling his bowl and said around a mouthful, "Good! Well seasoned. What of you?"

"Cooking is my hobby," the old man replied, also with a full mouth. "I'm out here trying to think up a spell to fit a curse I cast on Itaskia."

"Sorcerer, huh?"

"Uhn. Aristithorn of Necremnos… you don't seem distressed." He sounded hurt.

"Should I be?" He tossed his head to get the ends of his blond hair out of his stew. "Judging by Zindahjira, a man's safe if he isn't jumped straight off. I don't have anything a wizard would want anyway. Can I have another bowl?"

"Help yourself. You've met the Silent One, eh? Biggest windbag in the trade."

"That's him. Say, what kind of curse are you brewing up?"

The old man snorted. "You been in the kingdom lately?"

"Left the city five days back."

"Ever hear of the King's proclamation about the ogre? The one that's been stealing maidens and the like, not the one who robs travelers. *He* has a license, and pays his taxes."

"Heard somebody finally got him. Why? You the fellow?"

"Got him *and* two of his brothers who were helping handle a surfeit of maidens."

"And Norton wouldn't pay, eh?"

"No!"

"Should've expected it. How'd you get old, being so naïve? He promises his daughter every time there's trouble. What happened to the maidens?"

"Well, after stoning me for ruining what they said was a good thing, I suppose they went home and made do with ordinary men. There'll be a passel of ugly, warty, hairy little bastards born come spring. I hope they all grow up trollish and go into the independent ogre business. Serve Norton right."

"What're you going to do about it?"

"Don't know. When he refused me Yselda, I cast the first curse I thought of. Said that, starting the seventh day after I left, Itaskia would be stricken by total silence until Norton pays."

"Hey, that's good!" Bragi chuckled, speaking more clearly as his belly filled and his mouthfuls grew smaller. "I've got some friends there that need just that. How're you going to do it?"

"That's my problem. I don't know. Never tried anything like it. Wish I'd thought before I opened my mouth. Norton's probably still laughing."

"Be good if you could do it. Might get Yselda after all. Some woman, from all I've heard. A little skinny, but…."

"What? How?"

Bragi considered a moment, said, "Put yourself in Norton's place. King in a city with no sound. Like everyone's deaf, eh? Everything would have to be in writing, eh? How many written promises can a man break before he gets hung from his own rafters? A liar like Norton would sell his mother to keep on cheating. Mark me, Norton'll have his daughter up for whoever gets rid of the silence. Bet?"

The wizard grunted thoughtfully. Bragi imagined fiery lines from dreadful tomes where spells were written in blood on parchments of virgins' skins, bound in dragon hide, raging before his eyes.

"What do you want with Yselda, anyway? I thought sorcerers had to do without, or lose their powers."

"I'm old, ready to retire. I want to raise roses and practice the magicks of love."

"At your age? She'll kill you inside a week."

"No, no. I'm a wizard, remember? All my abstentions of three hundred years are stored up inside me, ready to go. I can hold my own even against Yselda."

"I suppose it's possible," Bragi muttered. "What's she got to say about it?"

"She didn't like me until I mentioned my wizard's savings. Ha! Then she pressed my case more passionately than I. That fool Norton is blind. The Palace Guards stand in line at her door, and the idiot thinks I want her as a source of virgin's blood."

Laughter, uproarious. Every man within a hundred miles of Itaskia knew at least a dozen ribald stories about the Princess's boudoir adventures. She was a girl of fiery nature, and always kept a fireman handy.

"Oh! What magicks would come of using her blood!" Bragi roared. "She'd wreck your whole profession. So! What about the spell?"

The sorcerer grunted noncommittally. He and Bragi started as an idea occurred to both. As one, they said, "I'll make you a deal…."

An hour found diabolical plots plotted and wicked agreements agreed.

The next two days were dull. Bragi was accustomed to bloody action or drunken inaction. Neither was available here. He amused himself by devouring vast quantities of Aristithorn's excellent stews.

The day the curse was to be fulfilled, Bragi made a point of staying out of the way. Aristithorn was uncertain he could cast the necessary spells, was terrified of his all-too-probable failure. However, he would hazard it. Bragi fled camp, following a desire to be at a safe distance when the wizard started summoning demons.

He sat on the earth in the forest, leaning against a tree, watching the squirrels at play among the autumn leaves. His pleasures were simple. But even that little amusement was soon denied him. Wails and demonic howls from Aristithorn's conjurations frightened the animals. Then the outcry died and the forest became unnaturally silent. The northman grew worried. He was working up the courage to investigate when, "Ho! Bragi! Come on in! I've done it!"

He found the ancient dancing around his pentacles. "Tomorrow I go," he said. "You'd better write the messages. But how'll I understand the answers? I can't read."

"What's to understand?" the wizard asked. "Just give him the list of demands, then sit tight till you get the woman and gold. What could be easier?"

"Norton taking my head."

"There is that chance, true."

"Can I hear the one to Yselda? You were up awful late with it."

The wizard stirred through a mound of dramaturgical gear and came up with a smallish scroll. "To the Princess Yselda, Duchess of Scarmane, et cetera, greetings from the great thaumaturge Aristithorn, Archimage of Necremnos, Lord of Eldritch Sprites…."

"Why do all magicians brag so?"

"Huh? We have to! Nobody else will. Necromancy's a hard way to make a living. Everyone cheats us. Knights try to kill us. Devils are after our souls. Everyone, everywhere, insists we're evil. Hell of a life! Praise for our modest efforts has to come from somewhere, so we do the applauding ourselves…."

"Maybe. Write. Save the speeches for Yselda. I'm leaving at first light. That'll give me a little time to scout before I stick my head in the dragon's lair."

"Uhm!" the wizard grunted, already writing. Tongue protruding from the side of his mouth. "Have you memorized the way back to the road?"

"Yes."

Bragi left at sunrise and was more than halfway to the city by nightfall. He rose with the sun again and by late afternoon had camped atop a hill two miles from the city walls. From there, he watched amazedly as refugees dismally came out Itaskia's gates and marched toward the boundaries of silence. He saw many a stout wife dragging her man toward where she could catch up on her backlog of nagging. Compulsive talkers shouted with glee when they were free of the curse and could once more bore their neighbors with tales of themselves. Bragi found he was tempted to leave, to let the silence go on, but thoughts of his share of the profits strengthened his determination.

He slept late next morning, did not ride till mid-morning. The flow of refugees had not slackened. Fighting their flow, he took until noon to reach the gates where he gave the guard officer the first of several scrolls.

Bragi was surprised by the gloominess of the city, then realized how many little noises he had always taken for granted. The song of wind was gone. The humming of insects. The creaks and groans of wagon wheels. The sounds of hooves on pavement. The silence was unnerving. He was beginning to understand the mood of the fleeing thousands.

The northman's scroll cheered the sour guard captain. The soldier quickly delivered him to the palace and King's herald. The herald got a second letter, danced with joy. He directed Bragi's attention to a poster. The northman was certain it was another of Norton's proclamations. He nodded.

The Vizier himself soon appeared, ushered Bragi into the Royal Presence. Here he delivered a scroll to the King. While Norton anxiously poured over the text, Bragi slipped a letter to Yselda. She read and laughed. Then, knowing there was nothing to do but wait, he sat on the floor, leaned against a pillar, and went to sleep.

Mountains of parchments and buckets of ink were used during an argument between Norton and his advisers, the latter pleading for accession to Aristithorn's demands. Bragi went unnoticed only because his prodigious snoring was inaudible. Later, however, someone did notice him and decided he might be pressured into betraying the wizard. Bragi was given parchments dripping doom and golden promises. He grinned at them all. Considering the direness of some of the threats, Norton soon concluded he could not read.

Bragi—always wearing his lack wit's smile—considered the Royal argument. It seemed the King's advisers wanted to pay Aristithorn. The King refused to give up a politically valuable daughter. The Vizier, however, found Norton's weakness.

The King, so the Vizier argued, would be lord of an empty city if the silence continued—the people were fleeing in thousands. Where, when the people were gone, did the Crown expect to apply taxes?

A telling blow! If there was anything Norton enjoyed more than lying, it was taxing his subjects to staggering. Insufferable demand, with no return, had made Norton one of the better known tyrants of his end of the world. Other monarchs envied him. These were distinctions he would not willingly surrender. Therefore, after breakfast, he put on his sad face and sent for Yselda. Sorrowfully, he told her what he had to do.

Yselda tearfully made apparent her willingness to sacrifice herself for her people.

Norton seemed delighted with Yselda's sorrow—not suspicious because her possessions were already waiting on a cart at the palace gate. However, he shrugged that off as he had all the other oddities about his child—unaware she had needs other than those complementing his own.

Bragi and the woman quickly departed.

His daughter gone, the King dried his tears and turned to business. He sent his bodyguard after the two, with orders to slay the northman and sorcerer. The wizard's death should cancel all his spells. He would then have his daughter back and could put her to good use.

However, a chuckling Aristithorn was watching from afar.

Bragi and Yselda left the silence, rode up a tall hill, over, and entered a smallish wood. Behind them, outside the wood, shimmering appeared, coalesced into duplicates of the couple. The specters rode at right angles to the path of those they imitated.

Norton's soldiers topped the hill, followed the decoys. Only later did they notice the chimeras had no cart—and then it was too late to find Bragi's carefully concealed trail. Somewhere afar, an old man chortled at his deception, then, weary, retired.

Bragi and Yselda covered most of the distance to the wizard's camp before nightfall. Yselda had ridden silently the afternoon long, eyes always on the northman. He grew wary of the hungers he saw there. He had his own desires, and one of the strongest was to avoid antagonizing Aristithorn.

But there was no avoiding the trap—all too well did the woman know how to bait it. Bragi was a long time getting to sleep. And rode with guilt next morning. He was surprised when the wizard greeted him pleasantly.

"Hai!" the old man cried when they rode up. "So Norton *can* be beaten. Wonderful—wonderful—wonderful! Hello, my dear. Did you have a pleasant journey?"

"Indeed I did, Thorny," she replied, sighing. "Indeed I did."

A suspicious look passed across Aristithorn's face, but he was too eager to waste time worrying. "Thank you, thank you," he said to Bragi. "I hope you did well too."

Grinning, the northman held up a sack with the mark of the Itaskian Treasury.

"Ah, good. My friend, you've helped an old man beyond all hope of repayment. If you ever need a friend, drop by my castle in Necremnos. It's the one with the chained chimeras guarding the gates and the howls coming from inside—I suppose I'll give that up, now I'm retiring. Drop by any time. I've got to go. The silence will end when I do. One more magick, then I'll get to the business of renouncing my vows."

The wizard was so excited he flubbed his incantation three times. The fourth, while Bragi watched, saw woman, sorcerer, cart, and two donkeys vanishing in a fearsome cloud of smoke.

Shrugging the affair off as profitable and amusing, but of no great import, Bragi returned to Itaskia. He stopped by the Red Hart Inn for a stoop with old friends.

But the story did not end so easily. Bragi found himself outlawed for his part in the affair. Off he went, on an adventure into Freyland where he planned to liberate a fortune said to be lying in the heart of a certain mountain. The treasure he found—and the dragon guarding it. The worm won the ensuing battle handily.

The singed northman, outlawed all along the western coast, decided to impose upon Aristithorn's hospitality. The wizard welcomed him warmly, immediately took him to see his children. Yselda had recently given birth to a pair of sturdy little blond, blue-eyed sons.

Innocently, Bragi asked, "How old are they?"

"Two months," Yselda replied. Confirmation of his suspicions was in her face.

Aristithorn said something about it being time to feed the vampires in the basement. He shuffled off. Bragi and Yselda went for a walk in the garden.

"Is he the man he claimed?" the northman asked.

"Indeed! A one-man army on that battlefield. There's a problem, though. He abstained so long he can't father children. He doesn't know, I'm sure." A strange light twinkled in the Princess's eyes as she added, "It's a pity. He wants more children. So do I, but I just don't know how we'll manage...."

"If I can be of any help...."

Deep in the dungeons, Aristithorn hummed to himself as he tossed wriggling mice to his vampire bats while watching a garden scene in a magical mirror....

He'd lied when he said he was retiring.

Celibacy has nothing to do with his kind of magic.

He'd known of his sterility.

Trust a wizard no more than a King. They're all chess players.

FINDING SVALE'S DAUGHTER

After completing two vast, never published, lethally influenced by Tolkien, Eddison, and the Victorian fantasists, inscribed in a nineteenth-century writing style trilogies, I became intrigued by the simple storytelling of folk tales. I was especially fond of the folklore of Norway. That became a powerful influence in the creation of both Bragi Ragnarson and his native Trolledyngja. The first few centuries after Norway's at-point-of-sword conversion to Christianity gave rise to many interesting tales as the Old Gods receded—much more slowly in the mountains and remote provinces, naturally. The Old Ones lived on as lesser, wicked supernatural beings. The Oskorei is sometimes identified with the Aesir. A character type identifiable as Thor can be found in tales as late as the first half of the twentieth-century—though the Thunderer has been demoted all the way to drunken troll.

This story, appearing for the first time, and "Silverheels" later, fit equally well into the Trolledyngja of the Dread Empire world or that of twelfth-century Norway.

From small bricks like this, never-to-see-the-light novels like The King of Thunder Mountain *and two others would arise—and in their turn provide the soil from which* A Shadow of All Night Falling *sprang. Nepanthe and the Storm Kings, Varthlokkur and others, had a long, quiet history ere ever they stepped onto the public stage.*

Tröndelag was wild country inhabited mainly by trolls and *huldre*-folk. Hifjell Mountain frowned down on Alstahaug village like a brooding giant. On Hifjell's skirts Dark Wood began, a dense pine forest where wolves prowled and the Hidden People spent summer nights in dances to the wicked Old Gods. Few Alstahaugers were brave enough to climb the mountain. Especially not Svale Skar, the village chieftain.

There was one old man, Ainjar, though, who came and went in Dark Wood. He had courage enough for all the villagers. They believed him almost as brave as the King.

Ainjar had no family save a one-eyed dog name Freki. He made his living hunting in Dark Wood. When he needed something that the forest could not provide he brought furs to town.

Grownups did not trust Ainjar because of the dark places he walked, but their children loved him. He always had time to describe a *huldre* wedding or trolls brawling by throwing boulders from wall to wall of canyons deep in the mountains. They thought his tales were tall but he told them well.

Svale Skar awaited Ainjar's coming from Dark Wood with deepening dread.

When a lamb or chicken disappeared everyone knew the *huldre* had been up to mischief and thought little more of it. It was the way of the land and the forest dwellers. But this had been an evil year all round. Right here in Tröndelag, at Stikklestad, there had been a great battle. The King himself had fallen. Before his death he had built bridges and strongholds, had bested giants and trolls, and had driven the wickedest things deep into the mountains or the icy northern wastes. Now he was gone. The new conqueror king, far, far away, had no time to shield his remote new subjects.

The old evils had begun to return.

Sons and daughters and wives had begun to disappear.

Svale's little girl, Frigga, was among the missing.

"Ainjar," he said when the old man finally came down from the mountain, "you wander Dark Wood. You have converse with the *huldre*-folk. Have you heard anything of my little Frigga?"

The old man's dog regarded him with bared teeth.

No one liked Svale Skar. He was a troublemaker. He always drank too much, then started something.

"Svale, you talk too loud, you brag too much, and you're cruel to your wife and children. The *huldre* wise would say you deserve your suffering. So you surprise me now, showing this spark of goodness. For the first time in your life, I think, you want to ask something not for your own sake. I'll ponder that while I deliver my furs to Fat Jens."

Ainjar returned from the furrier's with a smaller pack and lighter step. "Svale, I can give you no good news. This evil plagues the Hidden Folk, too. The *huldre* wise say the *Oskorei* has returned."

"The *Oskorei*? The Terrible Host?"

It was an army of evil spirits. The fallen King had banished it northward, to the realms of always cold. Old tales told of the *oskoreien* raging through the night, astride fire-breathing black stallions whose hooves struck lightning off the sides of mountains, hunting souls unlucky enough not to be safely home by dark. Their hunting horns could still be heard mourning on winter's bitterest northern winds.

"The Wild Hunt!" Svale stammered, frightened. "What can we do?"

Ainjar stared up the dusty path, tugged his ragged gray beard. "I wonder, are there any brave men left? Men like Hatchet-Face Svien, who plundered the Hifjell troll? Somebody who could lay hands on an iron sword?"

Hatchet-Face Svien had lived in nearby Aalmo. Svale often bragged that Alstahaug's cowards were braver than Aalmo's heroes.

His bluff had been called. He owned the only sword in Alstahaug. He had it of his grandfather, whose father had taken it a-reaving in the old days. He had always considered it only a keepsake.

"I have an iron sword."

Ainjar pretended surprise. "Yes? Good. I'll wait here."

Svale was scared but his neighbors had overheard. He got the rusty sword, a blanket, and a bag of food. He could do nothing but shake and stammer Frigga's name when his wife asked where he was going.

A mile into Dark Wood they found a fairy ring. Seven worn, rune-carved stones stood round its edges. Svale thought he saw shadows darting amongst the trees in the twilight.

"I've brought the man," Ainjar said.

Seven old *huldre* stepped into the circle from behind the standing stones. They were the wise of the Hidden People.

The oldest said, "So. Bold Svale Skar himself. In Dark Wood. Though I live another thousand years, no greater wonder shall I see. We have brought the *hulder*."

A young *hulder* entered the circle. He carried a spear with a silver head.

"This is Sköl," said the chieftain. "He's taken a vow not to speak till his son is free."

"We go, then," Ainjar said. "To Thunder Mountain. Fetch me my staff and cloak."

Svale started shaking all over again. Thunder Mountain lay far inland. The ancient stronghold of the *Oskorei* supposedly lay at its heart.

Ainjar led. Svale followed. Sköl came last. Freki ranged ahead. After four hard days, in forests that Svale thought haunted, they reached the foot of Thunder Mountain.

Svale had thought Dark Wood menacing when seen from Alstahaug, then terrifying once it surrounded him. On Thunder Mountain it was worse. There the forest grew dense as night, up to the snow line, and seemed eager to gulp him up. Wolves called on the mountainside.

"How much farther?" Svale's feet ached. Like most people of his time, he had never before strayed more than a few miles from home.

"To the snow line. Where that small hump sticks out like a nose. And now I must leave you."

"But...."

"But me no buts, Svale Skar. Freki!"

"But...."

"You will know what to do when the time comes."

"But...." He found himself talking to Ainjar's back. And Sköl had started climbing the mountain. He ran to catch up, his sword clanking.

Sköl did not camp with sundown. *Huldre*-folk were at home with night. But he did slow for Svale's sake.

They heard children and women crying as they neared the hump. The weeping came from a patch of deep darkness. Then there was evil laughter and the sounds of terrible horns, followed by a clatter and clank like a whole kitchen of pots and pans rattling together. Sköl guided Svale into hiding behind some ragged bushes.

A full orange moon rose. Sköl waited as patiently as the mountain. Svale tried not to fidget and scratch. His sword scraped against something every time he twitched.

The pots and pans noise got louder.

Suddenly, from the patch of darkness, a stream of horsemen galloped, all troll-huge and dark. The horses were bigger than any Svale had ever seen. Their eyes burned red. Their breath came in tongues of fire. Their hooves rang like thunder and struck fountains of sparks before, with a blast of horns, the Terrible Host stampeded across the sky like a flight of snow geese trails bits of fire.

Sköl touched Svale's arm, pointed.

Crossing the moon was something Svale had thought less probable than the return of the *Oskorei*.

"*Linnorm*," he murmured. The great northern dragon.

Astride it, vast cloak flapping, a rod of fire in one hand, was a man. "The Dragon King," Svale whispered, awed. He hadn't ever believed those old stories.

Wings beating with the sounds of gongs, the dragon raced after the Terrible Host. In moments, over westward peaks, there were rumbles and flashes as if a sudden, savage storm had rolled in off the sea.

Sköl pointed toward the cave. Shaking, Svale followed him inside.

The dark veil parted. They could see by torches burning within. Svale understood. Silver and iron were the banes of magic.

Echoed weeping drew them deeper into the earth, to a great cavern that was furnished like a castle's interior.

The missing wives and children were chained to its walls, weeping like lost souls. The stewpots of the *Oskorei* were deep.

Troll women, slaves of the Terrible Host, tended fires and their masters' housekeeping.

Svale spied Frigga sleeping in the lap of a woman from Aalmo.

He had bad habits, but he was not stupid. He did not run to the child. He knew the troll women would seize him and shove him into a cook pot. His old sword would not scratch their stony hides.

They were a problem.

Svale had a thought. It must be near dawn outside.

All trolldom resented what Hatchet-Face Svien had done to their cousin on Hifjell.

"Halvor laughed when the white cock crowed," Svale shouted. "But Hatchet-Face runs like the wind." The trolls dropped their work. Svale scampered back up the tunnel, singing as he went.

Sköl turned toward the wall. He became invisible. *Huldre*-folk can vanish anywhere. The trolls rushed past without seeing him at all.

Svale ran. His blisters became big as eggs. His legs grew heavy. But he ran all the way to the cave entrance, then down into Dark Wood. The troll women were so angry they chased him till Old Sun rose and turned them to stone.

Leading them away was the bravest thing Svale had ever done.

Climbing Thunder Mountain and descending to its heart again was the hardest. Day was almost done when, on feet that were coals of pain, Svale penetrated the dark veil again. It was fully dark when, with Sköl and the prisoners, he came out again. He was cheerful despite his misery, and undaunted by the journey yet to be made homeward.

He and Sköl found their way blocked by a dark rider on a dark horse. The chieftain of the *oskoreien*. His armor was badly battered, his mount was wounded in a dozen places, but both were alive and angry. Smoke trailed from the stallion's nostrils. The King of the *oskoreien*'s eyes were ruby coals behind his slitted visor.

The prisoners shrieked and fled into the cavern.

Sköl gripped his spear and braced himself.

Svale started to run but found his Frigga looking his way from the cave's mouth. He could not flee before her very eyes. He turned and readied his sword.

Their enemy drew a great black blade. Bloody fires flickered along its edge. And by that token they knew the Dragon King had been slain.

Silver and iron. Not even the lord of the *Oskorei*'s magic could withstand that combination. Svale's old sword rang and reeled beneath the enemy's strokes, yet shattered that black, haunted blade. The shards scattered across the mountainside, starting small fires where they fell. Sköl stabbed with his spear. It squealed through a chink in battered dark armor. The lord of the *Oskorei* roared, clutched his side. Lightning and thunder ripped across the night. A sudden, hard rain began to fall. The great black stallion reared, screamed, then galloped into the sky, trailing fire as he carried his master to the safety of his ice castle beneath the midnight sun.

Lightning and thunder continued to rip the night. The rain squelched the fires on Thunder Mountain.

Svale and Sköl laughed and hugged one another, and congratulated one another on how brave they were, and in small soft voices each admitted that he was lying, that he had been scared to death. It made a bond of brotherhood, that shared fear.

Then they called their people out of the mountain and Sköl guided them home.

Svale Skar returned to Alstahaug a changed man. His neighbors did not want to believe his story, but could not help themselves. He no longer started trouble. Neither did he drink to excess, brag, nor treat his family unkindly. It seemed that, in the crucible of his adventure, he had learned to appreciate things of real value.

He pursued no new adventures, though now he no longer feared Dark Wood. He became a quiet man and wise chieftain who, once each year, went to Hifjell Mountain where he and Sköl would join in a journey to a cairn the Hidden People had built for Ainjar and Freki.

After the great storm-battle in the sky the night the two raided Thunder Mountain the *huldre*-folk had found the old man and dog mysteriously slain in the forest.

Only Svale and Sköl and, perhaps the *huldre* wise, suspect whom Ainjar and Freki really were.

Never again did the Terrible Host rage through the mountains and valleys of Tröndelag, though the old folks say you can still hear the devil drumbeats of fiery hooves and the wail of evil horns from the snowfields and glaciers of the far north. They say that when the northern lights are dancing the King of the *Oskorei* is remembering and breathing fire.

GHOST STALK

This story appeared in the May 1978 issue of The Magazine of Fantasy & Science Fiction. *It was the first of a series of novelettes about the crew of* Vengeful Dragon. *At one time I attempted to cobble them together into a fix-up novel but there were no takers. The story was well-received critically and garnered a number of Nebula Award recommendations.*

I

It seemed we had been aboard the *Vengeful D.* forever, madly galloping the coasts from Simballawein to The Tongues of Fire. We looked toward land with the lust of stallions for mares beyond a twelve-foot fence. But our barrier was far less visible. It consisted solely of Colgrave's will.

"Going to the Clouds of Heaven next time I hit Portsmouth," said Little Mica, bending over his needle. He was forever patching sail. "Best damned cathouse on the coast. Best damned cats. Going to make them think Old Goat God himself has arrived." He giggled.

It was Subject Number One with Little Mica. It was with most of us. I had never met a sailor who was not drunk or horny. He would be both if he had his feet on dry land

"Runt like you couldn't satisfy a dwarf's grandmother," Student remarked from behind the inevitable book. They dueled with insults awhile. There was little else to do. We were running before a steady breeze.

During the exchange Student's eyes never left his book.

It was one we had taken off a Daimiellian two-master months earlier. We were due to take another vessel soon. (Maybe The One. I hoped. I prayed. Colgrave had vowed to remain at sea till he found her.) Our stores were running low. There was mold down to the heart of the bread. Maggots were growing in the salt pork, which had gotten wet in a recent storm. There was no fruit to fight the scurvy. And we were down to our last barrel of grog. One lousy barrel would not last me long.

I had no stomach for a beach raid just there, much as I wanted to feel earth and grass beneath my soles. We were a half-dozen leagues north of Cape Blood, off Itaskian coasts. Those were shores Trolledyngjans habitually plundered. And it was their season for hell raising. Coast watchers were, likely, considering us with cold, hard eyes at that moment.

"Sail ho!"

Men scrambled, clearing the decks. I glanced up. As usual, Lank Tor, our chief boatswain, was in the crow's nest. He was as crazy as the Old Man.

Colgrave stalked from his cabin. As always, he was armed and clothed as if about to present himself at court. The boatswain's cry, like a warlock's incantation, had conjured him to the weather decks. "Where away?" He would not go below till we had caught her. Or she shook us. *That* seldom happened.

I peered to seaward. There were always squalls off Cape Blood. That day was no exception, though the storm was playing coy, lying on the horizon instead of embracing the coast. Prey ships liked to duck in to escape. The rocky shoreline offered no hope better than drowning amidst wreckage and thundering surf.

"On the bow!" Tor shouted. "Just round the point and making the land-ward tack."

"Ah-ha-ha-ha," the Old Man roared, slapping his good thigh.

His face had been destroyed by fire. The whole left side was a grotesque lava flow of scar tissue. His left cheekbone showed an inch-square iceberg tip of bare bone.

"We've got her. Had her before we ever saw her."

Cape Blood was a long, jagged, desolate finger of rock diddling the ocean across the paths of cold northern and warm southern currents. If the ship *were* round the point and on a landward tack, she was almost certainly caught. We had a strong breeze astern. She would have to shift sail for a long seaward tack, coming toward us, piling onto the rocks round the headland. That turn, and bending on sail, would take time too.

"Shift your course a point to starboard," Colgrave roared at the helmsman. Toke, our First Officer, so summarily relieved of his watch, shrugged and went to watch Hengis and Fat Poppo, who had the chip log over the side.

"Making eight knots," he announced a moment later. The Old Man eyed the sails. But there was no way we could spread more canvas. With a breeze like the one we had we always ran hell-bent, hoping to catch somebody napping.

"She's seen us," Tor shouted. "Starting to come around. Oh! A three-master. Caravel-rigged." We were a caravel ourselves, a stubby, pot-bellied vessel high in the bows and stern.

The Old Man's face brightened. Glowed. The ship we were hunting was a caravel. Maybe this was The One.

That was what we called her aboard *Vengeful Dragon*. No one knew her true name, though she had several given her by other sailors. *The Ghost Ship. The Hell Ship. The Phantom Reaver.* Like that.

"What colors?" Colgrave demanded.

Tor did not answer. We were not that close. Colgrave realized it and did not ask again.

I did not know if the phantom were real or not. The story had run the western coast almost since the beginning of sea trade, changing to fit the times. It told of a ghost ship crewed by dead men damned to sail forever, pirating, never to set foot on land, never to see Heaven or Hell, till they had redeemed themselves for especially hideous crimes. The nature of their sins had never been defined.

We had been hunting her for a long time, pirating ourselves while we pursued the search. Someday we would find her. Colgrave was too stubborn to quit till he had settled his old score. Or till we, like so many other crews who had met her, fed the fish while she went on to her next kill.

The Old Man's grievance involved the fire that had ruined his face, withered his left arm, and left him with a rolling limp, like a fat galleon in a heavy ground swell. The phantom, like so many pirates, always fired her prey when she finished with them. Colgrave, somehow, had survived such a burning.

His entire family, though, had gone down with the vessel.

The Captain, apparently, had been a rich man. Swearing he would find The One, he had purchased the *Vengeful Dragon*. Or so the story went, as it had been told to us.

None of us knew how he had gotten rich in the first place. All we knew about him was that he had a terrible temper, that he compensated for his disfigurement by dressing richly, that he was a genius as a pirate, and that he was absolutely insane.

How long had we been prowling those coasts? It seemed an age to me. But they had not caught us yet, not the Itaskian Navy, or the witch-mastered corsairs of the Red Isles, or the longshipmen of Trolledyngja, nor the warships of the many coastal city-states. No. We caught them, like spiders who hunted spiders. And we continued our endless hunt.

Always we hunted. For the three-master caravel with the deadman crew.

II

"Steward!" Colgrave called. "Half pint for all hands." The Old Man seldom spoke at less than a bellow.

Old Barley flashed a sloppy salute and went looking for the key to the grog locker. That was my cue. Grog had been scarce lately. I shuffled off to be first in line.

From behind his book Student remarked to Little Mica, "Must be rough to be a wino on the *Vengeful D.*"

I threw him a daggers look. He did not glance up. He never did. He was not interested in observing the results of his razor-tongued comments.

As always, Priest fell in behind me, tin cup in hand. Service aboard *Vengeful Dragon* and a taste for alcohol were all we had in common. I suppose, though, that that made him closer to me than to anybody else. He was universally, thoroughly hated. He was always trying to save our souls, to renounce sin and this mad quest for a phantom killer little more evil than we.

Priest was strange. He was blue-assed hell in a boarding party. He went in like he meant to cutlass his devil right back to Hell.

The Kid and my friend Whaleboats jockeyed for the third position, till the Old Man turned his one ice-blue eye their way. The Kid did a fast fade. He was supposed to be on watch.

Kid had not been with us long. We had picked him up off a penteconter in the Scarlotti Gulf. We had taken her in full view of Dunno Scuttari's wharves. Their little navy had been too scared to come out after us.

Kid was crazy-wild, would do anything to get attention. He and I did not get along. I reminded him of the headmaster of the orphanage he had been fleeing when he had stowed away aboard the penteconter.

I had heard that that headmaster had been murdered, and arson, that had taken a score of lives, had been committed on the orphanage. The Kid would not say anything one way or the other

We kept our sins to ourselves.

Few of us got along. *Dragon* remained taut to her main truck with anger and hatred.

Ah. A life on the rolling wave, a cruise of the *Vengeful D.*, buccaneering with sixty-eight lunatics commanded by the maddest captain on the western ocean.... Sometimes it was Hell. Sheer, screaming Hell.

Old Barley was having trouble finding the key. The old coot never could remember where he had put it so he would not miss it next time he needed it.

"Shake a leg down there, buzzard bait. Or I'll bend you to the bowsprit for the gulls."

That would get him moving. Barley was a coward. Scared of his own shadow. You told him something like that, and he thought you were serious, he would carve you into pieces too small for fish bait. He was the only man aboard meaner than Colgrave and deadlier than Priest.

Curious what fear could do to a man.

Little Mica, leaning on the rail, said, "I can see her tops."

"So who cares?" Whaleboats replied. "We'll see all we want in an hour." He had been through the stalking dance so often it was all a dreadful bore for him now.

Whaleboats had picked up his nickname long ago, in an action where, when we had been becalmed half a mile from a prospective victim, he had suggested we storm her from whaleboats. It had been a good idea, except that it had not worked. They had brought up their ballast stones and dropped them through the bottoms of our boats. Then the breeze had freshened. We had had to swim back to *Dragon* while they sailed off. That vessel was one of the few that had gotten away.

Mica persisted. "Why's she running already? She can't know who we are."

"What difference does it make?" Whaleboats growled. "Barley, if you're not up here in ten seconds...."

"Ask Student," I suggested. "He's got all the answers." But some he would not tell, like how to retire from the crew.

She was running because she had to. Anyone beating round Cape Blood who encountered a vessel running before the wind did so. Nine times out of ten, the second vessel was a pirate who had been lying in ambush behind the headland. I had never understood why the Itaskian Navy did not keep a squadron on station there, to protect their shipping. Maybe it was because the weather was always rotten. That day's fairness was unusual in the extreme.

Nervously, I glanced at the squall line. Had it moved closer? I hated rough weather. Made me sick. Grog only made it worse.

Old Barley showed up with the bucket he had tapped off the barrel. There had better be some on the three-master, I thought. Doing without made me mean.

The Old Man stood behind Barley, beaming at us like a proud father. For that moment you would have thought he had completely forgotten his prey in his concern for his crew.

Dragonfeathers. The hunt was all that ever mattered to him.

He would sacrifice everyone and everything, even himself, to fulfill his quest. And we all knew it.

I thought, I could reach out with my fish knife ... *schlock-schlock*, and spill his guts on the deck. End it all right now.

I would have to remind Tor to get sand up from ballast before we closed with the caravel. To absorb the blood. He never remembered. He forgot a lot from day to day, remembering only his name and trade. He came to every battle with the eagerness of a male virgin.

It would have been easy to have gotten Colgrave. He was so vulnerable. Crippled as he was, he was no infighter. But I did not try. None of us ever did, though we all thought about it. I could see the speculation on a dozen faces then.

So easy. Kill the crazy bastard, run *Dragon* aground, and forget hunting spook ships.

You'll never do it, never do it, echoed through my mind.

Any other crew on any other ship would have strangled the insane sonofabitch ages earlier.

III

"I can see her mainsail," said Little Mica. "She's shifting sail again."

"Speed it up, Barley," said the Old Man. He put that cold eye on me as I tried to sneak my cup in again. A half pint was barely enough to warm the throat.

Better be hogsheads full on that three-master, I thought.

"Looks like she's trying for the squall," Tor called down. "I make her a Freylander. She was showing personal colors but got them in before I could read them."

Ah. That meant there was someone important aboard. They thought maybe we would not try as hard if we did not know.

Freyland lay west of Cape Blood, a dozen leagues to seaward where it came nearest the mainland. The caravel must have been making the run from Portsmouth to Songer or Ringerike, an overnight journey.

We seldom prowled the coasts of the island kingdom because the ghost ship seldom appeared there. We left Freyland to our competitors, the Trolledyngjans.

Colgrave's expression—what could be read through the scars—was deflated. Not The One. Again. Then he reconsidered. The flight and flirting with colors could be a ploy. He had done the same himself, to lull a Red Islander or Itaskian.

"Shift your heading another point to starboard," he ordered. "Bosun, come down and prepare the decks."

Lank Tor descended as agilely as an ape. Only the Kid scrambled through the rigging more quickly. But Kid sometimes fell.

A loud thump on the main deck, waking you in the night, told you he had been showing off again.

As Tor hit the deck he began growling orders through a grin of anticipation.

He enjoyed these bloodlettings. They were the only times he felt alive. The boring interim periods were the devil's price he paid for his moments of bloody ecstasy. The lulls were not bad for him, though. His memory was so weak it seldom reached back to our last conquest.

One of his mates began issuing weapons. I took a cutlass, went below for the bow and arrows I kept by my hammock, then repaired to my station on the forecastle deck. I was the best archer aboard. My job was to take out their helmsman and officers.

"I'd shoot a lot straighter with a little more grog in me," I grumbled to Whaleboats, who had charge of the forward grappling hooks.

"Couldn't we all. Couldn't we all." He laughed. "Talk about your straight shooting. I ever tell you about the thirteen-year-old I had in Sacuescu? Don't know where she learned, but she came well trained. Positive nympho. Male relatives didn't approve, though." He drew back his left sleeve to expose a long jagged scar on the roll of muscle outside the shoulder socket. "Two hundred fifty yards, and me running at the time."

I daydreamed while pretending interest. He had told the story a hundred times. Without improving it, the way most of us did. I don't think he remembered having told it before.

No imagination, Whaleboats. The sea ran in long, yard-tall, polished jade swells. Not a fleck of white. No depth. I could not see in. It must have been calm for days. There was none of the drifting seaweed usually torn up by the Cape's frequent storms.

The next one would be bad. They always were when they saved their energies that way.

The ship's pitch and roll were magnified on the forecastle deck, which was twenty feet above the main. My stomach began to protest. I should have saved the damned grog for later.

But then there would have been less room for spirits from the caravel.

The wind was rising, shifting. We were nearing the squall. Little rills scampered over the larger swells.

We were getting nearer Cape Blood, too. I could hear the muted growling of the surf, could make out the geysers thrown up when a breaker crashed in between rocks, shattered, and hurled itself into the sky.

The caravel was less than a mile away. She was showing her stern now, but we had her. Just a matter of patience.

Barley and Priest came up, leading several of the best fighters. It looked like Colgrave planned to board forecastle to stern castle. That was all right by me. It was all over but the killing, once we seized their helm.

Whaleboats spit over the rail. He was so unkempt he was disreputable even among us. "Maybe there'll be women," he mused. "Been a long time since we took one with women."

"Save one for the Virgin." I chuckled. That was the Kid's other name. It got used mostly when somebody was baiting him.

Whaleboats laughed too. "But of course. First honors, even." Then his face darkened. "One of these days we're going to catch another wizard."

They had tried it before.

It was our one great fear. Battles we could win when they were man against man and blade against blade. We were the meanest fighters on the western ocean. We had proven it a hundred times. But against sorcery we had no protection save the grace of the gods.

"Itaskia. We've hurt them most. They'll send out a bait ship with a first-rate witch-man aboard. Then what good our luck?"

"We managed before."

"But never again. I might take Student up on it." He did not say what.

The pirates of the Red Isles had tried it. It had been a close thing. We had been lucky, that time, that Colgrave was too crazy to run. Barley had gotten the sorcerer an instant before he could unleash a demon that would have scattered *Dragon* over half the western ocean.

Our competitors in the islands were not fond of us at all. We showed their vessels the same mercy we gave any others.

Each man of us prayed that we would find The One before some eldritch sea-fate found us.

I could make out faces on the caravel. Time to get ready. I opened their waterproof case and carefully considered my arrows. They were the best, as was my bow. Worth a year's hire for most men. Time was, I had made their price hiring them, and myself, out for a month.

I studied, I touched, I dithered. I finally selected the gray shaft with the two red bands.

Whaleboats observed the ritual with amusement, having failed to entice anyone into a wager on which I would choose. I always took the same one in the end. It was my luckiest shaft. I had never missed with it.

Someday I would exchange arrows with the archer aboard the phantom. They said he was sure death inside three hundred yards. I did not believe he could possibly be as deadly as I as long as I had the banded lady.

It would be interesting, if dangerous, meeting him.

The caravel was trying to trim her canvas. One of the cutlass men guffawed and shouted, "Fart in them! That'll give you all the wind you need."

I wondered what it was like to look over your taffrail and see certain death bearing down. And know there was not a thing you could do but wait for it.

IV

The caravel ran straight away, under full canvas. But the gap narrowed steadily. I could make out details of weapons and armor. "They've got soldiers aboard!"

"Uhm. A lot of them." That was Tor, who had the sharpest eyes on *Vengeful D.* He had known for some time, then.

I turned. The Old Man had clambered up to the poop, stood there looking like some dandified refugee from Hell.

"'Bout close enough for you to do your stuff," said the boatswain, tapping my shoulder.

"Yeah?" It was a long, long shot. Difficult even with the banded arrow. Pitch, roll, yaw. Two ships. And the breeze playing what devil's games in between? I took my bow from its case.

It was worth a year's pay to most men. A magnificent instrument of death. It had been designed solely for the killing of men and custom-crafted to my hands and muscles. I ran my fingertips lightly over its length. For a long time the weapon had been my only love.

I had had a woman once, but she had lost out to the bow.

I bent it, strung it, took out the banded arrow.

They were making it difficult over there, holding up shields to protect their helmsman. They had recognized us.

The banded lady never missed. This time was no exception. At the perfect instant she lightninged through a momentary gap between shields.

The caravel heeled over as she went out of control. She slowed as her sails spilled wind. Panic swept her poop. We raced in.

Colgrave bellowed subtle course changes at our own helmsman. Our sails came in as we swept up.

One by one, I sped my next eleven shafts. Only two failed finding their mark. One was the treacherous blue and white I had threatened to break and burn, it seemed, a thousand times.

The Old Man brought our bows alongside their stern with a touch so deft the hulls barely kissed, as Barley, Priest, and their party leapt over. The shambles I had made of the other poop left no contest. We controlled her immediately.

Sails cracked and groaned as both vessels took them in. Our bows crept past the Freylander's waist.

Whaleboats threw his grapnel. I helped heave on the line.

Screaming, our men poured over the main deck rail to assault the mob awaiting them. They were regular soldiers, Freylander troops tempered in a hundred skirmishes with Trolledyngjan raiders. Once Whaleboats made fast, I resumed plying my bow, using scavenged Freylander arrows.

Crude things, they were unfit to caress a weapon like mine. No wonder they had not harmed any of us.

I dropped a score into the melee, probing for officers and sergeants, then took out a bothersome pair of snipers in the caravel's rigging. They had been plinking at the Old Man, who stood like a gnarled tree defying a storm, laughing as arrows streaked around him

He would be some match for the dead captain of the phantom.

The caravel's poop was clear. Barley and Priest were holding the ladders against counterattacks from below. The men with them threw things at the crowd on the main deck. I decided to recover my arrows before some idiot trampled them, went aft.

The uproar was overwhelming. Shouts. Clanging weapons. Shrieks of pain. Officers and sergeants thundering contradictory orders. The sides of the vessels ground together as the seas rolled on beneath them. And the Old Man still laughed crazily on the poop. He and I were the only ones who remained aboard.

He nodded. "As always, well done."

I gave him an "it was nothing" shrug. When the stern castles rolled together, I jumped across.

My feet came down in a pool of blood, skidded away. Down I went, my head bounding off the rail.

Colgrave laughed again.

It was nearly over by the time I came around. A handful of soldiers were defending a hatchway forward. Most of our men were pitching corpses overboard. They were eying that hatchway hungrily. Feminine wailing came from behind it. Priest and Barley were getting ready for the final rush.

I staggered up, planning to help with a few well-placed arrows.

Damn! My head! And the Freylander seemed to be rolling badly.

It was not my imagination. The squall was closer. It would arrive in a few hours.

That was time enough for recreation. And to find the grog.

V

It had been another of those good battles. I sipped from a quart tankard I had found in the Freylander captain's cabin. No serious injuries for our boys. Lots of cuts and scratches, a bashed head here and a broken finger there. Nothing permanent. The gods must, as Colgrave claimed, have favored our mission. They seldom allowed any of us to come to harm.

The men were having a grand time down on the main deck. Twelve women. A genuine princess and her ladies-in-waiting. What Whaleboats called a jackpot ship. The Virgin, I saw, was not anymore. He abandoned his conquest, scrambled into the Freylander's rigging, began dancing on a yardarm. He was naked from the waist down.

His sureness in the tops, his fearlessness, was his great talent. He showed it off too much.

Whaleboats, a keg of priceless Daimiellian brandy under one arm, a woman's satin bolster under the other, joined me on the poop. "Another master stroke." He nodded toward Colgrave, who still stalked Dragon's poop, muttering, cursing the luck that kept him from finding The One.

Student joined us, glancing at Whaleboats questioningly. Whaleboats shrugged.

Student had found himself some new books. "Squall's moving in," he observed. The water had become a bluish gray showing freckles and stripes of white. The seas were running closer together.

"Going to be a blue-assed bitch of a storm," I prophesied. "The way it's taking its time."

Little Mica was the next of the clique to arrive. He was half-naked, sweat-wet. "The chunky one's not bad." He grinned. His performance had been up to brags.

He was carrying several pounds of gold and silver. We had collected a lot in our time. So much we used it for ballast. Once we found and destroyed The One, we planned to return landside rich as princes.

"That fool Kid's gonna break his neck yet."

He was hopping on one foot, on the tip of the yard, while hosing spurts of piss into the gap between ships.

He suddenly yelled wildly, threw up an arm, bounced his butt off the yard and plunged seaward, limbs flailing. The seamen roared as he did a perfect belly-buster. The ships nudged together. Everyone not otherwise occupied manned the rail.

"I told you...."

"Hold it." The Old Man was peering intently with his one eye. I saw it, too, then. Coming out of an arm of the squall that had reached landward north of us. "Two of them. Longships. Trolledyngjans."

They were no more than three miles away. Their sails were fat with wind and distinct as they spotted us and altered course. One was a black sail bearing a scarlet wolf's head. The other was a yellow-red striped one bearing a black ax.

They were coming after us. Already they were putting their shields on their gunwales and taking in their sails so they could unstep their masts. They looked quick and practiced. Old hands.

Gloating, no doubt, about having caught a competitor with his pants down.

The Old Man bellowed, bellowed, bellowed. Not much sense came through, but the men, drunk though they were, reacted. A storm of booty flew from vessel to vessel. Fat Poppo chucked the naked princess over. She screeched as she landed on her shapely little derriere. Lank Tor, laughing, planted a slobbery, wine-dark kiss on her tender young lips, tossed her back. He clouted Poppo when the fat man protested.

"Fire time," said Student. He looked at Whaleboats in a way that must have had meaning. My friend hurried down the ladder after him.

In moments cutlasses were chopping at lines. Bow and arrows in one hand, half-empty tankard in the other, I watched the deck force make sail. They kept tripping over plunder.

When the proper combination of rolls arrived, I casually stepped from rail to rail without losing a drop of my drink.

"Fo'c'sle," Colgrave growled. I nodded. "Wolf's Head first." I was not so far gone that I could not remember which had been which before they had gotten their sails in.

The Old Man was going to fight. Of course. He always fought. He would fight if the whole damned Itaskian Navy were coming down. He believed in his mission and that he was invincible because the gods were on his side.

The northmen were just a mile away when we finally got under way. Their oars worked with the swift precision of a centipede's legs.

Old hands. They needed no drummer to keep the cadence. They would be tough fighters.

Smoke poured from the Freylander. Naked women reached out to us, pleading.

"She's not burning right," said Mica, who had followed me to the forecastle.

As we drew away, the women abandoned the rail, began scurrying around with buckets.

"Student and Whaleboats better stay out of the Old Man's way," I replied. Colgrave would not be pleased.

He set a course angling seaward, squallward, across the bows of the Trolledyngjans. Any fugitive would have done the same, hoping to evade their first rush and get into the weather before they could come round and overhaul. The ax ship sheered to cut us off and to maneuver so they could board us over both rails. Less than half a mile separated us.

Old hands, yes, but they did not know us. They must have been used to working the coasts of Freyland. Seemed to me there was a good chance they had come over specifically to take the fish we had caught already. There was a big king at Songer, and a scattered gaggle of smaller ones who, nominally, owed him allegiance. The little kings plotted against the big one, and one another, constantly. They were not above tipping the Trolledyngjans to an opportunity to plunder their rivals.

Politics is one specialized field of sin I haven't the wit to comprehend.

A quarter mile. I caressed the banded arrow. Except for Mica, she and I were alone this time. Any fighting would take place on the main deck because the longships had such low freeboard. And it would involve only the ax ship. I kissed the arrow. After all our time together, I thought, we were finally going to part.

Time. The Old Man threw the helm over hard. *Dragon* staggered. The sails rumbled and cracked as they spilled wind.

I sent the banded arrow on her final flight. Ever faithful, as that slut of a wife in Itaskia could not be, she sped to the northern helmsman's heart. He sagged against his rudder arm. Wolf's Head heeled and bucked.

We took her directly amidships, our bows surging up and over, grinding and crunching her into driftwood and halves. Her mast, which had been shipped lengthwise atop her deck thwarts, levered up, speared through, and tangled in our sprit rigging. As we ploughed the wreckage, we staggered and shuddered like a fat lady donning a corset.

Little Mica yipped. A huge, incredibly hairy barbarian with mad blue eyes came up the mast one-handed, lugging an immense battle-ax. He sprang over the rail, howled. While he chased Mica, I dug up a boathook, then smacked him behind the ear. He was so huge it took both of us to dump him overboard. The water revived him. He splashed, cursed. The last I saw of him, he was swimming strongly toward the Freylander.

Our turn brought us round on a southerly course once more. We ploughed through the wreckage. I stared down at bearded warriors busy drowning, clinging to debris, calling for help. The other Trolledyngjan had turned to pick up survivors but had second thoughts now that we were coming back.

They surely thought we were berserkers then, mad killers. Losing some of the precision they had shown earlier, they stepped their mast, made sail, and fled toward the squall.

I groaned, rubbed my stomach in anticipation. Colgrave would not turn loose. No matter that we were shipping water forward and a dozen men had to go to the pumps. No matter that we were drunk on our asses and exhausted from a battle already fought. He had been challenged. He would respond if it meant chasing the Trolledyngjan off the edge of the world.

VI

The waves stood taller and taller, the sea became leadish gray with ever more white running the ridges and faces of the swells. Spray salted my lips even there on the forecastle deck. *Dragon* bucked and rolled, her timbers protesting. Splatters of rain beaded on the decks. The air grew cooler. The Trolledyngjan entered the squall and gradually faded from visibility.

This was more her sort of weather. Her high, curved bows, broad beam, and shallow draft made it possible for her to ride up and down even the most awesome waves—as long as she met them bow on. With her low freeboard she could ship a lot of water fast. I suspected she would put out a sea anchor once she was safely concealed in the storm.

Dragon's altitude, fore and aft, had not been designed with waves in mind. The castles were meant to provide an advantage in battle. They made us a tad top-heavy and wind-vulnerable. In rough weather they existed solely to compound my misery.

There was a lot of wind in that squall. And Colgrave had reduced sail only as much as absolutely compelled by the need to keep *Dragon* from being torn apart. The rigging cracked, screamed, groaned, as if a hundred demons were partying there. A topsail tore with a *sh-whack!* like the fist of a giant whooshing into a stone wall, began popping and cracking in the gale. Only ribbons remained by the time they got it in.

The Kid was up there, helping cut parts free. Some thoughtful soul had remembered to fish him out as we were getting under way. He was a lucky little bastard.

I was rather pleased. Though he had little use for me, I liked him. As much as I liked anyone. He reminded me of myself when I was a lot younger.

He knew that he had been lucky. He was not clowning anymore. He was even using a safety harness.

I collected my weapons and cases. I had to take them below and care for them. Moisture and salt could ruin them forever. Colgrave did not protest. Everyone else, cook included, had to drop everything to work ship, but I was exempted. I was the thunderbolt, the swift, deadly lightning, that determined the course of battles the moment they were joined. Colgrave did not value me as a human being, but he did value my skills and weapons.

The seas were thirty feet tall and gray-black when I dragged myself back topside. My guts were flooding back and forth between my toes and ears. But I had to help with the work. We had reached a point where we were not only pursuing our mad captain's mission, we were fighting to survive.

Every man had found some way to rope himself to his station. Floods raged round the tossing decks, threatening anyone not securely tied. It was a long, watery walk home.

A caravel was not designed to endure that.

I staggered, splashed around, lost a stomach full, snagged the rail in time to save myself. Fat Poppo handed me a safety line. I joined the men trying to control the canvas the Old Man insisted we show.

Lank Tor, the crazy bastard, was in the crow's nest, watching for the Trolledyngjan. He should have been down on the main deck showing off his sea wisdom, not up there proving he had a pig-iron gut. My stomach revolted just at the thought of being up where the mast's height magnified motion horrendously.

We did not regain contact till the weak light began fading from the gray, thick storm. In the interim I found too much time to think and remember, to be haunted by the woman in Itaskia.

She had not been bad, as wives went, but had been short on understanding. And too willful. The conclusion of the El Murid Wars had made jobs for bowmen scarce. You had needed to be related to someone. I had not been. And had not known anything else but farming. I had had enough of that as a boy. She had nagged about the money. It had been good in the war years and she had developed tastes to suit. So I had done a spot of work for Duke Greyfells. Some men had died. She had sensed their blood on my hands. That had led to more nagging, of course. There is just no pleasing them. Whatever you try, it's wrong. It had gotten so bad that I had started spending more time at the Red Hart than in our tenement room.

In alcohol I had found surcease, though more from a critical self than from a wife who, despite making her points in the most abrasive manner possible, had been right. But a man can't shake the pain he carries around inside him. All he can do is try deadening it. In my case that just made the wife situation worse.

There had come an evening when I arrived home early—or late, considering I had been gone three days—and had learned how she had been able to maintain our standard of living, how she had been obtaining the silver I stole to maintain my alcoholic tranquility.

It had been a double blow. A gut-wrecked and a rabbit punch. Your wife is seeing someone else. That is a decker, but you can get up and learn to live with it. But when you find out that there has been a parade, and you're living off the proceeds....

I swear by the Holy Stones, for all our troubles, I never laid a hand on that woman before, not even when roaring drunk. Not once, even provoked.

A couple of men died, and the woman, and I went on the run, bitter, never quite sure just what had come over me, why, or what it had all been about. Not long afterward, Colgrave had scavenged me off a ship he had taken and shanghaied me as replacement for a man who had been washed overboard earlier.

There were sixty-eight stories as shameful, or worse, lurking aboard the *Vengeful D*. Few of us talked about them. The Old Man's tale, if he had one, was his alone. All we knew was the story about the fire.

Student, though, thought he had guessed it. And claimed he knew how to get off *Dragon*, to where he wanted to be. He caused a lot of frowns and nervous questions when he talked like that.

He never would elaborate.

VII

The men were grumbling seditious by the time we spied the Trolledyngjan again. For hours we had been pushing westward, either into the heart of the ocean or onto the rocky coasts of southern Freyland. We had left the waters we knew far behind. Though not one of us had been ashore in a long time, we liked it handy just in case. We were not deep-water sailors. Losing all touch seemed a nightmare.

Colgrave stood on the poop like a statue, staring straight ahead, as if he could see through the spray and waves and rain. Reports of cracked planking, broken frames, and water gushing in as fast as the pumpers could bail, bothered him not at all. He persevered. That, if any one word ever did, encapsulated him perfectly. He persevered.

Dragon larked about on the shoulders of seas as huge as leviathans.

"I see her!" Lank Tor cried. How? I wondered. I could barely see *him*. But it was my cue. I recovered my weapons, repaired to the forecastle deck.

I could see her from there. She was a specter fading in and out almost dead ahead.

The problem was the size of the seas. She swooped down one side like a gull diving, vanished in a trough, then staggered up the next wave like an old man in an uphill race. Her sail had been torn to tatters. Her crew had been unable to unstep their mast. Now they huddled on their oar benches, trying to keep their bows into the waves. They had no protection from Mother Ocean's worst. They were brave, hardy men. What would they do if she swamped?

I never had much use for Priest. But when he clambered up to join me he looked so puzzled and pathetic that I could not ignore him. "What's up?"

"Whaleboats and Student. They're gone

"Gone? What do you mean, gone?" Whaleboats. My only friend. He could not abandon me.

Where the hell could he go? *Dragon*'s rails were the edge of our world.

"Over the side, I guess. Nobody's seen them since they fished the Kid out." He paused, stared at the sea with the look that usually presaged a sermon. Awe, I think you could call it. "The Old Man wanted to talk to them. About why the Freylander didn't burn. One-Hand Nedo says he saw them dump most of the oil into the drink instead of on the deck."

"Whaleboats?" Student, maybe. He had been spooky, unpredictable. But not the biggest woman-hater on the *Vengeful D*. The screams of a tormented female had been like the voices of harps to Whaleboats.

"Yes."

"Strange. Very strange." The man who had fished the Kid out of the drink at Dunno Scuttari had also gone over the side in a few hours. Was the Kid a jinx? I did not think so. Losing someone was unusual, but not unprecedented. In fact, the Old Man had kept the Kid mostly because we had lost another man a week earlier.

And the rebellion? Their failure to fire a captured vessel? That was beyond my comprehension.

"Whaleboats? Really?"

There had to have been more there than met the eye. I could feel it. It was something outside the normal ken, something almost supernatural. The same something that had gotten Priest into such a state.

I could sense some terribly important revelation hovering on the marches of realization, teasing, taunting, a butterfly of truth on gossamer wings. Gods were trying to touch me, to teach me. I pictured Student's dusky face, peeping over the inevitable book. His eyes were merry with the mockery he had always shown when he hinted around his secret.

Maybe he *had* known the way home. But miles at sea, amidst a storm, seemed a strange place and time to start the journey. There was nothing off *Dragon* but drowning and the teeth of fishes.

Or had they swum to the Freylander? They could have expected no mercy from possible rescuers.

Nobody died on the *Vengeful D*. Not in my memory, anyway, though that gets cloudier as it goes back toward my coming aboard. The battles might be fierce, gruesome, and bloody. The decks might become scarlet and slippery. Toke, who doubled as our surgeon (a profession he once had pursued), might stay busy for days sewing wounds, cauterizing, and setting bones, but none of us passed into the hands of Priest for burial with the fishes. All his prayers he had to save for the souls of our enemies.

We, like *Dragon* herself, wore a thousand exotic scars, but, as Colgrave said, the gods themselves guarded us. Only restless, treacherous Mother Ocean could steal a soul from *Vengeful D.*

It was no wonder the Old Man could hurl ship and crew against odds that would have assured mutiny on the most disciplined Itaskian man-o'-war. We believed ourselves immortal. Excepting Old Barley, we dreaded only the completion of our quest and the wizard trap that someone, someday, surely would spring.

What would become of our band of cutthroats if we found The One, or if the gods withdrew their favor?

We closed with the Trolledyngjan. Descending darkness, more than the storm, obscured her now. Still, when we were both at wave crest, I could see the pale faces of their chieftains. They showed fear, but also the dogged determination to die fighting that animates all northmen. We could expect them to turn on us soon.

A *creak-clump* sound drew my attention. The Old Man had come forward. How he had managed, I could not guess. He leaned on the rail while we ran up and down several watery mountains. The ship's motion did not discomfit him at all.

My guts were so knotted that it had become impossible for me to keep heaving them up.

"Can you do it?" he finally asked. "The helmsman?"

I shrugged. "In this? I don't know. I can try." Anything to end the chase and get *Dragon* out of that gray sea hell. He would not break off till we had made our kill.

"Wait for my signal." In a journey that was almost an epic, he returned to the poop. As darkness thickened, he brought *Dragon* more and more abreast of the Trolledyngjan.

She crested. He signaled. I sped my second-best shaft.

She was not the banded lady. She wobbled in the gale, failed the clean kill.

The helmsman had to drown with the others.

Out of control, the Trolledyngjan turned sideways as she slid into a trough, broached.

She survived one wave, but the next swamped her.

One arrow. One deadly shaft well sped, and our part was over. The terrible, terrible sea would do the rest.

Now we could concentrate on surviving. And I could look forward to respite from that constant roar and plunge.

VIII

Smooth sailing was a long time coming. We had to wait for a lull before putting about, lest we share the northman's fate. Then we drove back into it, the wind an enemy as vicious as the waves. We made headway only slowly. Three torturous days groaned past before we staggered through a rainy curtain and saw land and quieter seas once more.

The Old Man's dead reckoning was uncanny. He brought us back just two leagues south of Cape Blood.

But the caravel, that we had halfway hoped to find still adrift, had vanished. We would get no chance to finish plundering her.

Colgrave growled, "Tor, up top. Quick now." He surveyed the sea suspiciously.

Someone had come along. There was no other explanation. The caravel was not on the rocks. And those women, courtiers all, would never have worked ship well enough to have sailed her away. Itaskians summoned by the coast watchers? Probably.

They could be hanging around.

The work began. *Dragon* had taken a vicious pounding. She was leaking at a hundred seams. We had cracked planks forward from the ramming of the Trolledyngjan. Their condition had been worsened by days of slamming into heavy seas. The rigging looked like something woven in a mad war between armies of drunken spiders. Dangling cables, torn sheets, broken spars were everywhere aloft. We needed to pull the mizzenmast and step a spare, and to replace the missing foretopmast. We had enough replacements on board, but would have to plunder new spares off our next victim.

And stores. We had not gotten much off the Freylander. What had become of the keg Whaleboats had plundered, I wondered. I doubted that he had taken it over the side with him.

That was a good sign. I do not worry about alcohol when I'm seasick.

We had the mizzen half pulled, the foretop cleared, sails scattered everywhere for Mica's attention, and half the lines and cables down.

It was the perfect time.

And the enemy came.

As always, Lank Tor saw her first. She came out of the foul weather hugging the cape. Matter-of-factly, he announced, "Galleon, ho. Two hundred fifty tonner, Itaskian naval ensign."

Equally calmly, Colgrave replied, "Prepare for action, Bosun. Keep the repair materials on deck." He climbed to the poop. "And watch for more."

It was my turn. "Signals ashore. Mirrors, looks like." There were flashes all along the coast.

"Coast watchers. They'll be calling everything out of Portsmouth." Colgrave resumed his laborious climb.

We wasted no time trying to run. In our state it was hopeless. We had to fight, and count on our fabulous luck.

"Could be three, four hundred men on one of those," Barley muttered as he stalked past with the grog bucket. He was so damned scared I expected him to wipe them out single-handedly.

"Sail!" someone cried.

A little slooplike vessel, long, low, lateen-rigged, had put out from a masked cove. No threat.

"Messenger boat," said Fat Poppo, who had been in the Itaskian Navy at one time. "She'll log the action and carry the report to the Admiralty."

We did not like one another much, we followers of the mad captain's dream, but we were a team. We made ready with time to spare.

The Itaskian came on as if she intended ramming.

She did! She was making a suicide run with the messenger standing by, if needed, to collect survivors.

The Old Man bent on a main topsail and a storm spritsail, just enough to give us steerage way. At precisely the appropriate instant, he dodged.

The galleon rolled past so closely we could have jumped to her decks. She was crammed with marines. The snipers in her rigging showered me with crossbow bolts.

I leaned back and roared with laughter. Their best effort had but creased my right sea boot.

Each of my shafts took out a Crown officer. Our men drew blood with a storm of javelins.

To ram had been their whole plan. Going away in failure, they seemed at a loss.

Wigwag signals came from the sloop. They were in a cipher Poppo could not read.

"They'll be back," Priest predicted. It was no great feat of divination.

Already they were taking in sail, preparing to come about. This time they would not roar past like a mad bull.

"Find me some arrows!" I demanded. "Tor...."

"On the way," the boatswain promised, gaze fixed on the Itaskian.

I touched the hilt of my cutlass. It had been a long time since I had had to use one. I expected to this time, though. We had to take that galleon so I could recover my arrows. And get at their grog. Itaskians always carried a stock.

Our luck had held that far. There was but one casualty during the first pass. The Kid. He had fallen out of the rigging again. He was just dazed and winded. He would be all right.

The crazy little bastard should have broken every bone in his body.

The moment the Itaskian was clear, Tor put everyone to work.

Colgrave was crazier than I thought. He meant to try dodging till we completed repairs.

They let us get away with it one more time. They had little choice, really. We had the wind. I put down as many officer-killing shafts as I could. But they were prepared for me. Their decision-makers remained hidden while they were in range.

The repair parties succeeded in one thing: freeing most of the men from the pumps. We needed them.

Third time past, the Itaskian sent over a storm of grappling hooks. Despite flailing axes and busy swords and my carefully targeted arrows, they pulled us in, made us fast.

It began in earnest.

How long had it been since we had had to fight on our own decks? I could not remember the last time. But Itaskian marines overran the rail, swarmed aboard, coming and coming over the piles of their own dead. My god, I thought, how many of them are there? The galleon had them packed in like cattle.

I expected them to drive for our castles, to take out Colgrave and myself, but they disappointed me. The point of their assault was the mainmast.

I soon saw why. A squad of sailors with axes went to work on it.

The Old Man thundered at Barley and Priest. They went after the ax men. But the Itaskian marines kept ramparts of flesh in their path.

It was up to me. Ignoring the endless sniper fire, I sped arrow after arrow. That eventually did the trick, but not before they had injured the mainmast grievously.

A grappling hook whined past my nose. What now?

The Itaskian sailors still aboard the galleon were throwing line after line in our rigging.

It was insane. Suicidally insane. No ship, knowing us, tried to make it impossible for us to get away. No. Even the proudest, the strongest, made sure *they* could escape. At least two hundred dead men littered *Dragon*'s decks. Blood poured from our scuppers. And still the Royal Marines clambered over the hills of their fallen.

What drove them so?

The assault's direction shifted from the mainmast to the forecastle. Despite vigorous resistance, the Itaskians broke through to the ladders. I downed as many snipers as I could before, putting my bow carefully out of harm's way, I drew my cutlass and began slashing at helmeted heads.

It had been a long time, but my hand and arm still knew the rhythms. Parry, thrust, parry, cut. No fancy fencing. Riposte was for the rapier, a gentleman's weapon. There were no gentlemen on the *Vengeful D.* Just damned efficient killers.

The Itaskian captain sent the remnants of his sailors in after the marines. And, a grueling hour later, he came over himself, with everyone left aboard.

IX

As always, we won. As always, we left no survivors, though in the end we had to hunt a few through the bowels of their ship. An enraged Barley had charge of that detail.

The long miracle had persisted. Once those of us who were able had thrown the Itaskians to the fishes, it became apparent that not one man had perished. But several wished that they had.

I paused by Fat Poppo, who was begging for someone to kill him. There was not an inch of him that was not bloody, that had not been slashed by Itaskian blades. His guts were lying in his lap.

Instead of finishing him, I fetched him a cup of brandy. I had found Whaleboats's keg. Then, accompanied by Little Mica, who did not look much better than Poppo, I crossed to the galleon.

I wanted to find a clue to the cause of their madness. And a chance to be first at their grog.

Priest had had the same idea. He was wrecking the galley as we passed through.

Screams came from up forward. Barley had found a survivor.

We found the brig.

"Damned," said Mica. "Ain't he a tough one?"

Behind bars was the Trolledyngjan we had thrown overboard. Must be important, I thought, or he would be sleeping with the fishes. Probably some chieftain who had made himself especially obnoxious.

My banded arrow lay in his lap.

I gaped. She had found ways to come home before, but never by such an exotic route.

Mica was impressed too. He knew what that arrow meant to me. "A sign. We'd better take him to the Old Man."

The Trolledyngjan had been eying us warily. He jumped up laughing. "Yes. Let's go see the mad captain."

Colgrave listened to what I had to say, considered. "Give him Whaleboats's berth." He turned away, eye burning a hole in the southern seascape. The messenger vessel still lay there, watching.

I returned to the Itaskian for the banded arrow's sisters.

Ordinarily I did not do much but speed the deadly shafts. I was a privileged specialist, did not have to do anything unless the urge hit me. But now everyone had to cover for those too sliced up to rise, yet too god-protected to die. Not being much use in the rigging, I manned a swab.

They had caught us good, had tangled us thoroughly. It would take all night to get free, and another day to replace the masts. The main, now, would have to go too.

"They'll be here before we're ready," said Mica, passing on some errand.

He was right. All logic said we had sailed into a trap, and even now the ladies of Portsmouth were watching the men-o'-war glide ponderously down the Silverbind Estuary.

The Old Man knew. That was why he kept glaring southward. He was thinking, no doubt, that now he would never catch The One.

Me? All I wanted was to get away alive.

I hoped Colgrave still had a trick or two up his elegant sleeve.

Poppo waved weakly. I abandoned my swab to fetch him another brandy.

"Thanks," he gasped. Grinning, "I know now."

"What's that?"

"The secret. Student's secret,"

"So?"

"But I can't tell you. That's part of it. You've got to figure it out yourself."

"Not Whaleboats."

"Smarter than he looked, maybe. Back to your mopping. And think about it."

I thought. But I could not get anything to click. It was a good secret. I could not even define its limits, let alone make out details.

It had caused Whaleboats and Student to do something completely out of character: fake the fire aboard the Freylander.

Darkness closed in. It was the most unpromising night I had ever seen. Signal fires blazed along the coast. The messenger moved closer, to keep better track of us.

Those of us who were able kept on working. By first light we had stripped the Itaskian of everything useful and had freed *Dragon*. The Old Man spread the fore mainsail and, creeping, we made for the storm.

"There they are."

This time I paid attention to Mica. This time it was important.

Lank Tor and the Old Man, of course, had known for some time.

There were sails on the horizon. Topsails. Those of seven warships, each the equal of the one we had taken. No doubt there were smaller, faster vessels convoying them.

The messenger stayed with us, marking our slow retreat.

The gods were not entirely with us anymore. The squall line retreated as we approached, remaining tantalizingly out of reach. Soon it broke free of Cape Blood and began drifting seaward.

"We could try for Freyland...." I started to say, but Mica silenced me with a gesture.

There was a second squadron north of the Cape. Three fat galleons eager to make our acquaintance.

"We're had. What's that?"

Something bobbed on the waves ahead. Low, dark. Gulls squawked and flapped away as we drew nearer.

It was a harbinger of what Itaskia's Navy planned for us.

Trolledyngjans from Wolf's Head had managed to assemble a raft and start paddling for land. They had not made it. Itaskian arrows protruded from each corpse. The gulls had been at their faces and eyes.

"Always the eyes first," said Mica. He glanced at the wheeling birds, shivered.

"That," I said, "is the only ghost ship we're ever going to see."

The repairs went on and on. The Old Man stood the poop as stiffly as if this were just another plundering-to-be. Not till after they had drawn the noose tight did he act. And then he merely went below to change into fresher, dandier clothing.

Ten to one, and all of them bigger. How much can the gods help? But they took no chances. They surrounded us carefully, then slowly tightened their circle.

When it was almost time, I paused to speak to my banded arrow. This time, I told her, we were going to do a deed that would re-echo for decades. It would be our only immortality.

But they gave me no opportunity to employ her.

Two fat galleons moved in on our sides. We killed and killed and killed, till the sea itself turned scarlet and frothed with the surging to and fro of maddened sharks. They cut us up one by one till, like Fat Poppo, we could do nothing but squat in our own gore and watch the destruction of our shipmates.

The first pair of vessels eventually pulled away so another pair could put their marines aboard. And so on. And so on. Such determination. That Freylander must have been far more important than we had thought.

There came a time when I was alone on the forecastle, Colgrave was alone on the poop, and the Kid was alone in the rigging. Then even we had been cut down.

The Itaskians cleared their countless dead while, unable to interfere, we lay in our own blood. Would they fire us, as we had done to so many victims? No. Gangs of sailors came over and took up the repair work we had started.

I supposed they were planning to take us into Portsmouth. Our trials and executions would make a huge spectacle.

It would be the events of the decade.

X

The Itaskians worked a day and a night. Dawn proved my pain-fogged speculations unfounded.

The messenger ship then drew alongside. Just one man came aboard. He wore the regalia of a master sorcerer of the Brotherhood.

This was the man we had feared so long, the one against whom we had no defense. His was the mind, no doubt, which had engineered our destruction. He had been subtle. Not till now had we suspected the presence of a magical hand. Knowing he was there, Colgrave might have gone another way.

He surveyed *Dragon* with a pleased look, then went aft to begin a closer inspection. He started with the Old Man.

One by one, working his way forward, he paused over each man. Finally, he climbed the forecastle ladder and bent over me.

"So, Archer," he murmured. I clutched the banded arrow beneath my broken leg and wished I had the strength to drive her into his chest. I had not felt so much rage, so much hatred, since the night that I had killed my wife. "Your long journey is almost done. You're almost there. In just a few hours you'll have your heart's desire. You'll meet your ghost ship after all."

He must have said the same thing to the others. *Dragon* fairly quivered with anger and hatred. Mine was so strong I half sat up before I collapsed from pain and the weight of the spells he had spun about us.

"Farewell, then," he chuckled. "Farewell all!" A minute later he was aboard his sloop. Her crew cast off. By then the galleons had fled beyond the southern horizon.

I could still hear his voice, singing, as the sloop pulled away. At first I thought it imagination. But it was not. He was chanting up some new sorcery. The old began to relax.

My anger broke that enchantment's limits. I rolled. I found my bow. Ignoring nerves shrieking with the pain in my leg, I surged upward.

Three hundred yards. He had his back to me, his arms raised in an appeal to the sky. "This's the flight for which you were made." I kissed the banded lady good-by.

I fell as she left the bow, cursing because I would be unable to follow her final flight.

She was faithful to the last.

The skull-pounding chant became an endless tortured scream.

All the thunders of the universe descended at once.

I had let fly seconds too late.

The first thing I noticed was the gentle whisper of the ship moving slowly through quiet seas. Then the damp fog. I rolled onto my back. The mist was so dense I could barely make out the albatross perched on the fore truck. I sat up.

There was no pain. Not even the ache of muscles tormented by the exertions of combat. I rubbed my leg. It was whole. But I had not imagined the break. There was a lump, no longer tender, at the fracture site. My cuts, scrapes, and bruises had all healed, their only memorial a few new scars.

It takes months for bones to knit, I thought.

I stood, tottered to the rail overlooking the main deck. The bone held.

My shipmates, as puzzled as I, were patting themselves, looking around, and murmuring questions. Fat Poppo kept lifting his shirt, fingering the line across his belly, then flipping his shirt down and glancing around in embarrassed disbelief. Lank Tor stared upward, mouthing a silent "How?" over and over.

The sails were aloft and pregnant with wind.

I turned slowly, surveying the miracle. Maybe we *were* beloved of the gods, I thought.

The fog seemed less dense ahead. Light filtered through.

The Old Man sensed it too. He began clumping round the poop in suspicious curiosity, leaning on the rails, the stern sheets, trying to garner some hint of what had happened.

He paused, stared past me.

In a voice that was but a ghost of his usual thunder, he called Toke and Lank Tor, conferred. In minutes, quietly, they were about their work. He called to me to keep a sharp lookout.

The boatswain and First Officer took in sail.

XI

And now we drift, barely making steerage. Every man remains self-involved in the mystery of our survival.

The fog *is* thinning. I can see the water now, like polished jade, an algae-rich soup in which the only ripples are those made by *Dragon*'s cutwater.

Yet there is a breeze up top. Curious.

A dozen birds are perched in the tops, silently watching us, moving only when the Kid or another topman pushes by. Spooky.

The Old Man is as much at a loss as anyone. He is ready for anything, expects nothing good. He sends one of Tor's mates round to make sure we are all fully armed.

The fog gradually breaks into patchlets. But the low sky remains solidly overcast. It is no more than two hundred feet up. It is so thick, the light is so diffuse, that there is no telling exactly where the sun stands. Sometimes the cloud dips down, and the maintop ploughs through, swirling it like a spoon does cream in a cup of tea.

I check my arrows, mourn my banded lady. She was a truer love than any I have ever known, was faithful to the end. Not like this blue and white. She is as fickle as that bitch I killed in Itaskia.

Heart's desire. The dead sorcerer promised. Then what am I doing here, sailing to a rendezvous with the ghost ship? A queasiness not of wind or wave stampedes through my stomach. I will face a grim opponent, if the wizard did not lie. And without my deadly lady. The bowman there, they say, is at least as good as I.

This is my desire? Then I have fooled myself more thoroughly than anyone else.

I wish I could talk to Colgrave, to make sure there aren't any last-minute changes in plan.

Like a chess opening thoroughly planned beforehand, our initial moves will go by rote. We have discussed them a hundred times. We have taken a score of vessels in dress rehearsal.

I am the Old Man's key piece, his queen. He relies on me heavily. Perhaps too heavily.

I am supposed to take out that legendary bowman first. Before he can get me. Then I take the dead captain, the helmsman, anyone taking their places, and, as we go hand to hand, their deadliest fighters.

Dragon's prow slices through a final cloud.

I see her! A caravel emerging from a fog bank directly ahead, bearing down on us. I wave to Colgrave.

It's Her. The One. The Phantom. I can smell it, taste it. Its taste is fear. The sorcerer did not lie. Even from here I can see the bowman on her forecastle deck, glaring our way.

The butterflies grow larger

Colgrave shifts our heading a bit to starboard. The reaver immediately does the same. We have barely got steerage way, but it seems we are rushing toward one another at the breakneck speed of tilting knights. I glance at Colgrave. He shrugs. How and when I act is up to me.

I take my second-best arrow and lay it across my bow. "Now, if you ever aspired to greatness, is the time to fly true," I whisper. My hands are cold, moist, shaky.

We proceed in near silence, each man awed by what we are about to attempt. The ghost makes not a sound as she bears down, evidently intending a firing pass similar to our own. Even the birds, usually so raucous, are still. Colgrave stands tall and stiff, refusing to make himself a difficult target. He has complete confidence in my skill and the protection of the gods.

He is positively aglow. This is the end to which he has dedicated his life.

Momentarily, I wonder what we will really do if by some chance we are the victors in this encounter. Will we beach the *Vengeful D.* and haul our treasures ashore as we have always said? But where? We must be known and wanted in every kingdom and city-state fronting the western ocean.

Four hundred yards. The phantom seems a little hazy, a little undefined.

For a moment I suspect my eyes. But, no. It's true. There is an aura of the enchanted about her.

There would be, wouldn't there?

Three fifty. Three hundred yards. I could let fly now, but it does not feel right.

There is something strange about the reaver, something I cannot put my finger on.

Two-fifty. The crew are getting nervous. All eyes are on me now. Two hundred. I cannot wait any longer. He won't

I loose.

As does he, at virtually the same instant.

His shaft moans past my ear, nicking it, drawing a drop of blood. I stoop for another, cursing. I missed too.

The butterflies have grown as big as falcons. I send a second arrow, and so does he. And we both miss, by a wider margin.

Does he have the shakes too? He is supposed to be above that, is supposed to be far better than he has shown. The Phantom has never met a foe she needed fear.

But she has never met us. Perhaps fear is why we have never been able to track her down. Perhaps she has heard how terrible her stalkers can be.

One-fifty. I miss twice more. Now it has become a matter of pride. He can miss forever, so far as I'm concerned, but I've got a reputation to uphold and a nervous crew to reassure.

Another miss. And another. Damned! What is wrong with me?

Student's mocking grin comes haunting. I frown. Why now?

One hundred yards. Toe-to-toe. And I'm down to just one arrow. Might as well kiss it all good-by. We have lost. This feckless blue and white will miss by a mile.

But a dead calm comes over me. Disregarding my opponent, who, I suppose, has been toying with me, I ready the shot with tournament care.

It goes.

A thunderbolt strikes me in the chest. The bow slides from my fingers. The crew moan. I clutch the arrow….

A blue and white arrow.

I can hear Student laughing now. And, with blood dribbling from the corners of my mouth, I grin back. So that's his secret.

It's a good one. A cosmic joke. The sort that sets the gods laughing till their bellies ache and then, ever after, when they remember, is good for a snicker.

My opponent falls as I fall. I wind up seated with my back against the rail, watching as the grapnels fly, as the ships come together, as the faces of the men portray a Hell's gallery of reactions.

I suppose we'll drift at the heart of this circular mile forever, tied to ourselves, to our sins.

It's too late for redemption now.

FILED TEETH

This story is a collateral sequel to the novel All Darkness Met. *It appeared in the anthology* Dragons of Darkness, *edited by Orson Scott Card, a companion volume to* Dragons of Light. *Michael Whelan produced an absolutely stunning cover painting based upon "Filed Teeth" — which ended up on* Dragons of Light *because the artist doing that cover did not deliver his work on time. Whelan also did a fine interior illo of Lord Hammer, which has appeared on magazine and book covers around the world. And which resides proudly in my library now.*

I

Our first glimpse of the plain was one of Heaven. The snow and treacherous passes had claimed two men and five animals.

Two days later we all wished we were back in the mountains.

The ice storm came by night. An inch covered the ground. And still it came down, stinging my face, frosting the heads and shoulders of my companions. The footing was impossible. We had to finish two broken-legged mules before noon.

Lord Hammer remained unperturbed, unvanquishable. He remained stiffly upright on that red-eyed stallion, implacably drawing us northeastward. Ice clung to his cowl, shoulders, and the tail of his robe where it lay across his beast's rump. Seldom did even Nature break the total blackness of his apparel.

The wind hurtled against us, biting and clawing like a million mocking imps. It burned sliding into the lungs.

The inalterable, horizon-to-horizon bleakness of the world gnawed the roots of our souls. Even Fetch and irrepressible Chenyth dogged Lord

Hammer in a desperate silence.

"We're becoming an army of ghosts," I muttered at my brother. "Hammer is rubbing off on us. How're the Harish taking this?" I didn't glance back. My concentration was devoted to taking each next step forward.

Chenyth muttered something I didn't hear. The kid was starting to understand that adventures were more fun when you were looking back and telling tall tales.

A mule slipped. She went down kicking and braying. She caught old Toamas a couple of good ones. He skittered across the ice and down an embankment into a shallow pool not yet frozen.

Lord Hammer stopped. He didn't look back, but he knew exactly what had happened. Fetch fluttered round him nervously. Then she scooted toward Toamas.

"Better help, Will," Chenyth muttered.

I was after him already.

Why Toamas joined Lord Hammer's expedition I don't know. He was over sixty. Men his age are supposed to spend winter telling the grandkids lies about the El Murid, Civil, and Great Eastern Wars. But Toamas was telling *us* his stories and trying to prove something to himself.

He was a tough buzzard. He had taken the Dragon's Teeth more easily than most, and those are the roughest mountains the gods ever raised.

"Toamas. You okay?" I asked. Chenyth hunkered down beside me. Fetch scooted up, laid a hand on each of our shoulders. Brandy and Russ and the other Kaveliners came over, too. Our little army clumped itself into national groups.

"Think it's my ribs, Will. She got me in the ribs." He spoke in little gasps. I checked his mouth.

"No blood. Good. Lungs should be okay."

"You clowns going to talk about it all week?" Fetch snapped. "Help the man, Will."

"You got such a sweet-talking way, Fetch. We should get married. Let's get him up, Chenyth. Maybe he's just winded."

"It's my ribs, Will. They're broke for sure."

"Maybe. Come on, you old woods-runner. Let's try."

"Lord Hammer says carry him if you have to. We've still got to cover eight miles today. More, if the circle isn't alive." Fetch's voice went squeaky and dull, like an old iron hinge that hadn't been oiled for a lifetime. She scurried back to her master.

"I think I'm in love," Chenyth chirped.

"Eight miles," Brandy grumbled. "What the hell? Bastard's trying to kill us."

Chenyth laughed. It was a ghost of his normal tinkle. "You didn't have to sign up, Brandy. He warned us it would be tough."

Brandy wandered away.

"Go easy, Chenyth. He's the kind of guy you got to worry when he stops bitching."

"Wish he'd give it a rest, Will. I haven't heard him say one good word since we met him."

"You meet all kinds in this business. Okay, Toamas?" I asked. We had the old man on his feet. Chenyth brushed water off him. It froze on his hand.

"I'll manage. We got to get moving. I'll freeze." He stumbled toward the column. Chenyth stayed close, ready to catch him if he fell.

The non-Kaveliners watched apathetically. Not that they didn't care. Toamas was a favorite, a confidant, adviser, and teacher to most. They were just too tired to move except when they had to. Men and animals looked vague and slumped through the ice rain.

Brandy gave Toamas a spear to lean on. We lined up. Fetch took her place at Lord Hammer's left stirrup. Our ragged little army of thirty-eight homeless bits of war-flotsam started moving again.

II

Lord Hammer was a little spooky…. What am I saying? He scared hell out of us. He was damned near seven feet tall. His stallion was a monster. He never spoke. He had Fetch do all his talking.

The stallion was jet. Even its hooves were black. Lord Hammer dressed to match. His hands remained gloved all the time. None of us ever saw an inch of skin. He wore no trinkets. His very colorlessness inspired dread.

Even his face he kept concealed. Or, perhaps, especially his face….

He always rode point, staring ahead. Opportunities to peek into his cowl were scant. All you would see, anyway, was a blackened iron mask resembling a handsome man with strong features. For all we knew, there was no one inside. The mask had almost imperceptible eye, nose, and mouth slits. You couldn't see a thing through them.

Sometimes the mask broke the colorless boredom of Lord Hammer. Some mornings, before leaving his tent, he or Fetch decorated it. The few designs I saw were never repeated.

Lord Hammer was a mystery. We knew nothing of his origins and were ignorant of his goals. He wouldn't talk, and Fetch wouldn't say. But he paid well, and a lot up front. He took care of us. Our real bitch was the time of year chosen for his journey.

Fetch said winter was the best time. She wouldn't expand.

She claimed Lord Hammer was a mighty, famous sorcerer.

So why hadn't any of us heard of him?

Fetch was a curiosity herself. She was small, cranky, long-haired, homely. She walked more mannish than any man. She was totally devoted to Hammer despite being inclined to curse him constantly. Guessing her age was impossible. For all I could tell, she could have been anywhere between twenty and two hundred.

She wouldn't mess with the men.

By then that little gnome was looking good.

Sigurd Ormson, our half-tame Trolledyngjan, was the only guy who had had nerve enough to really go after her. The rest of us followed his suit with a mixture of shame and hope.

The night Ormson tried his big move Lord Hammer strolled from his tent and just stood behind Fetch. Sigurd seemed to shrink to about half normal size.

You couldn't see Lord Hammer's eyes, but when his gaze turned your way the whole universe ground to a halt. You felt whole new dimensions of cold. They made winter seem balmy.

Trudge. Trudge. Trudge. The wind giggled and bit. Chenyth and I supported Toamas between us. He kept muttering, "It's my ribs, boys. My ribs." Maybe the mule had scrambled his head, too.

"Holy Hagard's Golden Turds!" Sigurd bellowed. The northman had ice in his hair and beard. He looked like one of the frost giants of his native legends.

He thrust an arm eastward.

The rainfall masked them momentarily. But they were coming closer. Nearly two hundred horsemen. The nearer they got, the nastier they looked. They carried heads on lances. They wore necklaces of human finger bones. They had rings in their ears and noses. Their faces were painted. They looked grimy and mean.

They weren't planning a friendly visit.

Lord Hammer faced them. For the first time that morning I glimpsed his mask paint.

White. Stylized. Undeniably the skullface of death.

He stared. Then, slowly, his stallion paced toward the nomads.

Bellweather, the Itaskian commanding us, started yelling. We grabbed weapons and shields and formed a ragged-assed line. The nomads probably laughed. We were scruffier than they were.

"Gonna go through us like salts through a goose," Toamas complained. He couldn't get his shield up. His spear seemed too heavy. But he took his place in the line.

Fetch and the Harish collected the animals behind us

Lord Hammer plodded toward the nomads, head high, as if there were nothing in the universe he feared. He lifted his left hand, palm toward the riders.

A nimbus formed round him. It was like a shadow cast every way at once.

The nomads reined in abruptly.

I had seen high sorcery during the Great Eastern Wars. I had witnessed both the thaumaturgies of the Brotherhood and the Tervola of Shinsan. Most of us had. Lord Hammer's act didn't overwhelm us. But it did dispel doubts about him being what Fetch claimed.

"Oh!" Chenyth gasped. "Will. Look."

"I see."

Chenyth was disappointed by my reaction. But he was only seventeen. He had spent the Great Eastern Wars with our mother, hiding in the forest while the legions of the Dread Empire rolled across our land. This was his first venture at arms.

The nomads decided not to bother us after all. They milled around briefly, then rode away.

Soon Chenyth asked, "Will, if he can do that, why'd he bring us?"

"Been wondering myself. But you can't do everything with the Power."

We were helping Toamas again. He was getting weaker. He croaked, "Don't get no wrong notions, Chenyth lad. They didn't have to leave. They could've took us slicker than greased owl shit. They just didn't want to pay the price Lord Hammer would've made them pay."

III

Lord Hammer stopped.

We had come to a forest. Scattered, ice-rimed trees stood across our path. They were gnarled, stunted things that looked like old apple trees.

Fetch came down the line, speaking to each little band in its own language. She told us Kaveliners, "Don't ever leave the trail once we pass the first tree. It could be worth your life. This is a fey, fell land." Her dusky little face was as somber as ever I had seen it.

"Why? Where are we? What's happening?" Chenyth asked.

She frowned. Then a smile broke through. "Don't you ever stop asking?" She was almost pretty when she smiled.

"Give him a break," I said. "He's a kid."

She smiled a little at me, then, before turning back to Chenyth. I think she liked the kid. Everybody did. Even the Harish tolerated him. They hardly acknowledged the existence of anyone else but Fetch, and she only as the mouth of the man who paid them.

Fetch was a sorceress in her own right. She knew how to use the magic of her smiles. The genuine article just sort of melted you inside.

"The forest isn't what it seems," she explained. "Those trees haven't died for the winter. They're alive, Chenyth. They're wicked, and they're waiting for you to make a mistake. All you have to do is wander past one and you'll be lost. Unless Lord Hammer can save you. He might let you go. As an object lesson."

"Come on, Fetch. How'd you get that name, anyway? That's not a real name. Look. The trees are fifty feet apart...."

"Chenyth." I tapped his shoulder. He subsided. Lord Hammer was always right. When Fetch gave us a glimmer of fact, we listened.

"Bellweather named me Fetch. Because I run for Lord Hammer. And maybe because he thinks I'm a little spooky. He's clever that way. You couldn't pronounce my real name, anyway."

"Which you'd never reveal," I remarked.

She smiled. "That's right. One man with a hold on me is enough."

"What about Lord Hammer?" Chenyth demanded. When one of his questions was answered, he always found another.

"Oh, he chose his own name. It's a joke. But you'll never understand it. You're too young." She moved on down the line.

Chenyth smiled to himself. He had won a little more.

His value to us all was his ability to charm Fetch into revealing just a little more than she had been instructed. Maybe Chenyth could have gotten into her.

His charm came of youth and innocence. He was fourteen years younger than Jamal, child of the Harish and youngest veteran. We were all into our thirties and forties. Soldiering had been our way of life for so long we had forgotten there were others. Some of us had been enemies back when. The Harish bore their defeat like the banner of a holy martyr....

Chenyth had come after the wars. Chenyth was a baby. He had no hatreds, no prejudices. He retained that bubbling, youthful optimism that had been burned from the rest of us in the crucible of war. We both loved and envied him for it, and tried to get a little to rub off. Chenyth was a talisman. One last hope that the world wasn't inalterably cruel.

Fetch returned to Lord Hammer's stirrup. The man in black proceeded.

I studied the trees.

There was something repulsive about them. Something frightening. They were so widely spaced it seemed they couldn't stand one another. There were no saplings. Most were half dead, hollow, or down and rotting. They were arranged in neat, long rows, a stark orchard of death....

The day was about to die without a whimper when Lord Hammer halted again.

It hadn't seemed possible that our morale could sink. Not after the mountains and the ice storm. But that weird forest depressed us till we scarcely cared if we lived or died. The band would have disintegrated had it not become so much an extension of Lord Hammer's will.

We massed behind our fell captain.

Before him lay a meadow circumscribed by a tumbled wall of field stone. The wall hadn't been mended in ages. And yet....

It still performed its function.

"Sorcery!" Brandy hissed.

Others took it up.

"What did you expect?" Chenyth countered. He nodded toward Lord Hammer.

It took no training to sense the wizardry.

Ice-free, lush grass crowded the circle of stone. Wildflowers fluttered their petals in the breeze.

We Kaveliners crowded Fetch. Chenyth tickled her sides. She yelped, "Stop it!" She was extremely ticklish. Anyone else she would have slapped silly. She told him, "It's still alive. Lord Hammer was afraid it might have died."

Remarkable. She said nothing conversational to anyone else, ever.

Lord Hammer turned slightly. Fetch devoted her attention to him. He moved an elbow, twitched a finger. I didn't see anything else pass between them.

Fetch turned to us. "Listen up! These are the rules for guys who want to stay healthy. Follow Lord Hammer like his shadow. Don't climb over the wall. Don't even touch it. You'll get dead if you do."

The black horseman circled the ragged wall to a gap where a gate might once have stood. He turned in and rode to the heart of the meadow.

Fetch scampered after him, her big brown eyes locked on him.

How Lord Hammer communicated with her I don't know. A finger-twitch, a slight movement of hand or head, and she would talk-talk-talk. We didn't speculate much aloud. He was a sorcerer. You avoid things that might irritate his kind.

She proclaimed, "We need a tent behind each fire pit. Five on the outer circle, five on the inner. The rest here in the middle. Sentinels will be posted."

"Yeah?" Brandy grumbled. "What the hell do we do for wood? Plant acorns and wait?"

"Out there are two trees that are down. Take wood off them. Pick up any fallen branches this side of the others. It'll be wet, but it's the best we can do. *Do not* go past a live tree. Lord Hammer isn't sure he can project his protection that far."

I didn't pay much attention. Nobody did. It was *warm* there. I shed my pack and flung myself to the ground. I rolled around on the grass, grabbing handfuls and inhaling the newly mown hay scent.

There had to be some dread sorceries animating that circle. Nobody cared. The place was as cozy as journey's end.

There is always a price. That's how magic works.

Old Toamas lay back on his pack and smiled in pure joy. He closed his eyes and slept. And Brandy said nothing about making him do his share.

Lord Hammer let the euphoria bubble for ten minutes.

Fetch started round the troop. "Brandy. You and Russ and Little, put your tent on that point. Will, Chenyth, Toamas, yours goes here. Kelpie....” And so on. When everyone was assigned, she erected her master's black tent. All the while Lord Hammer sat his ruby-eyed stallion and stared northeastward. He showed the intensity of deep concentration. Was he reading the trail?

Nothing seemed to catch him off guard.

Where was he leading us? Why? What for? We didn't know. Not a whit. Maybe even Fetch didn't. Chenyth couldn't charm a hint from her.

We knew two things. Lord Hammer paid well. And, within restrictions known only to himself, he took care of his followers. In a way I can't articulate, he had won our loyalties.

His being what he was was ample proof, yet he had won us to the point where we felt we had a stake in it too. We wanted him to succeed. We wanted to help him succeed.

Odd. Very odd.

I have taken his gold, I thought, briefly remembering a man I had known a long time ago. He had been a member of the White Company of the Mercenaries' Guild. They were a monastic order of soldiers with what, then, I had thought of as the strangest concept of honor....

What made me think of Mikhail? I wondered.

IV

Lord Hammer suddenly dismounted and strode toward Chenyth and me. I thought, thunderhead! Huge, black, irresistible.

I'm no coward. I endured the slaughterhouse battles of the Great Eastern Wars without flinching. I stood fast at Second Baxendala while the Tervola sent the *savan dalage* ravening amongst us night after night. I maintained my courage after Dichiara, which was our worst defeat. And I persevered at Palmisano, though the bodies piled into little mountains and so many men died that the savants later declared there could be no more war for generations. For three years I had faced the majestic, terrible hammer of Shinsan's might without quelling.

But when Lord Hammer bore down on me, that grim death mask coming like an arrowhead engraved with my name, I slunk aside like a whipped dog.

He had that air. You *knew* he was as mighty as any force of Nature, as cruel as Death Herself. Cowering was instinctive.

He looked me in the eye. I couldn't see anything through his mask. But a coldness hit me. It made the cold of that land seem summery.

He looked at Chenyth, too. Baby brother didn't flinch.

I guess he was too innocent. He didn't know when to be scared.

Lord Hammer dropped to one knee beside Toamas.

Gloved hands probed the old man's ribs. Toamas cringed. Then his terror gave way to a beatific smile.

Lord Hammer strode back to where Fetch pursued her regular evening ritual of battling to erect their tent.

"You're a damned idiot, girl," she muttered. "You could've picked something you could handle. But no, you had to have a canvas palace. You knew the boys would just fall in love and stumble all over themselves to help. Then you hired lunks with the chivalry of tomcats. You're a real genius, you are, girl."

The euphoria had reached her too. Usually she was louder and crustier.

Chenyth volunteered. Leaving me to battle with ours.

That little woman could shame or cajole a man into doing anything.

I checked Toamas. He was sleeping. His smile said he was feeling no pain. "Thanks," I threw Lord Hammer's way, softly. No one heard, but he probably knew. Nothing escaped him.

When the tents were up Fetch chose wood-gatherers. I was one of the losers.

"Goddamned, ain't fair, Brandy," I muttered as we hit the ice. "Them sumbitches get to sit on their asses back there...."

He laughed at me. He was that kind of guy. No empathy. And no sympathy even for himself.

Some lessons have to be learned the hard way.

The circle had turned me lazy. Malingering is a fine art among veterans. I decided to get the wood-gathering over with.

What I did was go after a prime-looking dead branch lying just past the first standing tree. I mean, how hard could it be to find your way back when all you had to do was turn around?

I whacked and hacked the branch out of the ice. All the while Brandy and the others were cussing and fussing behind me as they wooled a dead tree.

I turned to go back.

Nothing.

I couldn't see a damned thing but ice, those gnarled old trees, and more ice. No circle. No woodcutters.

The only sound was the ice crackling on branches as the wind teased through the forest.

I yelled.

Chips of ice tinkled off the nearest tree. The damned thing was laughing! I could feel it. It was telling me that it had me, but it was going to play with me awhile.

I even felt the envy of neighboring trees, the hatred of a brother, who had scored....

I didn't panic. I whirled this way and that, moving a few steps each direction, without surrendering to terror. Once a man has faced the legions of the Dread Empire, and has survived nights haunted by the unkillable *savan dalage*, there isn't much left to fear.

I could hear the others perfectly when I turned my back. They were yelling at me, each other, and Lord Hammer. They thought I had gone crazy.

"Will," Brandy called. "How come you're jumping around like that?"

"Tree," I said, "you're going to lose this round."

It laughed in my mind.

I started backing up. Dragging my branch. Feeling for any trace of foot-steps I had left coming here.

Good thinking. But not good enough. The tree hadn't exhausted its arsenal.

A branch fell. A big one. I dodged. My feet slipped on the ice. I cracked my head good. I wasn't thinking when I got up. I started walking. Probably the wrong way.

I heard Brandy yelling, "Will, you stupid bastard, stand still!"

And Russ, "Get a rope, somebody. We'll lasso him."

I didn't understand. My feet kept shuffling.

Then came the crackle of flames and stench of oily smoke. It caught my attention. I stopped, turned.

My captor had become a pillar of fire. It screamed in my mind.

Nothing could burn that fast, that hot. Not in that weather. But the damned thing went up like an explosion.

The smell of sorcery fouled the air.

The flames peaked, began dying. I could see through.

The circle and my friends glimmered before me. Facing the tree, a few yards beyond, stood Lord Hammer. He held one arm outstretched, fingers in a King's X.

He stared at me. I peered into his eye slots and felt him calling. I took a step.

It was a long, long journey. I had to round some kink in the corridor of time before I got my feet onto the straight-line path to safety.

I made it.

Still dragging that damned branch.

I stumbled. Lord Hammer's arm fell. He caught me. His touch was as gentle as a lover's caress, yet I felt it to my bones. I had the feeling that there was nothing more absolute.

I got hold of myself. He released me.

His shoulders slumped slightly as he wheeled and stalked back to the circle. It was the first sign of weariness he had ever shown

I glanced back.

That damned tree stood there looking like it hadn't been touched. I felt its bitterness, its rage, its loss…. And its siren call.

I scooted back inside the circle like a kid running home after getting caught pulling a prank.

V

"Chenyth, it was on fire. I saw it with my own eyes."

"I saw what happened, Will. Lord Hammer just stood there with his arm out. You stopped acting goofy and came back."

The campfires cast enough light to limn the nearest trees. I glanced at the one that had had me. I shuddered. "Chenyth, I couldn't get back."

"Will...."

"You listen to me. When Lord Hammer says do something, do it. Mom would kill me if I didn't bring you home."

She was going to get nasty anyway. I had taken Chenyth off after she had sworn seven ways from Sunday that he wasn't going to go. It had been a brutal scene. Chenyth pleading, Mom screaming, me ducking epithets and pots.

My mother had had a husband and eight sons. When the dust of the Great Eastern Wars settled, she had me and little Chenyth, and she hadn't seen me but once since then.

Then I had come back with my story about signing on with Lord Hammer. And Chenyth, who had been feeding on her stories about Dad and the rest of us being heroes, decided he wanted to go too.

She told him no, and meant it. It was too late to do anything about me, but her last child wasn't going to be a soldier.

Sometimes I was ashamed of sneaking him out. She would be dying still, in tiny bits each day. But Chenyth had to grow up sometime....

"Hey! Listen up!" Fetch yelled. "Hey! I said knock off the tongue music. Got a little proclamation from the boss."

"Here it comes. All-time ass-chewing for doing a stupid," I said.

She used Itaskian first. Most of us understood it. She changed languages for the Harish and a few others who didn't. We drifted toward the black tent.

From the heart of the meadow I could see the pattern of the fire pits. Each lay in one of the angles of a five-pointed star. A pentagram. This meadow was a live magical symbol.

"It'll only be a couple days till we get where we're heading. Maybe sooner. The boss says it's time to let you know what's happening. Just so you'll stay on your toes. The name of the place is Kammengarn." She grinned, exposing dirty teeth.

It took a while. The legend was old, and didn't get much notice outside Itaskia's northern provinces, where Rainheart is a folk hero.

Bellweather popped first. "You mean like the Kammengarn in the story of Rainheart slaying the Kammengarn Dragon?"

"You got it, Captain."

Most of us just put on stupid looks, the southerners more so than those of us who shared cultural roots with Itaskia. I don't think the Harish ever understood.

"Why? What's there?" Bellweather asked.

Fetch laughed. The sound was hard to describe. A little bit of cackle, of bray, and of tinkle all rolled into one astonishing noise. "The Kammengarn Dragon, idiot. Silcroscuar. Father of All Dragons. The big guy of the dragon world. The one who makes the ones you saw in the wars look like crippled chickens beside eagles."

"You're not making sense," Chenyth responded. "What's there? Bones? Rainheart killed the monster three or four hundred years ago."

Lord Hammer came from his tent. He stood behind Fetch, his arms folded. He remained as still, as lifeless, as a statue in clothes. We became less restive.

He was one spooky character. I felt my arm where he had caught me. It still tingled.

"Rainheart's successes were exaggerated," Fetch told us. She used her sarcastic tone. The one that blistered obstinate rocks and mules. "Mostly by Rainheart. The dragon lives. No mortal man can kill it. The gods willed that it be. It shall be, so long as the world endures. It is the Father of All Dragons. If it perishes, dragons perish. The world must have its dragons."

It was weird. The way she changed while she was talking. All of a sudden she wasn't Fetch anymore. I think we all sneaked peeks at Lord Hammer to see if he were doing some ventriloquist trick.

Maybe he was. He could be doing anything behind that iron mask.

I wasn't sure Lord Hammer was human anymore. He might be some unbanished devil left over from the great thaumaturgy confrontations of the wars.

"Lord Hammer is going to Kammengarn to obtain a cup of the immortal Dragon's blood."

Hammer ducked into his tent. Fetch was right behind him.

"What the hell?" Brandy demanded. "What kind of crap is this?

"Hammer don't lie," I replied.

"Not that we know of," Chenyth said.

"He's a plainspoken man, even if Fetch does his talking. He says the Kammengarn Dragon is alive, I believe him. He says we're going to kype a cup of its blood, there it is. I reckon we're going to try."

"Will...."

I went and squatted by our fire. I needed a little more warming. The dead wood of the forest burned pretty ordinarily.

The men were quiet for a long time

What was there to say?

We had taken Lord Hammer's gold.

Even professional griper Brandy didn't say much by way of complaint.

Mikhail had been right. You went on even when the cause was a loser. It became a matter of honor.

Ormson killed the silence. His action was a minor thing characteristic of his race, but it divided the journey into different phases, now and then, and inspired the resolution of the rest of us.

He drew his sword, began whetting it.

The stone made a *shing-shing* sound along his blade For an instant it was the only sound to be heard.

We were old warriors. That sound spoke eloquently of battles beyond the dawn. I drew my sword....

I had taken the gold. I was Lord Hammer's man.

VI

A metallic symphony played as stones sharpened swords and spearheads. Men tested bowstrings and thumped weathered shields. Old greaves clanked, leather armor, too long unoiled, squeaked.

Lord Hammer stepped from his tent. His mask bore no paint now. Only chance flickers of firelight revealed the existence of anything within his cowl.

When his gaze met mine I felt I was looking at a man who was smiling.

Chenyth fidgeted with his gear. Then, "I'm going to see what Jamal's doing."

He sheathed the battered sword I had given him and wandered off. He didn't cut much of a figure as a warrior. He was just a skinny blond kid who looked like a gust of wind would blow him away, or a willing woman turn him into jelly.

Eyes followed him. Pain filled some. We had all been there once. Now we were here.

He was our talisman against our mortality.

I started wondering what the Harish were up to myself. I followed Chenyth. They were almost civil while he was around.

They were ships without compasses, those four, more lost than the rest of us. They were religious fanatics who had sworn themselves to a dead cause. They were El Murid's Chosen Ones, his most devoted followers, a dedicated cult of assassins. The Great Eastern Wars had thrown their master into eclipse. His once vast empire had collapsed. Now, according to rumor, El Murid was nothing but a fat, decrepit opium addict commanding a few bandits in the south desert hills of Hammad al Nakir. He spent his days pulling on his pipe and dreaming about an impossible restoration. These four brother assassins were refugees from the vengeance of the new order....

Defeat had left them with nothing but one another and their blades. About what victory had given us.

Harish took no wives. They devoted themselves totally to the mysteries of their brotherhood, and to fulfilling the commands of their master.

No one gave them orders anymore. Yet they had sworn to devote their lives to their master's needs.

They were waiting. And while they waited, they survived by selling what they had given El Murid freely.

Like the rest of us, they were what history had made them. Bladesmen.

They formed a cross, facing their fire. Chenyth knelt beside Jamal. They talked in low tones. The others watched with stony faces partially concealed by thin veils and long, heavy black beards. Foud, the oldest, dyed his to keep the color. They were all solid, tough men. Killers unfamiliar with remorse.

All four held ornate silver daggers.

I stopped, amazed.

They were permitting Chenyth to watch the consecration of Harish kill-daggers. It was one of the high mysteries of their cult.

They sensed my presence, but went on removing the enameled names of their last victims from amidst the engraved symbols on the flats of their blades. Those blades were a quarter-inch thick near the hilt. The flat ran half the twelve-inch length. Each blade was an inch wide at its base.

They seemed heavy, clumsy, but the Harish used them with terrifying efficiency.

One by one, oldest to youngest, they thrust their daggers into the fire to extinguish the last gossamer of past victims' souls still clinging to the deadly engraving. Then they laid their blades across their hearts, beneath the palms of their left hands. Foud spoke a word.

Chenyth later told me the ritual was couched in the language of ancient Ilkazar. It was an odd tongue they used, like nothing else I've heard.

Foud chanted. The others answered.

Fifteen minutes passed. When they finished even a dullard like myself could feel the Power hovering round the Harish fire.

Lord Hammer came out of his tent. He peered our way briefly, then returned.

The four plunged their blades into the fire again.

Then they joined the ritual everyone else had been pursuing. They produced their whetstones.

I considered Foud's blade. Nearly two inches were missing from its length. It had been honed till it had narrowed a quarter. The engraving was almost invisible. He had served El Murid long and effectively.

His gaze met mine. For an instant a smile flickered behind his veil.

This was the first any of them had even admitted my existence.

A moment later Jamal said something to Chenyth. The younger Harish was the only one who admitted to understanding Itaskian, though we all knew the others did too. Chenyth nodded and rose.

"They're going to name their daggers. We have to go."

Times change. Only a few years ago men like these had tried to kill Kavelin's Queen. Now we were allies.

The glint in Foud's eye told me that things might be different now if he had been the man sent then.

The Harish believed. In their master, in themselves. Every assassin who consecrated a blade was as sure of himself as was Foud.

"What're they doing here?" I muttered at Chenyth. I knew. The same as me. Doing what they knew. Surviving the only way they knew. Still…. The Harish revered their Cause, even though it was lost.

They wanted to bring the Disciple's salvation to the whole word, using every means at their disposal.

Toamas was awake and chipper when we got back. "I ever tell about the time I was with King Bragi, during the El Murid Wars, when he was just another blank shield? It was a town in Altea…."

I guess that kept us going, too. Maybe one mercenary in fifty thousand made it big. I guess we all had some core of hope, or belief in ourselves, too.

VII

"All right, you goat-lovers! Drag your dead asses out. We got some hiking to do today."

Fetch had a way with words like no lady I've ever known. I slithered out of my blankets, scuttled to the fire, tumbled some wood on, and slid back into the wool. That circle may have been springish, but there was a nip in the air.

Chenyth rolled over. He muttered something about eyes in the night.

"Come on. Roll out. We got a long walk ahead."

Chenyth sat up. "Phew! One of these days we've got to take time off for baths. Hey. Toamas. Wake up." He shook the old man. "Oh."

"What's the matter?"

"I think he's dead, Will."

"Toamas? Nah. He just don't want to get up." I shook him.

Chenyth was right.

I jumped out of there so fast I knocked the tent down on Chenyth. "Fetch. The old man's dead. Toamas."

She kicked a foot sticking out of another tent, gave me a puzzled look. Then she scurried into the black tent.

I tried to look inside. But there were inside flaps too.

Lord Hammer appeared a moment later. His mask was paintless. His gaze swept the horizon, then the camp. Fetch popped out as he started toward our tent.

Chenyth came up cussing. "Damnit, Will, what the hell you…." His jaw dropped. He scrambled out of Lord Hammer's path.

Fetch whipped past and started hauling tent away. Lord Hammer knelt, hand over Toamas's heart. He moved it to the grass. Then he walked to the gap we thought of as a gate.

"What's he doing?" Chenyth asked.

"Wait," Fetch told him.

Lord Hammer halted, faced left, began pacing the perimeter. He paused several times. We resumed our morning chores. Brandy cussed the gods both on Toamas's behalf and because he faced another miserable breakfast. You couldn't tell which mattered more to him. Brandy bitched about everything equally.

His true feelings surfaced when he was the first to volunteer to dig the old man's grave.

Toamas had saved his life in the mountains.

"We Kaveliners got to stick together," he muttered to me. "Way it's always been. Way it'll always be."

"Yeah."

His family and Toamas's lived in the same area. They had been on opposite sides in the civil war with which Kavelin had amused itself during the interim between the El Murid and Great Eastern Wars.

It was one of the few serious remarks I had ever heard from Brandy.

Lord Hammer chose the grave site. It butted against the wall. Toamas went down sitting upright, facing the forest.

"That's where I saw the thing last night," Chenyth told me.

"What thing?"

"When I had guard duty. All I could see was its eyes." He dropped a handful of dirt into the old man's lap. The others did the same. Except Foud. The Harish Elder dropped onto his belly, placed a small silver dagger under Toamas's folded hands.

We Kaveliners bowed to Foud. This was a major gesture by the Harish. Their second highest honor, given a man who had been their enemy all his life.

I wondered why Foud had done it.

"Why did he die?" Chenyth asked Fetch. "I thought Lord Hammer fixed him."

"He did. Chenyth, the circle took Toamas."

"I don't understand."

"Neither do I."

I wondered some more. Ignorance and Lord Hammer seemed poles apart.

Maybe he had known. But I couldn't hate him. The way Fetch talked, thirty-seven of us were alive because Toamas had died. The circle certainly was more merciful than the forest.

Lord Hammer gestured. Fetch ran to him. Then he ducked into his tent while she talked.

"Get with it. We've got a long way to go. We'll have to travel fast. Lord Hammer doesn't want to spend any more lives. He wants to leave the forest before nightfall."

We moved. Our packs were trailing odds and ends when we started. Our stomachs weren't full. But those were considerations less important than enduring the protection of another circle.

As we were leaving I noticed a flower blooming in the soft earth where we had put Toamas down. There were dozens of flowers along the wall. The few places where they were missing were the spots where Lord Hammer had paused in his circuit of the wall.

What would happen when all the grave sites were full?

Maybe Lord Hammer knew. But Hammer didn't have much to say.

We passed another circle about noon. It was dead.

The day was warmer, the sky clear. The ice began melting. We made good time. Lord Hammer seemed pleased.

I stared straight ahead, at Russ's back, all morning. If I looked at a tree I could hear it calling. The pull was terrifying

Chenyth seized my arm. "Stop!"

I almost trampled Russ. "What's up?" Lord Hammer had stopped.

"I don't know."

Fetch was dancing around like a barefoot burglar on a floor covered with tacks. Lord Hammer and his steed might have been some parkland pigeon roost, so still were they. We shuffled round so we could see without leaving the safety of the trail.

We had come to a clearing. It was a quarter mile across. What looked like a mud-dauber's nest, the kind with just one hole, lay at the middle of the clearing. It was big. Like two hundred yards long, fifty feet wide, and thirty feet high. A sense of immense menace radiated from it.

"What is it?" we asked one another. Neither Lord Hammer nor Fetch answered us.

Lord Hammer slowly raised his left arm till it thrust straight out from his shoulder. He lifted his forearm vertically, turning the edge of a stiffened hand toward the structure. Then he raised his right arm, laying his forearm parallel with his eyeslits. Then he stiffened his hand, facing the structure with its edge.

"Let's go!" Fetch snapped. "Follow me." She started running.

We whipped the mules into a trot, ran. We weren't gentle with the balky ones.

We had to go right along the side of that thing. As we approached, I glanced back. Lord Hammer was coming, his mount pacing slowly. Hammer himself remained frozen in the position he had assumed. He was almost indiscernible inside a black nimbus.

His mask glowed like the sun. The face of an animal seemed to peep through the golden light.

I glanced into the dark entry to that mound. Menace, backed by rage and frustration, slammed into me.

Lord Hammer halted directly in front of the hole. The rest of us raced for the forest behind the barrow.

Fetch was scared, but not scared enough to pass the first tree. She stopped. We waited.

And Lord Hammer came.

Never have I seen a horse run as beautifully, or as fast. It may have been my imagination, or the way the sun hit its breath in the cold, but fire seemed to play round its nostrils. Lord Hammer rode as if he were part of the beast.

The earth shuddered. A basso profundo rumble came from the mound.

Lord Hammer swept past, slowing, and we pursued him. No one thought to look back, to see what the earth brought forth. It was too late once we passed that first tree.

"Will," Chenyth panted. "Did you see that horse run? What kind of horse runs like that, Will?"

What could I tell him? "Sorcerer's horse, Chenyth. Hell horse. But we knew that already, didn't we?"

Some of us did. Chenyth never really believed it till then. He figured we were giving him more war stories.

He never understood that we couldn't exaggerate what had happened during the Great Eastern Wars. That we told toned-down stories because there was so much we wanted to forget.

Chenyth couldn't take anything at face value. He worked his way up the column so he could pump Fetch. He didn't get anything from her, either. Lord Hammer led. We followed. For Fetch that was the natural order of life.

VIII

We passed another dead circle in the afternoon. Lord Hammer glanced at the sun and increased the pace.

An hour later Fetch passed the word that we would have to stop at the next circle—unless it were dead.

Dread sandpapered the ends of our nerves. The men who had stood sentry last night had seen too much of the things that roamed the forest by dark. And Hammer's reluctance to face the night.... It made the price of a circle almost attractive.

Even thirty-seven to one aren't good odds when my life is on the line.

I've been risking it since I was Chenyth's age, but I like having some choice, some control....

The next circle was alive.

Darkness was close when we reached it. We could hear big things moving behind us, beyond the trees. Hungry things. We zipped into the circle and pitched camp in record time.

I stood sentry that night. I saw what Chenyth had seen. It didn't bother me much. I was a veteran of the Great Eastern Wars.

I kept reminding myself.

Lord Hammer didn't sleep at all. He spent the night pacing the perimeter. He paused frequently to make cabalistic passes. Sometimes the air glowed where his fingers passed.

He took care of us. Not a man perished. Instead, the circle took a mule.

"Butcher it up," Fetch growled. "Save the good cuts. Couple of you guys dig a hole over there where I left the shovel."

So we had mule for breakfast. It was tough, but good. Our first fresh meat in weeks.

We were about to march when Fetch announced, "We'll be there tomorrow. That means goof-off time's over. Respond to orders instantly if you know what's good for you."

Brandy mumbled and cussed. Chenyth wasn't any happier. "I swear, I'm going to smack him, Will."

"Take it easy. He was in the Breidenbacher Light. I owe him."

"So? They got you out at Lake Turntine. That was then. What's that got to do with today?"

"What it's got to do with is, he'll kick your ass up around your ears."

"Kid wants to duke it out, let him, Will. He's getting on my nerves too."

"Stow it," Fetch snarled. "Save it for the other guys. It's time to start worrying about getting out alive."

"What? Then we'd have to walk all the way back." Brandy cackled.

"Fetch, what's this all about?" Chenyth asked.

"I already told you, question man."

"Not why."

She scowled, shook her head. I asked, "Weren't you ever young, Fetch? Hey! Whoa! I didn't mean it like that."

She settled for the one shin-kick. Everybody laughed. I winked. She grinned nastily.

Brandy and Chenyth forgot their quarrel.

Chenyth hadn't forgotten his question. He pressed.

"All I know is, he wants the blood of the Father of Dragons. We came now because the monster is sluggish during the winter. Now why the hell don't you just jingle the money in your pocket and do what you're told?"

"Where'd you meet him, Fetch? When?"

She shook her head again. "You don't hear so good, do you? Long ago and far away. He's been like a father. Now get your ass ready to hike." She tramped off to her position beside Lord Hammer's stallion.

The woman had the least feminine walk I've ever seen. She took long, rolling steps, and kind of leaned into them.

"You ask too many questions, Chenyth."

"Can it, will you?"

We were getting close. Not knowing, except that we were going to go up against a dragon, frayed tempers. Chenyth's trouble was that he hadn't had enough practice at keeping his mouth shut.

Noon. Another barrow blocked our trail. We repeated our previous performance. The feeling of menace wasn't as strong. The thing in the earth let us pass with only token protest.

The weather grew warmer. The ice melted quickly, turning the trail to mud.

Occasionally, from ridge tops, we saw the land beyond the forest. Mountains lay ahead. Brandy moaned his heart out till Fetch told him our destination lay at their feet. Then he bitched about everything happening too fast.

Several of those peaks trailed dark smoke. There wasn't much snow on their flanks.

"Funny," I remarked to Chenyth. "Heading north into warmer country."

We passed a living circle. It called to us the way the trees called to me.

An end to the weird, wide forest came. We entered grasslands that, within a few hours, gave way to rapidly steepening hills. The peaks loomed higher. The air grew warmer. The hills became taller and more barren. Shadows gathered in the valleys as the sun settled toward the Dragon's Teeth.

Lord Hammer ordered us to pitch camp. He doubled the sentries.

We weren't bothered, but still it was a disturbing night. The earth shuddered. The mountains rumbled. I couldn't help but envision some gargantuan monster resting uneasily beneath the range.

IX

The dawn gods were heaving buckets of blood up over the eastern horizon. Fetch formed us up for a pep talk. "Queen of the dwarves," Brandy mumbled. She *was* comical, so tiny was she when standing before a mounted Lord Hammer.

"Lord Hammer believes we are about three miles from the Gate of Kammengarn. The valley behind me will lead us there. From the Gate those who accompany Lord Hammer will descend into the earth almost a mile. Captain Bellweather and thirty men will stay at the Gate. Six men will accompany Lord Hammer and myself."

Her style had changed radically. I had never seen her so subdued.

Fetch was scared.

"Bellweather, your job will be the hardest. It's almost certain that you will be attacked. The people of these hills believe Kammengarn to be a holy place. They know we're here. They suspect our mission. They'll try to destroy us once we prove we intend to profane their shrine. You'll have to hold them most of the day, without Lord Hammer's help."

"Now we know," Brandy muttered. "Needed us to fight his battles for him."

"Why the hell else did he hire us?" Chenyth demanded.

Lord Hammer's steed pranced impatiently. Hammer's gaze swept over us. It quelled all emotion.

"Lord Hammer has appointed the following men to accompany him. Foud, of the Harish. Aboud, of the Harish. Sigurd Ormson, the Trolledyngjan. Dunklin Hanneker, the Itaskian. Willem Clarig Potter, of Kavelin. Pavlo della Contini-Marcusco, of Dunno Scuttari." She made a small motion with her fingers, like someone folding a piece of paper.

"Fetch!..."

"Shut up, Chenyth!" I growled.

Fetch responded, "Lord Hammer has spoken. The men named, please come to the head of the column."

I hoisted my pack, patted Chenyth's shoulder, said, "Do a good job. And stay healthy. I've got to take you back to Mom."

"Will...."

"Hey. You wanted to be a soldier. Be a soldier."

He stared at the ground, kicked a pebble.

"Good luck, Will." Brandy extended a hand. I shook. "We'll look out for him."

"All right. Thanks. Russ. Aral. You guys take care." It was a ritual of parting undertaken before times got rough.

The red-eyed horse started moving. We followed in single file. Fetch walked with Bellweather for a while. After half an hour she scampered forward to her place beside Lord Hammer. She was nervous. She couldn't keep her head or hands still.

I glanced back, past Ormson. "Fight coming," I told the Trolledyngjan. Bellweather was getting ready right now.

"Did you ever doubt it?"

"No. Not really."

The mountains crowded in. The valley narrowed till it became a steep-sided canyon. That led to a place where two canyons collided and became one. It had a flat bottom maybe fifty yards across.

It was the most barren place I had ever seen. The boulders were dark browns. The little soil came in lighter browns. A few tufts of desiccated grass added sere browns. Even the sky took on an ochre hue....

The blackness of a crack in the mountainside ahead relieved the monochromism.

It was a natural cleft, but there were tailings everywhere, several feet deep, as if the cleft had been mined. The tailings had filled the canyon bottom, creating the little flat.

I searched the hillsides. It seemed I could feel eyes boring holes in my back. I looked everywhere but at that cavern mouth.

The darkness it contained seemed the deepest I had ever known.

Lord Hammer rode directly to it.

"Packs off," Fetch ordered. "Weapons ready." She twitched and scratched nervously. "We're going down. Do exactly as I do."

Bellweather brought the others into the flat. He searched the mountainsides too. "They're here," he announced.

War howls responded immediately. Here, there, a painted face flashed amongst the rocks.

Arrows and spears wobbled through the air.

There were a lot of them, I reflected as I got myself between my shield and a boulder. The odds didn't look good at all.

Bellweather shouted. His men vanished behind their shields....

All but my baby brother, who just stood there with a stupefied look.

"Chenyth!" I started toward him.

"Will!" Fetch snapped. She grabbed my arm. "Stay here."

Brandy and Russ took care of him. They exploded from behind their shields, tackled the kid, covered him before he got hurt. That got his attention. He started doing the things I had been teaching the past several months.

An arrow hummed close to me, clattered on rock. Then another. I had been chosen somebody's favorite target. Time to worry about me.

The savages concentrated on Lord Hammer. Their luck was poor. Missiles found him repulsive. In fact, they seemed to loath making contact with any of us.

Not so the arrows of Bellweather's Itaskian bows.

The Itaskian bow and bowman are the best in the world. Bellweather's men wasted no arrows. Virtually every shaft brought a cry of pain.

Then Lord Hammer reached up and caught an arrow in flight.

The canyon fell silent in sheer awe.

Lord Hammer extended an arm. A falling spear became a streak of smoke.

The hillmen didn't give up. Instead, they started rolling boulders down the slopes.

"Eyes down!" Fetch screamed. "Stare at the ground."

Lord Hammer swept first his right hand, then his left, round himself. He clapped them together once.

A sheet of fire, of lightning, obscured the sky. Thunder tortured my ears. My hearing recovered only to be tormented anew by the screams of men in pain.

It had been much nastier above. Dozens of savages were staggering around with hands clasped over their eyes or ears. Several fell down the slope.

Bellweather's archers went to work.

"Let's go." Fetch said. "Remember. Do exactly what I do."

The little woman was scared pale. She didn't want to enter that cavern. But she took her place beside Lord Hammer, who laid a hand atop her disheveled head.

His touch seemed fond. His fingers toyed with her stringy hair. She shivered, looked at the ground, then stalked into that black crack.

He only touched the rest of us for a second. The feeling was similar to that when he had caught me after my run-in with the siren tree. But this time the tingle coursed through my whole body.

He finished with Foud. Once more he swept hands round the mountainsides, clapped. Lightning flashed. Thunder rolled. Bellweather's archers plied their bows.

The savages were determined not to be intimidated.

Lord Hammer dismounted, strode into the darkness. The red-eyed stallion turned round, backed in after us, stopped only when its bulk nearly blocked the narrow passage. Hammer wound his way through our press, proceeded into darkness.

Fetch followed. Single file, we did the same.

X

"Holy Hagard's Golden Turds!" Sigurd exploded. "They're on fire."

Lord Hammer and Fetch glowed. They shed enough light to reveal the crack's walls.

"So are you," I told him.

"Eh. You too."

I couldn't see it myself. Sigurd said he couldn't, either. I glanced back. The others glowed too. They became quite bright once they got away from the cavern mouth. It was spooky.

The Harish didn't like it. They were unusually vocal, and what I caught of their gabble made it sound like they were mad because a heresy had been practiced upon them.

The light seemed to come from way down inside the body. I could see Sigurd's bones. And Fetch's, and the others' when I glanced back. But Lord Hammer remained an enigma. An absence. Once more I wondered if he were truly human, or if anything at all inhabited that black clothing.

After a hundred yards the walls became shaped stone set with mortar.

That explained the tailings above. The blocks had been shaped *in situ.*

"Why would they do that?" I asked Sigurd

He shrugged. "Don't try to understand a man's religion, Kaveliner. Just drive you crazy."

A hundred yards farther along the masons had narrowed the passage to little more than a foot. A man had to go through sideways.

Fetch stopped us. Lord Hammer started doing something with his fingers.

I told Sigurd, "Looks like the dragon god isn't too popular with the people who worship him."

"Eh?"

"The tunnel. It's zigzagged. And the narrow place looks like it was built to keep the dragon in."

"They don't worship the dragon," Fetch said. "They worship Kammengarn, the Hidden City. Silcroscuar is blocking their path to their shrines. So they blocked him in in hopes he would starve."

"Didn't work, eh?"

"No. Silcroscuar subsists. On visitors. He has guardians. Descendents of the people who lived in Kammengarn. They hunt for him."

"What's happening?"

Lord Hammer had a ball of fire in his hands. It was nearly a foot in diameter. He shifted it to his right hand. He rolled it along the tunnel floor, through the narrow passage.

"Let's go!" Fetch shrieked. "Will! Sigurd! Get in there!"

I charged ahead without thinking. The passage was twenty feet long. I was halfway through when the screams started.

Such pain and terror I hadn't heard since the wars. I froze.

Sigurd plowed into me. "Go, man."

An instant later we broke into a wider tunnel.

A dozen savages awaited us. Half were down, burning like torches. The stench of charred flesh fouled the air. The others flitted about trying to extinguish themselves or their comrades.

We took them before the Harish got through.

Panting, I asked Sigurd, "How did he know?"

Sigurd shrugged. "He always knows. Almost. That first barrow...."

"He smelled their torches," Foud said. The Harish elder wore a sarcastic smile.

"You're killing the mystery."

"There is no mystery to Lord Hammer."

"Maybe not to you." I turned to Sigurd. "Hope he's on his toes. We don't need any surprises down here."

Lord Hammer stepped in. He surveyed the carnage. He seemed satisfied.

Several of the savages still burned.

Fetch lost her breakfast.

I think that startled all of us. Perhaps even Lord Hammer. It seemed so out of character. And yet.... What did we know about Fetch? Only what we had seen. And most of that had been show. This might be the first time she had witnessed the grim side of her master's profession.

I don't think, despite her apparent agelessness, that she was much older than Chenyth. Say twenty. She might have missed the Great Eastern Wars too.

We went on, warriors in the lead. The tunnel's slope steepened. Twice we descended spiraling stairs hanging in the sides of wide shafts. Twice we encountered narrow places with ambushes like that we had already faced. We broke through each. Sigurd took our only wound, a slight cut on his forearm.

We left a lot of dead men on our back trail.

The final attack was more cunning. It came from behind, from a side tunnel, and took us by surprise. Even Lord Hammer was taken off guard.

His mystique just cracked a little more, I thought as I whirled.

There was sorcery in it this time.

The hillmen witch-doctors had saved themselves for the final defense. They had used their command of the Power passively, to conceal themselves and their men. Our only warning was a premature war whoop.

Lord Hammer whirled. His hands flew in frenetic passes. The rest of us struggled to interpose ourselves between the attackers and Lord Hammer and Fetch.

Sorceries scarred the tunnel walls. The shamans threw everything they had at the man in black.

Their success was a wan one. They devoured Lord Hammer's complete attention for no more than a minute.

We soldiers fought. Sigurd and I locked shields with Contini-Marcusco and the Itaskian. The Harish, who disdained and reviled shields, remained behind us. They rained scimitar strokes over our heads.

The savages forced us back by sheer weight. But we held the wall even against suicide charges.

They hadn't the training to handle professional soldiers who couldn't be flanked. We crouched behind our shields and let them come to their deaths.

But they did get their licks in before Lord Hammer finished their witch-doctors and turned on them.

It lasted no longer than three minutes. We beat them again. But when the clang and screaming faded, we had little reason to cheer.

Hanneker was mortally wounded. Contini-Marcusco had a spearhead in his thigh. Sigurd had taken a deep cut on his left shoulder.

Fetch was down.

Me and the Harish, we were fine. Tired and drained, but unharmed.

I dropped to my knees beside Fetch's still little form. Tears filled my eyes. She had become one of my favorite people.

She had been last in line, walking behind Lord Hammer. We hadn't been able to get to her.

She was alive. She opened her eyes once, when I touched her, and bravely tried one of her smiles.

Lord Hammer knelt opposite me. He touched her cheeks, her hair, tenderly. The tension in him proclaimed his feeling. His gaze crossed mine. For an instant I could feel his pain.

Lord, I thought, your mystique is dying. You care.

Fetch opened her eyes again. She lifted a feeble hand, clasped Lord Hammer's for an instant. "I'm sorry," she whispered.

"Don't be," he said, and it felt like an order from a god. The fingers of his left hand twitched.

I gasped, so startling was his voice, so suddenly did the Power gather. He did something to Fetch's wounds, then to Sigurd's, then to Contini-Marcusco's. Hanneker was beyond help.

He turned, faced downhill, stared. He started walking.

We who could do so followed.

"What did he do?" I whispered to Sigurd.

The big man shrugged. "It don't hurt anymore."

"Did you hear him? He talked. To Fetch."

"No."

Had I imagined it?

I glanced back. The Harish were two steps behind us. They came with the same self-certainty they always showed. Only a tiny tick at the corner of Aboud's eye betrayed any internal feeling.

Foud smiled his little smile. Once again I wondered what they were doing here.

And I wondered about Lord Hammer, whose long process of creating a mythic image seemed to be unraveling.

A mile down into the earth is one hell of a long way. Ignoring the problem of surviving the dragon, I worried about climbing back out. And about my little brother, up there getting his blooding....

I should have stayed with Chenyth. Somebody had to look out for him....

"I have taken the gold," I muttered, and turned to thoughts of poor Fetch.

Now I would never learn what had brought her here. I was sure we wouldn't find her alive when we returned.

If we returned.

Then I worried about how we would know what Lord Hammer would want of us.

I needn't have.

XI

The home hall of the Father of All Dragons was more vast than any stadium. It was one of the great caverns that, before Silcroscuar's coming, had housed the eldritch city Kammengarn.

The cavern's walls glowed. The ruins of the homes of Kammengarn lay in mounds across the floor. As legends proclaimed, that floor was strewn with gold and jewels. The great dragon snored atop a precious hillock.

The place was just as Rainheart had described. With one exception.

The dragon lived.

We heard the monster's stentorian snores long before we reached his den. Our spines had become jelly before we came to that cavern.

Lord Hammer paused before he got there. He spoke.

"There are guardians."

"I wasn't wrong," I whispered.

The others seemed petrified.

The voice came from everywhere at once. It was in keeping with Lord Hammer's style. Deep. Loud. Terrifying. Like the crash of icebergs breaking off glaciers into arctic seas. Huge. Bottomless. Cold.

Something stepped into the tunnel ahead. It was tall, lean, and awkward in appearance. Its skin had the pallor of death. It glistened with an ichorous fluid. It had the form of a man, but I don't think it was human.

Fetch had said there would be guardians who were the descendants of the people of Kammengarn. Had the Kammengarners been human? I didn't know.

The guardian bore a long, wicked sword.

An identical twin appeared behind it. Then another. And another.

Lord Hammer raised his hands in one of those mystic signs. The things halted. But they would not retreat.

For a moment I feared Lord Hammer had no power over them.

I didn't want to fight. Something told me there would be no contest. I am good. Sigurd was good. The Harish were superb. But I knew they would slaughter us as if we were children.

"Salt," Lord Hammer said.

"What the hell?" Sigurd muttered. "Who carries salt around?..."

He shut up. Because Foud had leaned past him to drop a small leather sack into the palm of Lord Hammer's glove.

"Ah!" I murmured. "Sigurd, salt is precious in Hammad al Nakir. It's a measure of wealth. El Murid's true devotees always carry some. Because the Disciple's father was a salt caravaneer."

Foud smiled the smile and nodded at Sigurd. Proving he wasn't ignorant of Itaskian, he added, "El Murid received his revelation after bandits attacked his father's caravan. They left the child Micah al Rhami to die of thirst in the desert. But the love of the Lord descended, a glorious angel, and the child was saved, and made whole, and given to look upon the earth. And, Lo! The womb of the desert brought forth not Death, but the Son of Heaven, El Murid, whom you call the Disciple."

For a moment Foud seemed almost as embarrassed as Sigurd and I. Like sex, faith was a force not to be mocked.

Lord Hammer emptied the bag into his hand.

Foud flinched, but did not protest. Aboud leaned past Sigurd and me, offering his own salt should it be needed.

Lord Hammer said no more. The guardians flinched but did not withdraw.

Hammer flung the salt with quick little jerks of his hand, a few grains this way, a few that.

Liverish, mottled cankers appeared on the slimy skin of the guardians. Their mouths yawned in silent screams.

They melted. Like slugs in a garden, salted.

Like slugs, they had no bones.

It took minutes. We watched in true fascination, unable to look away, while the four puddled, pooled, became lost in one lake of twitching slime.

Foud and Aboud shared out the remaining salt.

Lord Hammer went forward, avoiding the remains of the guardians. We followed.

I looked down once.

Eyes stared back from the lake. Knowledgeable, hating eyes. I shuddered.

They were the final barrier. We went into the Place of the Dragon, the glowing hall that once had been a cavern of the city Kammengarn.

I began to think that, despite the barriers, it was too easy, without Lord Hammer. Mortal men would never have reached Kammengarn.

"Gods preserve us," I muttered.

The Kammengarn Dragon was the hugest living thing I've ever seen. I had seen Shinsan's dragons during the wars. I had seen whales beached on the coast....

The dragons I had seen were like chicks compared to roosters. The flesh of a whale might have made up Silcroscuar's tail. His head alone massed as much as an elephant.

"Reckon he'd miss a cup of blood?" Sigurd whispered.

The northmen and their gallows humor. A strange race.

The dragon kept on snoring.

We had come in winter, according to Fetch, because that was the best time of year. I suppose she meant that dragons were more sluggish then. Or even hibernated.

But at that depth the chill of winter meant nothing. The place was as hot as an August noon in the desert.

We flanked Lord Hammer. Sigurd and I to his right, the Harish to his left. Hammer started toward the dragon.

The monster opened an eye. Its snakelike tongue speared toward Lord Hammer.

I interposed my shield, chopped with my sword. The tongue caromed away. My blade cut nothing but air.

A mighty laugh surrounded us. It came from no detectable source.

"You made it, fugitive. Ah. Yes. I know you, Lord Hammer. I know who you are. I know what you are. I know more than you know. All tidings come to me here. There are no secrets from me. Even the future is mine to behold. And yours is a cosmic jest."

Lord Hammer reacted only by beginning a series of gestures, the first of which was the arm cross he had used at the barrows in the forest.

The dragon chuckled. "You'll have your way. And be the poorer for it." It yawned.

My jaw sagged. The teeth in that cavernous mouth! Like the waving scimitars of a horde of desert tribesmen....

Laughter assailed the air. "I have been intimate with the future, refugee. I know the vanity of the course you have chosen. Your hope is futile. I know the joke the Fates have prepared. But come. Take what you want. I'll not thwart you, nor deny the Fates their amusement."

The dragon closed his eye. He shifted his bulk slightly, as if into a more comfortable position.

Lord Hammer advanced.

We stayed with him.

And again I thought it was too easy. The monster wasn't making even a token attempt to stop us.

That matter about the Fates and a cosmic joke. It reminded me of all those tales in which men achieved their goals only to discover that the price of success was more dear than that of failure.

Lord Hammer clambered up the mound of gold and jewels, boldly seizing a gargantuan canine to maintain his balance.

My stomach flopped.

The dragon snored on.

Sigurd started grabbing things small enough to carry away. I selected a few souvenirs myself. Then I saw the contempt in Foud's eyes.

He seemed to be thinking that there were issues at stake far greater than greed.

It was an unguarded thought, breaking through onto his face. It put me on guard.

"Sigurd," I hissed. "Be ready. It's not over."

"I know," he whispered. "Just grabbing while I can."

Lord Hammer beckoned. I scrambled across the treacherous pile. "Cut here." He tapped the dragon's lip where scaly armor gave way to the soft flesh of the mouth. "Gently."

Terror froze me. He wanted me to cut that monster? When it might wake up? What chance would we have?…

"Cut!"

Lord Hammer's command made the cavern walls shudder. I could not deny it. I drew the tip of my blade across dragon flesh.

Blood welled up, dribbled down the monster's jaw.

It was as red as any man's. I saw nothing remarkable about it, save that men had died for it. Slowly, drop by drop, it filled the ebony container Lord Hammer held.

We waited tensely, anticipating an explosion from the monster. Dragons had foul and cunning reputations, and that of the Kammengarn Dragon outstripped them all.

I caught a smile toying with Aboud's lips. It was gone in an instant, but it left me more disturbed, more uncertain than ever.

I searched the cavern, wondering if more guardians might not be creeping our way. I saw nothing.

Sigurd bent to secure one more prize jewel….

And Lord Hammer screwed a top onto his container, satisfied.

Foud and Aboud surged toward him. Silver Harish kill-daggers whined through the air.

I managed to skewer Aboud and kick Foud in one wild movement. Then my impetus carried me down the mountain of treasure to the cavern floor. Golden baubles gnawed at my flesh.

Sigurd roared as he hurled himself at Foud, who was after Lord Hammer again. I regained my feet and charged up the pile.

A gargantuan laughter filled the caverns of Kammengarn.

Foud struck Lord Hammer's left arm, and killed Sigurd, before he perished, strangling in the grip of Lord Hammer's right hand.

Aboud, though dying, regained his feet. Again he tried to plant his kill-dagger in Lord Hammer's back.

I reached him in time. We tumbled back down the pile.

Lord Hammer flung Foud after us.

Aboud sat up. He had lost his dagger. I saw it lying about five feet behind him. Tears filled his eyes as he awaited the doom descending upon him.

"Why?" I asked.

"For the Master. For the blood of the dragon that would have made him immortal, that would have given him time to carry the truth. And for what was done to him during the wars."

"I don't understand, Aboud."

"You wouldn't. You haven't recognized him as your enemy."

Lord Hammer loomed over us. His left arm hung slackly. The kill-dagger had had that much success.

Lord Hammer reached with his right, seizing Aboud's throat.

The Harish fought back. Vainly.

I recovered his dagger during the struggle. Quietly, carefully, I concealed it inside my shirt. Why I don't know, except that the genuine article was more valuable than anything in the dragon's hoard.

"Come," Lord Hammer told me. Almost conversationally, he added, "The dragon will be pleased. He's hungry. These three will repay him for his blood." He strode to the gap where the guardians had perished. Their hating eyes watched us pass.

I had to strain to keep pace with him. By the time we reached Fetch I was exhausted. Hanneker had expired in our absence.

"We rest here," Lord Hammer told me. "We will carry these two, and there may be ambushes." He sat down with his back against one wall. He massaged his lifeless arm.

The image had slipped even more. He seemed quite human at that moment.

"Who are you?" I asked after a while.

The iron mask turned my way. I couldn't meet his gaze. The Power was still there.

"Better that you don't know, soldier. For both our sakes."

"I have taken the gold," I replied.

I expect he understood. Maybe he didn't. He said nothing more till he decided to go.

"It's time. Carry Fetch. Be wary."

I hoisted the little woman. She seemed awfully heavy. My strength had suffered. The mountains. The forest. The fighting. The tension, always. They ground me down.

We met no resistance. Only once did we hear what might have been men. They avoided us.

We rested often. Lord Hammer seemed to be weakening faster than I, though his resources were more vast. Maybe the Harish kill-dagger had bitten more deeply than he let on.

"Stop," he gasped. We were close to the end of the tunnel. I dropped Fetch.

Men's voices, muted, echoed along the shaft. "Chenyth." I started on.

"Stay." The command in Hammer's voice was weak, but compelling.

He moved slowly, had trouble keeping his feet. But he negated the spells that made us glow. "We must rest here."

"My brother...."

"We will rest, Willem Potter."

We rested.

XII

Outside ambushed us.

The sun had set. No moon had risen. The stars didn't cast much light. Bellweather had lighted no fires. We were suddenly there, beside Lord Hammer's stallion.

The last dozen yards we had to step over and around the dead and wounded. There were a lot of them. I kept whispering Chenyth's name. The only man I could find was Brandy. The griper had been dead for hours.

"They've killed or captured most of the animals," Bellweather reported. Lord Hammer grunted noncommittally. "We've killed hundreds of them, but they keep coming. They'll finish us in the morning. This is serious business to them."

"Chenyth!" I called.

"Will? Will! Over here."

I hurried over. He was doing sentry duty. His post was an open-topped bunker built of the corpses of savages.

"You all right?" I demanded.

"So far. Brandy and Russ and Aral are dead, Will. I'm sorry I came. I'm tired. So tired, Will."

"Yeah. I know."

"What happened down there?"

"It was bad." I told him the story.

"The other Harish. Will they?..."

"I'm sure their daggers are consecrated to the same name."

"Then they'll try again?"

"They made it? Then we'd better warn...."

A shriek ripped the air.

I hurled myself back toward Lord Hammer. I arrived at the same time as the Harish. Blades flashed. Men screamed. Lord Hammer slew one. I took the other. Bellweather and the others watched in dull-eyed disbelief.

Before Jamal died he cursed me. "You have given the Hammer his life," he croaked. "May that haunt you all the ages of earth. May his return be quickened, and fall upon you heavily. I speak it in the Name of the Disciple."

"What did he mean, Will?" Chenyth asked.

"I don't know." I was too tired to think. "They knew him. They knew his mission. They came to abort it. And to capture the dragon's blood for El Murid." I glanced at Lord Hammer. He had begun a sorcery. His voice sounded terribly weak. He seemed the least superhuman of us all. My awe of him had evaporated completely.

He was but a man.

"Maybe they were right," Chenyth suggested. "Maybe the world would be better without him. Without his kind."

"I don't know. His kind are like the dragon. And we have taken the gold, Chenyth. It doesn't matter who or what he is."

Sleep soon ambushed me. The last thing I saw was a ball of blue light drifting into the rocks where the savages lurked. I think there were screams, but they might have come in my dreams.

They took me back to the wars. To the screams of entire kingdoms crushed beneath the boots of legions led by men of Lord Hammer's profession. Those had been brutal, bitter days, and the saddest part of it was that we hadn't won, we had merely stopped it for a while.

My subconscious mind added the clues my conscious mind had overlooked.

I awakened understanding the Harish.

"His name is a joke," Fetch had said.

It wasn't a funny one. It was pure arrogance.

One of the arch-villains of the Great Eastern Wars had been a sorcerer named Ko Feng. He had commanded the legions of the Dread Empire briefly. But his fellow wizards on the Council of Tervola had ousted him because of his unsubtle, straightforward, expensive, pounding military tactics. For reasons no one understood he had been ordered into exile.

His nickname, on both sides of the battle line, had been The Hammer.

Aboud had told me he was my enemy....

The savages bothered us no more. Lord Hammer's sorcery had sufficed.

Only a dozen men were fit to travel. Chenyth and I were the only surviving Kaveliners....

Kavelin had borne the brunt of the Great Eastern Wars. The legions of the Dread Empire knew no mercy. The nation might never recover....

I was sitting on a rock, fighting my conscience. Chenyth came to me. "Want something to eat?"

"I don't think so.

"What's the matter, Will?"

"I think I know who he is. What he's doing. Why."

"Who?"

"Lord Hammer."

"I meant, who is he?"

"Lord Ko Feng. The Tervola. The one we called The Hammer during the wars. They banished him from Shinsan when it was over. They took his immortality and drove him onto exile. He came for the dragon's blood to win the immortality back. To get the time he needed to make his return."

"Oh, Gods. Will, we've got to do something."

"What? What's the right thing? I don't *know* that he's really Ko Feng. I do know that we've taken his gold. He's treated us honorably. He even saved my life when there was no demand that he do so. I know that Fetch thinks the world of him, and I think well enough of Fetch for that to matter. So. You see what's eating me."

My life wasn't usually that complicated. A soldier takes his orders, does what he must, and doesn't much worry about tomorrow or vast issues. He takes from life what he can when he can, for there may be no future opportunity. He seldom moralizes, or becomes caught in a crisis of conscience.

"Will, we can't turn an evil like Ko Feng loose on the world again. Not if it's in our power to stop it."

"Chenyth. Chenyth. Who said he was evil? His real sin is that he was the enemy. Some of our own were as violent and bloody."

I glanced back toward the split in the mountain. The giant black stallion stood within a yard of where Lord Hammer had posted him yesterday. Hammer slept on the ground beneath the animal.

Easy pickings, I thought. Walk over, slip the dagger in him, and have done.

If the horse would let me. He was a factor I couldn't fathom. But somehow I knew he would block me.

My own well-being wasn't a matter of concern. Like the Harish, it hadn't occurred to me to worry about whether or not I got out alive.

I saw no way any of us could get home without Lord Hammer's protection.

Fetch dragged herself to a sitting position.

"Come with me," I told Chenyth.

We went to her. She greeted us with a weak smile. "I wasn't good for much down there, was I?"

"How you feeling?" I asked.

"Better."

"Good. I'd hate to think I lugged you all the way up here for nothing."

"It was you?"

"Lord Hammer carried the Scuttarian."

"The others?"

"Still down there, Love."

"It was bad?"

"Worse than anybody expected. Except the dragon."

"You got the blood?"

"We did. Was it worth it?"

She glanced at me sharply. "You knew there would be risks. You were paid to take them."

"I know. I wonder if that's enough."

"What?"

"I know who Lord Hammer is, Fetch. The Harish knew all along. It's why they came. I killed two of them. Lord Hammer slew two. Foud killed Sigurd. That's five of the company gone fighting one another. I want to know what reason there might be for me not to make it six and have the world rid of an old evil."

Fetch wasn't herself. Healthy she would have screeched and argued like a whole flock of hens at feeding time. Instead, she just glanced at Lord Hammer and shrugged. "I'm too tired and sick to care much, Will. But don't. It won't change the past. It won't change the future, either. He's chasing a dead dream. And it won't do you any good now." She leaned back and closed her eyes. "I hated him for a while, too. I lost people in the wars."

"I'm sorry."

"Don't be. He lost people, too, you know. Friends and relatives. All the pain and dying weren't on our side. And he lost everything he had, except his knowledge."

"Oh." I saw what she was trying to say. Lord Hammer was no different than the rest of us leftovers, going on being what he had learned to be.

"Is there anything to eat?"

"Chenyth. See if you can get her something. Fetch, I know all the arguments. I've been wrestling with them all morning. And I can't make up my mind. I was hoping you could help me figure where I've got to stand."

"Don't put it on me, Willem Potter. It's a thing between you and Lord Hammer."

Chenyth brought soup that was mostly mule. He spooned it into Fetch's mouth. She ate it like it was good.

I decided, but on the basis of none of the arguments that had gone before.

I had promised myself that I would take my little brother home to his mother. To do that I needed Lord Hammer's protection.

I often wonder, now, if many of the most fateful decisions aren't made in response to similarly oblique considerations.

XIII

I need not have put myself through the misery. The Fates had their own plans.

When Lord Hammer woke, I went to him. He was weak. He barely had the strength to sit up. I squatted on my hams, facing him, intimidated by the stallion's baleful stare. Carefully, I drew the Harish kill-dagger from within my shirt. I offered it to him atop my open palms.

The earth shook. There was a suggestion of gargantuan mirth in it.

"The Dragon mocks us." Lord Hammer took the dagger. "Thank you, Willem Potter. I'd say there are no debts between us now."

"There are, Lord. Old ones. I lost a father and several brothers in the wars."

"And I lost sons and friends. Will we fight old battles here in the cupped hands of doom? Will we cross swords even as the filed teeth of Fate rip at us? I lost my homeland and more than any non-Tervola could comprehend. I have nothing left but hope, and that too wan to credit. The Dragon laughs with cause, Willem Potter. Summon Bellweather. A journey looms before us."

"As you say, Lord."

I think we left too soon, with too many wounded. Some survived the forest. Some survived the plains. Some survived the snows and precipices of the Dragon's Teeth. But we left men's bones beside the way. Only eight of us lived to see the plains of Shara, west of the mountains, and even then we were a long way from home.

It was in Shara that Lord Hammer's saga ended.

We were riding ponies he had bought from a Sharan tribe. Our faces were south, bent into a spring rain.

Lord Hammer's big stallion stumbled.

The sorcerer fell.

He had been weakening steadily. Fetch claimed only his will was driving him toward the laboratories where he would make use of the dragon's blood....

He lay in the mud and grass of a foreign land, dying, and there was nothing any of us could do. The Harish dagger still gnawed at his soul.

Immortality rested in his saddlebags, in that black jar, and we couldn't do a thing. We didn't know how. Even Fetch was ignorant of the secret.

He was a strong man, Lord Hammer, but in the end no different than any other. He died, and we buried him in alien soil. The once mightiest man on earth had come to no more than the least of the soldiers who had followed him in his prime.

I was sad. It's painful to watch something magnificent and mighty brought low, even when you loath what it stands for.

He went holding Fetch's hand. She removed the iron mask before we put him into the earth. "He should wear his own." She obtained a Tervola mask from his gear. It was golden and hideous, and at one time had terrorized half a world. I'm not sure what it represented. An animal head of some sort. Its eyes were rubies that glowed like the eyes of Lord Hammer's stallion. But their inner light was fading.

A very old man lay behind the iron mask. The last of his mystique perished when I finally saw his wizened face.

And yet I did him honor as we replaced the soil above him.

I had taken his gold. He had been my captain.

"You can come with us, Fetch," Chenyth said. And I agreed. There would be a place for her with the Potters.

Chenyth kept the iron mask. It hangs in my mother's house even now.

Nobody believes him when he tells the story of Lord Hammer and the Kammengarn Dragon. They prefer Rainheart's heroics.

No matter. The world goes on whether geared by truth or fiction.

The last shovelful of earth fell on Lord Hammer's resting place. And Chenyth, as always, had a question. "Will, what happened to his horse?"

The great fire-eyed stallion had vanished.

Even Fetch didn't know the answer to that one.

CASTLE OF TEARS

There was some serendipity associated with the publication of this story. It appeared in the special Fritz Leiber issue of Whispers *in October 1979. But it was written in September1969, in Fritz's two-room apartment in Venice, California, during several weeks I spent there with him after the death of his wife, Jonquil. We wrote back to back, sometimes using one another's characters in walk-ons, he producing much of the very dark stuff that became part of* Swords Against Death.

The manuscript of this bears the title "Keeper of Shadows." I don't recall the reason for the change.

He thought he would never see the day, but, when Bragi Ragnarson reached Itaskia's South Fortress, he could not restrain a sigh of pleasure. His adventure in the south, that had included a forced march back through dark jungles and strange dangers, made him realize just how safe he felt in a city he knew. Once despised Itaskia seemed a suburb of Heaven.

He wandered slowly through the slums of Wharf Street South, his immediate destination the Red Hart Inn at the intersection of Wharf and Love Lane. He smiled hugely as he entered.

Yalmar glanced up from his mug-washing. "I see ye're back, freeloader. Ye lose yer meal ticket somewhere else?" Though it had been a year the man made their parting seem like it had been yesterday.

"Yalmar, you're beautiful," the shaggy blond mercenary boomed. He tossed a coin. "How's that? A stoop of your best."

Yalmar filled a mug, not with his finest.

"Where's my change?" the big man asked as he lifted it.

"What change?" Yalmar pulled a box from beneath his counter, extracted a long, tattered account sheet. "Subtracting the value of one new obol of Hellin Daimiel, ye still owe two sovereigns gold, three crowns silver, and tuppence. A small fortune. If yer father hadn't been a friend...."

"Bah! Gotta find a tavern where the keeper's illiterate."

"Them's the kind where they want cash in advance," Yalmar countered. "And where's yer knavish accomplices, Mocker and Haroun?" Yalmar obviously hoped they had perished somewhere along the way.

"Went to Portsmouth. A woman. They'll be along."

Yalmar groaned.

A tall, thin, gray, nervous man oozed into the tavern. With a hand raised high, finger pointing at the ceiling, he started toward the mercenary. "Mr. Ragnarson?..."

"Yes?" Someone must have heard he was coming. Curious.

"Uh..."

"Something to drink? Yalmar, just don't stand there."

"Ain't heard the ring of his money...."

The thin man glanced around distastefully. The Red Hart was no upper-crust watering hole. He mumbled, "Oh, I think not."

"So what do you want?" Ragnarson was in an amiable mood, though this type usually spelled trouble.

"You return at an opportune moment. My Lord... uh..." The thin man leaned close to whisper, "My Lord, the Duke Greyfells, would be grateful and generous, if you'd undertake a most delicate piece of work."

"Greyfells?" The Duke was a bad man to deal with. A political manipulator for whom he had worked previously and as near an arch-villain and arch-traitor as Itaskia's recent history boasted. And a treacherous master. One risked the evidence-erasure of the assassin's blade if one's task were politically motivated.

Yet Ragnarson needed money, and Greyfells' favor. His departure from Itaskia had been clouded by the demands of creditors and the displeasure of this same Duke. Many dangerous men had to be satisfied if he were to stay on long.

He laughed thunderously, slapped the thin man's back. "Hah! Good! Who does he want murdered this time?"

"Ssshh! It's nothing illegal."

"He wants me to do something legal? Remarkable! Will wonders never cease? Yalmar, you ever heard of anybody coming down here looking for honest men? Hey, why not hire me through the Mercenaries' Guild?"

"Ssshh! Too many people would become involved. We have to keep a low profile on this. It's politically sensitive."

Ragnarson wondered if Greyfells had ever so much as futtered a Love Lane strumpet without agonizing over the political considerations. "Well, what is it, man?"

"He'd like you to go into the Forest of Night...."

"The who?"

"The Forest of Night."

"That's what I thought. You'd better start making sense." It was becoming hard to maintain a cheerful outlook. The sordid, scheming side of Itaskia was one he had overlooked in his joy of return.

"Alright. One who is called the Keeper of Shadows is holding the Heart of Lorraine, which belongs to the Duke's daughter. He has it locked away in the Castle of Tears in the Forest of Night. The Duke requires its return. The girl lies in enchanted sleep whilst...."

"Gah! Yalmar, give us a quart here. This crap can't be listened to sober." He was well-traveled. He had heard of none of these before. A quirky little nervous moth began fluttering about in his stomach.

"Hrumph! See here! The Duke *must* have his daughter back. She's pledged to the Lord of Four Towers. It's a union of such potential that My Lord dares not lose it."

"So fetch up a ransom."

"The ransom would have to be Lorraine herself, so to speak."

"I don't understand."

"Neither do I. I merely report what My Lord tells me."

"Another mug, damn it, Yalmar." The taverner had not delivered the quart. "Go away, skinny man."

"Would this change your mind?" The whisperer angrily slapped five gold sovereigns onto the counter.

Ragnarson didn't look up, though the sum was magnificent. But Yalmar recognized the set of his shoulders. He scooped three coins into his cash-box, made change.

"Ye're on the right path," he told the thin man. "Prime the pump." To Ragnarson, "We're even. But there's the others." And, "One on the house." He drew a quart of the good ale this time.

Five more sovereigns appeared. In Itaskia's barter economy this was a fortune. But Ragnarson rolled his shoulders in a mighty stretch and yawn, as if bored. He had left a lot of debts. Five more sovereigns. Bragi combed his golden hair with his fingers. Coins. The mercenary picked his nose.

"Right, then," the thin man snapped in exasperation. "How much?"

"Two hundred?"

The messenger sputtered, mumbled incoherently, then gasped, "I'm not buying a regiment! I want just one reliable man. Thirty, tops. Then I go elsewhere."

"Done," said Ragnarson, who would have taken the job for the original five if the man hadn't been so eager and his creditors so numerous and bloodthirsty.

"There're conditions."

"That figures. Let's hear them."

"First, the job must be completed within forty-three days. The wedding cannot be delayed longer. Second, you have to return the Heart to Castle Greyfells. It is there Lorraine lies enchanted. Don't waste time and don't fail your trust. My Lord isn't a forgiving man."

"All right. Where's this Forest of Night?"

"I don't know."

"What? How the hell am I supposed to lift something I don't even know where it's at?"

"That's why you're being paid."

"I knew there'd be a catch. All right. Castle Greyfells in forty-three days. Now go away and let me get drunk."

The money was gone, scattered hopelessly in a frenzy of drinking, wenching, and debt-paying. A week of the six had vanished as well. And he had done nothing yet. Could he explain a failure to the Duke's man, whom he had seen watching him more than once? Not likely. And there was no backing out now. The Duke's vengefulness was widely known and farther reaching.

Where to begin? Who knew about the places unknown? A sorcerer, perhaps.

"I'll try Visigodred," he mumbled to himself as he rose from the curb where he had spent the night.

A second week had passed before, riding a "borrowed" horse, he spied the gothic spires of Castle Mendalayas, home of the sorcerer Visigodred. Shivers ran down his spine. What would his welcome be? Warlocks were notoriously unpredictable.

Nervously, he used the great brass death's head knocker. A minute passed. Then the gate swung inward on hinges which groaned like souls in torment. A muted, melodious voice said, "Come in, come in."

A groom awaited him. Saying nothing, the man took Bragi's horse, indicated another man waiting on the steps of the inner fortress. The latter guided Ragnarson to the wizard.

To his surprise, Bragi found Visigodred pleased to see him. "I get so few visitors, you know," said the tall, longly bearded man. "Scared, I suppose. It's been too peaceful since last you visited. But why should you fear me? That business is done. How are your friends?"

Ragnarson shrugged. "Haven't seen them for a while. They have their own interests."

"What brings you here, then? Business, I presume. This's no pleasure palace."

"Business, yes. In a place called the Forest of Night. If I can locate it. I hoped you could help."

"Hmm. How so?"

"Well, tell me where to find the Keeper of Shadows, the Castle of Tears, and the Forest of Night."

"You shouldn't want to know. All are euphemisms for darker things. The first you'll find in the second, and the second surrounded by the third, and all neither here nor there."

"Ah-huh. That tells me a lot. How do I get there?"

"'Walk the left hand by the right,
To the Forest of the Night,
Not of this world, nor of any,
But in Darkness, 'twixt the many....'"

"You're not helping."

"An old canta from my apprenticeship. For a small fee of a promise of service in the future, I could send you, though my advice, as a friend, would be to stay away."

"What kind of service?"

"I'd let you know when I needed it."

"When?"

"I'd call when I called."

"Bah! Your first apprenticeship course must have been plain and fancy obfuscation."

"Remember Greyfells' wrath. His gold can buy a long dagger."

"So. You already know what's going on."

Visigodred smiled enigmatically, shrugged. "I know everything, and nothing. I see all, and am blind."

"Talk endlessly and say nothing," Ragnarson concluded. "Alright, I'll do it. But it can't be anything bigger than the service you do me."

"But of course. I'm just trying to cover costs, you see. This's a non-profit business. Just a hobby. I make my living from the vineyards."

"Sure. Look, I've only got four weeks. I'd love to hang around and chat about old times, but...."

"Of course. I understand. Come to the study."

Ragnarson followed Visigodred into a large, gloomy room filled with thousands of books, with cabinets of rare coins, cut crystal, antique weapons. The man was an avid collector and amateur historian. His major claim to fame was his having reconstructed the Lost Passages of Thislow by raising the shade of the poet and compelling him to re-write them. Thus he justified his dabbling in the Black Arts.

"Stand over there." The sorcerer waved an arm as he settled onto a tall stool beside a cluttered table. "Directly over the silver star in the pentagram on the floor there."

Ragnarson moved to the star. He hadn't the least idea what Visigodred meant to do.

"Hair of the toad and tooth of the frog,
Eye of the newt and toe of the hog...."

"Hold it, damn it!" Ragnarson thundered. "What the hell are you doing?"

"Sending you to the Forest of Night. That was what you wanted, wasn't
it?"

"Yeah, but...."

"But what?"

"I thought I'd need a few minutes to get ready. A little up front about
what to expect. You know."

"Pointless. No one's ever ready. You decide, you'd better go, get what you
want, and get out. When you're ready to come back, you say, 'Shoshonah
heluska e irmilatrir eskonagin.'"

"Eh?"

"Shoshonah heluska e irmilatrir eskonagin."

"Right. Anything else?"

"Some advice. Don't waste time. It flows differently in the Forest. Passes
slower. Stay a week and you might return to find me an old man. If you
could get back at all."

"Why's that?"

"Who can say? The gods? The Forest lies in the time river of eternity,
where sentience alone enforces familiarities on the fabric of a space with
no reasonable substance."

"How can I tell when to get out?"

"That's knowledge hidden even from me. Perhaps when you feel the
incantation slipping from your mind. The Forest experience is unique to
each visitor. You make of it what you will. The only way to discover your
own version is to go there."

"So send me."

As Ragnarson spoke, the wizard sketched a fiery mystical sign in the air
before him. The mercenary's universe reeled. There was a gut-wrenching
twist, then blackness.

Blackness surrounded him when he wakened. His first panicky thought
was that he had been blinded. Then he began to discern objects around
him, though by what means he couldn't determine. There was no light
source. No stars, no moon.

Around him were black-trunked trees leafed with metallic ebon leaves,
and beneath him lay a carpet of dark crystalline grass. Above him lay a
deeper blackness, an infinite, hungry darkness that could hardly be called
a sky.

He rose and turned slowly. Everywhere, the same thing. Blackness and
trees. "The Forest of Night," he murmured. It echoed mockingly in the

stillness. He shuddered, felt his weapons to make sure they were in trim. He turned again till he found a direction that felt right, started walking.

He had begun to worry about the time before he finally encountered a break in the Forest.

Light! Through the quiet trees came a greenish light. Witch light. His breath came more quickly. He walked faster, crouched more, took more precautions against discovery.

Before him, surrounded by a broad, blackly watered moat and black-grassed glen, stood a strangely shifting and shapeless black edifice. It had many tall, tube-like spires, each of which had tear-shaped bulges slowly working down their heights. Sparks of almost invisibly pale green light appeared briefly in what might have been windows.

"The Castle of Tears," he muttered. He had thought that the name had to do with pain or sorrow.

He invested an estimated quarter hour in catching his breath and over-coming his awe. Then, very slowly, sword in hand, he stalked toward the castle. He stopped at the moat, leaned back, considered the towers. The great teardrops slowing ran down the pipe stems and disappeared behind the shifting walls.

Something stirred the surface of the moat. He caught a glimpse of an oily back, shuddered, began following the bank.

Again and again he caught a flicker of motion as some creature roiled the stagnant waters. Perhaps it was best he didn't get a direct view.

He came to a narrow drawbridge. The gate beyond was open. Trap-wary, Ragnarson cautiously stepped onto the bridge. Nothing happened. Five rapid steps took him to the gate, which seemed alive. Its shape, width, and height constantly changed. He entered the courtyard beyond. A greenish mist filled the place. It stirred and boiled, yet was not there to his touch.

Growing more uncertain, and increasingly time-worried, Ragnarson crossed to steps leading to the only doorway in sight.

Within lay a room lighted in green mist, revealing nothing threatening. He cautiously stalked ahead... and found himself surrounded by a great weep-ing, as of ghost voices from afar. He whirled, saw nothing but shadows.

The weeping went on. The shadows stirred. But nothing threatened him.

Once more he modified his theory about the fortress's name. The weep-ing....

Speculation would not get him the Heart. He began searching.

He wandered for what might have been hours, constantly worrying the passage of time. He climbed and descended strangely shifting stairways, ventured into a hundred oddly shaped rooms. Always he was surrounded by blackness and haunted by patchlets of weeping, shadow-containing green mist.

Then he entered a hall where the mist was dense. The weeping was louder. Shadows swirled around him as he pushed through the fog, swarming over him. His fear grew as the weeping became like the wailing of women over a field of ten thousand fallen. Ragnarson at last realized that he had entered a place that was vastly more than a haunted castle in a strange forest. He realized it was a place beyond forests, beyond worlds, beyond times. A place where gods or demons dwelt.

He went on.

He found a small door. A red light glowed from beyond it. Shadows swirled and moaned as he approached. He intuited that he had reached his goal.

Two steps took him to where a small calamander chest rested, lid open. Within lay a glowing heart-shaped ruby. "The Heart." He reached for it.

"Yes," said a whisper from behind him.

Ragnarson whirled. His sword leapt out as swiftly as an adder's strike.

And encountered nothing. Yet a creature stood before him, unharmed.

"The Heart of Lorraine," the creature whispered. "Very precious to me. Why do you want it?"

"To return it to Duke Greyfells, to whom it belongs. So his daughter can be freed from an enchantment and marry the Lord of Four Towers."

"Greyfells doesn't own the Heart. No man can trade a Heart like so many pounds of cabbage. It belongs to Lorraine, to be given when and where she wills. It's here because she wills it to be. I, and only I, have the power to remove it against her will."

"What is this place?" Ragnarson asked, closing the calamander chest, slipping it into his jerkin.

"This is the place beyond places, the end after ends. It has many names. It is the gathering place of the shades of hopes that have died, and I am their keeper. The Heart is mine."

"And yet I must have it."

"And yet you must have it." The Keeper shifted form. "I will think on it. It may be that all can gain heart's desire, including myself. Return to the gate. Your time grows short. I will meet you there."

Ragnarson went. As he understood it he was in Hell. And soon might be trapped there forever. Fear lent speed. He reached the gate in a quarter of the time it had taken to find the Heart.

The Keeper of Shadows was waiting. Thick green mists surrounded him.

"I have considered," said the specter. "You may take the Heart. Thus, Greyfells will gain his wish. Yet he will be disappointed. You, too, shall see a wish fulfilled, yet learn despair. And you will have to flee Greyfells, though you fulfill your commission. Now speak your words and go. Your time is short and I have not yet prepared a place for your dream."

A wall arose as the shadows protested an escape from the Castle of Tears.

Ragnarson bowed, muttered, "Shoshonah heluska e irmilatrir eskonagin."

Something stirred in the Forest of Night. Leaves long unmoved sighed. Trees bent toward the mercenary as if loath to let him escape.

The wind arrived. For an instant it opened the mist surrounding the Keeper.

Ragnarson screamed. He had seen the true face of Despair.

He woke in the center of the pentagram whence he had departed Mendalayas. Visigodred poured fiery liquid into his mouth. "Four weeks. I'd begun to fear you'd stayed too long. But you got what you went after?"

"Uhm. Four weeks? I was only there a day. Wouldn't want to go back."

"We'll all go sometime. A part of us. Well, we'd best get you moving toward Greyfells. You have less than two days." Castle Greyfells lay some sixty miles east of Mendalayas.

Ragnarson gagged on another draught of liquid, spat, staggered up, snatched up the casket. "Yeah. It'll be a hell of a ride. Thanks for helping."

"Helped myself while I was at it. The pledge of service. I'll collect. And I needed the exercise." Making small talk, the wizard led him to the courtyard, where a page had his horse ready.

A minute later Ragnarson galloped toward Greyfells.

He rode that horse till she collapsed, stole another, and continued till he reached Castle Greyfells. He arrived barely a half hour before his deadline.

Ragnarson was impressed by the castle's size and stories he had heard of its unique construction.

There was a remarkable structure, called the Echo Tower, which guarded the gate. Greyfells, pathologically afraid of treachery, had had the sorcerer Silmagester contrive him a structure in which there could be no secret communications. The slightest whisper there could be heard for miles around. As Ragnarson approached, a sentinel was muttering about the weather, which threatened rain.

The man from the Red Hart waited at the gate. "Well, it's about time! You have it?"

"Yes. And hell's own time getting it. Thirty sovereigns aren't enough."

"You knew there would be risks."

"But the risk of soul?"

"Let's have it."

"No."

"There're a thousand men here. They could kill you before you escaped."

"No doubt. But I'd destroy the Heart before I died."

"Uhn. Thief." He drew a small sack from within his shirt. "I haven't time to argue. The wedding's too close. Give me the casket."

Ragnarson surrendered the Heart, seized the purse, galloped away. As he wheeled, he noticed Greyfells himself running toward the Echo Tower. He thought little of it till, moments later, as he rounded that same tower's exterior, he heard a scream from its parapet.

Looking upward, he saw the Duke waving the casket before a slim young woman.

"I'll never marry that savage!"

"You will!"

"Never! Sooner the Keeper of Shadows."

"Do as I say."

"Sooner the Keeper."

"Lorraine!..."

The woman hurled herself into space. She plummeted toward the moat. Ragnarson sprang from his saddle, ran to the waterside, waded in, grabbed a handful of hair. He managed to keep her breathing, but could do nothing about her crushed insides. She kept gasping, "Sooner the Keeper of Shadows."

Ragnarson looked up angrily. Beauty ruined, life wasted.... Men were coming. He didn't know their intent, didn't care to learn it. He jumped into his saddle, galloped away. The frustrated curses of Greyfells, amplified by the Echo Tower, pursued him.

He remembered the prediction of the Keeper. Yes. Everyone had gained a wish, yet had been disappointed.

He shrugged. Of such unpleasant yarn did the Norns weave lives—and deaths. He had seen youth and beauty destroyed many times. This world might well be the true Forest of Night and Castle of Tears.

He would forget his own disappointment sooner than would any of the others.

The extorted purse contained disks of lead.

CALL FOR THE DEAD

This was the second Vengeful Dragon *story. It appeared in* The Magazine of Fantasy & Science Fiction *for July 1980. It proved that few endings are irrevocably final. It received numerous excellent reviews, many Nebula Award recommendations, and was a finalist on the Balrog Awards ballot for best short fantasy of 1980.*

I

The figure wore scarlet.

It had a small, hairless skull. Its face was as delicate as that of a beautiful woman. A rouge colored its lips. Kohl shadowed its eyes. Zodiacal pendants hung from its earlobes. Yet no observer could have sworn to its sex.

Its eyes were closed. Its mouth was open.

It sang.

Its song was terror. It was evil. Its voice stunk with its own fear.

Its lips did not move while the words came forth.

A dark basaltic throne served as its chair. A pentagram marked the floor surrounding it. That Stygian surface seemed to slope away into infinity. The arms of the pentagram, and the cabalistic signs filling them, had been sketched in brilliant reds and blues, yellows and greens. The colors rippled and changed to the tempo of the song. They surrendered to momentary flashes of silver, lilac, and gold.

Perspiration dribbled down the satin-smooth effeminate face. Veins stood out darkly at its temples. Neck and shoulder muscles became knots and cords. Small, slim, delicate hands clawed at the arms of the throne. The fingernails were long, curved, sharp, and painted the color of fresh blood.

Torches surmounting the throne's tall back flickered, growing weaker and weaker.

The song faltered....

The figure surged, drew upon some final bastion of inner resource. A scream ripped from its throat.

The darkness gradually withdrew.

The figure slowly stood, arms rising. Its song/scream transmuted into a cry of triumph.

Its eyes opened. They were an incredible cerulean blue, almost shining. And they were incalculably malevolent.

Then the darkness struck. A finger came from behind, swiftly, coiling round its victim like a python of night. Tendrils of the tentacle thrust into the sorcerer's nostrils and open mouth.

II

The caravel revolved slowly in an imperceptible current. The sea was cool and quiet, a plain of polished jade. Neither fin nor wind rippled its lifeless surface. It looked as unyielding as a serpentine floor.

I stared as I had for ages. It was there, but I no longer saw it.

Fog domed the place where *Vengeful Dragon* lay becalmed. It made granite walls where it met the quiet sea, but overhead it thinned. Daylight leaked through.

How many times had the sun come and gone since the gods had abandoned us to the spite of that Itaskian sorcerer? I had not counted.

Sometimes, when I tried hard enough, I drifted away from my body. Not far. The spells that bound us were of the highest order.

It pleased me that I had slain the spell-caster. If ever I escaped this pocket hell and encountered him in the afterworld, I would attack him again.

I could get free just enough to survey the scabby remnants of my drifting coffin.

Emerald moss clung to her sides. It crept a foot up from her waterline. Colorful fungi gnawed at her rotting timbers. Her rigging dangled like strands of a broken spider's web. Her sails were tatters. Their canvas was old and brittle and would crumble at the first caress of wind.

The decks were littered with fallen men.

Arrows protruded from backs and chests. Limbs lay twisted at odd, painful angles. Bowels lay spilled upon the slimy planks. Gaping wounds marked every body, including mine.

Yet there was no blood. Nor any corruption.

Not of the biological kind. Morally, *Dragon* had been the cesspool of the world.

Sixty-seven pairs of eyes stared at the gray walls of our tiny, changeless universe.

Twelve black birds perched in the savaged tops. They were as dark as the bottom of a freshly filled grave. There was no sheen to their feathers. Only the movement of their pupilless eyes betrayed their claim to life.

They knew neither impatience, nor hunger, nor boredom. They were sentinels standing guard over the resting place of old evil.

They watched the ship of the dead. They would do so forever.

They had arrived the moment our fate had overtaken us.

Suddenly, as one, twelve heads jerked. Yellow eyes peered into the thinner fog overhead. One short screech filled the heavy air. Dark pinions drummed a frightened bass tattoo. The birds fled clumsily into the granite fog.

I had never seen them fly. Never.

A shadow, as of vast wings, occluded the sky without actually blocking the light.

I suffered my first spate of emotion in ages. It was pure terror.

III

The caravel no longer revolved. Its battered prow pointed an unerring north-northeast. A tiny swale of jade bowed around her cutwater. A shallow depression bordered her stern.

Vengeful D. was moving.

Dark avians wheeled round her splintered masts, retreated in consternation.

Our captain lay on the caravel's high poop, beneath the helm, clad in rags. Once they had been noble finery. He still clutched a broken sword. He was Colgrave, the mad pirate.

Not all Colgrave's wounds had come in our last battle. One leg had been crippled for years. Half his face had been so badly burned that a knoll of bone lay exposed on his left cheek.

Colgrave had been the worst of us. He had been the cruelest, the most wicked of men.

Our fell commander had collapsed atop several men. His eyes still stared in fiery hatred, burning like the lamps of Hell. For Colgrave, Death was a temporary lover. A woman he would betray when his time came.

Colgrave was convinced of his immortality, of his mission.

Stretched on the high forecastle deck, in rags as dark as the loss of hope, lay another man. A blue and white arrow protruded from his chest. His head and shoulders lay propped against the vessel's side. His hating eyes stared through a break in the railing opposite him. His face was shadowed by ghosts of madness.

He was me.

I hardly recognized him anymore. He seemed more alien than any of my shipmates.

I remembered him as a grinning young soldier, a cheerful boy, a hero of the El Murid Wars. He had been the kind you wanted your daughters to meet. That man on the forecastle deck, beyond his obvious injuries, had wounds to the bones of his soul. Their scars could be seen by anyone. He looked like he had endured centuries of hurt.

He had dealt more than he had received in his thirty-four years.

He was hard, bitter, petty, vicious. I could see it, know it, and admit it when looking at him from my drifting place amidst the rigging. I could not from inside.

He was not unique. His shipmates were all hating, soul-crippled men. They hated one another more than anything else. Except themselves.

A seven-legged spider limped down my right shoulder, across my throat, and out along my left arm. The arachnid was the last living creature aboard *Dragon*. She was weakening in her relentless quest for one more victim.

The spider's odyssey took her out onto the pale white of a hand still gripping a powerful bow. My bowstring had parted long ago, victim of rot and irresistible tension.

I felt her…! My skin twitched beneath her feet.

The spider scuttled into a crack between planks and observed with cold, hungry eyes.

My eyes itched. I blinked.

Colgrave shuddered. One spindly arm rose deliberately. Colorless fingers brushed the helm. Then his hand fell, stirred feebly in the slime covering the deck.

I tried moving. I could not. What a will Colgrave had!

It had driven us for years, compelling us when no other force in Heaven or Hell could move us.

A shadow with saffron eyes wheeled above us. It uttered short, sharp cries of dismay.

Tendrils of the darkness that could not be seen were weaving new evils on the loom of wickedness of our accursed ship. And the watchers could do nothing. The sorcerer who had summoned them, who had commanded them and who had charged them with watching and bearing tidings, was no more.

I had silenced his magical songs forever with a last desperate shaft from my bow.

The birds could fly to no one with their fearful news. Nor could anyone liberate them from their bondage.

One by one my shipmates stirred the slightest, then returned to their long rests.

Sometimes in darkness, sometimes in light, the caravel glided northward. The shadow-weaver ran its shuttle too and fro. No foul weather came to nag at our ragged floating Hell. The fog surrounding us neither advanced nor receded, nor did the water we sailed ever change. It always resembled polished jade.

My shipmates did not move again.

Then darkness descended upon me, the oblivion for which I had longed since my realization that *Vengeful Dragon* was not just another pirate but a seagoing purgatory manned by the blackest souls of the western world....

And while I slept in the embrace of the Dark Lady, the weaver weaved. The ship changed. So did her crew. And the watchbirds followed in dismay.

IV

A dense fog gently bumped Itaskia's South Coast. It did not cross the shoreline. The light of a three-quarters moon gleamed off its low-lying upper surface. It looked like an army of cotton balls come to besiege the land.

A ship's main truck and a single spar cut the fog's surface like a shark's fin, moving north.

The moon set. The sun rose. The fog dissipated gradually, revealing a pretty caravel. She had a new but plain look, like a miser's beautiful wife clothed in homespun.

The fog dwindled to a single irreducible cloud. That refused to disperse. It drifted round the ship's decks. Black birds dipped in and out.

I began to itch all over. My skin twitched. Awareness returned. Straining, I opened my eyes.

The sun blazed in. I decided to roll over instead.

It was the hardest thing I had ever done. A physical prodigy.

Battered old Colgrave staggered to his feet. He leaned on the helm and scanned the gentle sea. He wore a bewildered frown.

Here, there, my shipmates stirred. Who would the survivors be? Priest, the obnoxious religious hypocrite? The Kid, whose young soul had been blackened by more murders than most of us older men? My almost-friend, Little Mica, whose sins I had never discovered? Lank Tor? Toke? Fat Poppo? The Trolledyngjan? There were not many I would miss if they did not make it.

I climbed my bow like a pole. I could feel the expression graven on my face. It was wonder. It tingled through me right down to my toenails.

We had no business being anywhere but perpetually buried in that sorcerer's trap.

I scanned the horizon suspiciously, checked the main deck, then met my Captain's eye. There was no love between us, but we respected one another. We were the best at what we were.

He shrugged. He, too, was ignorant of what was happening.

I had wondered if he had not brought the resurrection about by sheer force of will.

I bent and collected an oiled leather case. Inside lay twelve arrows, labeled, and several new bowstrings. My bow, which had been exposed for so long, had been restored by careful oiling and rubbing. I strung and tested it. It remained as powerful as ever. I did not then have the strength to bend it completely.

A dozen men were afoot. They searched themselves for wounds that had disappeared during the darkness.

I wondered how many had shared my vigil of impotent awareness, denied even the escape of madness.

They started checking each other.

I looked for Mica. I spotted the little guy studying himself in a copper mirror. He ran fingers over a face that had been half torn away.

Everyone was recovering.

I descended to the main deck and strolled aft. *Dragon* was in the best shape I had ever seen. She had been *renewed*....

I walked stiffly. The others moved jerkily, like marionettes manipulated by a novice. I reached the ladder to the poop as vanguard of a committee. Our First Officer and Boatswain, Toke and Lank Tor, had joined me. Old Barley tagged along, hoping the Old Man would order a ration of rum.

Barley was one of the alcoholic in-group. Priest was another. He was watching Barley closely. Barley always did the doling.

Rum! My mouth watered. Only Priest could outdrink me.

Colgrave shooed his deck watch down the starboard ladder.

Why hadn't our mysterious benefactors done a full repair job on the Captain? I looked round. Several men had not been restored completely. We were as we had been the day we had stumbled into the Itaskian sorcerer's trap.

Colgrave was first to speak. He said, "Something happened." Not an ingen-ious deduction.

My response was no more brilliant. "We've been called back."

Colgrave's voice had a remote, sepulchral timbre. It seemed to reach us after a journey up a long, cold, furniture-crowded hallway. There was no force in it. It had no volume, and very little inflection

"Tell me something I don't know, Bowman," Colgrave growled.

The lack of love between us was not unique. This crew had shipped together, and fought together, by condemnation of the gods. We cooperated only because survival demanded it.

"Who did? Why?" I demanded. Again I scanned the horizons.

I was not a lone watcher. We had powerful enemies along these coasts. Dread enemies, they had at their disposal the aid of men like the one who had banished us to that enchanted sea.

"We don't have time to worry about it." Colgrave threw a spidery hand at the coast. "That's Itaskia, gentlemen. We're only eight leagues south of the Silverbind Estuary."

The Itaskian Navy had sent that sorcerer after us. Itaskians hated us. Especially Itaskian merchants. We had plundered them so often that we used gold and silver for ballast.

We had preyed on them for ages, slaughtering their crews and burning their ships during our relentless search for what, in the end, had proven to be ourselves.

The great naval base at Portsmouth lay just inside the mouth of the Estuary.

"Coast watchers have spotted us by now," Colgrave continued. "The news will have reached Portsmouth. The fleet will be coming out."

It did not occur to us that we could have been forgotten. Or that we might not be recognized. But we did not know how long we had been gone, nor did *Dragon* look the same.

"We better get this bastard headed out to sea," Tor said. "Head for the nether coast of Freyland. Hole up in a cove till we know what's happening. Some timbre entered the boatswain's voice. It smelled of fear.

We had never been well-known in the island kingdoms. Seldom had we plundered there.

"We'll do that. Meantime, check out this tub from stem to stern. Check the men. Tor, take a look round from the tops. They could be after us already."

Tor had the best eyes of any man I've ever known.

The crew milled below, touching each other, speculating in soft tones. Their voices, too, sounded remote. I do not know why that was. It soon corrected itself.

"First watch," Tor called. "Rigging. Prepare to shift sail for the seaward tack."

They moved slowly, stiffly, but sorted themselves out. Some clambered into the rigging. Lank Tor said, "Ready to shift course, Captain."

Colgrave spun the wheel. Tor bellowed to the topmen.

Nothing happened.

Colgrave tried again. And again. But *Vengeful D.* would not respond.

We just stood round staring at one another till Kid called down, "Sail ho!"

V

"Boatswain, see to the weapons," Colgrave ordered.

I looked at him narrowly. A fire was building within him. Action imminent. The old Colgrave flared through, despite what we had endured, despite what we had learned about ourselves. "See that sand is scattered on the decks. Barley! One cup for all hands. Bowman. Take yours first. Go to the forecastle."

Our gazes locked. I had had my fill of killing. At least for this madman.

But the compulsion was still there. The fire that forced a man to adapt his will to Colgrave's. I looked down like a kid who had just been scolded. I descended to the main deck.

Mica caught up with me. "Bowman. What's going on? What happened to us?"

He called me Bowman because he did not know my name. None of them did, unless Colgrave had penetrated the secret. It was one I could no longer answer myself.

Vengeful Dragon had a way of stealing memories. I could not remember coming aboard. I did remember murdering my wife and her lovers before I did. But what was her name...?

The curse of the gods lies heavy. To remember my crime, to remember the love and hate and pain that had gone into and pursued it, and yet to forget the very name of the woman I had killed.... And, worse, to have forgotten my own, so that the very cornerstone of my identity was denied me.... They award their penalties in cruel and ingenious ways, do the gods.

Some of the others remembered their names but had forgotten why they had committed their sins. That, too, was torture.

None of us remembered much of our life aboard *Vengeful Dragon*.

Colgrave and I had the murder of our families in common. That was not much of a foundation for friendship.

"I don't know, Mica. No more than you."

"I thought maybe the Old Man.... It scares me, Bowman. To be re-called...."

"I know. Think of the Power involved. The evils unleashed.... Come up to the forecastle with me, Mica."

He did not have anything else to do. He was our sail maker. Our sails were in chandler's shop condition.

We leaned against the rail, staring over the quiet green water at the tops of a pair of triangular sails.

"That's no Itaskian galleon," Mica observed.

"No." I debated for several seconds before I hinted at my suspicion. "Maybe the gods are tinkering with us, Mica." A gull glided across our bows. For a moment I marveled at its graceful flight. A shadow followed. One of the black birds.

"Suppose they're giving us another chance?"

He watched the black bird for several seconds. "How patient are they, Bowman? We had our chances in life. We had them in limbo, while we harried the coasts. And we didn't even recognize them."

"And maybe we couldn't. This ship.... We forget things. We stop thinking. We get like Lank Tor, who can't remember yesterday. Remember Student and Whaleboats?"

They had been friends of ours. They had disappeared during a terrible storm shortly before the sorcerer had caught us.

"Uhm."

We had never talked about it, but the suspicion could not be denied. There was a chance that Student and Whaleboats had found redemption. There was a connection between righteous deeds and disappearances from *Dragon*. It *had* to be more than coincidence. Our memories were reliable only back to the time Kid had come aboard, but since then several men had vanished. Each had been guilty of doing something truly *good* shortly before.

How Colgrave had screamed and cussed at Student and Whaleboats for not setting fire to that shipload of women....

"Student claimed there was a way out. Fat Poppo told me he figured it out too. I think there is. I think they found it. And I think I know what it is, now."

Mica did not say anything for at least a minute. Then, "Did you die at that place, Bowman?"

"What?" For some reason I did not want to tell him. "What place?"

"The foggy sea, dummy. Where we met ourselves and lost the battle."

Colgrave's habit was to destroy every vessel we encountered. We had entered that quiet place out of a deep fog, with a sorcerer's grim promise still ringing in our ears. Black birds had roosted in our tops and another ship had been headed our way. Colgrave, mad Colgrave, had ordered the attack. And when we had come to grips with the caravel, who had we found manning her but doppelgangers of ourselves...?

"Were you aware the whole time?"

"Yeah." The grunt liked to choke me getting out. "Every damned second. I couldn't sleep. I couldn't even go crazy."

He raised an eyebrow.

"All right. Crazier than I already am."

Mica grinned. "Sometimes, Bowman, I wonder if we're not just a little less wicked than we think. Or maybe it's pretend. We're great pretenders, the crew of the *Vengeful D*."

"Mica, you ain't no philosopher."

"How do you know what I am? I don't. I don't remember. But what I'm saying, man, is I think we all knew what was going on. Every minute. Even the Old Man."

"What's the point?"

"The sun rose and set a lot of times, Bowman. I didn't sleep either. That's a lot of time to think. And maybe change."

I turned my back to the rail. The crew were about ship's work. They were quieter than I remembered. Thoughtful. They moved less jerkily now.

How long had it been? Years?

"We don't look any different." Colgrave was the same old specter of terror there on the poop. He had changed clothing. He was clad in regal finery now. Clothes were his compensation for his deformity.

When he dressed this well, and kept to the poop instead of lurking in his cabin, he meant to spill blood.

"I mean different inside." He considered Colgrave too. "Maybe some of us can't change. Maybe there's nothing else in there."

"Or maybe we just don't understand." I suffered an insight. "The Old Man's scared."

"He should be. These are Itaskian waters. Look what they did already."

"Not just afraid of what they'll do if they catch us. We had that hanging over us before. It didn't bother anybody. Won't now. I mean scared like Barley. Of everything and nothing."

Old Barley was our resident coward. He was also the meanest fighter on the *Vengeful D*. His fear drove him to prodigies in battle.

"Maybe. And maybe he's changed, too."

"I haven't. Not that I can see."

"Look at your right hand."

I did. It was my hand, fore and middle fingers calloused from drawing bowstrings. "So?"

"Every guy here can tell you two things about your hands. If there's a ship in sight, your left will be holding a bow. And your right, when Colgrave lets you, will be hanging on to a cup of rum like it was your first-born child."

I looked at Mica. He smiled. I looked at my hand. It was naked. I looked down at the main deck, that I had crossed without thinking of rum. Barley was almost finished issuing the grog ration.

The craving hit me hard. I must have staggered. Mica caught my arm.

"Try to let it go, Bowman. Just this once."

I waved at Barley.

"Just to see if you can do it."

Why didn't he mind his own business? Gods, I needed a drink.

Then Priest caught my eye. Priest, the king of us alkies. The man who peddled salvation to the rest of us and remained incapable of saving himself.

Priest did not have a tin cup either. He leaned over the starboard rail. His expression said that his guts were tearing him apart. His need for a drink was devouring him. But he was not drinking. His back was to Barley.

"Look at Priest," I murmured.

"I see him, Bowman. And I see you."

The cramps started then. They pissed me off. I whirled and planted myself against the rail, mimicking Priest, overlooking the bowsprit. I tried to shut out the world.

"No way that pervert is going to outlast me," I declared.

Our bow began rising and falling gently. The water was assuming the character of a normal sea. Our resurrection was about finished.

I did not look forward to its completion. I could get seasick in a rowboat on a lake on a breezy day.

The other vessel was hull up on the horizon and headed our way fast.

I re-examined my bow and arrows. Just in case.

VI

Had we changed? The gods witness, we had. The two-master came in alongside, gently, and we did not swarm over her. We did not cast her screaming crew to the sharks. We did not set her aflame. We did not do anything but hold our weapons ready and wait.

Colgrave did not ask us to do anything more.

Mica and I surveyed our shipmates. I'm sure he saw as much wonder in my face as I saw in his.

We watched Colgrave almost constantly. The Old Man would determine the smaller vessel's fate. Like it or not, if he gave the order, we would attack.

"We're a pack of war dogs," I told Mica. "We might as well be slaves."

He nodded.

Never a word escaped our mad captain's mouth. That astonished him more than the rest of us, I think.

The ship lay bumping against *Dragon* for fifteen minutes. Her strangely clad, silent crewmen studied us. We studied them. Not a one would meet my eye. They knew who and what we were. We could smell the fear in them.

Yet they had come to us, and they stayed. And that was reason for us to fear.

The vessel had a small deckhouse amidships. Its door finally opened. Two more strangers stepped out, stationed themselves to either side. They studied us with startled, frightened eyes.

A person in red came forth, looked up.

"A woman!" Mica swore.

We did not have a reputation for being gallant.

"I don't think so...." But I could not be sure. I had never seen a bald woman. "But.... Call it an it."

Its incredible blue eyes stared in slight bewilderment. Unlike its shipmates, it did not fear us. It was confident.

I got the impression that we had been a disappointment. Because we had not conformed to our vicious reputation.

The urge to let an arrow fly was as strong in me as the need for a drink. I did not bend my bow.

One glance into those weird eyes was all I could handle. Incredible Power sparked them. They proclaimed their possessor a sorcerer greater than he who had banished us to fogs and leaden seas.

The creature also had that aura of command that animated Colgrave.

"This's the one who called us back," I whispered.

Mica nodded.

I had myself in control. I tested the draw of my bow.

Black birds wheeled overhead, screeching their consternation. One dove at the figure in red.

The figure raised a palm. It spoke a single word.

Feathers exploded. They spun down toward ships and sea, smoldering as they fell. The stench of burnt feathers assailed the air.

The naked albatross smashed into *Dragon*'s side. It broke its neck. It thrashed in the water briefly, then changed form. In seconds it became a thing like a snake of night. The thing wriggled away through water and air with lightning speed.

Its companions screeched once, then remained silent. They did not cease their endless patrol. They clearly preferred avoiding their comrade's liberation.

The figure in red said something.

Someone shouted orders in a strange language. Sailors threw grappling hooks over *Dragon*'s rail.

I looked at Colgrave. An arrow lay across my bow.

He made a slight negative head gesture.

"He *has* changed," I told Mica. "He says let them come." I looked again. Colgrave was instructing Toke and Lank Tor. They descended to the main deck.

They disposed the men in such fashion that they could attack the boarders from all sides.

We waited.

One of the smaller ship's officers came up. He looked round, saw the lay of things. He was not happy. He glanced at me. I half drew my bow. He cringed.

I laughed. Old Barley giggled. The crew took it up.

We were not kind people. We enjoyed tormenting our captives.

Again Colgrave gave me that little headshake. A nasty grin smeared his face too. He liked my joke.

More of them came. And more, and more.

"Mica, they're all coming over."

"Looks like."

They stood on the main deck, nervously watched Colgrave.

"Slide back and tell the Old Man we can sneak down and knock a hole in their bottom when they're all up here. If he wants."

Mica grinned. "Yeah." It was his kind of dirty trick. He liked sneaking.

I expect his sins involved some fancy sneakiness. He wasn't chicken, mind. Just the kind of guy who sees the advantages of back-stabbing. A low-risk type guy. He could handle himself face-to-face, when the stakes were high. He shoved through the strangers. They twisted away from him like he was a plague carrier.

I watched a grin spread across Colgrave's battered face. It was as lopsided as the altars of Hell. The muscles only worked on one side.

He liked it. My suggestion did not violate his inexplicable armistice with the creature in red.

Mica almost danced back to the forecastle.

The sorcerer boarded last. Its crew surrounded it. It disappeared among them. They were all bigger.

I laughed, catching the creature's attention. I again half drew my bow.

It looked at me with no apparent fear, but I knew better. I knew I could take the sorcerer if just one instant's gap opened through those body-guards.

We had not been stripped of our defenses. I could get an arrow from here to there quicker than the creature could blink.

It knew too. That was why it had brought its whole crew. In the time it would take us to kill them, it could perform the sorceries needed to save itself.

It, too, concentrated on Colgrave.

The Old Man's eye flicked my way just once, for a tenth of a second.

Mica and I rolled over the rail into the ratlines, transferred to the other vessel's stays, got down to her deck in seconds.

"Bowman, you see about sinking her. I'll go through the cabin."

"Good thinking. But look for something besides loose gold."

He gave me a look.

I looked back. Gold was Mica's weakness. Whenever we took a ship, he spent most of the celebration scrounging gold and silver. He brought it back, and we took it down and put it in ballast, never knowing what we would ever do with it.

That was one tough little ship. It took me twenty minutes to chop a decent hole through her thin planking. By the time I finished I knew she would not sink before the strangers could get back aboard.

I chuckled. That made the joke richer.

I hustled back topside. We were taking too long. "Mica!" I called softly. "Come on. We haven't got all day."

He poked his head out the deckhouse door. "Here. Take some of this crap."

He had gotten some gold, of course. But not much. The rest seemed to be books, papers, and the thing-gobbies sorcerers have to have to be comfortable doing their nasties.

VII

I rolled over *Dragon*'s rail expecting all eyes to be looking my way.

None were. None did. The strangers were crowded against the base of the poop. Colgrave stood above them, a mocking smile on half his face. Everybody stared at him like he was some demon god.

Sometimes I thought he was myself.

The men were impatient. The strangers felt it. Their fear was about to become panic. Only the will of the creature in red kept them from running.

Mica handed up our plunder. I concealed it beneath a spritsail lying on the forecastle deck. Mica rolled over the rail.

Colgrave's glance flicked our way. His smile stretched. He terminated the audience with a shrug and a turned back.

The creature in red started back to its vessel. Its followers surged around it, eager to be gone.

I half drew my bow for the third time.

The creature in red smiled at me.

That made me mad. I would have let fly had Colgrave not shook his head.

Nobody mocked the Bowman....

Then they were gone, their vessel turning away and heading back whence it had come. They stood around watching us, as if to make sure we did not change our minds about letting them go.

Their ship was a foot lower in the water already. Soon they would realize that she was not responding properly. They would discover the hole....

I had cut it too big for them to keep afloat by pumping. And I doubted that they would be able to get a good patch on it. I slapped Mica's back. "Let's take the stuff to the Old Man."

It was not a chore that pleased me. Though it was unavoidable, I plain did not like being anywhere near Colgrave. But with Student gone, he was the only reader left aboard.

Anyway, he needed to know what we had. If anything.

He stirred through the pile. Mica's personal plunder he pushed to one side. Mica took it below. The rest Colgrave sorted into three piles. A half-dozen items he just flipped over his shoulder, over the rail, into the sea. Then he examined the piles again. He deep-sixed several more items.

Toke, Tor, and I watched in silence. Colgrave kept dithering, poking. I don't think he knew what he had. But Colgrave was not the kind to admit ignorance.

Finally, I could stand no more. "What did they want?" I demanded.

"The usual," Colgrave replied without looking up. "A little murder. A little terror. With his enemies on the bull's-eye, of course. Not ours."

"His?"

"I think it was a he. You cut a big hole, Bowman?"

"Big enough. It'll stop them." He seemed so damned blasé after what had been done to us. Was he still trusting in divine protection? After the Itaskian sorcerer? If so, he was a fool.

That was one thing that had never been pinned on Colgrave.

"Tor, go to the masthead. Let us know when they go dead in the water. Toke, make sail for Freyland. I think she'll respond now."

I watched while Colgrave examined several books. He seemed awfully undignified, sitting on the deck with his legs crossed. Finally, "Captain, what're we going to do?"

He peered at me with that one evil eye till I thought he was going to have me thrown to the sharks. One did not address Colgrave. Colgrave called one to the presence.

He finally replied, "It would be a raid to belittle anything we've ever tried. Portsmouth itself. Burn the docks. Burn the town. Kill everybody we can."

"Why?"

"I didn't ask, Bowman." His voice was cold and hard. He was tired of my questions. Yet I remained where I was. He *had* changed. He was more open than ever I had seen. "He ordered us. We haven't yet tested the limits of his control. We may not be able to do otherwise."

"And we do have our grievances."

"Yes. We have scores to settle with Portsmouth."

Dragon shifted her heading to north-northeast. We were on course for the island kingdoms.

"The little sail maker must have missed something," Colgrave said. "There's nothing here we can use. All we can do is deny this stuff to him."

"She's taking in sail, Captain," Tor called down. A vast amusement filled his voice.

The story had passed through the crew, spread by Mica. There was a lot of laughter.

I looked north. I could barely make out the other vessel.

Damn, did that Tor have eyes.

Excellent eyes. "Sail ho!" he called a moment later. "She's a big one. War galleon, by her look."

His arm thrust aft. Colgrave and I turned.

We could just make out her maintops. I looked at Colgrave.

I could see the torment in him. The need.... He had to have bloodshed the way I had to have rum, had to use my bow.

"She's an Itaskian," Tor called a few minutes later. The bloodlust filled his voice. He, too, needed the killing.

Nervousness and uncertainty washed the main deck. The men no longer had the absolute confidence that had impelled them before our capture.

Dragon had changed indeed. And was changing still.

"Maintain your heading, First Officer," Colgrave finally croaked.

It tore him up to say it, but he did.

A breeze came up. It took us on our port quarter, setting us to landward. The more we turned to seaward, the harder it blew.

The smell of wizardry tainted it.

Colgrave gathered Mica's plunder, took it to his cabin, then returned to the poop. He said nothing more. The stubborn Colgrave of old, he kept *Dragon*'s course inalterably fixed on Freyland.

We passed within three hundred yards of the sorcerer's ship. Its crew were too busy keeping from drowning to pay attention. Several called for help. We sailed on.

Colgrave laughed at them. I'm sure his voice carried that far.

The breeze died soon afterward, as the other ship began going under. I guess the wizard needed to concentrate on surviving.

One round for us.

We took orders from nobody. Not even those who pretended to be our saviors.

That is what Tor said the thing in red claimed when it had spoken to Colgrave. It had wanted to bargain.

To bargain? I thought. Then its hold on us could not be as strong as it would like.

I smiled. And stood on the forecastle looking forward to the coasts of Freyland. It had been a long time since we had sailed them.

The black birds circled overhead. After a time, one by one, they settled into our tops. They seemed less outraged than they had been.

VIII

Spring had only recently conquered the western shores of Freyland. The cove where we anchored was surrounded by low, forested hills blushing green. The afternoons were warm and lazy.

There was nothing to do. For the first time since I had come aboard. *Dragon* was in perfect repair. Half the ship's work being done was stuff Toke and Lank Tor conjured up because they did not have anything to do either. For several days we just plain loafed.

But in the background lurked the nagging questions, the aching doubts. What would Colgrave decide? Would it be the right thing?

"Right thing?" Mica demanded. Pure amazement animated his features. "What the hell kind of question is that, Bowman?"

He and I and Priest had rigged us a couch of folded sail and were lying back staring at cloud castles while dangling fishing lines over the side. Fishing was something I had not done since boyhood.

I could not remember that far back. I just knew that I had liked to fish.

"It's a valid question," Priest insisted. "We have come to the crossroads of righteousness, Sailmaker. We stand at the forking of the way...."

"Oh, knock it off, Priest," I grumbled. "Don't you ever give up?"

"I think I got a bite," he replied.

"Take it easy, Bowman," Mica said. "He's getting better."

That he was, I had to admit. I used to loathe Priest because he insisted on being our conscience while remaining one of the worst sinners himself.

Priest dragged a small fish over the side. "I'll be damned."

"Doubtless. We're all damned. We have been for ages."

"That's debatable. I meant the fish."

It was a little speckled sand shark about sixteen inches long. Not exactly what we were after. I started to smash its head with my heel.

"Why don't you just throw it back?" Mica asked. "It ain't hurting nothing."

Trouble was, the shark did not want to go. Not with our help. Its little jaws kept going chompity-chomp. Its skin sandpapered the hide off my fingers when I tried to hold it so Priest could get his hook back.

It died before we could save it.

"You was talking about doing the right thing," Mica told me. "What made you say that? I've never heard the Bowman talk that way before."

I gave him a look.

Priest took his side. "He's right. Colgrave's the only man here meaner than the Bowman."

I did not agree. At least, I had never thought of it that way. I rated Priest and Old Barley meaner than me any day.

The Kid came up and joined us. He had been keeping a low profile lately. He seemed to be completely tied up inside himself. Ordinarily, he was our number-one showoff, our number-one mouth man.

I was at the end of the sail couch. He sat down beside me.

Amazing.

I kind of liked the Kid. Really. He reminded me of myself when I was younger. But he had no use for me. I never understood, unless it was true that I looked like somebody he had hated before coming aboard.

"Hey, Bowman. What do you think?" he asked.

"Hunh? About what, Kid?" Why was he asking me? Anything.

"About this. About us coming back." He sat up, started making himself a fishing line of his own. He fumbled around. It was obvious that he had never fished in his life. I helped him get it right.

And I asked him why he was asking me.

"Because you're the smart guy now that Student's gone. Toke. Lank Tor. They're just zombies. And the Old Man wouldn't give me the time of day if I begged."

"Kid. Kid. I...." I let it drift off unsaid.

"What?"

I forced it. "I never much cared about anybody. But it hurts me to see you here, so young."

He looked at me strangely, then smiled. That smile was worth a ton of gold. "I earned it, Bowman."

"Didn't we all?" Mica mused.

"That we did," Priest declared. "The sins on our souls…." He shut himself off, said instead, "The question is, are we going to go right on deserving it?"

Mica got a bite. He hauled in another goddamned shark. This one was more cooperative. Or we had gotten better at handling them.

"Kid, I don't know what to think. That's the gospel. I'm lost. I go half crazy worrying about it sometimes."

A body plopped down the other side of Kid. I glanced over. It was the Trolledyngjan, the final addition to our mad crew. We had picked him up off an Itaskian warship we had taken in our next-to-last battle. He had been confined to her brig.

He had a name, Torfin something, but nobody ever used it. He was one long drink of silence. I don't think he had spoken twenty words the whole time he had been aboard. He did not say anything now. He just looked at me and Mica.

We had tried to kill him once. Before he had become part of our crew. Back when we were raiders. We had attacked his ship. He had tried boarding us. Me and Mica had dumped him into the drink.

And then he had turned up aboard the Itaskian, and Colgrave had decided he ought to replace Student or Whaleboats.

A treaty of forgiveness passed between us without words being spoken.

The Trolledyngjan said, "There be tales told in the Fatherland of the *Oskorei*. The Wild Hunt. They be souls of the damned who ride Hell's stallions through the high range hunting the living."

The Kid passed him a hook and some line. He started fiddling with it.

"What're you driving at?" I asked.

"We be the *oskoreien* of the sea." He baited his hook and flipped it over the side. We waited. Finally, he continued. "They tell of the Wild Hunt that they be hating none so much as they be hating one another."

We waited some more. But that was all he had to say.

It was enough. It made me think.

He had stated a truth and posed a question in a characteristically oblique Trolledyngjan manner.

Hatred had always been the one shared, unifying emotion aboard *Dragon*. And we hated each other more than any outsiders.

Only, we were getting along now. More or less.

The others saw it too. Even the Kid. "What's it mean, Bowman?" the boy asked.

"I don't know."

The changes were progressing. I no longer knew myself. If ever I had.

Fat Poppo laboriously clambered to the forecastle deck. His appearance was another declaration of how the crew regarded me.

"Welcome to the philosophy klatch, Poppo," I said. "What brings you dragging your ass all the way up off the main deck?" He seldom moved if he did not have to, so fat and lazy was he.

He dropped to his knees behind me, whispered, "In the trees across the cove. Under the big dead one you guys been calling the hanging tree."

I looked. And I saw what he meant.

There were four of them, and they wore livery. Soldiers.

The honeymoon was over. "Mica, slide down and dig up the Old Man. Tell him to take a gander at what we've got under the hanging tree. Try to keep it casual."

Colgrave had been holed up in his cabin since we had dropped anchor. He was studying the wizard's things. He would not appreciate being disturbed.

But this was important.

Maybe I made a mistake. The rest of us might not have been recognized. We were well-known, but there was nothing really unique about our appearances. Not the way Colgrave's was unique.

I reached for my bow and quietly strung it behind the mask of the railing.

IX

Colgrave strode from his cabin dressed for a day at court. Mica dogged along behind him as he climbed to the poop. He turned his one grim eye on our watchers.

"The dead captain!"

It carried clearly over the water. Brush crackled. I leapt to my feet and pulled an arrow to my ear.

"It's them! That's the Archer!"

"Bowman. Let them run."

I relaxed. Colgrave was right. Wasting arrows had no point. I could not get them all. Not through the trees.

Still, a gesture seemed necessary.

One turned, stared back through a small opening in the foliage. He bore a spade-shaped shield. A griffin rampant was its device. I let fly with a waste arrow, a practice arrow. It pierced the griffin's eye.

I still had it. After however long it had been, my shafts still flew true.

The soldier's jaw dropped. I bowed mockingly.

"That wasn't smart," Priest told me.

"Couldn't help myself. I had to do it."

The black birds above cursed me in their squawky tongue. I glared my defiance.

My archery was my one skill, my one way of defying the universe and its perversity. The gesture had been important to me. It was a statement that the Bowman existed, that he was well, that his aim was still deadly. It was a graffito on the walls of time, screaming I AM!

Colgrave beckoned.

I shook in my sea boots. I was going to catch hell for defying orders....

But he did not mention my shot. Instead, he gathered Toke, Lank Tor, and myself, and told us, "The decision is at hand. Within two days the whole island will know we've returned. They'll know in Portsmouth in three days, in Itaskia in four. They won't endure us anymore. Our return will scare them so much that they'll send out every ship they have. They won't trust warlocks this time. They'll destroy us absolutely, with fire, at whatever cost we demand."

He stared at the western sea, his one good eye gazing on sights the rest of us could never see. He said again, "At whatever cost we demand."

Tor giggled. Fighting was his only love, his only joy. He did not care whether he would win or lose, only that he would be able to swing a blade in another battle. He was the same old Tor. I did not think there was anything in him capable of change. He was a hollow man.

Toke said, "There's no hope, then? We have to depart this plain memorialized by mountains of dead men and seas scattered with burning ships?"

I sighed. "There's nowhere to run, Toke. Destiny's winds have blown us into the narrow channel. We can't do anything but ride the current."

Colgrave looked at me strangely. "That's odd talk from you, Bowman."

"I feel odd, Captain."

"There's still the sorcerer who recalled us," he said. "And we aren't forgotten of the gods. Not completely." He glanced at the black birds.

The creatures strained their necks toward us.

I surveyed my long-time home. Forward, against the base of the forecastle, I could discern a tiny, almost invisible patchlet of dark fog. I had not noticed it since the day the sorcerer had boarded us. I imagined it had always been there, unnoticed because it stayed behind the corner of my vision.

"I'll give my orders in the morning," Colgrave declared. "For today, celebrate. Our final celebration, Tor. See to the arms. Toke, tell Barley to use his keys."

My guts snapped into an agonized knot. Rum...!

"We'll sail at dawn," the Old Man told us. "Be ready. I'll tell you our destination then."

He scanned us once with that wicked eye, and it seemed that there was pain and care in his gaze. He left us there, stunned, and returned to his cabin.

Emotion? In Colgrave? It was almost too much to bear.

I returned to the forecastle and plopped my ass down between the Kid and Little Mica. I leaned back and stared at the clouds, at the green hills where four terrified soldiers were racing to unleash the hounds of doom. "Damned!" I muttered. "Damned. Damned. Damned."

The Kid was first to ask, "What did you say, Bowman?"

I glared at the hills as if my gaze could drop those Freylanders in their tracks. "We sail with the morning tide. He hasn't decided where or why."

The Trolledyngjan hooked a sand shark. We went through the routine, dumped it back.

"Think it's the same one?" Priest asked. "It don't look any different."

"Why would it keep coming back?" Mica wanted to know.

The Kid asked me, "What do you think he'll decide, Bowman?"

"To spill blood. He's still Colgrave. He's still the dead captain. He only knows one way. The only question is who he'll go after."

"Oh."

"Give me a line." I baited my hook and flipped it over the rail. "Priest, Barley's passing out grog." I needed a drink something cruel. But I was not going to give in first.

I watched the torment in his face. And he watched it in mine as he replied, "Don't think so, Bowman. Too far to walk. Besides, I'm getting a nibble."

He got the nibble, but I caught the fish. It was the same damned shark. What was the matter with that thing? Couldn't it learn?

Dragon rocked gently on quiet swells. A breeze whispered in the trees surrounding the cove. We kept catching that sand shark and throwing it back, and not saying much, while the sun dribbled down to the horizon behind us.

X

Toke, Lank Tor, and I clambered up to the poop. The crew gathered on the main deck, their eyes on the Old Man's cabin door. The sun had not yet cleared the hills to the east.

"Tide's going to turn soon," Toke observed.

"Uhm," I grunted.

Lank Tor shuffled nervously. The blood-eagerness in him seemed tempered by something else this morning. Had the changes begun to reach even him?

Colgrave came forth.

The crew gasped.

Tor, Toke, and I leaned over the poop rail to see why.

He wore old, battered, plain clothing. It was the sort a merchant captain down on his luck might wear. There wasn't a bit of color or polish on him.

A new Colgrave confronted us. I was not sure I liked it. It made me uneasy, as if the man's style of dress were the root of our failures and successes.

He ignored everybody till he had reached the poop and surveyed his surroundings. Then, "Make sail, First Officer. North along the coast, two points to seaward. They're watching. Let them think we're bound for North Cape."

Toke and Tor went to get anchor and sails up. I stood beside Colgrave searching the shore for this morning's watchers.

He said, "We'll keep this heading till we're out of sight of land. Then we'll come round and run south. We'll stay in the deep water."

I shuddered. We were not deep-water sailors. Though hardly any of us had set foot on dry land in years, we did not want to let it out of sight. Few of us had been sailors before fate shanghaied us onto this devil ship.

And deep water meant heavier seas. Seas meant seasickness. My stomach was in bad enough shape, having had no rum.

"What then?" I asked.

"Portsmouth, Bowman."

"The wizard wins? *Dragon* runs to his beck? We do his murders for him?"

"I don't know, Bowman. He's the crux. He's the answer. Whatever happens, it'll revolve around him. He's in Portsmouth. We'll take our questions to him."

There was uncertainty in Colgrave's voice. He, the megalithic will round which my universe turned, no longer knew what he was doing. He just knew that something had to be done.

"But Portsmouth? You're sure?"

"He's there. Somewhere. Masquerading as something else. We'll find him." There was no doubt in him now. He had selected a course. Nothing would turn him aside.

I could not fathom Colgrave's thinking. He wanted to take *Dragon* into the very den of our enemies? Just to confront that sorcerer again? It was pure madness.

No one had ever accused Colgrave of being sane. Only the once had he come out a loser.

We sailed north. We turned and ran south once Tor could no longer discern land from the maintop. A steady breeze scooted us along. By nightfall, according to Toke, we had come back south of the southernmost tip of Freyland. But Colgrave did not alter course till next morning. Several hours after dawn he ordered a change to a heading due east.

He shifted course a point this way, a point that as we sailed along. He had Toke and Tor put on or take off canvas.

A plan was shaping in his twisted mind.

Time lumbered along. The sun set, and it rose. Tension built up till we were all ready to snap. Tempers flared. Some of the old hatred returned.

We were not very tolerant of one another.

The sun set again.

I had seen Colgrave's matchless dead reckoning before. I was not over-whelmed when he brought *Dragon* into the mouth of the Silverbind Estuary with the same accuracy I showed in speeding a shaft to its target.

We were all dismayed. To a man we had hoped that he would change his mind, or that something would change it for him.

We had not seen one ship during our time at sea.

They had taken our false trail for true. The fleet had cleared Portsmouth only that morning, heading north in hopes of catching us in the wild seas between Freyland and Cape Blood. The only vessels we saw now, as we eased along the nighted Itaskian coast, were fishing boats drawn up on the beaches for the night.

Watch fires burned along the Estuary's north shore. They winked at us as if secretly blessing our surreptitious passage.

Those winks conveyed messages. A steady flow were coming from the north. Fat Poppo tried reading them but the Itaskians had changed their codes since he had been in their navy.

No one noticed our little caravel creeping along through the moonless night.

The lights of Portsmouth appeared on our starboard bow. Little bells tinkled over the water ahead. Poppo softly announced that he had spotted the first channel-marker buoy.

Its bell pinged happily in the gentle swell.

Colgrave sent Tor to the forecastle to watch the markers.

He meant to try the impossible. He meant to take *Dragon* up the chan-nel by starlight.

Colgrave's confidence in his destiny was justified. *Dragon* was surely a favored charity of the gods that night. The breeze was absolutely perfect for creeping from one bell buoy to the next. The current did not bother us at all.

We penetrated the harbor basin two hours after midnight. Perfect timing. The city was asleep. Colgrave warped *Dragon* in to a wharf with a precise beauty that only a sailor could appreciate.

Fear had the ship by the guts. I was so rattled that I don't think I could have hit an elephant at ten paces. But there I was on the forecastle, ready to cover the landing party.

Priest, Barley, and the Trolledyngjan jumped to the wharf. They searched the darkness for enemies. Mica and the Kid jumped. Others threw them mooring lines. They made fast in minutes. The gangplank went down for the first time in anyone's memory. Toke and Tor started ushering the men ashore. Tor made sure they were armed.

Some did not want to go.

I was one. I had not set foot on any land in so long that I could not remember what it was like.... And this was the country of my birth. This was the land of my crimes. This land loved me no more, nor wanted its sacred soil defiled by the tread of my murderer's feet....

Nor did I want to do any sorcerer's bloodletting.

Colgrave beckoned.

I had to go. I relaxed my grip on my bow, descended to the main deck, crossed to the gangplank.

Only the Old Man and I remained aboard. Toke and Tor were trying to maintain order on the wharf. Some of the men were trying to get back to the ship, to escape stable footing and everything that land meant. Others had fallen to their knees and were kissing the paving stones. Some, like Barley, just stood and shook.

"I don't want to return, either, Bowman," Colgrave whispered. "My very being whines and pules. But I'm going. Now march."

The old fire was in his eyes. I marched.

He had not changed clothing. He still wore rags and tatters. Following me down the gangplank, he looped a piece of cloth across his features the way they do in the deserts of Hammad al Nakir.

Colgrave's presence made the difference. The men forgot their emotions. Toke quickly arranged them in a column of fours.

A late drunk staggered out of the darkness. "Shay...." he mumbled. "What're.... Who're...." He almost tripped over me and Colgrave.

He was an old man young. A beggar, by his look, and a cripple. He had only one arm, and one leg barely functioned. He reeked of cheap, sour wine. He stumbled against me again. I caught him.

"Thanks, buddy," he mumbled. His breath was foul.

My god, I thought. This could be me if I keep on the grog.... I forced honesty. I was looking at what I had been when I had committed my murders, and most of the time since.

All I could see was ugliness.

The drunk stared at me. His eyes grew larger and larger. He glanced over the crew, peered at the Old Man.

A long, terrified whine, like the plea of a whipped cur, ripped from his throat.

"Priest!" the Old Man snapped.

Priest materialized.

"This man recognizes us. Man, this is Priest. Do you know him, too? You do? Good. I'm going to ask some questions. Answer them. Or I'll let Priest have you."

The drunk became so terrified that for several minutes we could pry no sense from him at all.

He did know us. He had been a sailor aboard one of the warships that had helped bring us to our doom. He had been one of the few lucky survivors. He remembered the battle as if it had taken place yesterday. Eighteen years and a sea of alcohol had done nothing to erase the memories.

Eighteen years! I thought. More than half my lifetime…. The life I had lived before boarding *Vengeful D*. The whole world would have changed.

Colgrave persisted with his questions. The old sailor answered willingly. Priest shuffled nervously.

Priest had been the great killer, the great torturer, back when. He had loved it. But the role did not fit him anymore.

Colgrave learned what he wanted. At least, he learned all the drunk had to tell.

A moment of decision arrived. The old sailor recognized it before I did.

It was the moment when a man should have died, based on our record.

A black bird squeaked somewhere in *Dragon*'s rigging.

"There is a ship at the wharf," Colgrave said. "Barley! The keys." Barley came. Colgrave gave the keys to the drunk. He stared at them as if they fit the locks in the one-way gates of Hell.

"You will board that ship," Colgrave told him. His tone denied even the possibility that his will might be challenged. "You will stay there, drinking the rum behind the lock those keys fit, till I give you leave to go ashore."

The watchbird squawked again. Excited wings punished the night air.

Fog started drifting in from the Estuary. Its first tendrils reached us.

The drunk looked at Colgrave, stunned. His head bobbed. He ran toward *Dragon*.

XI

"Bowman, come," Colgrave said. "You've been to Portsmouth before. You'll have to show me the way to the Torian Hill."

I did not remember ever having been to Portsmouth. I told him so, and suggested that Mica be his guide. Mica was always talking about Portsmouth. Mostly about its famous whorehouses, but sometimes about its people and their strange mores.

"You will remember," Colgrave told me. He used the same tone that he had directed at the drunk.

I remembered. Not much, but enough to show him the way to the Torian Hill, which was the area where the mercantile magnates and high nobility maintained their urban residences.

Dawn launched its assaults upon the eastern horizon, though in the fog we were barely aware of it. We began to encounter early risers. Some instinct made them avoid us.

We passed out of the city proper, into the environs of the rich and powerful. Portsmouth was not a walled city. There were no gates to pass, no guards to answer.

We broke from fog into dawn light halfway up the Torian Hill.

It was not like I remembered it. Mica's expression confirmed my feeling.

"There's been a war pass this way," he said. "Only a couple years ago."

It was obvious. They were still picking up the pieces. "Where are we going?" I asked Colgrave.

"I don't know. This's the Torian Hill?" Mica and I both nodded.

Colgrave dug round inside his rags, produced a gold ring.

"Hey!" Mica complained. "That's...." He shut up.

A glance from Colgrave's eye could chill the hardiest soul.

"What is it?" I asked Mica.

"That's my ring. I took it off the wizard's ship. He said I could have it. I put it down in the ballast with my other things."

"Must've been more than just gold."

"Yeah. Must have been." He eyed Colgrave like a guy trying to figure how best to carve a roast.

He would not *do* anything. We all had those thoughts sometimes. Nobody ever tried.

Colgrave forced the ring onto a bony little finger, closed his eyes.

We waited.

Finally, "That way. The creature is there. It sleeps."

I caught the change from *he* to *it*. What had changed Colgrave's mind? I did not ask. During the climb he had become the mad captain again.

People began to notice us. They did not recognize us, but we were a piratical crew. They got the hell away fast.

Some were women. We had not laid hands on women in ages....

"Sailmaker." Colgrave said it softly. Mica responded as though he had been lashed. He forgot women even existed, let alone the one he had begun stalking.

We came to a mansion. It skulked behind walls that would have done a fortified town proud. The stone was gray, cold limestone still moist from the fog.

"Bowman, you knock." He waved everyone against the wall, out of view of the gateman's peephole.

I pounded. And pounded again.

Feet shuffled behind the heavy gate. The shield over the peephole slid aside. An old man's eye glared through. "What the hell you want?" he demanded sleepily.

Colgrave dropped the cloth concealing his face. "Open the gate." He used the voice that had made Mica forget a skirt, that had driven a drunk aboard *Dragon*.

The old man croaked, "Gah…. Gah…."

"Open the gate," Colgrave told him.

For a moment I did not think that he would.

The gate creaked inward an inch.

Colgrave hit it with his shoulder. I lunged through after him, nocking an arrow. Colgrave seized the gateman's shirt, demanded, "Where us he? The thing in red?"

I do not think he knew the answer. But he talked.

Something growled. Barley eased past us and opened the mastiff's skull with a brutal sword stroke. Priest silenced a second growler.

Men charged toward us from behind shrubbery, from behind trees. They had no intention of talking things over. They had blades in their hands and murder on their minds.

Yet it was not an ambush. Ambushers do not pull their pants on as they attack.

"I don't think we be welcome," the Trolledyngjan drawled laconically.

I sped a half-dozen arrows. Men dropped. The crew counter-charged the rest.

"Do it quietly!" Colgrave ordered.

They did. Not a word was spoken. Not a warcry disturbed the morning song birds. Only the clang of blades violated the stillness.

I sped a couple more arrows. But the men did not need my help. They had the defenders outnumbered. I turned to Colgrave.

He had the gatekeeper babbling. Aside, he told me, "Lock the gate." I did.

"Come on, Bowman." Colgrave stalked toward the mansion. He left the gatekeeper lying in a widening lake of blood.

A black bird scolded from the limestone wall.

This was the Colgrave of old. This was the mad captain who killed without thought or remorse, who fed on the agony and fear of his victims….

The creature in red was not going to be pleased with him.

I recovered my spent arrows, running from victim to victim so I could keep up with the Old Man. I recognized some of the dead. They had crewed the sorcerer's ship.

The thing they dreaded had overtaken them after all.

"Where are we headed?" I asked Colgrave.

"Cellars. The thing's got to be hiding under the house somewhere."

"Hey! What's going on?" A sleepy, puzzled, powerfully built gentleman of middle years had come onto the mansion's front porch. He still wore his night clothes. Servants peeped fearfully from the doorway behind him.

I never found out who he was. Somebody important. Somebody who had thought he could get the world by the ass if he allied his money and political pull with the magical might of the creature in red. Somebody driven by greed and addicted to power. Somebody laboring under the false impression that his mere presence would be enough to cow low-life rogues like ourselves. Somebody who did not know that deals with devils never come out.

He was in for a big disappointment quick. Nobody faced Colgrave down.

The Old Man grabbed him exactly the way he had grabbed the gateman. The man lunged, could not break Colgrave's hold. "The thing in your cellar. What is it?"

The man's struggles ceased. He became as pale as a corpse. "You know?" he croaked. "That's impossible. Nobody knows. He said that nobody would ever find out...."

"He did? Who is he? What is he?" Aside, "Tor. Toke. Surround the house. Be ready to fire it if I call."

"No! Don't burn...."

"Colgrave does whatever he damn well pleases. Answer me. Where is he? Why did he call us back...?"

"Colgrave?"

"Colgrave. Yes. That Colgrave."

"My God! What has he done?"

I bowed mockingly. "They call me Bowman. Or the Archer."

He fainted.

The servants scattered. Their screams dwindled into the depths of the house.

"Priest. Barley. Mica. Bowman. Trolledyngjan. Come with me." Colgrave stepped over our host, into the house.

"Catch one of the servants."

Mica came up with one in seconds. She was about sixteen. His leer betrayed his thinking.

"Not now," Colgrave growled.

Mica, too, was reverting.

"Girl," Colgrave said, "show us the way to the cellar."

Whimpering, she led us to the kitchens.

"Barley, you go down first."

Barley took a candle. He was back in a minute. "Wine and turnips, Captain."

"Girl, I'll give you to Mica if...."

Something screeched. Lamps overturned and pottery broke in a room behind us. I whirled. A black bird waddled into the kitchens.

I said, "She probably doesn't know, Captain. It's probably a hidden doorway."

Hatred flamed from Colgrave's eye when he glanced my way. "Uhm. Probably." He fingered the gold ring he had plundered from Mica's hoard. "Ah. This way."

We surged back into the front rooms. Everyone pounded panels. "Here," said Colgrave. "Trolledyngjan."

The northman swung his ax. Three resounding blows shattered the panel.

A dark, descending stairway lay behind it. I seized a lamp.

"Barley goes first," the Old Man said. "I'll carry the lamp. Bowman. I want you behind me with an arrow ready."

It would be tight for drawing, but I had my orders.

XII

The stair consisted of more than a hundred steps. I lost count around eighty. It was darker than the bottom side of a buried coffin.

Then light began seeping up to meet us. It was a pale, spectral light, like the glow that sometimes formed on our mastheads in spooky weather. Colgrave stopped.

I glanced back up. The servant girl stood limned in the hole through the panel. The waddling silhouette of a black bird squeezed past her legs. Another fluttered clumsily behind her, awaiting its turn.

We went on. The stair ended. An open door faced its foot. The pale light came splashing through, making Barley look like a ghost.

He went on. He was shaking all over. There was nothing in the universe more deadly than a terrified Barley.

Colgrave followed him. I followed Colgrave. Priest, Mica, and the Trolledyngjan crowded us. We spread out to receive whatever greeting awaited us. Barley was a step or two ahead.

The creature in red reposed on a dark basaltic throne. The floor surrounding it had been inscribed with a pentagram of live fire. The signs and sigils defining its angles and points wriggled and gleamed. The floor itself seemed darker than a midnight sky.

This was the source of light. The only source. There were torches atop the red thing's throne, but they were not alight.

The creature's eyes were closed. A gentle smile lay upon its delicate lips.

"Kill it?" I whispered to Colgrave. I bent my bow.

"Wait. Move aside a little and be ready."

Barley started forward, blade rising. Colgrave caught his sleeve.

At the same instant one of the black birds flopped past us, positioned itself in Barley's path.

"We're here," Colgrave said softly, to himself. "So what do we do now?"

He had altered again. Once more he was the mellowed Colgrave. The old Colgrave did not know the word *we*.

"You don't know?" I whispered.

"Bowman, I'm a man of action. Action begets action, till resolution...."

My goal has been to get here. I haven't thought past that. Now I must. For instance, what happens if we do kill this thing? What happens if we don't? To us, I mean. And to everyone else. Those aren't the kinds of things Colgrave usually worries about."

I understood. Tomorrow had never mattered aboard *Dragon*. Life on that devil ship had been a perpetually frozen Now. Looking backward had been a glance at a foggy place where everything quickly became lost. Looking ahead had consisted of waiting for the next battle, the next victim ship, with perhaps hope for a little rape or drunkenness before we fired her and leaned back to enjoy the screams of her crew. Tomorrow had always been beyond our control, entirely in the hands of whimsical gods.

They had taken remarkable care of us for so long, till they slipped us that left-handed one with the Itaskian sorcerer....

Here we stood at a crossroads. We had to decide on a path, and both went down the back side of a hill. We could only guess which was the better.

If we could even glean a hint of what they were. The trails were virtually invisible from this side of the crest.

"Ready your arrows, Bowman," Colgrave told me. "If he needs it, put the first one between his eyes. Or down his throat. Don't give him time to cast a spell."

"What'll your signal be?"

"You make the decision. There won't be time for signals."

We locked gazes. This was a new Colgrave indeed. Technique was my private province, but the decision to shoot had never been mine.

"Think for *Dragon*," he said. And I realized that that was what *he* was trying to do, and had been for the past several days. And Colgrave was unaccustomed to thinking for or about anyone but himself.

As was I. As was I.

A tremor passed through my limbs. Colgrave saw it. His eyebrows rose in question.

"I'll be all right." I nocked a different arrow. The motion was old and familiar. My hands stopped trembling. "You see?"

He nodded once, jerkily, then spun to face the creature in red.

It remained unchanged. It slept, wearing that insouciant smile. "Wake him up," Colgrave ordered.

Barley started forward.

"Don't enter the pentacle!" the Old Man snapped. "Find another way."

The Trolledyngjan took an amulet from round his neck. "This be having no potency here anyway," he said. He flung it at the sleeper.

It coruscated as it flew. It trailed smoke and droplets of flame. It fell into the sorcerer's lap.

The creature jumped as if stung. Its eyes sprang open. I pulled my arrow to my ear.

Mine were the first eyes it met. It looked down the length of my shaft and slowly settled back to its throne, its hand folded over the amulet in its lap. We had dealt it a stunning surprise, but after that first reaction it hid it well. It turned its gaze from me to Colgrave.

They stared at one another. Neither spoke for several minutes. Time stretched into an eternity. Then the thing in red said, "There is no evading fate, Captain. I see what you mean to do. But you cannot redeem yourself by killing me instead of those whom *I* desire slain. In fact, unless I misread you, you have slain to reach me. Wherefore, then, can you expect redemption?"

His lips were parted a quarter inch, still smiling. They never moved while he spoke. And I was never sure whether I was hearing with my ears or brain.

I do not know what was on Colgrave's mind. The sorcerer's remarks did not deflate him. So I presume that he had seen the paradox already.

"Nor can you win redemption simply through performing acts. There must be sincerity." There was no inflection in his voice, but I swear he was mocking us.

I remembered an old friend who had disappeared long ago. Whaleboats had never been very sincere. Unless he had hidden it damned well.

"The damned can be no more damned than they already are," Colgrave countered. A grim rictus of a smile crossed his tortured face. "Perhaps the not-yet-damned can be spared the horror of those who are."

My eyes never left my target, but my mind ran wild and free. This was Colgrave, the mad captain of the ghost ship? The terror of every man who put to sea? I had known him forever, it seemed, and had never sensed this in him.

We all have our mysterious deeps, I guess. I had been learning a lot about my shipmates lately.

"There is life for you in my service," the sorcerer argued. "There is no life in defying me. What I have once called up I can also banish."

"This be no life," the Trolledyngjan muttered. "We be but *oskoreien* of the sea."

Priest nodded.

Barley was poised to charge. Colgrave caught his sleeve lightly. Like the faithful old dog he was, Barley relaxed.

I relaxed too, letting my bow slack to quarter pull. It was one of the most powerful ever made. Even I could not hold it at full draw long.

I stopped watching the sorcerer's eyes. There was something hypnotic about them, something aimed specially at me.

His hands caught my attention. They began moving as he argued with Colgrave, and I ignored his words for fear there would be something compelling hidden in his voice. His hands, too, were playing at treacheries.

I whipped my shaft back to my ear.

His hands dropped into his lap. He stopped talking, closed his eyes.

A wave of power inundated me. The creature was terrified of me! Of *me!*

It was the power I had felt as *Dragon*'s second most famous crewman, while standing on her poop as we bore down on a victim, my arrows about to slay her helmsman and officers. It was the power that had made me the second most feared phenomenon of the western seas.

It was the absolute power of life and death.

And in that way, I soon realized, he was using me too.

I had the power, and he did fear me, but he was playing to my weakness for that power, hoping that it would betray me into his hands. In fact, he was counting on using all our weaknesses....

He was a bold, courageous, and subtle one, that creature in red. Whatever the stakes in his game, he was not reluctant to risk losing. Not one man in a million would have faced *Dragon*'s crew for a chance at an empire, let alone have recalled us from our fog-bound grave.

He spoke again. And again he made weapons of his hands, his eyes, his voice. But he no longer directed them my way.

He chose Barley. It made a certain sense. Barley was the most wicked killer of us all. But I held the power of death, and Barley would have to get past Colgrave and Priest to take it away from me.

He whirled and charged. And the Trolledyngjan smacked the back of his head with the flat of his ax. Barley pitched forward. He lay still. Colgrave knelt beside him, his eye burning with the old hatred as he glared at the creature in red.

I nodded to the Trolledyngjan. I was pleased to see that I was not alone in my awareness of what the sorcerer was doing.

"I think you just made a mistake," Colgrave said.

"Perhaps. Perhaps I'll send you back to your waiting place. There are other means to my ends. But they're much slower...."

"You shouldn't ought to have done that," Priest said. "Barley was my friend."

What? I thought. You never had a friend in your life, Priest.

One of the black birds shrieked warningly. Colgrave reached out....

Too late. Priest's left hand blurred. A throwing knife flamed across the space between himself and the creature in red.

The sorcerer writhed aside. The blade slashed his left shoulder. His left hand rose, a finger pointing. He screamed something.

"Wizard!" I snarled.

And loosed my shaft.

It passed through his hand and smoked away into darkness. He looked down the length of my next shaft. His bloody hand dropped into his lap.

Pain and rage seethed in him, but he fought for control. He wadded his robe around his hand.

My gaze flicked to Colgrave. We had a stand-off here. And unless the Old Man did something, that wizard would pick us off one by one. Colgrave had to decide which way to jump.

Colgrave had to? But he had told me.... But....

XIII

All the black birds had joined us. They were big. I called them albatrosses, but their size was the only thing they had in common. They lined up between us and the wizard. Their pupilless yellow eyes seemed to take in everything at the same time.

They were doing their damnedest to make sure we knew they were there.

I had always been aware of them. For me they had become as much a part of *Dragon* as Colgrave or myself. What were they? Lurkers over carrion? Celestial emissaries? Sometimes, because I sympathized with their plight, I wanted to make them something more that what they were.

Those sentinels posted by a dead man were as trapped as we. Maybe more than we were. Their exit might be even narrower.

Neither Colgrave nor the creature in red paid them any heed. To those two the birds were squawking nuisances left from another time.

Those squawking nuisances had been trying to guide us since our recall. We had seldom heeded them. Maybe we should have.

Why were they trying to intercede? That had to be beyond their original writ. That, surely, had been but to keep their summoner informed of what was happening amongst *things* he could only banish, not destroy.

I suppose his last-second death compelled them to interpret their mission for themselves.

One squawked and threw itself into the pentagram.

There were sorceries upon that bird. It was nothing of this world. The spells shielding the thing in red were less efficacious against it than they had been against arrow, dagger, or amulet.

Nonetheless, it fell before it reached the sorcerer. The stench of smoldering feathers assailed my nostrils. Smoke boiled off the writhing bird. It emitted some of the most pathetic sounds I had ever heard.

Then, like the bird the sorcerer had downed at sea, it became a snake of smoke and slithered off like black lightning, through air and cellar wall....
I presumed.

The thing in red had begun some silent enchantment. We now faced it amidst a vast plain, walled by mists instead of limestone.

A second bird threw itself into the pentacle the instant the first changed and hurtled off.

It penetrated a foot farther. Then a third flopped clumsily forward, achieving perhaps fourteen inches more than the second.

Mica's voice echoed eerily from the mist behind us. "Captain. Bowman. Hurry up. There's a big mob in the street. They're armed. We're in trouble if they break in."

Another bird hurled itself at the sorcerer. This one managed to sink a beak into an ankle.

The sorcerer called down a thunderbolt. It scattered flesh and feathers.

Another leapt.

The Old Man said, "Have Toke and Tor gather the men behind the house, Sailmaker. If we're not up in ten minutes, go back to *Dragon*. Tell them not to wait for us. They'll have to clear the Estuary before the fleet gets back from Cape Blood."

"Captain!"

I could read Mica's thoughts. What would they do without Colgrave? *Dragon* would become lifeless without the dead captain's will animating it.

"Do as I say, Sailmaker."

Two black birds threw themselves into the pentacle together. The sorcerer got the first in midair. The second landed in his lap, tearing with beak and talons. They *had* to be driven by more than their original assignment. Maybe the gods were interceding....

Barley clambered to his feet with the Old Man's help. He was groggy. Colgrave dithered round him.

The grumble of a crowd working itself up reached the cellar.

We were in trouble.

"Maybe we ought to run for it," Priest suggested.

Colgrave hit him with that one cold eye. "Colgrave doesn't run." Then, "We have an enemy here." He indicated the thing in red. "He's decided to send us back. We have to stop him. Sixty men counting on us.... I don't want any of us to go back. It's forever this time."

"I'll buy that," I muttered. It reflected my thinking of the moment. But I was surprised to hear it from the Old Man. It was not his kind of thinking.

It seemed that the black birds had been trying to stop us from compounding our sins. That was all I could get their admonitory squawks to add to. "Sorry, guys," I murmured. A sin or two looked necessary for the greater welfare.

I did not want to see that quiet, fog-bound sea again. Eighteen years was long enough. The others felt the same.

I could see just one way out of it. Kill the sorcerer in red.

Another murder.

What was one more death on my soul? I asked myself. Not a penny-weight.

The last black bird hurled itself into the pentagram.

The sorcerer was covered with blood, reddening its clothing even more. Pain had destroyed the delicacy of its face. And yet a tiny smile began to stretch its lips again.

I drew to my ear and let an arrow fly.

The others had the same idea at the same instant. The Trolledyngjan hurled his ax. Priest and Barley flung themselves against the waning Power of the pentagram. Colgrave drew his blade and followed at a more casual pace. The Trolledyngjan whipped out a dagger and joined him. My arrow and the Trolledyngjan's ax did not survive the smashing fist of a lightning bolt. Both weapons touched the creature in red, but only lightly.

The last bird became another serpent of night and slithered off to wherever they went when they devolved.

The spells protecting the sorcerer gnawed at Priest and Barley. They screamed like souls in torment.

And kept on.

They were Colgrave's favorite hounds, those two. Because nothing stopped them.

They had been the two most dreaded in-fighters on the western sea.

A continual low moan emanated from the Trolledyngjan. Colgrave made no sound at all. He just leaned ahead like a man striding into a gale, his eye fixed on the sorcerer's throat.

Priest and Barley went down. They writhed the way the birds had. But they kept trying to get to the creature in red. Barley's blade struck sparks from the stone beside the wizard's ankle.

Its smile grew larger. It thought it was winning.

I sped three arrows as fast as I could.

The first did no good at all. The second pinked him lightly. It distracted him for an instant.

His attackers surged at him, threatening to bury him.

I sent my third arrow beneath Colgrave's upraised arm. It buried itself in the creature's heart.

The Old Man's blade fell. It sliced the flesh away from one side of that delicate face.

The thing slowly stood. A mournful wail came from between its motionless lips. The sound rose in pitch and grew louder and louder. I dropped my bow and clapped my hands over my ears.

That did not help. The sound battered me till I ached.

The Trolledyngjan was down with Priest and Barley. I did not expect them to rise ever again.

The creature in red touched Colgrave. My captain started to drop too.

He fell slowly, like a mighty kingdom crumbling.

"Go, Bowman," he told me in a voice that was hardly a whisper, yet which I heard through the sorcerer's wail. "Take *Dragon* back to sea. Save the men."

"Captain!" I seized his arm and tried to drag him away. The thing in red touched him. The touch anchored the Old Man.

"Get the hell out of here!" he growled. "I'll handle him."

"But...."

"That's an order, Bowman."

He was my Captain. These were my comrades. My friends.

"Will you get the hell gone?"

He used the old Colgrave's voice. It was strong. Compelling. I could defy it then no more than ever before. I seized my bow and fled.

XIV

The others had needed little urging to make a run for it. Mica and the Kid were the only ones hanging around when I hit the mansion's door. Not counting the owner and half an army of citizens headed our way.

It was your basic mob. A ravening killer monster made up of harmless shopkeepers. An organism without fear because it knew its components were replaceable.

Mica screeched. "Come on, Bowman! You going to wait till they tie you to a burning stake?"

I was not as numb as I looked. I was looking for the thousand-eyed monster's brain cells. I had eight good arrows left.

But Mica was right. The mob did not have a brain. Random fragments had begun vandalizing the grounds.

I took off round the side of the house.

As we loped along, the Kid asked, "What happened down there? Where's Barley and Priest and the Trolledyngjan and the Old Man?"

"Down there. All gone but the Old Man and the sorcerer. The thing is all chopped up, but it's still alive."

"You left him there?"

"He made me, Kid. You ever win an argument with Colgrave?"

He just grinned.

"Hold up for a second, Bowman," Mica panted. We were in the street now and drawing some startled looks. "What happens when they go?"

"What?"

"Colgrave runs us. What do we do without him? And that wizard called us back. What happens when he dies? To his spells?"

"Oh. Man, I don't know." I was no expert on wizardry. Some sorceries devolved with the death of the sorcerer, and some did not. I could not tell him what he wanted to know.

There were shouts behind us. I wheeled. Part of the mob was after us.

"Let's take them," the Kid said.

There were about twenty of them. For a *Dragon* sailor, protected by the Bowman, the odds did not look bad.

The earth started quivering like a bear in restless slumber. The timbers of nearby buildings creaked.

Our pursuers stopped, looked back.

We could see the steep tiled roofs of the mansion. Cracks lightninged across them. They began sagging, as if some huge invisible hand were pressing downward....

The cracks leaked a black fog that looked first cousin to the one that dogged *Vengeful D.* The breeze did nothing to disperse it.

"Let's hike," I said. "While they're distracted. Maybe we can catch the others."

I was afraid Toke and Tor would sail without us.

Could anger be an absolute? The cloud over the mansion said it could be. I felt it from a quarter-mile away.

That shadow was a being. It echoed the feeling I had been given by the creature in red. I now understood our ambiguous reactions to the sorcerer. He or she had no meaning if the thing were not human at all.

It was not alone. A second being held it in a death grip. That being radiated an absoluteness too, an utter refusal to yield to any other will.

"Colgrave," I whispered.

Colgrave had been a man, of that there was no doubt. But he had been larger than life and animated by a determination so unswerving that it had made him a demigod.

"Children of evil." Mica muttered.

We resumed walking toward the waterfront. No one interfered. We were forgotten.

The Torian Hill shook like a volcano about to give birth.

"What?" I asked.

"We are all children of evil," Mica said.

"What're you talking about?" He was off on some sideways line of thought, saying the obvious and not meaning what he was saying. "Keep stepping. I don't think the Old Man will win this one."

"He already has, Bowman. He's forced that thing to take it's natural form. Look, it's fading. It can't stay here that way."

He was right. The thing was evaporating the way a cloud of steam does.

So was the thing created by the will of my Captain.

In minutes they were gone.

There were tears in my eyes. Mine. The Bowman's. And I was the deadliest, coldest, most remorseless killer ever to sail the western seas, excepting only the man for whom my tears fell.

I had hated him with a passion as deep and black and cold as the water in the ocean's deepest deeps. Yet I was weeping for him.

I averted my face from the others.

I had not wept since I did not know when. Maybe after I had killed my wife, when I had been alive and still one of the smaller evils plaguing the world.

We reached *Dragon*. They had the mooring lines in but the gangplank still down. The crew manned the rail. Their eyes were on the hills behind the city. Their faces showed relief when we raced onto the wharf. Then dismay when they realized we three were the last.

They had the drunk at the head of the gangplank, holding him like a hostage against Portsmouth's ill-will.

"The others?" Toke asked.

"They won't be coming," I replied.

"What do we do?"

"You're asking me?" He was First Officer. He should have taken charge.

He looked me in the eye. He did not have to speak to tell me that he was no Colgrave, that he was incapable of commanding *Vengeful Dragon*.

I glanced around. Every eye fixed me with that same expectant stare.

I am the Bowman, I thought. Second only to Colgrave.... Second to none, now. "All right. Mica. Take the old guy and leave him on the wharf. Healthy. Tor, stand by to make sail."

Some of them looked at me oddly. Letting the drunk go was not *Dragon*'s style.

But *Dragon* had changed. We had learned, just a little, the meaning of pity and mercy.

"Give him something to tell his grandkids," I remarked to Tor, whose disappointment was obvious. He was the most bloodthirsty and unchanged member of the crew.

A breeze rose as the gangplank came in. It was a perfect breeze. It would carry us into the channel at just the right speed. I assumed Colgrave's old place on the poop and peered at the sky. "You still with us?" I murmured.

I started. For an instant I thought I saw faces in the racing clouds. Strange, alien faces with eyes of ice, in which no hint of motivation could be read.

Was this what Colgrave had seen? Had he just looked up whenever he wanted to know if the gods were still with us?

I had a lot to learn if I was going to replace the Old Man.... I looked at the clouds again. I saw nothing but clouds. Imagination?

I paused to reflect on the fact that I was the only survivor among *Dragon*'s four greatest evils.

Why? What had they done that I had not? Or was it the reverse?

The crew seemed thin. How many had been redeemed? "Toke, take a muster."

"I have, Captain. We lost five besides those you know. One-Hand Nedo. Fat Poppo...."

"Poppo? Really? He said he knew.... I'm glad for him. But we'll miss them all."

"We will, Captain."

Mica's "We are all children of evil" returned to me. I think I understood now. He was stating the reason why I could not understand why some had been redeemed and some not. The evil in us was such that we could not recognize facts laid openly before us. It would take a moment of truth, an instant of revelation, to drive the message home.

I remembered sitting with Priest and Mica and the Kid, fishing, pulling in a sand shark that just could not quit hitting our hooks. I glanced at the clouds and wondered if they would quit trying to teach that stupid shark.

XV

The dividing line between the sea and the Silverbind's flood is as sharp as a pen stroke. Turgid brown against slightly choppy jade. The two do not mix till you are out of sight of land.

Dragon is in the brown, straining toward the green. We have bent on every piece of canvas we can find. Lank Tor is up top yelling things nobody wants to hear.

"Another one, Captain. On the starboard quarter."

Their sails crowd the north. They came back in a hurry.

I try to think like Colgrave. What would he do?

Colgrave would fight. Colgrave always fought.

I try to remember his face. I cannot. The forgetfulness of *Dragon* is at work. Before long he, and the others, will be completely forgotten and we'll have a whole new style.

It is necessary. Colgrave was incapable of backing down. But *Dragon* is no longer invincible. These Itaskians' fathers proved how vincible we are. They just have to be willing to pay an extreme price.

I look at the clouds. "You tired of hauling in the same stupid sharks?"

A distant cloud wears a face for an instant. I swear it sticks out its tongue.

The tongue is lightning. It stabs the sea. "Steer for that," I order. The helmsman shifts our heading.

Another bolt falls. Then another and another. The sky grows dark. The wind picks up. *Dragon* fairly dances toward the sudden foul weather. The sails in the north seem to bounce in anger as this slim chance to escape develops.

"Damn you!" I shake a fist at the sky. For an instant I think I hear mocking laughter.

The seasickness is grinding my entrails already. It will be tearing me apart after we hit the storm.

The gods do have senses of humor. But the level seems to be that which ties the tails of cats for draping over clotheslines.

Lightning bolts are falling like the javelins of a celestial army. The helmsman is nervous. He keeps glancing my way, awaiting the order to turn away. Others join him.

Nobody asks questions.

My predecessor trained them well.

Now the bolts are hitting the sea around us. We have never seen anything like this....

"Tor?"

"They're coming after us, Captain."

Those bold, brave fools. They would be. They know the game well now. They know they have to be as determined as we.

The granddaddy bolt of them all hits the mainmast. Tor shrieks. The mast snaps. Topmen scream. The Kid tumbles through the rigging and hits the main deck with a thud I can hear over the roar of wind and sea. The masts, the spars, the lines and stays all begin to glow. *Dragon* crawls with a pale, cold fire that must be visible for miles.

She rides up a mountainous wave and plunges down its nether side.

Darkness comes, sudden and sharp as a sword stroke.

I am striding across the poop when it does, intending to take a look at the Kid.

I trip into the rail when the light returns as suddenly as it went. I catch myself, look around.

We are in a bank of dense fog. The sea is absolutely still. "Damned! No."

The fog thins quickly. I can see my command.

The men are scattered over the decks, motionless, eyes glassy. I know where we are, what has happened. We have returned to the beginning, and Colgrave's sacrifices were in vain.

The jokes of the gods can be damned cruel.

The fog gives way. We glide into the heart of a circle of lifeless jade sea. Lethargy gnaws at me. It takes all my will to take up my bow so I can use it as a prop on which to lean.

I will not go down. I will not fall. I refuse. *They* do not have the Power....

Dragon eases to a stop and begins revolving slowly in the imperceptible current. The featureless face of the fog slides past. The mist overhead is light sometimes, and sometimes dark. It does not make an exciting day. Before long I lose interest in counting the days.

It will not be long before I cease to think at all.

Till then, I must try to find the answer. What did I do wrong?

SEVERED HEADS

The following story is one of my favorites of everything that I've done. Partly, that is, because it was so very successful, having been reprinted so many times overseas that it earned me more, in its time, than most of my novels had. Then, too, at its core lie elements of a family legend.

I

Narriman was ten when the black rider came to Wadi al Hamamah. He rode tall and arrogant upon a courser as white as his djellaba was black. He looked neither right nor left as he passed among the tents. Old men spat at his horse's hooves. Old women made warding signs. Children and dogs whined and fled. Makram's ass set up a horrible braying.

Narriman was not frightened, just confused. Who was this stranger? Why were her people frightened? Because he wore black? No tribe she knew wore black. Black was the color of ifrits and djinn, of the Masters of Jebal al Alf Dhulquarneni, the high, dark mountains brooding over Wadi al Hamamah and the holy places of the al Muburak.

Narriman was a bold one. Her elders warned her often, but she would not behave as fit her sex. The old ones shook their heads and said that brat of Mowfik's would be no good. Mowfik himself was suspect enough, what with his having gone to the great wars of the north. What business were those of the al Muburak?

Narriman stayed and watched the rider.

He reined in before her father's tent, which stood apart, drew a black rod from his javelin case, breathed upon it. Its tips glowed. He set that glow against the tent, sketched a symbol. The old folks muttered and cursed and told one another they'd known despair would haunt Mowfik's tent.

Narriman ran after the stranger, who rode down the valley toward the shrine. Old Farida shouted after her. She pretended not to hear. She dodged from shadow to shadow, rock to rock, to the hiding place from which she spied on the rites of her elders.

She watched the rider pass through the Circle with arrogance unconquered. He did not glance at Karkur, let alone make obeisance and offerings. She expected the Great Death to strike him ere he left the Circle, but he rode on, untouched. She watched him out of sight. Narriman stared at the god. Was Karkur, too, a frightened antique? She was shaken. Karkur's anger was a constant. Each task, each pleasure, had to be integrated with his desires. He was an angry god. But he had sat there like a red stone lump while a heathen defiled his Circle.

The sun was in the west when she returned to camp. Old Farida called her immediately. She related what she had seen. The old folks muttered and whispered and made their signs.

"Who was he, Farida? What was he? Why were you afraid?"

Farida spat through the gap in her teeth. "The Evil One's messenger. A shaghûn out of the Jebal." Farida turned her old eyes on the Mountains of a Thousand Sorcerers. She made her magic sign. "It's a mercy your mother didn't live to see this."

"Why?"

But just then the guard horn sounded, ending on a triumphant note. The hunters had returned. Karkur had favored the tribe. Narriman ran to tell her father about the stranger.

II

Mowfik had an antelope behind his saddle, a string of quail, a brace of hares, and even a box terrapin. "A great hunt, Little Fox. Never was it so fine. Even Shukri took his game." Shukri could do nothing right. He was, probably, the man Narriman would wed, because she was her mother's daughter.

Her father was so pleased she did not mention the stranger. The other hunters heard from the old ones. Dour eyes turned Mowfik's way. Narriman was afraid for him till she sensed that they felt pity. There was a lot of nodding. The stranger's visit confirmed their prejudices.

Mowfik stopped outside their tent. "Little Fox, we won't sleep much tonight. I hope you've gathered plenty of wood."

She heard the weariness in his voice. He had worked harder than the others. He had no woman to ride behind and clean game, no woman to help here at home. Only old Farida, his mother's sister, bothered to offer.

Narriman took the quail and hares, arranged them on a mat. She collected her tools, stoked up the fire, settled down to work.

The sun settled westward and slightly south. A finger of fire broke between peaks and stabbed into the wadi, dispelling shadows. Mowfik glanced up.

He turned pale. His mouth opened and closed. Finally, he gurgled, "What?"

She told him about the rider.

He sat with head bent low. "Ah, no. Not my Little Fox." And, in response to an earlier question. "There are those even Karkur dares not offend. The rider serves one greater than he." Then, thoughtfully, "But perhaps he's shown the way. There must be a greater reason than a feast when game runs to the hunter's bow." He rose, walked into the shadows, stared at those dread mountains that no tribe dared invade. Then he said, "Cook only the meat that might spoil before we get it smoked."

"Tell me what it means, Father."

"I suppose you're old enough. You've been Chosen. The Masters sent him to set their mark. It's been a long time since the shaghûn came. The last was in my mother's time."

III

Mowfik had been north and had bathed in alien waters. He could think the unthinkable. He could consider defying the Masters. He dug into his war booty to buy Makram's ass. He loaded all he possessed on two animals and walked away. He looked back only once. "I should never have come back."

They went north over game trails, through the high, rocky places, avoiding other tribes. They spent twelve days in the hills before descending to a large oasis. For the first time Narriman saw people who lived in houses. She remained close to Mowfik. They were strange.

"There. In the east. That is el Aswad, the Wahlig's fortress." Narriman saw a great stone tent crowning a barren hill. "And there, four days' ride, lies Sebil el Selib, the pass to the sea." He pointed northeast. His arm swung to encompass the west. "Out there lies the great erg called Hammad al Nakir."

Heat shimmered over the Desert of Death. For a moment she thought she saw the fairy towers of fallen Ilkazar, but that was imagination born of stories Mowfik had brought home from his adventures. Ilkazar had been a ruin for four centuries.

"We'll water here, cross the erg, and settle over there. The shaghûn will never find us."

It took eight days, several spent lost, to reach Wadi el Kuf, the only oasis in the erg. It took fourteen more to finish and find a place to settle.

The new life was bewildering. The people spoke the same language, but their preoccupations were different. Narriman thought she would go mad before she learned their ways. But learn she did. She was the bold one, Mowfik's daughter, who could question everything and believe only that which suited her. She and her father remained outsiders, but less so than among their own people. Narriman liked the settled people better. She missed only old Farida and Karkur. Mowfik insisted that Karkur was with them in spirit.

IV

Narriman was twelve when the rider reappeared.

She was in the fields with her friends Ferial and Feras. It was a stony, tired field. Ferial's father had bought it cheap, offering Mowfik a quarter interest if he would help prove it up. That morning, while the children dug stones and piled them into a wall, Mowfik and his partner were elsewhere. Feras had been malingering all morning, and was the scorn of Narriman and his sister. He saw the rider first.

He was barely visible against a background of dark rocks and shadow. He was behind a boulder which masked all but his horse's head. But he was there. Just watching. Narriman shuddered. How had he found them?

He served the Masters. Their necromancy was great. Mowfik had been foolish to think they could escape

"Who is he?" Ferial asked. "Why are you afraid?"

"I'm not afraid," Narriman lied. "He's a shaghûn." Here in the north some lords had shaghûns of their own. She had to add, "He rides for the Masters of the Jebal."

Ferial laughed.

Narriman said, "You'd believe if you had lived in the shadow of the Jebal."

Feras said, "The Little Fox is a bigger liar than her namesake."

Narriman spit at his feet. "You're so brave, huh?"

"He doesn't scare me."

"Then come with me to ask what he wants."

Feras looked at Narriman, at Ferial, and at Narriman again. Male pride would not let him back down.

Narriman had her pride too. I'll go just a little way, she told herself. Just far enough to make Feras turn tail. I won't go near him.

Her heart fluttered. Feras gasped, ran to catch up. Ferial called, "Come back, Feras. I'll tell Father."

Feras groaned. Narriman would have laughed had she not been so frightened. Feras was trapped between pride and punishment.

The certainty of punishment made him stick. He meant to make the whipping worth the trouble. No girl would outbrave him.

They were seventy yards away when Feras ran. Narriman felt the hard touch of the shaghûn's eyes. A few steps more, just to prove Feras was bested.

She took five long, deliberate steps, stopped, looked up. The shaghûn remained immobile. His horse tossed its head, shaking off flies. A different horse, but the same man.... She met his eyes.

Something threw a bridle upon her soul. The shaghûn beckoned, a gentle come hither. Her feet moved. Fifty yards. Twenty-five. Ten. Her fear mounted. The shaghûn dismounted, eyes never leaving hers. He took her arm, drew her into the shadow of the boulder. Gently, he pushed her back against the rock.

"What do you want?"

He removed the cloth across his face.

He was just a man! A young man, no more than twenty. He wore the ghost of a smile, and was not unhandsome, but his eyes were cold, without mercy.

His hand came to her, removed the veil she had begun wearing only months ago. She shivered like a captive bird.

"Yes," he whispered. "As beautiful as they promised." He touched her cheek.

She could not escape his eyes. Gently, gently, he tugged here, untied there, lifted another place, and she was more naked than at any moment since birth.

In her heart she called to Karkur. Karkur had ears of stone. She shivered as she recalled Mowfik saying that there were powers before whom Karkur must nod.

The shaghûn piled their clothing into a narrow pallet. She gasped when he stood up, and tried to break his spell by sealing her eyes. It did no good. His hands took her naked flesh and gently forced her down.

He drove a burning brand into her, punishing her for having dared flee. Despite her determination, she whimpered, begged him to stop. There was no mercy in him.

The second time there was less pain. She was numb. She ground her eyelids together and endured. She did not give him the pleasure of begging.

The third time she opened her eyes as he entered her. His gaze caught hers.

The effect was a hundred times what it had been when he had called her. Her soul locked with his. She became part of him. Her pleasure was as great, as all-devouring, as her pain the first time. She begged, but not for mercy.

Then he rose, snatched his clothing, and she cried again, shame redoubled because he had made her enjoy what he was doing.

His movements were no longer languid and assured. He dressed hastily and sloppily. There was fear in his eyes. He leaped onto his mount and dug in his heels.

Narriman rolled into a tight ball of degradation and pain, and wept.

V

Men shouted. Horses whinnied. "He went that way!"

"There he goes! After him!"

Mowfik swung down and cast his cloak over Narriman. She buried her face in his clothing.

The thunder of hooves, the cries of outrage and the clang of weapons on shields, receded. Mowfik touched her. "Little Fox?"

"Go away. Let me die."

"No. This will pass. This will be forgotten. There's no forgetting death." His voice choked on rage. "They'll catch him. They'll bring him back. I'll give you my own knife."

"They won't catch him. He has the Power. I couldn't fight him. He made me *want* him. Go away. Let me die."

"No." Mowfik had been to the wars in the north. He had seen rape. Women survived. The impact was more savage when the victim was one of one's own, but that part of him that was Man and not outraged father knew that this was not the end.

"You know what they'll say." Narriman wrapped his cloak about her. "Ferial and Feras will tell what they saw. People will think I went willingly. They'll call me whore. And what they call me I'll have to be. What man would have me now?"

Mowfik sighed. He heard truth. When the hunters returned, chastened by losing the man in their own territory, they would seek excuses for failing, would see in a less righteous light. "Get dressed."

"Let me die, Father. Let me take my shame off your shoulders."

"Stop that. Get dressed. We have things to do. We'll sell while people are sympathetic. We started over here. We can start again somewhere else. Up. Into your clothes. Do you want them to see you like this? Time to make the brave show."

All her life he had said that, whenever people hurt her. "Time to make the brave show."

Tears streaming, she dressed. "Did you say that to Mother, too?" Her mother had been brave, a northern girl who had come south out of love. She had been more outsider than Mowfik.

"Yes. Many times. And I should've held my tongue. I should've stayed in the north. None of this would have happened had we stayed with her people."

Mowfik's partner did not try to profit from his distress. He paid generously. Mowfik did not have to waste war booty to get away.

VI

A Captain Al Jahez, who Mowfik had served in the wars, gave him a position as a huntsman. He and Narriman had now fled eight hundred miles from Wadi al Hamamah.

Narriman began to suspect the worst soon after their arrival. She remained silent till it became impossible to deceive herself. She went to Mowfik because there was nowhere else to go.

"Father, I'm with child."

He did not react in the traditional way. "Yes. His purpose was to breed another of his kind."

"What will we do?" She was terrified. Her tribe had been unforgiving. The settled peoples were only slightly less so in these matters.

"There's no need to panic. I discussed this with Al Jahez when we arrived. He's a hard and religious man, but from el Aswad originally. He knows what comes out of the Jebal. His goatherd is old. He'll send us into the hills to replace him. We'll stay away a few years while he stamps your widowhood into everyone's mind. You'll come back looking young for your age. Men will do battle for such a widow."

"Why are you so kind? I've been nothing but trouble since the rider came down the wadi."

"You're my family. All I have. I live by the way of the Disciple, unlike so many who profess his creed only because it's politic."

"And yet you bow to Karkur."

He smiled. "One shouldn't overlook any possibility. I'll speak with Al Jahez. We'll go within the week."

Life in the hills, herding goats, was not unpleasant. The land was hard, reminding Narriman of home. But this was tamer country. Wolves and lions were few. The kids were not often threatened.

As her belly swelled and the inevitable drew near, she grew ever more frightened. "Father, I'm not old enough for this. I'm going to die. I know it."

"No, you won't." He told her that her mother, too, had grown frightened. That all women were afraid. He did not try to convince her that her fears were groundless, only that fear was more dangerous than giving birth. "I'll be with you. I won't let anything happen. And Al Jahez promises he'll send his finest midwife."

"Father, I don't understand why you're so good to me. And I'm baffled as to why he's so good to you. He can't care that much because you rode in his company."

Mowfik shrugged. "Perhaps because I saved his life at the Battle of the Circles. Also, there are more just men than you believe."

"You never talk about the wars. Except about places you saw."

"Those aren't happy memories, Little Fox. Dying and killing and dying. And in the end, nothing gained, either for myself or for the glory of the Lord. Will you tell the young ones about these days when you're old? Those days weren't happy, but I saw more than any al Muburak before or since."

He was the only one of a dozen volunteers who survived. And maybe that, instead of the foreign wife, was why he had become an outcast. The old folks resented him for living when their own sons were dead.

"What will we do with a baby, Father?"

"What? What people always do. Raise him to be a man."

"It'll be a boy, will it?"

"I doubt me not it will, but a girl will be as welcome." He chuckled.

"Will you hate him?"

"We are talking about my daughter's child. I can hate the father, but not the infant. The child is innocent."

"You did travel in strange lands. No wonder the old ones didn't like you."

"Old ones pass on. Ideas are immortal. So says the Disciple."

She felt better afterward, but her fear never evaporated.

<h2 style="text-align:center">VII</h2>

"A fine son," the old woman said with a toothless smile. "A fine son. I foretell you now, little mistress, he'll be a great one. See it here, in his hands." She held the tiny, purplish, wrinkled, squalling thing high. "And he came forth with the cap. Only the truly destined, the chosen ones, come forth with that. Aye, you've mothered a mighty one."

Narriman smiled though she heard not a tenth of the babble. She cared only that the struggle was over, that the pain had receded. There was a great warmth in her for the child, but she hadn't the strength to express it.

Mowfik ducked into the tent. "Sadhra. Is everything all right?" His face was pale. Dimly, Narriman realized he had been frightened too.

"Both came through perfectly. Al Jahez has a godson of whom he can be proud." She repeated her predictions.

"Old Mother, you'd better not tell him that. That smacks of superstition. He's strict about religious deviation."

"The decrees of men, be they mere men or Chosen of the Lord, can't change natural law. Omens are omens."

"May be. May be. Shouldn't you give her the child?"

"Aye. So I should. I'm hogging him because one day I'll be able to say I held such a one." She dropped the infant to Narriman's breast. He took the nipple, but without enthusiasm.

"Don't you worry, little mistress. Soon he'll suckle hearty."

"Thank you, Sadhra," Mowfik said. "Al Jahez chose well. I'm in both your debts."

"It was my honor, sir." She left the tent.

"Such a one, eh, Little Fox? Making him the Hammer of God before he draws his first breath."

Narriman stared up at him. He wasn't just tired. He was disturbed. "The rider?"

SEVERED HEADS — 195

"He's out there."

"I thought so. I felt him."

"I stalked him, but he eluded me. I didn't dare go far."

"Perhaps tomorrow." As she drifted into sleep, though, she thought, You'll never catch him. He'll deceive you with the Power. No warrior will catch him. Time or trickery will be his death.

She slept. And she dreamed of the rider and the way it had been for her the third time.

She dreamed that often. It was one thing she kept from Mowfik. He would not understand. She did not understand herself.

Maybe she *was* a whore at heart.

VIII

Narriman called the child Misr Sayed bin Hammad al Muburaki, meaning he was Misr Sayed son of the desert, of the al Muburak tribe. Hammad could be a man's name also, so it became that of her missing husband. Misr's grandfather, however, called him Towfik el-Masiri, or Camel's Feet, for reasons only he found amusing.

Misr grew quickly, learned rapidly, and was startlingly healthy. Seldom was he colicky or cranky, even when cutting teeth. He was happy most of the time, and always had a big hug for his grandfather. Narriman remained perpetually amazed that she could feel so much love for one person. "How do women love more than one child?" she asked.

Mowfik shrugged. "It's a mystery to me. I was my mother's only. You're your mother's only."

The first two years were idyllic. The baby and the goats kept them too busy to worry. In the third year, though, Mowfik grew sour. His heart was not in his play with Misr. One day Narriman found him honing his war sword and watching the hills. Then she understood. He expected the rider.

The prospect fired her fantasies. She ached for the shaghûn. She held her left hand near the fire till pain burned the lust away.

Shortly after Misr's third birthday Mowfik said, "I'm going to see Al Jahez. It's time you became Hammad's widow."

"Will we be safer there? Won't the shaghûn just ride in like he did before?"

"Al Jahez thinks not. He thinks the priests can drive him away."

Narriman went to the tent flap, surveyed the unfriendly hills. "Go see him. I'm afraid to go back where people might cry shame, but I'm more scared of the shaghûn."

"I'd hoped you'd feel that way."

She had begun to relax. The night had passed without incident. Mowfik should be back by noon. If she could stay too busy to worry....

It was almost noon when Misr called, "Mama, Grandpa coming." She sighed, put her mending aside, and went to meet him.

"Oh, no. Karkur defend us." Misr could not be blamed for his mistake. He'd seldom seen anyone but Mowfik on horseback.

The shaghûn was far down the valley, coming toward her. He seemed larger than life, like a far city seen through the shimmer over the great erg. He came at an unhurried walk. The rise and fall of his animal's legs was hypnotic. He did not seem to draw any closer.

"Go into the tent, Misr."

"Mama?"

"Do it. And don't come out till I tell you. No matter what."

"Mama, what's wrong?"

"Misr! Go!"

"Mama, you're scaring me."

She gave him her fiercest look. He scooted inside. "And close the flap." She turned. The rider looked twice as big but no nearer. His pace was no faster. The pain in her heart grew with the heat in her loins. She knew he would take her, and her evil side called to him eagerly.

He came closer. She thought of running into the hills. But what good that? He would hunt her down. And Misr would be left alone.

She snatched the bow Mowfik used for hunting, sped an arrow toward the rider. She missed.

She was good with that weapon. Better than her father, who remained perpetually amazed that a woman could do anything better than a man. She should not have missed. She sped a second and third arrow.

Each missed. The fourth plucked at his djellaba, but only because he was so close. There was no fifth. She had seen his eyes.

The bow fell from her hand. He dismounted and walked toward her, reaching.

Only one moment from the next hour stuck with her. Misr came outside, saw the rider thrusting into her, ran over and bit him on the buttocks. That would remain with her forever, in that mixture of amusement and pain such a thing could recall.

Afterward he stared into her eyes. His will beat against her. She dwindled into sleep.

Cursing wakened her. It was the violent cursing of savagery and hatred. She was too lazy to open her eyes.

She recalled the inexorable approach of the man in black coming up the valley on a line as straight as the arrow of time. She recalled his touch, her fevered response. She felt the sun on her naked shame. She flew up, wrapped herself in discarded clothing.

Mowfik belabored a fallen tree with his axe, cursing steadily. He blasphemed both Karkur and the Lord of the Disciple. She scrambled into her clothing, frightened.

Exhaustion stopped Mowfik. He settled on the tree trunk and wept. Narriman went to comfort him.

"It's all right, Father. He didn't hurt me. He shamed me again, but he didn't hurt me." She put her arms around him. "It'll be all right, Father."

"Little Fox, he took Misr. It wasn't you this time."

IX

Narriman changed, hardened, saddened. The Narriman of Wadi al Hamamah would not have recognized her. That Narriman would have been terrified by her.

Mowfik took her to see Al Jahez. The captain was properly outraged. He set his men to scouring the country. He sent an alarm across the kingdom. He appealed to the Most Holy Mrazkim Shrines for a Writ of Anathema, and for prayers for the Lord's intervention.

"And that is all I can do. And it's pointless. He won't be seen. Those who serve the Masters come and go as they please."

"Can't somebody do something?" Narriman demanded. "How long has this been going on? How many women have had to suffer this?"

"It's gone on forever," Al Jahez said. "It went on throughout the age of Empire. It went on before the Empire was born. It'll go on tomorrow, too."

"Why isn't it stopped?"

"Because no one can stop it. One of the Emperors tried. He sent an army into the Jebal. Not one man returned."

She was venting frustration. She knew the futility of battling the Masters. No, this was personal. This was between herself and one shaghûn. The Masters were but shadows beyond the horizon, too nebulous to factor into the emotional equation.

"That man took my son. *My* son. I don't recognize his claim. He did nothing but force me onto my back."

"Narriman?" Mowfik said, baffled.

"I want my son back."

"We can't do anything about that," Al Jahez said. "The shaghûn is who he is, and we're who we are."

"No."

"Narriman?" Again Mowfik was puzzled.

"I thought about this all day, Father. I'm going after Misr."

Al Jahez said, "But you're a child. And a woman."

"I've grown up in the past few years. I'm small, but I'm no child. As to my sex, say what you will. It won't change my mind."

"Narriman!"

"Father, will you stop saying that? You stood by me when I begged you not to. You drowned me in love I did not deserve. Stand by me now. Give me what I need to get Misr back. Teach me what I need to know."

Al Jahez shook his head. "Mowfik, you were right. She *is* remarkable."

"Little Fox…. It would take so long. And I'm not rich. I can't afford weapons and mounts and…."

"We have a horse. We have a sword. You were a soldier. I can survive in the wilderness. I was of the al Muburak."

Mowfik sighed. "The sword is too heavy, girl."

Narriman glanced at Al Jahez. The captain tried to disappear amongst his cushions.

"Little Fox, I don't want to lose you too. I couldn't bear that." Mowfik's voice cracked. Narriman glimpsed a tear in the corner of one eye. This would cost him dearly from his beggared emotional purse.

He did not want to see her ride away. His heart said he would not see her again.

That dark rider had stolen her from him as surely as he had stolen Misr. She threw her arms around Mowfik. "Father, I have to do this. Wouldn't you come after me?"

"Yes. Yes. I would. I understand that."

Al Jahez said, "This isn't wise. The impossibility of dealing with the shaghûn and the Jebal aside, what would happen to a young woman alone? Even honest men would consider her fair for a moment's sport. Not to mention slavers and bandits. The Disciple instituted a rule of law, little one, but the Evil One, as ever, rules most of the land."

"Those are problems to face when they arise." What he said was true. She could not deny that. Women had no legal status or protection. When the shaghûn forced her onto her back he injured her father, not her. An unattached woman was not a person.

Her resolve was not shaken. Damned be the problems, and anyone who stood in her way.

X

When she wanted something badly Narriman got her way. Mowfik surrendered in the end. Once he gave in, Al Jahez grudgingly endorsed her training.

Narriman pursued it with a dogged determination that, in time, compelled the respect of Al Jahez's men. She arrived early and left late, and worked harder than any boy.

She was hard. She ignored bruises and aches. Her instructors called her Vixen and backed away when the deadly fire rose in her eyes.

One day she browbeat Mowfik into taking her to the captain. She told Al Jahez, "I'm ready. I leave tomorrow."

Al Jahez addressed her father. "Will you permit this, Mowfik? A woman under arms. It's against nature."

Mowfik shrugged.

Narriman said, "Don't stall me. Father's done that for weeks. I'll go with or without your blessing."

"Mowfik, forbid this madness."

"Captain, you heard her. Shall I put her in irons?"

Al Jahez looked at her as if he would cage her for her own protection. "Then marry her to me, Mowfik."

Though struck speechless, Narriman understood. Al Jahez wanted the legal rights of marriage. So he could forbid, so he could call upon the law if she persisted. If she rebelled, they would hunt her like a runaway slave.

Pure terror gripped her. She stared at her father, saw him tempted.

"Captain, heart and soul cry for me to accept. But I can't. A stronger voice bids me let her go. No matter how it hurts me."

Al Jahez sighed, defeated. "As you will. Child. Bring your father no sorrow or shame." He scowled at her expression. "No sorrow or shame of your own doing. That which is done by a shaghûn isn't of your doing. They're like the great storms in the erg. A man—or woman—can but bow his head till they pass. Come. The priests will bless your quest."

They waited in their fine ceremonial raiment. Al Jahez's eyes twinkled. "You see? Even the old Captain begins to know you."

"Perhaps." She wondered if she was too predictable.

The ceremony was less important to her than to Mowfik and Al Jahez. She endured it for their sakes. She would ride with Karkur.

"Now then," Al Jahez said. "One more thing and I'll harass you no more. Gamel. The box."

A priest presented a sandalwood box. Al Jahez opened it. Within, on white silk, lay a pendant. It was a small, pale green stone not unlike many she had seen on the ground. Al Jahez said, "Perhaps this will be gift enough to repay you, Mowfik." And to Narriman, "Child, the Disciple teaches that even the acquiescence to sorcery is a sin, but men have to be practical. The Disciple himself has shaghûn advisers.

"The stone is an amulet. It will warn you if you are near one with the Power. It will begin to grow cooler when you're a mile away. When you're very near, it will shed a green light. It's the best weapon I can give you."

Narriman tried to control the shakes. She failed. Tears broke loose. She hugged the captain. He was so startled he jumped away, but his face betrayed his pleasure.

"Go with the Lord, Little Fox. And with Karkur if it pleases you."

"Thank you," she said. "For everything. Especially for being Father's friend."

Ah Jahez snorted. "Ah, child. What are we without friends? Just severed heads rolling across the sands."

XI

Narriman looked back just before Al Jahez's fortress passed out of sight. "That's yesterday." She looked southward, toward the great erg. "There lies tomorrow. Eight hundred miles." She gripped her reins, touched the amulet between her breasts, her weapons, the bag that Mowfik had filled with war booty when he thought she was not looking. He had done everything to dissuade her, and everything to help her.

She looked back again, wondering if their concepts of manhood and womanhood would compel them to send guardians.

"Go, Faithful," she told her mare. The fortress disappeared. Her heart fluttered. She was going. Alone. A severed head, rolling across the sand, cut off from her body—with a little help from the rider.

She pictured him as he had been the day he had taken Misr. She got that warm, moist feeling, but not as powerfully. Hatred had begun to quench that fire.

She wished there was a way a woman could do to a man what he had done to her.

The wilderness was all that she had been warned. It was bitter, unforgiving, and those who dwelt there reflected its harshness. Twice she encountered men who thought her a gift from heaven. The first time she outrode them. The second, cornered, she fought. And was surprised to find herself the victor.

Though she had told herself that she was the equal of any man, she'd never believed it in her heart. Could the wisdom of centuries be wrong? She rode away more mature, more confident.

The great erg was more vast than she remembered. It was hotter and more harrowing. She had no one and nothing to distract her.

"The severed head has to roll without its body." She put her thoughts into words often. Who was to hear?

She had no choice but to enter Wadi el Kuf. They were shocked to see her, a woman in man's wear, hung about with weapons, talking as tough as any wandering freesword. Even the whores were scandalized. Nobody knew what to make of her. She bought water, asked questions, and rode on before they regained their balance.

Someone came after her, but one arrow altered his ambitions.

She rode with dust devils as companions. The al Muburak believed dust devils were ifrits dancing. She called out, but they did not respond. After a few days she began to think oddly, to suspect them of being spies for the Masters. She mocked and taunted them. They ignored her.

Finally, she checked the amulet. Not only did it not shed light, it was not cool. "So much for old stories."

She rode out of the erg and paused at the oasis she had visited coming north. There, as at Wadi el Kuf, she asked about a man in black traveling with a child. There, too, no one had seen such a traveler.

"Of course," she muttered. "And maybe they're telling the truth. But he's human. He *had* to stop at Wadi el Kuf." But he need not have appeared as a shaghûn out of the Jebal, need he?

No matter. She knew his destination.

Fourteen days passed. She rode into Wadi al Hamamah.

The al Muburak were not there. It was the wrong time of year. They were farther west, stalking wild camels in hopes of adding to their herd.

She camped in the usual place. When night fell she went to Karkur.

After the proper greetings and obeisances, she told her story in case Mowfik was wrong about his being able to follow an al Muburak anywhere. Karkur sat and listened, firelight sending shadows dancing across his ugly face.

She said, "Father says you aren't as great as I thought. That others are more powerful so sometimes you don't dare help. But if there's a way you can, help me do what I have to do."

She stared at the image. The image stared back. Time passed. The fire died. The moon rose, filled the Circle with shifting shadows.

"Karkur, there's a man named Al Jahez. He follows the Disciple, but he's a good man. Could you reward him? Could you tell Father I've come here safely?"

She thought, I'm talking to a lump of rock as though it really could do something. "Tell Al Jahez the severed head goes daft after it's separated."

The moon was a great, full thing that inundated the wadi with silver light. She leaned back and stared.

Something startled her. Fool, she thought. You fell asleep. Her dagger filled her hand. She searched the shadows, saw nothing. She listened. Nothing. She sniffed the air. Again nothing.

She shivered. It was getting cold. Colder than she remembered the nights this time of year. She pulled her cloak tighter.

And realized that the cold radiated from one point. The amulet!

She snatched it out. Green! Glowing green. Had the shaghûn come out to meet her?

The stone flared. It crackled. An emerald snake writhed between it and Karkur. A cold wind swirled around the Circle. Dead leaves pattered against her. She glanced up. No. The sky was clear. Stars winked in their myriads. The moon shone benevolently.

The emerald snake turned amber shot with veins of blood. Narriman gasped. That was the combination they mentioned when they talked about the Great Death.

The snake died. The stone grew less cold, became just a small, pale green piece of rock lying in her hand. She stared at Karkur.

"What have you done? What have you given me? Not the power of the Great Death?"

The image stared back, as silent as ever. She was tempted to rant. But Karkur gave short shrift to ingrates. He was more a punitive than a helpful god. "But loyal to his people," she said. "Thank you, Karkur."

She hurried through the parting rituals and returned to camp. She fell asleep still astonished that Karkur had responded.

There were dreams. Vivid dreams. She rode into the Jebal, moving with an absolute certainty of her way. She knew exactly when to expect the first challenge.

The dream ended. The sun had wakened her. She felt fit and rested. She recalled every detail of the dream. She looked down the wadi. A dumb stone god? She examined Al Jahez's stone. It looked no less ordinary this morning.

XII

The trails were faint, but she followed them confidently. Once she noted an overturned stone, darker on the exposed side. Someone had been this way recently. She shrugged. The amulet would warn her.

The mountains were silent. All the world was silent when you rode alone. The great erg had been filled with a stillness as vast as that of death. Here it seemed there should be some sound, if only the call of the red-tailed hawk on the wing. But the only sounds were those of a breeze in scrubby oaks, of water chuckling in one small stream.

She moved higher and higher. Sometimes she looked back across the hills where the wadi lay, to the plains beyond, a distance frosted with haze. The al Muburak might profit from such a view.

Night fell. She made a fireless camp. She drank water, ate smoked meat, turned in as the stars came out.

She wakened once, frightened, but her stone betrayed no danger. The mountains remained still, though the wind made an unfamiliar soughing through nearby pines. She counted more than a dozen meteors before drifting off.

Her dreams were vivid. In one her father told Al Jahez he was sure she had reached Wadi al Hamamah safely

The mountains continued their rise. She rested more often. Come midday she entered terrain scoured by fire. That stark, black expanse was an alien landscape.

The trees changed. Oaks became scarcer, pines more numerous. The mountains became like nothing in her experience. Great looms of rock thrust out of their hips, the layering on end instead of horizontal. Even where soil and grass covered them she could discern the striations. Distant mountainsides looked zebra-striped in the right light.

Higher still. The oaks vanished. And then, in the bottom of one canyon, she encountered trees so huge a half dozen men could not have joined hands around their trunks. Narriman felt insignificant in their shadows.

She spent her fourth day riding up that canyon. Evening came early. She almost missed the landmarks warning her that she was approaching the first guardian. She considered the failing light. This was no time to hurry. She retreated and camped.

Something wakened her. She listened, sniffed, realized that the alarming agent was not external. She had dreamed that she should circle the watch post.

"Come, Faithful," she whispered. She wrapped the reins in her hand and led away.

She knew exactly where to go, and still it was bad. That mountainside was not meant for climbing. The brush was dense and the slope was steep. She advanced a few yards and listened.

The brush gave way to a barren area. The soil was loose and dry. She slipped several times. Then her mare went down, screaming and sliding. She held on stubbornly.

The slide ended. "Easy, girl. Easy. Stay still."

A glow appeared below. She was surprised. She had climbed higher than she had thought. The glow drifted along the canyon.

"I can't fail now. Not at the first hurdle."

Her heart hammered. She felt like screaming against clumsiness, stupidity, and the whim of fate.

The glow drifted down the canyon, climbed the far slope, came back. It crossed to Narriman's side and went down again. It repeated the patrol but never climbed far from the canyon floor. It never came close enough to make her amulet glow. It finally gave up. But Narriman did not trust it because it had disappeared. She waited fifteen minutes.

The sky was lightening before she felt comfortably past. She was exhausted. "Good girl, Faithful. Let's camp."

XIII

A horse's whinny wakened her. She darted to Faithful, clamped her hands over the mare's nostrils.

The sound of hooves on brookside stone came nearer. The amulet became a lump of ice. She saw flickers of black rider through the trees.

This one was stockier than her shaghûn.

Her shaghûn? Had he touched her that deeply? She looked inward, seeking the hatred of rider and love of son that had brought her to the Jebal. And it was there, the hatred untarnished by any positive feeling.

Then the rider was gone, headed down the canyon. Was he going to the guardian?

She had no dream memories of the canyon above the guardian. Why not? Couldn't Karkur reach into the realm of the Masters?

The uncertainty became too much. She dismounted and walked. No need to rush into trouble. Minutes later she heard a rhythmic thumping ahead. Something rumbled and crashed and sent echoes rumbling down the canyon. She advanced more carefully, sliding from cover to cover.

She did not know where they came from. Suddenly, they were there, across the brook. They walked like men but were shaggy and dark and tall. There were four of them. The biggest growled.

"Damn!" She strung her bow as one giant bellowed and charged.

Her arrow split its breastbone. It halted, plucked at the dart. The others boomed and rushed. She sped two quick arrows, missed once, then drew her saber and scampered toward a boulder. If she got on top....

Neither wounded monster went down. Both went for the mare. The others came for her.

Faithful tried to run, stumbled, screamed. The beasts piled on her.

Narriman drew her razor-edged blade across a wide belly. The brute stumbled a few steps, looked down at its wound, began tucking entrails back inside.

Narriman glanced at the mare as she dodged the other beast. The wounded creatures were pounding her with huge stones.

A fist slammed into Narriman's side. She staggered, gasped. Her attacker bellowed and closed in. She tried to raise her saber. It slipped from her hand. She hadn't the strength to grip it.

The thing shook her half senseless. Then it sniffed her and grunted.

It was something out of nightmare. The thing settled with Narriman in its lap, pawed between her thighs. She felt its sex swell against her back.

Was the whole Jebal rape-crazy? "Karkur!"

The thing ripped her clothing. Another grunted and tried to touch. The beast holding Narriman swung at it.

She was free for an instant. She scrambled away. The beast roared and dove after her.

She closed her hand on her amulet. "Karkur, give me the strength to survive this."

The beast snorted weirdly, uttered an odd shriek that tortured the canyon walls. It stumbled away, enveloped by an amber light laced with bloody threads.

Another beast came for her. Its cries joined those of the other.

Narriman scrambled after her saber. The last beast, with an arrow in its chest, watched her with glazed eyes, backed away. She arranged her clothing, ran to Faithful.

"Poor Faithful." What would she do now? How would she escape the Jebal without a horse for Misr?

The beasts in amber kept screaming. The Great Death was a hard death. It twisted their muscles till bones broke.

The screaming finally stopped.

She heard distant voices.

Hurriedly, she made a pack of her possessions, then climbed the canyon wall. She found an outcrop from which she could watch the mess she had fled.

Those things! She recalled their size and smell and was sick.

The investigators were ordinary men armed with tools. They became excited and cautious when they found the beasts. Narriman heard the word shaghûn used several times. "Keep thinking that," she murmured. "Don't get the ideas there's a stranger in the Jebal."

Her shakes faded. She offered thanks to Karkur and started across the mountainside.

What were those beasts? Those men feared them. She moved with saber in hand.

The investigators had come from a lumbering camp. She watched them drag a log up the road, toward the head of the canyon. Why? She shrugged. The Masters must want it done.

She took to that road once she passed the camp.

That afternoon she heard hoof beats. She slipped into the underbrush. "Oh, damn!" The horseman carried two of her arrows and Faithful's saddle. She strung her bow, jumped into the road, shouted, "Hey! Wait a minute!"

The rider reined in, looked back. She waved. He turned.

Her arrow flew true. He sagged backward. His horse surged forward. Narriman caught it as it passed. She dragged the body into the brush, mounted up wondering how soon he would be missed.

The canyon walls closed in. The brook faded away. She reached the summit. The road wound downhill, toward a far haze of smoke. There were a lot of hearth fires down there.

XIV

She traveled for two days. The only people she saw were men working logs down the road. She avoided them. She topped a piney ridge the second day and saw a city.

Thoughts of Misr nagged her. Should she go down now? She was ahead of news from the logging camp. But he might not be there. And she was tired. She was incapable of acting efficiently in a desperate situation. Her judgment might be clouded, too.

She settled down off the road. She would have loved a fire. The mountain nights were chilly. Gnawing dried meat, she grumbled, "I'd sell my soul for a decent meal."

Sleep brought dreams. They showed her the town, including a place where children were kept. She also saw a place where shaghûns lived, and beyond the city a tower that was an emptiness fraught with dark promise.

She wakened knowing exactly what to do. Come nightfall she would slip into the city, break into the nursery, and take Misr. Then she would flee, set an ambush down the trail and hope her shaghûn was the one who came.

Her plan died immediately. Her mount had broken its tether. Its trail led toward the city.

What would they think? Would they investigate? Of course. She'd best move elsewhere.

She trudged southward, circling the city. Time and again she went out of her way to avoid farmsteads. By nightfall she was exhausted again.

It had to be tonight, though. There was no more time.

What would she do for a mount? Her hope of escape hinged on her being able to lead the pursuit to ground of her own choosing.

She settled down near the city's edge. "Karkur, wake me when it's time."

It was a dark night. There was no moon. Clouds obscured the stars. Narriman arose shaking. Her nerves got no better for a long time.

The streets were strange for a girl who'd never walked pavement. Her boot heels kept clicking. Echoes came back off the walls. "Too quiet," she muttered. "Where are the dogs?"

Not a howl went up. Not one dog came to investigate. Her nerves only tautened. She began to imagine something watching her, the town as a box trap waiting for her to trip its trigger. She dried her hands on her hips repeatedly. The moths in her stomach refused to lie still. She kept looking over her shoulder.

She gave the place of the shaghûns a wide berth, closed in on the nursery. Why were the youngsters segregated? Was it a place for children like Misr? The city made no sense. She didn't try to make it do so.

The only warning was a rustle of fabric. Narriman whirled, saber spearing out. It was an automatic move, made without thought. She found herself face to face with a mortally wounded shaghûn.

He raised a gloved hand as he sank toward the pavement. His fingers wobbled. Sorcery! She hacked the offending hand, came back with a neck stroke. She cut him again and again, venting nervous energy and fear.

"What do I do with him?" she wondered. She examined him. He was no older than she. She felt a touch of remorse.

She glanced around. The street remained quiet. A convenient alleyway lay just beyond the body.

She wondered what he had been doing. Her dreams had suggested that no one wandered the streets after dark, save a night watchman with a special dispensation.

Had the horse alerted them? Were there more shaghûns to be faced? Her stomach cramped.

Maybe her father and Al Jahez were right. Maybe a woman *couldn't* do this sort of thing. "And maybe men feel as ragged as I do," she muttered. She dropped the body into shadow. "Give me an hour, Karkur." She went on to the nursery.

Anticipation partially overcame her reaction to the killing. She tried a door. It was barred from within. A second door proved as impenetrable. There was a third on the far side but she assumed it would be sealed, too.

Above, barely visible, were second-story windows, some with open shutters. If she could....

She spun into shadow and balled up, blade ready. A shape loomed out of the night, headed her way. Shaghûn! Were they all on patrol?

He passed just ten feet away. Narriman held her breath. What were they doing? Looking for her? Or was her fear wholly egotistical?

There was a six-foot-wide breezeway between the nursery and the building to its left. A stairway climbed the neighbor. A landing hung opposite a nursery window. Narriman secreted her possessions beneath the stair and crept upward. The stair creaked. She scarcely noticed. She could think of nothing but Misr.

The window was open. It was but a short step from the landing. She straddled the railing.

Someone opened the door to which the stair led. Light flooded the landing. A fat man asked, "Here, you. What's?...."

Narriman slashed at him. He grabbed her blade. Off balance, she almost fell. She clung to the railing. It creaked. She jumped for the window.

The fat man staggered, reached for her, ploughed through the railing. Narriman clung to the window's frame and looked down. The man lay twitching below. "Karkur, don't let him raise the alarm."

The room before her was dark. A child mumbled something. Behind Narriman, a woman called a question. Narriman eased into the room.

The child was not Misr.

Someone shrieked. Narriman glanced outside. A woman stood on the landing, looking down.

Narriman slipped into a hallway running past other bedrooms. Which one? Might as well start with the nearest.

She found her son in the fifth room she checked. He was sleeping peacefully. His face looked angelic. He seemed healthy. She threw herself on him, weeping, and remained lost within herself till she realized he was awake.

"Mama! What're you doing here?" Misr hugged her with painful ferocity. He cried too. She was glad. Her most secret fear had been that he would have forgotten her.

"I came to take you home."

"Where's Grandpa?"

"Home. Waiting for us. Come on."

"The man, Mama. The dark man. He won't let us." He started shaking. His body was hale but they had done something to his mind.

"He won't stop us, Misr. I won't let him. Get dressed. Hurry." People were talking in the hall.

Misr did as he was told. Slowly.

Someone shoved through the doorway. "What's going on?..."

Narriman's saber pricked his throat. "Over there."

"A woman? Who are you?"

She pressed the sword's tip a quarter inch into his chest. "I'll ask. You answer." He shut up and moved. Small children watched from the doorway. "How many shaghûns in this town?"

He looked strange. He did not want to answer. Narriman pricked him. "Four! But one went to the lumber camp three weeks ago. He hasn't come back. You're the boy's sister?"

"Misr, will you hurry?" Four shaghûns. But one was out of town and another was dead. A third roamed the streets. Was hers the fourth?

"You can't take the boy out of here, woman."

She pricked him again. "You talk too much. Misr!"

"He belongs to the Old Ones."

Misr finished and looked at her expectantly.

Now what? Go out the way she had come? She stepped behind her prisoner and hit him with her pommel. He sagged. Misr's eyes got big. She dragged him toward the hallway. He told the other children, "I'm going home with my mother." He sounded proud.

She was amazed at how he had grown. He acted older, too. No time for that. "Come here." She tossed him across to the landing, jumped, hurried him downstairs. She recovered her belongings.

The fat man's woman howled all the while. "Shut up!" The woman retreated, whimpering.

Narriman looked into the street. People were gathering. "Misr. This way." She withdrew into the breezeway. "A horse," she muttered. "Where do I find a horse?"

She was about to leave the breezeway when she heard someone running. "Get back, Misr. And be quiet." She crouched.

The runner turned into the breezeway. Shaghûn! He tried to stop. Narriman drove her blade into his chest. He staggered back. She struck again. This was the shaghûn who had missed her earlier.

She smiled grimly. Succeed or fail, they would remember her.

"Come on, Misr." People were shouting to her right. She headed left, though that was not the direction she preferred. Misr ran beside her. She searched her dream memories for a stable. She did not find one.

Hope of escape came out of a walking dream that hit like a fist, made her stumble.

Karkur wanted her to go eastward. There was a road through the mountains. They would not expect her to flee that way. If she reached the seacoast she could go north and recross the mountains at Sebil el Selib, where the Masters held no sway.

But this end of that road ran around the dread tower of her dreams. Who knew what the Masters would do? If their shaghûns were but shadows of themselves, how terrible might they be?

She was afraid but she did not stop moving. Karkur had not failed her yet.

And Karkur was right. It *was* the best way. She saw no one, and no one saw her. And the dark tower greeted her with an indifference she found almost disheartening. Was she that far beneath their notice? She had slain two of their shaghûns.

"Keep walking, Misr. We're going to get tired, but we have to keep walking. Otherwise the dark men will catch us."

His face puckered in determination. He stayed with her. The sun was high before she decided to rest.

XV

"Narriman!" The voice boomed through the forest, rang off the mountains. "Narriman!" There was an edge of anger to it, like hers when she was impatient with Misr.

It was him. He had not been deceived.

Misr snuggled closer. "Don't let him take me, Mama."

"I won't," she promised, disentangling herself. "I'll be back in a little while."

"Don't go away, Mama."

"I have to. You stay put. Just remember what happened last time you didn't do what I said." Damn! That was unfair. He would think the whole thing was his fault. She spat, strung her bow. Selected three good arrows, made sure her other weapons were ready. Then she went to hunt.

"Narriman!" He was closer. Why act as if he couldn't find her?

Karkur, of course. That old lump did not dare smash things up in the Jebal. He would not want his hand seen. But he could confuse his enemies.

Brush crackled. Narriman froze. He was close. She sank into a patch of shade, arrow on bowstring.

"Narriman!" His voice boomed. More softly, he talked to himself.

"Damned crazy woman. I'll use her hide to bind books." His anger was hard but controlled. Fear wriggled through Narriman's hatred.

Memories flashed. His ride down Wadi al Hamamah. Her rape. The day he had come for Misr. Her knees weakened. He was a shaghûn. He had conquered her easily. She was a fool to challenge him.

Brush crackled ever closer. She saw something white moving among the trees. His horse. That was him. Coming right to her.

There he was. Black rider. Nightmare lover. Misr's father. She pictured Mowfik and Al Jahez. "You!" she breathed. "For what you did to my father."

A twig snapped as she bent her bow. The horse's head snapped up, ears pricking. Her arrow slammed into its throat. It should have struck the shaghûn's heart.

The animal kept rising into a screaming rear, hooves pounding air. The rider went over backward. Narriman heard his breath explode when he hit ground.

Up she sprang. She let fly again. Her shaft passed though his djellaba as he rolled, pinned him for a second. In that second Narriman loosed her last arrow.

It glanced off his hip bone, leaving a bloody gash across his right buttock. He stumbled a step, fell, regained his feet with a groan.

Narriman drew her saber, stalked forward. Her mind boiled with all she wanted to say before she killed him.

He regained control, drew his own blade. A strained smile crossed his lips.

Narriman moved in carefully. I'll attack to his right, she thought. Make him put more strain on his wound. He's battered and bleeding. He'll be slow. I can wear him down.

"Little Fox. Little fool. Why did you come here? Outsiders don't come into the Jebal. Not and leave again."

There'll be a first, then, she thought. But she did not speak. Things she wanted to say rattled through her mind, but not one reached her lips. Her approach was as silent and implacable as his preceding her rapes.

She threw three hard, quick strokes. He turned them, but looked disturbed. She was not supposed to do this, was she? She was supposed to fall under his spell.

"Narriman! Look at me!"

She was caught by the command. She met his eye.

The fire ran through her. She ached for him. And to her surprise, she ignored it. She struck while his guard was loose, opened a gash on his cheek.

He went pale. His eyes grew larger. He could not believe it.

She struck again. He blocked her, thrust back, nearly reached her. He knew he was not dealing with a little girl anymore.

He beat her back, then retreated. A weird keening came from him, though his lips did not move. Leaves stirred. A cold wind rose. The tip of Narriman's saber drooped like a candle in the sun. She shifted it to her left hand, pulled her dagger and threw it. Mowfik had taught her that.

The dagger struck the shaghûn in the left shoulder, spun him. The cold wind died. Narriman moved in with her odd-looking saber. Fear filled the shaghûn's eyes.

He plucked the dagger from his wound and made those sounds again. His wounds began to close.

Surprise had been Narriman's best weapon. Fate had stolen that. She feared she had more than she could handle now.

She launched a furious attack. He retreated, stumbled, fell. She cut him several times before he rose.

But he had his confidence back. She could not kill him. He smiled. Arrow, saber, and dagger. She had exhausted her options. She did have poison. Would he step up and take it? She had a garrote given her by one of Al Jahez's men, half a love-offering and half a well-wish. But would he hold still while she used it?

Brush crackled. She whirled. "Misr, I told you...."

That shaghûn smashed into her, knocked her saber away. His fingers closed around her chin and forced her to turn toward him.

XVI

Lost! she wailed inside. She should have listened to Al Jahez and Mowfik. The fire was in her again and she could not stop him. He stripped her slowly, taking pleasure in her humiliation.

He pressed her down on the stones and pines needles and stood over her, smiling. He disrobed slowly. And Misr stood there watching, too terrified to move.

Tears streaming, Narriman forced her eyes shut. She had been so close! One broken twig short.

She felt him lower himself, felt him probe, felt him enter. Felt herself respond. Damn, she hated him!

She found enough hatred to shove against his chest. But only for an instant. Then he was down upon her again, forcing her hands back against her breasts. "Karkur," she wept.

The shaghûn moaned softly, stopped bucking. His body stiffened. He pulled away. The spell binding Narriman diminished.

"The Great Death!" she breathed.

It had him, but he was fighting it. Amber wriggled over him, flickering. There were few bloody veins in it. His mouth was open as though to scream, but he was gurgling a form of his earlier keening.

Narriman could not watch.

It did not occur to her that a mere shaghûn, even a shaghûn of the Jebal, could overcome Karkur's Great Death. He was but stalling the inevitable. She crawled to her discarded clothing.

Misr said something. She could not look at him. Her shame was too great.

"Mama. *Do* something."

She finally looked. Misr pointed.

The shaghûn's face was twisted. The muscles of his left arm were knotted. The bone was broken. But there was just one patch of amber left, flickering toward extinction.

He had bested the Great Death!

A silent wail of fear filled her. There was no stopping him! Raging at the injustice, she seized a dead limb and clubbed him. Misr grabbed a stick and started swinging too.

"Misr, stop that."

"Mama, he hurt you."

"You stop. I can do it but you can't." Did that make sense? I can murder him but you can't? No. Some things could not be explained. "Get away."

She swung again. The shaghûn tried to block with his injured arm. He failed. The impact sent him sprawling. The Great Death crept over him. She hit him again.

He looked at her with the eyes of the damned. He did not beg, but he did not want to die. He stared. There was no enchantment in his eyes. They contained nothing but fear, despair, and, maybe, regret. He was no shaghûn now. He was just a man dying before his time.

The club slipped from her fingers. She turned back, collected her clothes. "Misr, let's get our things." For no reason she could appreciate, she recalled Al Jahez's words about severed heads.

She collected the shaghûn's sword, considered momentarily, then gave him the mercy he had denied her.

"You killed him, Mama. You really killed him." Misr was delighted.

"Shut up!"

She could have closed her eyes to his screams, but his dying face would have haunted her forever. It might anyway.

When all else was stripped away, he had been a man. And once a mother had wept for him while a dark rider had carried him toward the rising sun.

Misr Sayed bin Hammad al Muburaki, the Hammer of God, would become a major player in desert politics in the later Dread Empire novels, just as Sadhra prophesied.

SILVERHEELS

The following wasn't originally intended for publication. It was written at the 1969 Clarion Workshop as a birthday gift for Fritz Leiber, one of whose loves was cats. Both he and Robin Wilson, the workshop director, insisted I market it.

This was my second sold and first published piece of short fiction. It was not, at the time, part of the Dread Empire world, that not having yet coalesced. But changing just a few words places it in the wild north of that world rather than the wild north of our own—though, as the name implies, Trolledyngja is a particularly remote mountain wilderness in our own world, armed with an ancient reputation for harboring all manner of the fey.

In the old days there was a man from Telemark, up in Lochlain, which you call Trolledyngja, who had a very strange adventure. His name was Olav and he lived in Rauland, beside Lake Totak. Everyone thought him a ne'er-do-well, because, instead of farming his land, he made his living by fishing the lake, and trapping in the forests covering the sides of the valley leading down to the lake's eastern edge. Olav did not mind what people thought. He was content with his own sort of friends.

Save for a few animals, old Olav had lived most of his life alone. He had just two friends at the time of his great adventure: a mare pony named Faith, and a black kitten with white paws, called Silverheels. A precocious kitten.

They were very close, those three, and some of the more credulous country folk thought Olav a wizard, or even one of the *huldre*-folk—the hidden people, the mischievous elves of that country—because he talked with his animal friends. But there was no truth to that rumor. He had merely saved a talent from childhood, a talent his neighbors had forgotten.

It was a fine, sunny day just before summer's start when Olav began his adventure. He had had a particularly fine catch the day before, so he called Faith and Silverheels, and said, "Friends, let's take this fish down to Rauland Market today. I need some salt, and a pink ribbon for Faith's mane."

So they got the fish, put them into two panniers on the pony's back, Olav set Silverheels up on top, and off they went to market. They had been walking about an hour when Faith noticed that Silverheels was sneaking fish from the baskets.

"Little thief, stop!"

"It's just a small one," said Silverheels, guiltily.

"But the fourth. And there'll be another, and another, and then how will Olav get the money to buy my ribbon?"

"Oh, don't worry, Faith," said Olav. "We have enough to get the ribbon. But if Silverheels steals another fish, we won't get him his bowl of cream." Olav always bought Silverheels a bowl of cream when they took fish down to Rauland town.

Silverheels liked his cream. He took his paws out of the basket and behaved very well. For a time.

Down around Lake Totak they walked, and came to the foot of Dovre Mountain, where trolls and *huldre*-folk were said to live. They reached a turn in the road where an old grandfather of trees had fallen across a huge boulder.

They met a strange man around the turn. Very old he was, dressed in a gray robe, and wearing a white beard so long it hung to his waist. He was leaning on an oaken staff in the middle of the road, humming to himself.

"Excuse me, sir," said Olav. "I have to get by so I can take my fish to Rauland. I have to get some salt, and a ribbon for my pony."

"He's not going to move," said Silverheels. "He's one of the *huldre*-folk."

The old man looked up then, staring at the kitten. Silverheels stared right back, his head cocked naughtily.

"Silverheels is right," Faith said. "He's the king of the *huldre*. My dam told me about him."

The old man turned his strange eyes on the pony. She backed a step away. Olav made signs against the evil eye, twice, hoping that would frighten the *hulder* away.

"I'll buy your mare and kitten," said the bearded man. Olav thought his eyes seemed on fire, so intense was his gaze. Frightened, he made the signs of Hammer and Star, from the new religion and the old, in appeal to whatever gods were watching, then replied, "I'll not sell my friends, all I have in the world."

"Well, if that's the case, you'll just have to come along too, Crazy Olav." Crazy Olav, that's what the villagers down in Rauland called him.

"Where?"

"A place with no name." The old man walked to the fallen tree and smote the boulder beneath with the tip of his staff. The sound was louder than the ringing of the alarm bell in the thane's watchtower, the other side of Rauland. As the ringing died, a large door opened in the side of the rock. Olav could see a passage, lit by smoky torches, waiting within. He made the Hammer and Star again.

The old man stepped through the doorway, then beckoned the three to follow. Then they realized they were *huldrin*, which is the name given those who are bewitched by a *hulder*. They could not keep their feet from starting down the path which led into the heart of the mountain.

Olav, Faith, and Silverheels followed the wizard through a long tunnel. It seemed it would take forever to get wherever they were bound.

Once they happened on a band of drunken trolls, but the old magician cast a spell so they would not be seen by the wicked *tusse*-folk. Had the trolls known of their visitors, they would have had a plump little pony for supper. And, perhaps, a kitten, or even a stringy old Trolledyngjan.

A while later, they came to caves where dwarves lived. Olav marveled at all the gold and silver the little smiths had.

After more weary travel, they came to the end of the tunnel. Olav immediately knew they were nowhere in Trolledyngja. He saw dragons soaring in the sky, *huldre* maidens catching sunbeams in great silver bowls, and he knew that they had entered *Utröst,* the land of the elves.

He and his friends followed the old wizard across a strange land, a land where it was always late afternoon, and, at last, came to a great castle with many towers, which sat high atop a hill. *Huldre* knights rode forth to greet them, hailing the wizard "King," confirming Faith's identification. Princesses lined the gray battlements over the gate, waving gaily colored handkerchiefs, bidding their father a welcome home. All the *huldre* squires and servants, dressed in their finest, were clustered at the drawbridge. The old man stopped and greeted each as he led his captives into the fortress.

Olav, Faith, and Silverheels whispered to one another, questioning these strange events, and wondering what they should do. They wanted to go home, but were unable to escape the spell the wizard had cast. Naturally, they were frightened for there were many tales told in Trolledyngja about the evil ways of some of the folk of *Utröst.*

Then little Silverheels succumbed to curiosity, and announced that he wanted to go on. Olav told him the tale of curiosity and the cat, but the kitten wouldn't listen.

The wizard led the way into a great hall where a huge meal was already set on the tables. There were just four places set: platters of meat for Olav and the king, a trencher heaped with fine fresh clover for Faith, and a little golden bowl of cream for Silverheels. Relieved, the three captives took their places at the Elfking's table.

When they were done, and after *huldre* maidens had brought out huge stoops of chilled ale for Olav and the king, it was time to talk.

"Why did you bring us here?" Silverheels asked.

"Ah, little kitten, you're a bold one, I see. I've brought you here because I want you to help my people, in a way only mortals are able. You see, there are a pair of terrible dragons, Ironclaw and Hookfang, who are destroying the kingdom. My people cannot stop them because it's impossible for one under-earth creature to slay another. Only a mortal can give the gift of death to a creature of *Utröst*. And these two dragons cannot be bested, save by being slain."

Olav and Faith shook with fear at the mere mention of dragons, for the *linnormen* have a dreadful reputation in their country, though no Trolle-dyngjan could truthfully claim to have seen one. But little Silverheels was undismayed. "Why don't you use your magic to make them go away, old wizard?"

"Because a wicked sorcerer of the east, of a land where the sun never shines, is using a magic greater than my own. The *linnormen* are proof from my power. These dragons can be slain only by a sword of steel, and only a mortal can stand the touch of iron."

"Then you were certain I would come too?" Olav asked.

"Yes, you're too fond of your friends to sell them to a stranger. And there was my spell."

"Am I not too old for such carryings on? Anyway, I've never held a sword in my life. I wouldn't know how to use one. How could I slay a dragon?"

"You can do it easy, Olav," said Silverheels, cocking his head at the old fisherman. "I think it'll be fun."

"You're just a kitten," Faith scolded. "You've never even caught a mouse. What would you know about dragons?"

Silverheels pretended he couldn't hear her, because he couldn't think of an answer. Olav and Faith argued with the king and Silverheels until late in the evening (it was always evening in that part of Elfland), but the question was finally settled in spite of any of their wishes.

When Olav and the king were many stoops of ale along, a young *hulder* knight came running in. He bore evil news. "Sire," he cried, "the dragons have come to the castle proper. The Red Dragon, Ironclaw, is setting fire to the fields in the west. The White Dragon, Hookfang, is burning the farmers' village to the east. The country folk are fleeing into the castle, but many have suffered grievous wounds where they were touched by drops of dragon fire."

Silverheels hopped from his stool to the top of the table. He danced with joy because he had a chance to see a real live dragon. Faith and Olav grew very frightened. They were older and wiser, and knew dragons were no fun. The king grew sad. "My enemy has brought evil to the walls of my people. It is sad that you will not help, Olav."

Olav, too, felt sad, but he had always considered himself a wise man. And a wise man knew better that to challenge the might of a dragon. There were many bleached bones to prove it.

Silverheels suddenly gave a little kittenish "miaow" of excitement. His sharp ears had caught the distant roaring of dragons. He leapt to the floor and scampered across the room. Over his shoulder, he called, "I'm going to see the *linnormen*."

"You come back here!" Olav cried. "Do you want to get burnt?"

Faith ran after the kitten, but Silverheels evaded her. As he went out the door, he called, "Old Olav, I think you're afraid."

That made Olav angry. "I'm no coward! I just know better than to get myself killed fighting dragons!"

"Old Olav, I think you're afraid."

Olav got madder. Without thinking, he snatched a heavy sword from the hands of a *hulder* knight wearing thick gloves, and went striding off after Silverheels. Faith looked at the old fisherman strangely, then timorously followed. Smiling, the Elfking came along behind the mare.

Silverheels skipped upstairs, pausing just often enough to taunt Olav into following. He led the way to the turret of a tall tower, the tallest of the castle. From that vantage point, both dragons, and the damage they were doing, could be seen.

In the west was the blood-red dragon called Ironclaw, and in the east, now destroying precious vineyards, was the ivory dragon called Hookfang. The monsters had already destroyed most of the *huldre* crops. The Elfking was red with rage, but he could do nothing to protect his people from this plague. The lightning-spells he cast, there on the heights of his tower, only served to draw the attentions of the dragons. Perhaps that was the idea he had in mind.

Ironclaw soared up in the west, blood against the sun. In the east, Hookfang spiraled into the sky, turning toward the castle, trailing smoke. Both dragons circled the tower widdershins. Ironclaw roared past at low altitude, a huge, winged snake. His talons and fangs gleamed in the evening sun, like golden scimitars. Smoke and fire trailed from his huge nostrils. Hookfang was close behind. The White Dragon was both larger and uglier, like a gigantic, winged crocodile. His smoke and fire seemed to cover half the sky.

The *huldre*-king told a hasty spell, then said, "Olav, the sword is iron. It is proof against all the magic of *Utröst*, but still must be used at the right time. You must use it only when you can smite the Red Dragon in the eye, or the White in the heart. Each is invulnerable, except in those places. I've erected a spell which will protect the top of this tower, and you, from their fire, but that protection will be destroyed the moment you strike your first blow. If you make that stroke count, you will need fear but one of them." Having said this, the Elfking hastily retreated into the tower. He slammed a heavy door behind him.

Olav was shaking. He tried the door, but found it locked from within.

"Old Olav, I think you're afraid!" said Silverheels. He thought it was all very exciting. Olav and Faith glared at him. He danced with joy at the prospect of a battle with dragons.

"Foolish kitten!" said Faith, shivering. "You'll dance to a different tune when the dragons come."

The dragons flew three times round the tower before diving at the three. First came Ironclaw, spouting smoke and flame, then the White Dragon, attacking with his claws. The flame of the first dragon was turned by the *huldre*-king's spell. The claws of the second were unable to reach the friends because they were crouched beneath the battlements. As Hookfang wheeled up into the endless evening sky, Silverheels jumped atop the ramparts. He arced his back, puffed up his fur, and said some very unkittenish things. Olav pulled him down just in time to escape Ironclaw's second attack.

The three crouched under those battlements for a long time. The two great dragons swooped and swooped above them, like falcons after prey. The king's spell turned fire, the stone turned claw, and it looked like nothing was going to happen. But old Olav was finding his lost courage by exposing himself each time he had to pull Silverheels down off the perilous battlements.

The dragons grew angrier and angrier because they were unable to harm these three puny enemies. Then Ironclaw, the elder of the two, swooped too low and caught a claw in a crack between stones. The talon broke. The Red Dragon sailed upward, bellowing terribly. Old Olav finally took heart. The dragons could be hurt after all.

When Ironclaw next came winging down, he tried to land on the small turret, apparently thinking he could win the battle simply by dropping his great weight atop the three. The three friends huddled beneath the battlements, trying to avoid claws and the great wind stirred by the *linnorm*'s wings. The Red Dragon was far larger than the space where he had landed. And was having difficulty maintaining his balance. Precocious little Silverheels decided to push him off the tower.

He sprang to the battlements again, began taunting the dragon. Ironclaw roared like a thunderstorm and loosed a tremendous lot of flame. Silverheels jumped, barely in time to make it back to the protection of the king's spell.

Worried about Silverheels, Olav jumped up and started after the kitten, but he was forced to jump out of the way of a giant claw. He tripped, flung his arms out to catch himself. The iron sword flew through the air and struck the Red Dragon full point in the eye. With a great scream, the *linnorm* fell backward off the tower, his wings beating like the cymbals of a mighty army.

Mystified, Olav collected the sword from where it had fallen after doing its deed, and went to peer over the ramparts. Faith and Silverheels joined him just in time to see the Red Dragon crash against the flagstones in the courtyard far below. "See," said the kitten. "I told you you could do it."

A shadow grew around them, becoming larger and deeper. Looking up, Olav saw Hookfang diving toward them in a fury. They scurried for protection below the battlements.

The White Dragon seemed about to repeat the mistake of the Red. It landed on the tower and immediately began stalking the three. Wishing to treat them cruelly for the slaying of the other, Hookfang withheld his fire.

"Faith, Silverheels, get behind me," Olav ordered as he hefted the sword and braced himself for battle. The kitten leapt to the ramparts, then bounced onto the pony's back. She got behind Olav, watching over his shoulder. The fisherman retreated as the dragon stalked closer.

Round and round the tower they went, the dragon advancing, Olav retreating, time and again thrusting the tip of his blade at a small red heart on the monster's ivory chest.

"Oh, look!" said Silverheels. "The Red Dragon's still alive." Olav glanced over the ramparts. Ironclaw was moving his wings feebly in the courtyard, twitching his armored tail, and spewing out gouts of flame.

"But dying," said Olav. "He won't live much longer."

At his words, the White Dragon made a thunderous, angry sound with his wings, and dove straight at Olav. Faith squealed with fright and ran. Silverheels leapt from her back to the battlements and started taunting the dragon. That kitten was either fearless or a fool. And what is it they say of the young?

Olav retreated as fast as his legs would carry him.

Faith was so frightened that she ran completely around the turret and butted into Hookfang's tail before she realized what she was doing. The dragon turned to snap at her.

"Whee!" Silverheels screamed. "The Red Dragon's dead!" He had been looking down into the courtyard and saw it happen. Then, with a grown-tom shriek, he leaped to the top of Hookfang's head. He tried to sink his little claws into the tremendous, fiery eyes, to blind the dragon so it could not see Faith. The eyes closed in self-defense and the *linnorm* began shaking, trying to shed the little nuisance.

Something happened. Time seemed to stop. Olav, who had been moving in with the sword, eyes on the little red heart, stopped moving. Faith stopped trying to get her legs untangled. Silverheels stopped clawing at the dragon's eyes. Hookfang moved only far enough to look down into the courtyard. A black mist had formed there, concealing the body of the Red Dragon. A soft, high-pitched keening sound came from the monster's throat. Then Olav, Faith, and Silverheels found themselves in the heart of a dense black cloud. They could see nothing.

A gust of wind blew the cloud away. Silverheels tried to move—and found his claws were caught in hair. And Olav had the funniest look on his face. The kitten looked down. Why, where was the dragon? He was perched atop a tall, beautiful, dark-haired woman in white, with tears like crystals sparkling in the corners of her eyes.

Olav looked at the tiny red heart over the woman's left breast. "Oh!" he said. "Well!" Leaning over the battlements, he saw a man in red lying on the flagstones. A mystery of Elfland.

"Why," said the voice of the Elfking, "you've caught the daughter of my arch-enemy. They took the forms of dragons so they could attack me."

"Oh," was all that Olav could say. He was watching the beautiful woman as she gently pulled Silverheels out of her hair, held his soft fur against her tear-streaked cheek. Silverheels winked at him.

"Well," said the king, "this calls for a feast, don't you think?" He started into the tower.

"Yes!" cried Silverheels. "A whole quart of cream! I'm a hero!"

"You're a naughty kitten," said Faith. "And if you had a place for it, I'd ask Olav to spank you."

"He was very brave," said the girl, in a voice as soft and beautiful as the breeze in the pines above Lake Totak.

"He was bad," said Olav, agreeing with Faith.

"Oh, no," she said with a pale smile. "He was a little soldier. A pity he was so brave on the side of evil."

"Evil?" asked all three.

"Yes." She brushed a tear away. "But I forget that you're mortals. Don't they tell stories about the *huldre* in the world of men?"

"Why, so they do," said Olav. He'd heard them all his life. And never a one was good. "Have we been tricked?" he asked. "Why were you fighting?"

"This was our castle, and these were our lands, before the *huldre* put spells on us and drove us into the land beyond the sunset."

"He said he was unable to put spells on you...."

"Only in our dragon form, where we were invulnerable to everything but mortal-wielded iron."

"I'm sorry," said Olav.

"And me," said Silverheels. "I made Olav do it."

"I might think of a place to spank you yet," Faith told him. She was remembering a pink bow she would probably never see.

"You are all forgiven," said the girl. "You didn't know."

"What will you do now?" Olav asked. He was sad because of what he had done.

"That will be up to the *huldre*-king, won't it?" she said. "They say he has many wicked instruments in his dungeons."

There was a tremendous festival that evening. The *huldre* came from miles around, to celebrate the victory. The party went on for hours and hours, for where the sun never sets the people need not hurry home. Olav drank the best ale of his experience but his thoughts were elsewhere. Faith was tempted with just oodles of the finest clover. Silverheels lapped cream until he was round as a ball. But he did not talk much, which was unusual. He always had something to say about everything.

At last, the great party came to an end. "What can I do to repay your kindness to my people?" the king asked. "Would you like a bucket of gold or a handful of rubies?"

Olav shook his head sadly. "No, no wealth. Maybe my salt, a ribbon for Faith, and a hand along the path home. I need nothing else. I have Faith, and Silverheels, and my nets and traps, and what more could a man desire?"

Silverheels had been whispering in Faith's ear. And she had been nodding her head sagely, with female wisdom. Said Silverheels, "Well, I have a request."

"Behave yourself!" said Olav.

"I want the girl," said Silverheels. "I claim her!" Well, how bold can one kitten be?

The king thought for a moment? "Why not? She'll be less of a threat in the world of men. She's yours."

"And I have a request," said Faith, and she whispered in the king's ear.

He chuckled, gave Olav a sly look. "Yes, I think that's perfect. He did kill her father. It would fill the spirit of the old laws. Your request, too, shall be granted."

Olav was mystified. He looked at Faith, but she ignored him. So. She had a secret. And would not tell him till she was ready.

"Come," said the king. "We'll find the girl, then show you home." And, shortly, they were under the mountain once more, going past the mines of dwarves and the place where trolls dwelt. The king opened the door in the boulder with his staff. He pointed to the place where he had met them. "There," he said. "I think we all have what we want. Farewell." And with that the king went back into the mountain. The door in the boulder closed as if it had never been.

Olav looked around, happy to be in his own land. He had always loved it, but now it was even better. He looked at Silverheels, thinking of punishments. The kitten was grinning. Why, so was Faith. And the girl, whose name he had discovered to be Amethyst, why, even she wore a tiny smile. Mysteriouser and mysteriouser.

The mystery was resolved when they came to the edge of the lake. At Faith's bidding, Olav looked down into the water—and saw a stranger's face. No, not a stranger's. His own, but forgotten, it had been so long ago. He was young, young as the girl. And his spirits were high, as they had not been for decades.

"Even the *huldre*," as she took his hand in hers, "can show an occasional kindness."

"Well!" said Olav. "Well! What do you think of that?"

"I think we ought to go home," said Silverheels. "I'm hungry."

"And the fish in my panniers are starting to smell," said Faith. "I want to smell nice when we see the priest."

"Yes, well, home," said Olav.

So they went to their little home above Lake Totak, unloaded the panniers, and went back to doing things as they had always been done, except that Olav and Amethyst went to see the priest. And, though she promised the priest she would forget all her witchcraft, well, there always seemed to be lots of ribbons for Faith, and Silverheels stayed fat on mysterious bowls of cream.

Oh, Silverheels never did get the punishment he deserved. That precocious kitten grew into one of the most mischievous and rascally toms ever to plague Rauland.

HELL'S FORGE

The third Vengeful Dragon *story, published here for the first time.*

I

A cold steel sea rolled in, poised, hurled itself against lead-colored rocks, exploded in a wall of silver froth, geysered toward a pewter sky. Chill mists raced inland, dampening ruins. A bitter wind tumbled ragged leaves around fallen buildings, sometimes humming like a giant unable to carry a tune. Here, there, scattering the dust of ages, it uncovered a fragment of mirror. Such shards freckled the dead city with points of light. At the heart of the ruin it gnawed a mound of sand supporting a heap of fallen masonry. In time, that heap collapsed.

Gray shadows moved through the gray city, beside the gray sea, under the cold gray sky. Where a fragment of mirror flickered, shadows gathered. Where the mound had fallen the revealed glass stood like a window into which shadows peered at another world.

The mirror reflected a city full of intercourse and commerce. The people there were not human. Their skins were a sallow, fish-belly color, tinged with olive-green. Their heads were vaguely snakelike.

The sun continued its westward course. Gray deepened into darkness.

The cold black sea rolled in, poised, hurled itself against rock like polished jet, exploded in a wall of luminescent froth, geysered toward the ink dark sky. The bitter wind scattered the mist, now so cold it formed films of ice. Mirror fragments glowed more dully. Behind the groan and hum of the wind a sound rose like that of a bell ringing. No, like a hammer striking an anvil, slowly, steadily, louder and louder.

II

A bell rang.

How long? Days? Half of eternity? Light and darkness alternated, approximating days. I did not keep track. I stood on the ship's poop, leaning on my bow, an everlasting statue. *Vengeful Dragon* drifted in lazy circles inside a changeless dome of fog.

The bell rang again.

Fifty-eight stone-still bodies lay scattered across the decks of the weathered caravel. She had been here long enough for moss and seaweed to cover her sides, climb her lines, and blanket the obsidian sea surrounding her.

Why was I noticing? I should be in mental limbo, staring fixedly across *Dragon*'s decks at nothing. Time should have no meaning. We were immune. We had paid time's price already, condemned by savage gods.

A bell rang once more, faintly and far away.

Something had changed. Something had wakened me. Something had shaken the hourglass and gotten the sands moving. Ah, no. Not again.

A clump of darkness lurked by the mainmast, no fatter than two fists held together. It had been there for as long as I could remember. And *Vengeful Dragon* was an old, old evil, having sailed the western sea, pirating, captained by mad Colgrave, for how long? Centuries, possibly. Till a great sorcerer banished us to this limbo in mist.

One last featherweight hint of the song of a bell.

Once, something recalled us. Rather than be used, we destroyed it. We lost crew, including the grand old madman himself. Colgrave passed command to me. I took *Dragon* to sea…. And…. Lightning struck. And we came back here. To the mist.

In those days I thought that lump of shadow served the creature who called us up. But that monster was extinct. And the shadow remained.

Now it spun like a pinwheel, tossing off dark sparks. Its center opened. Nothing shown through. Neither darkness nor light, color nor its absence. *Nothing.* The opening grew.

Nothing hung, sensed more than seen. Fear rattled me. I couldn't move, not so much as an eye.

Could they not let us be? Could they not learn? The world was a better place with us imprisoned. We were great devils, so wicked that the gods themselves had bound us to this ship for all time, in a vain pursuit of redemption.

Dragon shuddered. She rocked. Her bows turned. She was trying to get under way, I shrieked in the asylum of my mind. She shuddered again, trying to break the grip of motionless water thicker than cold molasses. A violent surge toppled me.

III

I could hear. I did not like what I heard. Boots with iron heels, down on the main deck. I heard them click on hard planking. My crew knew better than to scar the decks.

How did somebody get aboard? We were far from the world, halfway between Heaven and Hell.

A breeze fluttered the sails. Not good. *Dragon* could tear herself apart if she hit winds without a crew to tend her.

Crew. I assumed the men were as aware as I. Which meant they saw what was afoot down there. What did they feel? Fear? Hope? Rage? Most likely that. *Dragon* was always moved by rage and hatred. We were filled with those emotions in life.

I strained with all my will, trying to move. Nothing happened. Rage shook me. I hated the cloud that had quickened me, wanted to destroy the thing that had come onto my ship without my invitation.

A foot settled on my shoulder, pushed. Sprawled me on my belly. Someone took my bow. I raged. My bow meant everything. She was heart and soul of me, *was* me…. Hands dipped under my armpits, hoisted me, carried me to the rail, dumped me against it, upright.

Now I could see.

This sorcerer was less human than the last. It looked like a man in a fake fish skin, baggy and ill-tailored, wearing a snake's head mask.

Nothing like this existed in my world. Not even in myth or legend.

The wind in the rigging hummed. The sails snapped angrily. We might lose them. They had been up however long we'd been imprisoned in the fog. *Dragon*'s bows began to rise and fall. She was entering a living sea. I became queasy. I am one of those sailors who never gets used to the roll of the deep.

The mist thinned. I could do nothing but stare ahead. Fish moved in and out of sight as he took weapons from the men. A sudden, sharp pain suggested his motive. We were recovering.

The fool! All sorcerers are fools. Why would he feel secure if he took our weapons? This is *Vengeful D*. He must not have done his research.

Right then I would have tortured him cheerfully, just to hear him scream. I wanted somebody to hurt more than I did.

The sky ahead showed no hint of color. I caught glimpses of the water. The seas were running tall enough to wear white feathers in their hair. They were gray and cold. The wind, too, was chilly. I had that much sensation. I began to shiver. Straining, I forced my eyes shut. I opened them again, then concentrated on wiggling my fingers.

Fish was on the forecastle deck, collecting Little Mica's toys. Mica was looking my way, awareness in his eyes. I blinked. He replied with a blink of his own.

I used the roll of the ship to help me topple onto my belly. I closed my eyes and sought that reservoir of stubborn determination Colgrave had been able to tap at will. I brought one hand forward, then the other, shifted each leg. I pushed off the deck, stared at Fish.

He stared back, startled. I grinned demonically.

Inch by inch, I moved to the taffrail, lifted one hand slowly, grabbed. I dragged myself up. My left hand drew a boot knife the creature had over-looked. He had not bothered to search me.

Not smart. I flopped on my belly, over the rail. Fish did not understand how dangerous we were. He would be taught.

Somebody groaned down on the main deck. Lank Tor, the ship's boat-swain. Heaven couldn't help Fish if he got close to Tor. Tor existed to kill. And had not fed his need for an age.

Fish started to climb down from the forecastle. Behind, Mica pulled himself upright. He produced a throwing knife missed by the intruder.

Standing, I could see most of the men. They were stirring, eyes wide and white, features twisted. Fish's chances looked slim. Eyes tracked him, smoldering. Somebody would make a move soon.

Fish came up the poop ladder in a hurry. He asked something in a language I did not understand. I grinned again, thinking about the doom gathering behind him.

He moved to the rail where I would look at him. He spoke again in that unfamiliar tongue. I sneered. He shifted to badly accented Itaskian. "You are Bowman?"

I did not respond.

His features twisted. His expressions were not human. This would be anger or frustration. He pointed a finger with too many joints. Darkness crackled around his hand.

Pain slammed through me. I staggered, groaned.

"You will answer. Are you Bowman?"

"Yes." Softly. And flicked my gaze to one side, betraying a hint of a smile.

Startled, he turned.

I stuck a knife in a kidney. Or where a kidney would be in a man.

IV

Fish squealed. He jumped two yards, spun to face me. He reached back, with-drew the knife, stared at it momentarily, looked at me, faced forward.

Men were headed for the poop. The Kid and Lank Tor were on the ladders already. Kid had a knife between his teeth. Tor's was in his belt. The rest all had steel ready to do death.

Fighting pain, Fish flipped my knife overboard. He gobbled in that weird tongue.

So I got out another knife. I would rush him when Kid and Tor reached the heads of their ladders. Fish bit his last few words like they were enemy flesh. My knife began to hum. It got hot. I held on and started toward him.

A turnbuckle on the mainmast gave way. Rigging pulled loose. A yard came free and fell, tearing lines as it dropped.

The fool sorcerer wanted to disarm us using a spell that impacted iron. Iron and magic do not mix well. The ship had begun to fall apart around him. I laughed. "Standoff. Unless you don't care if you go down with us." He might *be* a fish.

He glared, hating. That was mutual. More so than should have been even with such as we, who hated all existence. Who wanted to rest in the surcease of our foggy limbo. He looked, then leapt over the rail, dropped to the main deck, hastened forward to the forecastle as Mica descended the other ladder. From the forecastle deck he planted a boot in Mica's face.

The crew surged after him. Knives flashed through the air, did no harm. The men failed to climb the ladders. Fish was more agile than they. He bounced from one ladder to the other while trying to find a spell to control us.

I was amused.

The weather worsened. I gathered Tor and Toke, my First Officer, at the base of the stern castle. "We have to mend that rigging. And get a proper spread of canvas on. We don't want to lose our sheets and the rest of the rigging."

Grumbling, they went to work. They were good sailors. We all are. We've had ages of practice.

A dozen men formed a skirmish line facing Fish. The rest worked ship. Our visitor was determined to interfere.

Mica reached the poop. "Take the helm," I said, before he told me what was on his mind. My stomach gnawed at me. A seasick captain. That's something.

After half an hour *Dragon* was riding the seas well enough, considering. Mica asked, "What're we gonna do?"

"About what?"

"Everything."

"Repair the rigging. Get rid of that thing up forward."

"And then what?"

"I don't know then what. Not yet."

"Consider the fact that he's not in this all alone."

"What?"

"Stands to reason, don't it? If he was good enough to get here on his own, and wake us up, on his own, then he ought to be good enough to keep us in line. He isn't. So somebody sent him."

I looked at the creature, there on the forecastle, watching us watching him. He seemed diminished, though not yet frightened. Mica was right.

The seas were running higher. I decided we would put out a sea anchor, reef back, and run with the wind. No point doing much else till dark came and the sky cleared enough to take star sights. I had to know where we were before I could make big choices.

I called the Kid. "Kid, you see what he did with our weapons when he took them?" I figured it was a good bet he hadn't disposed of them. Nobody would call us up without having a use for us. And we were useful only one way. To deal death and destruction. For that we needed arms.

The Kid shook his head. "I was facing the wrong way."

"Take Maggot and Hengis and Sharkey and search the ship. I want my bow."

The Kid grinned, glanced at our visitor, grinned even more. That little bastard was nasty. "Just wing him, eh? We could have some fun, then."

Mica and I exchanged glances.

V

The Kid found the weapons. I chose not to bend my bow. The seas were running taller. Day was fading. Chill spray made the weather decks misery incarnate. For Fish it was worse.

As the temperature fell he became sluggish. I recalled snakes and lizards from my life on land. All slow in the cold. I gave orders to stand easy and wait on nature.

We moved at midnight. Our vitality was almost wholly restored. Even so, he handed out bruises enough to go around. He tried spells that threatened to rip *Dragon* apart. Each failed because somebody broke his concentration by pounding him.

We tied and gagged him and threw him down on the main deck. Tor went down to the galley for coals and an iron rod. Got to have proper tools to do a proper job. Toke got the men working up forward, making repairs and adjusting sail.

The seas were running no higher. We were not in the trouble I had feared. Still, they kept me seasick. My temper was short.

Toke drew me aside. "We've got a problem, Captain."

"Such as?"

"She won't answer the helm."

"Eh? But Mica's been...."

"Steering a course somebody wants steered. Running with a wind taking us somewhere. I tried to bring her around, to see how she'd handle. I couldn't force her more than a point off the wind."

I scowled. Though it was dark, I could tell by the way *Dragon* rode that the seas were shifting to our portside, so that she yawed and rolled as well as pitched. Which would be why Toke wanted to turn off the wind. To keep our bows into the seas. "Do the best you can. Maybe we can convince our friend to help."

What did the shifting direction of the seas mean? My guess was, we were in shallow water. Or near land. Or both.

"Tor. Post lookouts." I left the poop to Mica, went down to examine our prisoner. "Ugly bastard, ain't he?"

"*What* is he?" Buckets wanted to know.

"I got no idea. We're going to ask. Get him strapped down. Let's see what's under those togs." He wore doublet and hose like they do in Hellin Daimiel, but with a definite alien turn.

He had no visible sex organs, and no hair. Naked, he was more lizard-like than ever. His skin even had a scaly texture. His back was darker and rougher than his front.

Tor returned from posting the lookouts. He drew his iron from his charcoal, spat upon it. The spittle hissed. "Need to let it cook a little more," he said. "Got to do these things right." He patted our prisoner's shoulder.

"Captain," Mica called. "Come here a minute."

"What for?"

"I think I hear something."

A moment later, as I strode toward the stern castle, a lookout called, "Break in the clouds ahead, Skipper. Looks like moonlight coming through."

He was right. I made a quick side trip, collected the sextant and navigational tables. I joined Mica. He asked, "Much for me to do?" He was our sail maker.

"Yes. One sheet is ripped all to hell. Two others need minor repairs. What did you want me to hear?"

"Be real quiet. Hold your breath. Listen."

I did. I heard wind and sea. Then, as *Dragon* crested a swell, I heard it. A single remote sound that might have been a bell.

"What direction?"

Mica pointed. Directly along the course we would have been making had we kept running with the wind instead of taking the point off it that we could steal.

Land? A warning to ships? I squinted. I could see nothing. But the bell notion seemed somehow familiar. I thought I'd heard the sound before but could not remember where or when.

VI

"Keep a sharp lookout," I told the watch. "And use your ears. We're coming up on something." I placed my sextant and book of tables in the rack provided, went back down to the main deck. "How's your rod, Tor? Ready?"

"Any time, Captain."

"Let's get started, then. Couple of you men keep him from flopping around." I leaned forward, so Fish could see me clearly. "Who are you?"

He looked back with blank eyes. He meant to play rough. I removed the gag. "It won't work. Eventually we'll give you more than you can handle. Save yourself the trouble."

He rolled his head slightly, plainly unaccustomed to that sort of communication.

"Name."

Headshake.

"Tor."

Again a response more powerful than any human would have managed.

We repeated the cycle four times. The bell kept getting closer. Only now it sounded like somebody hammering out horseshoes. Slowly.

"Lookouts. You see anything?"

"No, sir."

I checked the clear patch of sky. We were close. It was moving our way as we approached it. I glimpsed a full moon. A full moon but not *the* moon. Not unless we had been away so long the moon had grown larger and developed different acne.

Raw fear. A different moon? Impossible. I rushed to the poop and the sextant.

The men realized that the moon was not the one they knew.

We entered the break.

The constellations were all askew. A few stars looked like ones I'd used for taking sights but they were not in the right places in the sky.

I put the sextant aside. And as I did, I wondered, for half a second, how come I knew how to use it. I'd never picked one up before.

My curiosity slipped away as the distant blacksmith gave his anvil sudden hell. All I could see was a deeper darkness on the horizon, though it was hard to tell where the horizon ought to be.

A lookout called, "Think I see land, Captain."

"Keep a sharp watch, then. Doing any good, Tor?" I asked.

"Negative. He's stubborn."

"Toke, haul back on the canvas. We may be coming up on land." I returned to the interrogation.

The creature was in pain but pain had not broken him. His hate-filled eyes told me he had reserves left. "This isn't working. Any suggestions, Tor?"

"Not without knowing what it is."

I'd thought not. "Keep plugging." I went forward, to the forecastle deck, where I leaned against the rail, watched the horizon rise and fall. Something lay ahead. Besides the obvious ringing.

Once the forecastle had been my domain. When Colgrave was captain. I'd stood my station there when we attacked. I was the Bowman, feared all down the western coast. A coast that did not exist here, perhaps.

The strange stars began to disappear behind thickening clouds.

VII

Tor got a name. Nobody could pronounce it. Fish's translation went: Assistant-to-the-Great-Master-of-the-Hope-of-Callidor-Beside-the-Sea.

"Now we're getting somewhere," Tor observed with unwonted sarcasm.

The sky began to lighten, from black to shades of lead. There *was* land ahead. A low promontory jutted into the gray sea to starboard. We would have run aground there had we let the spell control our course. Great breakers smashed upon that shore, hurling mountains of foam at the sky. "Tor, put your toys away. I want everybody working. We've got to dodge that headland."

The banging of the anvil was so loud it hurt.

We passed the promontory, which sank slowly into the sea, becoming a rocky reef. Foam swirled around rocks that never quite broke water, fifty yards off our starboard beam. There were furiously treacherous currents, too.

We entered calmer water. The diminished seas were on our beam, now. *Vengeful D.* rode those poorly.

Hengis was on the helm. Little Mica was mending sails. Hengis called, "She won't respond to port, Captain."

Up I went, demanding more information.

"If I turn to starboard, she answers. But if I want to swing port, no dice."

I tried the helm. He was right. I could not muscle the rudder past midships. I had Tor check it. He could find nothing physically wrong. Still, I sent Toke below to rig the emergency steering arm. I doubted there would be time to use it.

Tor has the best eyes aboard. He spotted the ruins first. He pointed. I looked. "What?"

"Looks like a ruined city."

We moved closer. The rudder would permit nothing else. The ruins became more obvious. "You're right." I could see where streets had run, where buildings had stood.

The heavy-handed smith picked up the beat.

Dragon turned directly toward shore.

Nothing helped. Not even taking in all sail. We had one spot of luck. I managed to run aground on deep, fine sand. *Dragon* rode up the beach, canted over, halted.

In moments Toke and Tor had working parties over the side, belaying lines, getting *Vengeful Dragon* secured, lest unknown tides sweep her away or drive her onto the rocks above the beach. The Kid and our better fighters ranged inland a hundred yards, making sure no trouble surprised us while we worked.

I stood on the canted forecastle, bow in hand. Mica held my arrows. The old fever was in me. I wanted to kill somebody.

That had been with me since my dimly recollected time as a soldier. A fire in my soul both cruel and self-destructive. Once I hadn't noticed, hadn't cared, hadn't been aware. Now I was. But the fever remained, dark and deadly.

She was a good weapon, my bow. Crafted by the best boyer, accompanied by arrows from the hands of the best fletcher and best arrowsmith. Masterpieces of murder, all.

"What's up?" Mica asked softly.

"Eh?"

"I haven't seen your eyes so hot since the time we caught those two Trolledyngjan longships."

I fought the urge to lie. We are all liars aboard *Vengeful D.* Every man jack blames his situation on externals. "It's the devil inside. The beast that got me here. It's slavering eager to get loose."

"I thought so. Control it. We're riding the edge."

"What?"

"We're here. Again. Another chance." He glanced at the sky. The clouds moved oddly, their bellies boiling. If I turned my imagination loose I had no trouble seeing faces up there. Off north a few knife-slit gaps appeared in the overcast. Spears of sunlight stabbed through and struck what looked like distant fields of ice. "Would they let us be wakened otherwise?"

Little Mica was not religious. But he had developed a mystical quality, as though he was a nonbeliever chosen spokesman for the powers that shape the world.

His sins were as black as mine, else he would not be aboard *Vengeful Dragon.* But I counted on him to nurture what conscience I retained. "Maybe. And maybe we're somewhere where old debts don't matter."

"Huh?"

"This isn't the world where we died, Mica. But it's not Heaven or Hell, either. I don't know what it is."

"Scared?"

I battled the instant rage his suggestion stirred. "A little." Odd. Fear was a stranger. I'd never had anything to lose, nor had I entertained doubts about my own invulnerability. We sailed for generations without fear, till we fell foul of the sorcerer who first consigned us to the place where Fish had wakened us.

I stared at the dead city, the alien city. It was barely a ghost of a memory in stone. Whatever hand Fate held, it would be played out there.

The men finished making fast, awaited direction. "Muster on the beach,"

I said. "Tor, drag the prisoner down there."

VIII

They were not kind, getting Fish ashore. But he did not protest. Of course, somebody had replaced his gag, just in case he developed an itch to cast a vengeful spell.

"Turn him loose," I said. "Somebody wants us here, Fish can lead us to them."

Toke and Tor seemed reluctant to walk into something blind. Amazing. In times gone by they were fiery eager to jump into anything where they could cut somebody up.

The clouds still rolled weirdly overhead. The knife slits through which light fell were approaching the ruins. Seeing those hints of faces up there inspired me. "Aid us, O Great Ones, in this our hour of peril. Aid us, O Great Ones, in fulfilling the destiny you have set us." I'm not much at prayer.

The men gave me weird looks. Several snickered. For a moment I feared I'd made a wrong move. Colgrave had set the standard for leadership aboard *Vengeful Dragon*: be the meanest, scariest sonofabitch aboard. Then several others sent up clumsy prayers of their own. The slow change was continuing.

The clouds opened and dropped a beam of light on us briefly. Coincidence? Whatever, it buoyed morale dramatically.

The hammering in the ruins had diminished to a spine-tickling nuisance once *Dragon* beached herself. It waxed stronger now, demanding, firing my bloodthirsty mood. I do not like to be pressed.

"Billow. Three-Fingers. Walleye. Clabber. Stay here. Don't let nothing near the ship. The rest of you, form up. Tor. Toke. Take the flanks. Spread out. Mica. Kid. Stay with me." I tested the flex of my bow. She was as smooth and powerful as ever.

Toke and Tor spread the men. A sorrier, nastier bunch I couldn't imagine. They did not properly belong in this scene, but rather in a mad painter's portrait of a city being raped.

Fish just stood there. I gestured for him to go. He didn't move. He seemed frightened. But that was judging by human standards. Kid and Mica urged Fish along with the tips of their blades. He walked with difficulty.

I gave Toke and Tor the signal.

We reached the nearest ruins. They were extremely ancient. Up close, you could hardly tell that the stones once formed buildings. There was no evidence of occupation, present or past. Time had devoured everything but the stones themselves.

The bell sounded louder as we advanced. I had the men fashion earplugs. That helped only a little. We could *feel* the sound.

The slits in the clouds became more numerous. A dozen fingers of light played across the city. From the peak of a rubble pile I saw that it sprawled for miles. It had been vast in its time.

Kid grabbed my elbow, indicated a particular column of light. For a moment I saw nothing. Then light flashed, reflected. There were more flashes when the beam drifted. The ruins sparkled briefly.

I checked the other columns of light. Each trailed sparkles across the ruins. Curious.

Mica and the Kid yelped. There had been a brilliant flash directly ahead. A moment later a sailor called, "Skipper! Look here." He was on one knee. I knelt myself. A soft gleam shone between the stones, something in there giving off light.

"Dig it out." I glanced at Fish. He remained indifferent. He stared toward the source of the ringing.

The men dug out a triangle of glass an inch in its long direction. Its reverse was a grayish black. Its edges were the green of a deep tropical sea. It looked like a mirror shard, yet it reflected nothing. I moved it around, glimpsed something momentarily but could not catch it again.

We discovered scores of similar fragments, none bigger than the first. Occasionally, we found handfuls crushed to gravel. Mica chirruped, "That stuff would be worth a fortune back home. For making jewelry."

Typical Mica thinking. He always went for the treasure. *Dragon* used it for ballast. "Thought you were cured of that."

"Sure. Only...."

"On our way back. We'll fill a sack."

Kid found a fragment an inch across and round. He sailed it toward the apparent source of the ringing. "Gonna hammer that bastard when I get hold of him," he yelled.

"Keep moving," I said. "And be careful. We're getting close."

IX

I whirled, arrow drawn.

"What?" Mica demanded.

"Saw something. I thought."

"Know what you mean. I keep getting that myself. But there's never anything there."

A shadow moved in the corner of my eye. I looked. Nothing. The men were all uneasy. "Tor! Hold up." Time to call on his remarkable eyes. "You see anything? Like from the corner of your eye?"

"Shadows. Like they was from this thing." He indicated Fish with his cutlass. "Tell us about it."

Fish ignored him.

"Can I kill him, Captain?"

"Not yet. He might be useful. He don't make an effort, though, you can chop him into bait."

"Give me a go, too, Captain," Kid pleaded.

"Easy. We need to find out where we're at, why we're here, and how we get out."

We went on, the ringing engulfing us. I shivered in the chill. The grays grew grayer, though blades of light continued to scribble trails of sparkle. An occasional bright flash kept me on course.

The Kid scampered up every rubble heap. Atop one he froze, pointed. His mouth worked but no words came out. Cursing my tired old bones, I clambered up there.

Ahead stood a panel of bright light. Clouds of shadows boiled through the rocks around it. No corner of the eye stuff here. As Tor had said, they were shadows of Fish, racing over and under and around one another like maggots in an old carcass. The light was their focus.

At first glimpse it was blinding. In moments, though, it was bright only by contrast. I could look at it without discomfort.

It was a window. Things moved on the other side.

Mica grabbed a rock and cocked his arm. I yelled. Fish knocked the stone out of his hand, then hurled himself at the sheet of light.

Several men threw knives and javelins. I bent my bow, thought better of it. A javelin hit him an instant before he reached the light.

Shadows swirled. The great anvil rang angrily. Fish staggered, kept on. I nearly caught him. He did not move well on legs Tor had brutalized.

He hit the bright plane. And kept on going. Twisting. Foaming and twirling and twisting, inside and out, and around again…. Then he was over there. He staggered, fell, bleeding on a cobbled street. Others like him surrounded him immediately. They seemed horrified and frightened by his materialization.

I kept after him. And mashed my nose.

Men roared up, ready to break the glass. Or whatever it was.

"Hold it a damned minute!" I shouted. "Let's figure out what we've got here."

Shadows rolled around us, over us, assailing the window. Fish's passage through stirred them up thoroughly.

Occasionally a shadow fell on the plane in such a way that the glass acted as a mirror. Each reflection showed us another monster like Fish. And, now that Fish had passed through, the creatures on the other side seemed able to see the reflections from their side as well.

Which seemed to strike many with panic.

The hammering became frenzied. The shadows struck listening attitudes, then swarmed away, all headed the same direction.

The hammering stopped.

The silence was like the sudden absence of a murderous headache. My thoughts became clearer, more sensible. "Tor, pick six men and watch this thing. The rest of us will follow those shadows."

"Why watch it?" Tor wanted to know.

"To see what it does. Toke. Come on."

X

A reddish glow illuminated the flank of a huge rubble pile. There was a rent in the earth beside it. The glow came from that. Straggler shadows fluttered in. Each seemed to be carrying something.

"You going down there?" Mica asked. We could see nothing but red light from our vantage.

"We might find answers."

"Or we could head back to the ship."

"And then what? We've got to *do* something if we want to get out of here."

Toke agreed. "Whatever brought us here will be down there. Let's kill it." The fever smoldered in his eyes.

I went first. The gash narrowed quickly. I stopped thirty feet down, bent over with my hands protecting the back of my head. Stones and dirt pelted down. Toke slammed into me, then the Kid, Mica, Jo-Jo, and Blackie.

It was warmer down there. Though maybe that was just the absence of the wind. I wriggled out of the pile, slithered through a last narrow crack, stepped out into what must have been a deep basement once upon a time. Forty-five degrees to my left lay what looked like a lake of burning charcoal. Shadows dropped their tiny burdens into that. Beyond the smoldering lake was something resembling Fish, only twenty feet tall, seated, wearing eight arms. Several hands gripped hammers. Each hammer gleamed with fresh wear. The thing had eyes like jewels, in the finest tradition of horrible hidden idols. But these jewels were alive. They looked right through me, into the darkest folds of my soul.

A normal Fish thing sat in the monster's lap. It beckoned.

The crack opened higher than the basement floor. I jumped down. Dust puffed up. I slapped an arrow across my bow, made way for the others. "Toke. Send somebody up to tell Tor, then get this mob organized."

Confrontation time. Evening it up time. Straightening him out time. How dare he waken us?

This time I could not be direct. This time I had to find a way home before I could feed the devil to his own flames.

Shadows swarmed around us, over the walls, across the floor, in tens or hundreds of thousands. They danced upon the coals, dropping something that must have been fuel. There was an eager stink to their frenzy. They had been waiting a long time.

Why?

Toke wanted to kill the Fish right away. "Let him talk first," I suggested. "You want out of here, don't you?"

"Kill him and his spell dies with him."

True in some cases. "The Itaskians' didn't, though. We could end up trapped till we starve."

"Dead is dead, Bowman."

"Some ways dead must be less miserable than others. Stand easy." I moved toward the lake of coals.

Fish Junior beckoned me.

"You guys spread out," I said. "Cover me. Poke around. Cut loose if the big guy swings those hammers."

I walked forward. Mica and Kid stuck close, Kid hoping he'd get to do some damage. Fish shadows by the ten thousand boiled in excitement. I skirted the coals, which were warm but not really hot.

Fish Junior dropped off the idol's lap, came to meet me. The idol's eyes tracked me.

Some idol. It was alive. Or animate, anyway.

Anger kept me moving.

Anger is the fuel that fires us all.

Junior tried the gobble his predecessor had used. "Better try Itaskian, pal."

He faced his deity. If deity it was. The big guy rapped him lightly on the noggin with a hammer.

Mica snickered. Hysterically. Easy to understand. That hammer had to weigh fifty pounds. The anvil where it whacked out its mad music had been disfigured by endless pounding.

Junior hardly staggered. His face lighted with inner glow. He said, "I am *Something Unpronounceable* who is Speaker-of-Truth for Great-Master-of-the-Hope-of-Callidor-Beside-the-Sea. You are Bowman and the crew of the eternal voyager."

"Right first try. That the Great with the hammers?"

"His worldly avatar. He has no form. He is spirit. He fills all Callidor. And we fill Him." His gesture encompassed the agitated shadows. "We invoked Him in this form. He gave some of us flesh in turn. Including that traitor who abandoned us moments ago. He will forge new hope for all of us."

"Right." I had no idea what he was blathering about. "He the one that brung us here?"

Junior nodded. He had the gestures down better than Fish the First.

"Why? Get to the point. We ain't happy. You don't talk fast and sweet, you'll be sorry you woke us up."

"The Hope of Callidor is your hope. The Hope of Callidor is your Master. You must carry out His desires."

"I said get to the point."

He indicated the frenetic shadows. "We are all exiles." He shut his snake eyes. "Once Callidor was great. Once the Master was great and unchallenged. But cold devoured the world. We could live here no longer. The ancients created windows into other planes and migrated to friendlier climes. But some were not allowed to go. And others were forced to come back. We who were disdained eventually combined our wills into power enough to raise the Master in animate form. The Master searched the planes of existence for a key that would open the way. He found you. It took another age to bring you here. Now you will open the way and end our exile."

In a pig's eye. Or…. Maybe. His story contained suspicious gaps, but what the hell?

"How do we get out of here?"

"End our exile and the Master will send you back."

That simple, eh? Sure. "Yeah? What do we need to do? Get down to cases."

"It will be much easier now that an unbroken portal has been found. You will pass through that portal and seize control of it from that side. You will compel them to open the way for us."

"We can get through when you can't?" I had seen Fish the First do the deed.

"You have flesh. We do not. Excepting me. I was given form and flesh so the Master might communicate."

Mica touched my elbow lightly. Yeah. The bullshit was getting deep. We needed to consult. "We're going back over there. We're going to talk it over."

"Do not dally, Bowman."

He was eager, too.

XI

Mica was all set for a brawl. "That story stinks. The guy don't know how to lie."

"It has holes. He left out whatever he thought we wouldn't like. But that's not the point. We're in a corner, Mica. And I don't see any angles. We need more information."

Tor appeared in the crack in the basement wall. "Damn!" he whispered. "It's true." He hopped down.

"What's true?"

"One of them Fish guys came out of that damned mirror. Walked up on the other side, did him a weird dance and jumped at it. He turned inside out a couple times, then he was here. Couple of them shadows went the other way while he was in the mirror. Would you believe they grew bodies when they got over there? But the Fish guys over there whacked them with clubs and threw them back. Their bodies sort of evaporated till there wasn't nothing but shadows left."

"All right." I believed Tor. He lacked all imagination. "What about our old Fish?"

"They threw him back, too. All busted up. He wasn't very happy. He tried to say something but he all of a sudden started to steam. And scream. Then there wasn't nothing left but another one of them shadows."

"And this new Fish?"

"He grabbed holt of Buzzard Neck soon as he come through and pushed his forehead against Buzz's. We dragged him off and tied him up. He started yakking. He made enough sense that we listened some instead of just chopping him up. I come to get you."

I glanced behind me. The basement was still. The coals had faded some. The idol's eyes gleamed, fixed on me. "What did he say?"

"He said don't help them. This place is a prison." He grinned. "I guess for our kind of guys. Guys so black-hearted nothing can help them. The critter with the hammers is their devil."

"I see." I started pacing. That had helped Colgrave think. I kept one eye on the idol. Nothing happened over there.

"What do we do?" Mica asked.

"This news change anything?" I asked. "Are our balls still in a vise?"

He scowled. "Right."

"Right. Toke, keep an eye out here. I'm going topside. Mica. Kid. Tor. Come with me."

The men hoisted me to the crack. After minor physical miracles, I reached the surface. The others followed. For the Kid it was all in a day's fun. We went back to the portal. And there was a Fish, neatly trussed.

Who told a story identical to what Tor had related.

I sketched our situation. He didn't seem sympathetic.

"You expect me to save your asses out of the goodness of my heart? You don't know who we are, do you? Me, I don't have a heart." I glanced at the sky. Daggers of light still roamed the ruins. Hints of faces still marred the bellies of the clouds. "What the hell do you want?"

The new Fish admitted he had no idea who we were.

"Fool," I muttered. "Look at Buzzard Neck's memories."

He folded inside himself. In moments he came back looking bleak.

"Yeah," I said. "Now. Again. Why should we help? We got a shot at breaking even with the other gang."

"Let me take you to the other side. I am but a novice. Perhaps the Masters can explain better."

"Now you're talking. Cut him loose, guys." I flexed my bow. "Kid, you and Mica come with us. Stay in his pocket."

Kid giggled. Fish had no pockets. He wore doublet and hose.

A gang of Fishes watched from the other side. Our captive gestured. They gestured back, not happily. The signals got heated. Then the creatures over there relented.

I glanced at the clouds. They seemed less unfriendly. "How about a hint, then?" I muttered.

"Come," emissary Fish said.

"What do we do?"

"Just follow me." He marched forward.

The instant he touched the plane an angry clang rolled across the gray ruin. I hit the mirror a second later. Another blow on the anvil shook earth and Heaven.

XII

The heat over there was oppressive. The air was tropically muggy. The emissary became more spry quickly. On the Callidor side he had been pale and slow.

"Make this quick," I told him. "I have men back there and the head monster is swinging his hammer."

"It will take the Masters a few minutes to arrive."

"What happens if the others come here?" I asked the emissary. "You can't just send them back?"

"Not if they all come. Callidor has been a prison for ages. Those exiled there do not perish. There are more of them than there are of us. They would seize control. They would bring their dark master across. His rule would be restored. All the warmth would go out of this world, too.

"He was the Doom of Callidor. When his cult ruled. Their dark rites conjured him into that world. He devoured it. Sucked all the heat out. Our ancestors escaped here. Some of theirs did as well. We succeeded in sending them back to Callidor and banishing their Master to his native hell. Now they have conjured his avatar again. And he lusts after the warmth of the new world."

"Right." It made no sense. Gods and devils seldom do. I reflected on a lake of unnaturally cool coals. The guy with eight hands was feeding off their heat? Might mean something. Might not. I said, "That critter has got us in a bind. You don't want us to help him, you better make a deal to get us out."

The emissary's bosses showed up. They were old Fish. Their skins were baggy, colorless, and peeling. Though obviously distressed, they couldn't get hold of the concept of my problem being more important to me than was theirs.

I saw how they could solve it. Finish what they must have tried an age ago. Send a volunteer through to bust any doorways that remained unbroken. Then round up all the millions of fragments and grind them into shining sand. Take the sand out and dump it in the harbor, if they wanted to take it that far.

An hour of yammer wafted into the mists of history. Maddening, not to be able to solve things just by killing people. "You guys aren't even trying. We can't help." I told Mica, "We're on our own."

Mica had a glint in his eye. The Fish were getting to him. He had his eye on salvation and had stopped thinking clearly.

Clever was our only exit. I had recognized that early on. But was no closer to a solution. Clever and the Bowman are not historical complements.

And clever don't work on the gods. Especially devil gods. They have more practical experience.

My stance baffled the Fish. They understood me no better than I did them. "Send us back and say your prayers," I told them.

They decided to play the devil's game. They wouldn't let us go. So now I was two hops and a skip from home: the fog place, Callidor, and their world.

The rage broke through. They even set Mica off, and he wanted to help. But they made Kid angriest of all. He carved up three before I backed off enough to ply my bow.

The dust settled. Seven mutilated corpses lay scattered. Six badly injured survivors were eager to send us back to Callidor before we butchered their whole population.

Maybe they would become more reasonable once they had a chance to reflect on consequences yet to befall them.

XIII

When the dizziness cleared I told Mica, "If we could kick that devil's ass that way, maybe we'd be headed home."

He glanced up. I looked, too. Somebody wasn't pleased. The fingers of light were fewer and weaker. "Thanks for all the help," I said. And, "You get what you pay for." Their attitude was no better than that of the Fish people.

Angry ringing filled the dead city. It fired my rage. "Tor, keep a sharp watch."

Teeth rattling, I dropped into the basement temple, passing through a swarm of shadows carrying bits of fuel. The idol's arms worked mechanically, dropping blow after blow on the anvil. Sparks flew. Shadows swarmed, trying to feed a fire that was cold enough to lie down in. Between devil and anvil a Fish form wavered as it slowly gained substance.

Half my men were down, arms around their heads. Only Toke seemed unaffected. "What's happening?" I screamed.

"He figured out what you were doing. He got mad."

"Let's make him stop."

"Tried that."

I had given orders.

A dozen arrows stuck out of the idol. There were chop marks on it where blades had broken against it. Junior had been chopped up bad but was not yet defunct. God-forged, he was tougher than his cousins in the warm world.

I loosed an arrow. It struck a faceted eye, knocked out a chunk. The hammering stopped. The form taking shape shrieked, faltered, faded. Junior dragged himself my way, in great pain.

"I'm ready to talk," I said.

"You will open the way?"

"Maybe. I need guarantees."

"You are in no position to bargain."

"Of course I am. You want something desperately. I can provide it. That gives me a long lever. Because I don't have to deliver."

"Evil feeds on its environment," Mica muttered. He was covered with Fish gore. "Eventually, it must devour it."

What the hell did that mean? He was getting too weird. Unless he meant the devil having sucked the warmth out of this world.

Frantic shadows kept dragging bits of fuel in for the fire. The idol was sucking the warmth up fast.

Junior asked, "What guarantees would you like?"

How do you fix a devil so he can't cheat? "Free *Vengeful Dragon* from any compulsion. Make it impossible to place another compulsion on her. Give us you, armed with the skills and knowledge needed to return us to our own world."

Puzzled, Junior faced his god.

Mica whispered, "What good does that do?"

"Can't we make him do what we want? With time to work on him?"

"Yes. But...."

Junior faced me. "I now have the knowledge required to take you back. Your ship has been released. A new compulsion has been laid upon her. The Master himself will be unable to control her again."

Did I believe that? No. "Now we're getting somewhere."

Toke grumbled. He didn't like all the talking we did in the post-Colgrave era. Colgrave didn't talk, he acted. He stormed in and *compelled* fate to deliver.

"Is your Master tied to that idol?" Might as well go for it.

"He is bound there. Until we become strong enough to liberate him."

Excellent. I smiled evilly. That confirmed the accusations of the other Fish folk. I studied the big bugger. The notion was feeble but you can't win if you don't make a play.

"Here's the rest of the deal. I'll send men to my ship. They'll see how free she is. If she'll float all right and steer, we'll pull the idol out of here and take it aboard *Dragon*. Some of us will stay here and open the way. The rest will sail to our home world. If he's strong enough to bring us here, after putting one of you there, he can get back easy himself once you guys are ready to free him. After he brings the rest of us home, of course."

That sounded scatterbrained enough and left room enough for skullduggery on their part. It should tempt them. For my part, if I *had* to go through with it, most of the crew would be saved. Assuming the devil didn't skullduggle better than me.

Mica said, "Bowman, you can't sacrifice a whole world for our comfort. Besides...." He jammed a thumb skyward.

"Let them take care of their own problems." I wasn't sure the business of faces in the clouds wasn't just wishful thinking. If not, I didn't mind extortion in that quarter, either.

It was taking shape. I told Junior, "It's your play. You and him on the ship. You both take *Dragon* home. I'll leave my best men behind. As hostages, so to speak."

Junior did not like it. His master liked it less. He was suspicious. Rightly so. I said, "That's take it or leave it. We don't have anything to lose."

Mica protested again. I told him, "Go topside. Collect a couple bags of mirror grit. And stay out of my hair." He was supporting my plan without knowing it.

Junior fussed. He wanted to argue. He wanted to debate. I ignored him. I sent Toke and a gang to ready *Vengeful Dragon* to receive the idol, to ready booms to load it, to build a cart to carry it from here to there, to erect a crane we could use to hoist it out of the basement. To dig a hole through which the latter could be accomplished. All that would take a lot of work. Leaving everybody too tired to wonder much.

The devil saw holes in my plan that pleased him. He okayed the thing.

XIV

"It won't work, you know," Mica said, having crept up behind me as I stared into the pit being dug. An unstepped mast and bits of rigging had become a crane. Below, the anvil rang endlessly, forging new Fishes. Three helped dig. They worked without tiring. There is that about the darkness, wherever you find it. It will be more efficient than the light.

"I said it won't work," Mica repeated. "I won't let you...."

I laid my best Colgrave stare on him. He fell back, startled. I could have given him a hint. I didn't. What did not exist outside my brain could not betray me.

The ship was ready. Men not digging prepared a path over which a big crude cart could haul the idol. I beckoned Toke. "How're our stores?" We might be sailing the nether shore but our bodies still demanded *some* fuel.

"Better hope the men you leave can eat Fish food. Or rocks."

"Tight, eh?"

"The tightest." He glanced at the sky. To my surprise. I hadn't thought he would be sensitive to that. "What kind of dumb-ass gods make it so dead men have to eat?"

Somebody came to tell me, "The diggers are knocking dust off the overhead down there."

"Fine." I bellowed, "Put your backs into it, you scum!" I glanced up, trying to guess the time. I wanted to sail at dusk, with the ebb tide.

The daggers of light were back, more numerous. If that meant somebody topside had peeked into my head and approved, excellent. Just lend me a hand when the time comes. And don't tip the devil below.

The hammering rang on.

"Stop ignoring me," Mica said. "I won't let you do this."

"Hey! Toke!" I waved. "Come here!" Toke waved back. He climbed out of the pit. "I know you're bucking for a halo, Mica, but you ain't climbing over me to get it."

He pulled a knife. I shook my head sadly, noted that Junior had caught the action.

Toke arrived. "Toke, Mica tells me he needs thrown into chains."

Toke asked no questions. He circled while I stood fast. The men paused, leaned on their tools. This was the only challenge I had faced since Colgrave told me to take over.

Mica spun toward Toke. I clipped him on the back of the head. Angry, he whirled toward me. Toke cracked him one. I kicked at his knife hand, missed. Toke had better luck. The knife flipped straight up. I caught it on the fly, tucked it into my belt, told Toke, "You can turn him loose after we get home."

Toke had no trouble subduing Mica now. Mica isn't big.

Shouts rose from the pit. The devil's hammering had been shaking the earth. Men scrambled for handholds as the roof of the basement collapsed. Dust boiled up.

The hammering finally stopped.

Afterward, the men went down and cleared rubble off the idol. The crane swung out. Lines dropped. Sailors made them fast. We tried to pull the devil free.

We lifted him four feet before the lines parted. He fell. He was not happy. Junior ran in circles screeching and holding the sides of his head. Likewise, the three Fish laborers.

"Damned rotten rope," I muttered. "We've got to refit. Get that rubble cleared!" I checked the sky. "And move it! We don't have forever."

Second try we got him up and, with sufficient cursing, loaded him onto the cart. That bastard was big, though not as heavy as he looked. He peered down at us with his jewel eyes, one badly chipped and seemingly partly blind. I thought I saw him shiver.

I kept a straight face. Junior was headed my way. "He wants his anvil taken," he said.

"What the hell for?"

He responded with a very human shrug.

I could sense no danger in that. It was just more work than I wanted to do. I had the crane swing back and hoist the anvil. It was heavier than the idol.

"Get that sonofabitch rolling!" I yelled. Most of the men took up lines attached to the cart. I faced the crane. A small crew began disassembling it. "Hurry it up!" I told Junior, "You and your buddies help pull the cart."

"Where are the men you will leave here?"

"Already chosen. As soon as we get the big guy loaded I'll send them back. Come on. Let's go."

It took all day to drag the cart to the shore. We could not have made it without the help of the Fish critters. They were strong and tireless. We loaded the idol by torchlight. *Vengeful Dragon* canted dangerously during the hoisting. Down into the hold the thing went. Seamen placed timbers meant to keep it from shifting once we got out on the waves. The anvil went in. The only space for it was right in front of the devil. He might be able to whack it if he took a notion.

I told Junior, "Ask him not to make any music. He'll pound a hole right through our bottom. Then down we'll all go."

He did as I asked, returned topside, stood with me watching the crew replace the decking, step the masts, restring the rigging. "Too slow," I bellowed occasionally. I kept a sharp eye on Junior. The cold was slowing him down.

It was close to midnight before *Dragon* was ready. We had missed the tide but there were hints of a suspiciously convenient offshore breeze. And the overcast was thinning, letting flickers of moonlight sneak through.

"Now?" Junior asked.

"Now. Toke. You got the shore party." I watched the twenty-six-man gang form up on the sand, under the slow eyes of the spare Fishes. I told Junior, "Go below now. Tor, show him where." I had gotten a minute with the boatswain. That was set. But I hadn't yet been able to tell Toke. I jumped over the side, into water hip deep and frigid. Toke was all set to push *Dragon* off the beach. I whispered, "Let the men rest. Don't let those Fish push you around. Come sundown tomorrow, kill them. Then wait for us."

He raised one eyebrow.

"Just do it."

XV

Lank Tor came topside as I turned ship. "All set?" I asked.

"Yeah." He grinned. "Resting in the lap of his lord." He stepped to the

246 — GLEN COOK

rail. "We're riding damned low in the water, Captain. Better not hit any weather."

I glanced upward. There was definitely a moon backlighting the thinning clouds. "You heard the man."

The breeze freshened on cue. We put on sail, pulled away from land. Tor went to check our cargo. I raised an eyebrow when he returned. He smiled.

I took the helm, put it over gently, turning north.

Tor isn't too sharp, usually, but he understood that. He shifted sail with little fuss. The breeze shifted with us.

I tossed a cheery wave skyward.

The wind carried force enough for us to make good headway without *Dragon* burying her bows in oncoming seas. Our freeboard was so low we risked foundering if we did not avoid shipping water.

Even so, I had the hatches open. Spare sails shaded the deck so it would receive no direct sunlight come morning. I sent lookouts up to watch for hazards. I expected to encounter some.

The sun presented no problem next morning. The overcast was denser than ever, the air and sea colder. The weather was perfect.

Tor told me, "The Fish is bitching about the cold. Him and his boss can't hardly move."

"Tell him I don't make the weather."

"Suppose he wants to come topside?"

"Stall him."

"And if I can't?"

"Then let him come. He probably can't tell north from south."

"And if he catches on?"

"Then it's chains time." Or worse.

Tor stalled Junior all day, but soon after nightfall the Speaker-of-Truth came lumbering topside, animated by anger. "You betrayed us!" he raged. "Your men slew...."

"Aye," I muttered, and signaled Tor.

They chained Junior, gagged him, and tucked him away on the forecastle deck. Up there he could enjoy the maximum chill.

Below, the anvil yielded a tentative *clang* that echoed into the deep. For an instant *Vengeful Dragon* and the sea stood still. Then *Dragon* plunged forward again, shuddering.

The next *clang* did not come for several minutes. The third and fourth were more widely separated and weak. *Dragon* survived.

I had Mica brought topside. "Cold enough for you, runt?"

He would not speak to me.

"Not for me. That idol thing can still move its arms. But we're about to hear the last of him."

Mica eyed me, frowning.

"Yo!" a lookout called. "Iceberg! Two points off the port bow. Two miles out."

I held my course, studied the berg once it was close enough to make out. It was not big enough. We sailed on, Mica sullen beside me.

I found the right iceberg next morning. We were way north then, having run before a constant wind. The men were grumbling about the possibility of getting iced in. I put that horror out of mind. Eternity locked in the ice with that devil god? I refused to consider it. Cautious glances heavenward. I wondered.

I brought the ship alongside the berg, put a boat over, had the men shape the ice so we could lay alongside. Then it was undo rigging and unstep a mast, open the deck, hoist the big guy and swing him onto his frosty new home.

Several of his arms moved as he sat there. He tried to feed off the heat of our bodies. But our bodies had no heat. We had paid time's price already. Something else, the power of some divine curse, animated us now.

We put *Dragon* back into sailing shape and headed south. I watched the idol and his ice barge dwindle, amused. The old devil faced a different wind. Every iceberg in sight drifted with the breeze that drove us. Except his. His berg was headed north, toward colder climes.

I gave the sky a big grin. I wondered how the Hope of Callidor had managed to so offend the rest of the supernatural community. And guessed I'd never know. "Mica. You ready to forgive me?"

"I guess. What now?"

"We go pick up Toke and the boys. And hope them that live up top give us good winds south. We hope they're feeling generous, now we've done what they set us up to do. We have Junior take us home. He knows how to take us there."

"We didn't win anything, Bowman. We barely broke even."

"I'm thinking that might've been the whole point. To test us. To see how far we'd backslide. And we didn't." Truthfully, I did not think that was the real story at all. I was sure we had been a weapon in a scheme to get rid of a threat that was a lot bigger than we could imagine.

"How about that anvil? That thing has got to be dangerous."

Also more so than we were capable of understanding, I suspected. "I figure on dumping it after Junior takes us home. Somewhere deep. I don't see how it could hurt the Fish people from there."

He seemed satisfied. He went off to play with his sack of glowing gravel.

I stared at the gray, cold sea, wishing there were some way that anvil could be destroyed.

Evil never seemed to go away. Not forever.

Vengeful D. was concrete proof.

XVI

Junior is cooperating. He is deflated, having seen his god defeated by mere whatever we might be. And he doesn't want to ride the demon anvil down when we chuck it over the side.

I am afraid. I am not sure Junior's devil did not trick us and the gods alike. And I have mixed feelings about returning to the place of fog, though it offers a blessed surcease from pain.

Surcease must be in order. My mind is working too well. I have been remembering those atrocities I committed that got me condemned here. There is no end to the pain inside the dictatorship of memory.

A glance at the sky. "Wherever we end up, make it warm."

Lightning rips out of the fat-bellied clouds. The bolt strikes the maintop. Blue ghost fires roam the sails and stays.

Junior gets busy.

A black, spinning cloud forms on the main deck and grows rapidly, then devours *Vengeful Dragon* whole.

Oblivion descends. Oblivion engulfs. Oblivion rules.

Night Shade Books Is an Independent Publisher of Quality SF, Fantasy and Horror

ISBN: 978-1-59780-100-3, Trade Paperback; $15.95

Once a mighty kingdom reigned, but now all is chaos. In the vast reaches of the desert, a young heretic escapes certain death and embarks on a mission of madness and glory. He is El Murid—the Disciple—who vows to bring order, prosperity, and righteousness to the desert people of Hammad al Nakir. Inciting rebellion against the godless kingdoms as he plots to execute the justice of the desert, El Murid is the savior destined to build a new empire from the blood of his enemies. Or so it seems...

A Fortress in Shadow collects the two volumes that make up the prequel series to The Dread Empire. *The Fire in His Hands* and *With Mercy Toward None* were written and published after the first three books, but the war in the east chronicled herein precedes the events in *A Cruel Wind*. This volume also features an introduction by Steven Erikson.

Night Shade Books Is an Independent Publisher of Quality SF, Fantasy and Horror

ISBN: 978-1-59780-104-1 , Trade Paperback; $16.95

Before The Black Company... before The Garrett Files... Before the Instrumentalities of the Night... There was The Dread Empire. *A Cruel Wind: A Chronicle of the Dread Empire* collects the legendary Dread Empire trilogy: *A Shadow of All Night Falling*, *October's Baby*, and *All Darkness Met*, with an introduction by Jeff VanderMeer.

Across the mountains called Dragon's Teeth, beyond the chill reach of the Werewind and the fires of the world's beginning, above the walls of the castle Fangdred, stands Wind Tower, from which the Star Rider calls forth the war that even wizards dread. A war fought for a love. The love of a woman called Nepanthe, princess to the Storm Kings...

Night Shade Books Is an Independent Publisher of Quality SF, Fantasy and Horror

ISBN: 978-1-59780-148-5,
Mass Market Paperback; $7.99

Glen Cook delivers a masterpiece of galaxy-spanning space opera. For four thousand years, the Guardships ruled Canon space with an iron fist. Immortal ships with an immortal crew roamed the galaxy, dealing swiftly and harshly with any mercantile houses or alien races that threatened the status quo. But now the House Tregesser believes they have an edge; a force from outside Canon space offers them the resources to throw off Guardship rule. Their initial gambits precipitate an avalanche of unexpected outcomes, the most unpredicted of which is the emergence of Kez Maefele, one of the few remaining generals of the Ku warrior race—the only race to ever seriously threaten Guardship hegemony.

ISBN: 978-1-59780-119-5,
Mass Market Paperback; $7.99

The ongoing war between Humanity and the Ulant is a battle of attrition that Humanity is losing. Humans do, however, have one technological advantage—trans-hyperdrive technology. Using this technology, specially designed and outfitted spaceships —humanity's Climber fleet—can, under very narrow and strenuous conditions, pass through space undetected. *Passage at Arms* tells the intimate, detailed, and harrowing story of a Climber crew and its captain during a critical juncture of the war. Cook combines speculative technology with a canny and realistic portrait of men at war and the stresses they face in combat. *Passage at Arms* is one of the classic novels of military SF.

Find these Night Shade titles and many others online at http://www.nightshadebooks.com or wherever books are sold.

Night Shade Books Is an Independent Publisher of Quality SF, Fantasy and Horror

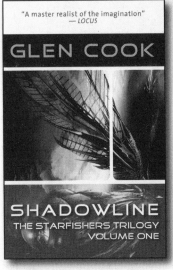

"A master realist of the imagination"
— *LOCUS*

GLEN COOK

SHADOWLINE
THE STARFISHERS TRILOGY
VOLUME ONE

ISBN: 978-1-59780-167-6,
Trade Paperback; $14.95

From Glen Cook, the master of modern heroic fantasy, comes *Shadowline*, the first novel in the Starfishers Trilogy, a seamless blend of ancient myth, political intrigue, and scintillating futuristic combat action.

Mercenary warlord Gneaus Julius Storm surveys his domain from the Fortress of Iron, his citadel among the stars. Surrounded by the mementos of his centuries of conquest, his hand-picked soldiers, and his sons, Gneaus has grown weary of warfare and his artificially extended life. But far away, on the burning half of the planet Blackworld, the armies of the galaxy are about to clash, battling for wealth unimaginable along the Shadowline.

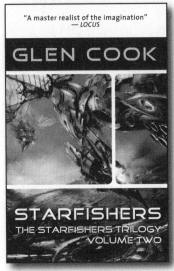

"A master realist of the imagination"
— *LOCUS*

GLEN COOK

STARFISHERS
THE STARFISHERS TRILOGY
VOLUME TWO

ISBN: 978-1-59780-168-3,
Trade Paperback; $14.95

Coming in October 2010
Stars' End
Volume Three of the Starfishers Trilogy
ISBN: 978-1-59780-169-0,
Trade Paperback; $14.95

From Glen Cook, *Starfishers*, the second novel in the Starfishers Trilogy.

Known as Starfishers, the High Seiners defy Confederation rule and Sangaree attack alike to skirt the dangerous boundaries of Stars' End, gathering their priceless cargo.

It is with the Starfishers of the harvestship *Danion* that Confederation agents Mouse Storm and Moyshe benRabi now fly and fight, probing the mysteries and myths of Stars' End, a strange fortress planet beyond the galactic rim, bristling with automatic weapons programmed to slaughter anyone fool enough to come into range. And where benRabi, a man of many names, must surrender his dreams and his mind itself to the golden dragons of space.

Glen Cook is the author of dozens of novels of fantasy and science fiction, including *The Black Company*, *The Garret Files*, Instrumentalities of the Night, and the Dread Empire series. Cook was born in 1944 in New York City. He attended the Clarion Writers' Workshop in 1970, where he met his wife, Carol. "Unlike most writers, I have not had strange jobs like chicken plucking and swamping out health bars. Only full-time employer I've ever had is General Motors." He currently makes his home in St. Louis, Missouri.